Swift

Swift

Alec Merrill

ARCHWAY PUBLISHING

Copyright © 2013 Alec Lindsay Merrill.

All rights reserved. No part of this book may be used or reproduced by any means, graphic, electronic, or mechanical, including photocopying, recording, taping or by any information storage retrieval system without the written permission of the publisher except in the case of brief quotations embodied in critical articles and reviews.

Archway Publishing books may be ordered through booksellers or by contacting:

Archway Publishing
1663 Liberty Drive
Bloomington, IN 47403
www.archwaypublishing.com
1-(888)-242-5904

Because of the dynamic nature of the Internet, any web addresses or links contained in this book may have changed since publication and may no longer be valid. The views expressed in this work are solely those of the author and do not necessarily reflect the views of the publisher, and the publisher hereby disclaims any responsibility for them.

Any people depicted in stock imagery provided by Thinkstock are models, and such images are being used for illustrative purposes only. Certain stock imagery © Thinkstock.

ISBN: 978-1-4808-0354-1 (sc)
ISBN: 978-1-4808-0356-5 (hc)
ISBN: 978-1-4808-0355-8 (e)

Library of Congress Control Number: 2013919986

www.alecmerrill.com

Printed in the United States of America

Archway Publishing rev. date: 11/6/13

Table of Contents

Chapter 1   Meat for the Table 1

Chapter 2   A Warning 9

Chapter 3   The Setup 17

Chapter 4   Headaches 33

Chapter 5   HMS Winchester 41

Chapter 6   Mess Mates 57

Chapter 7   Adjusting 81

Chapter 8   Learning the Ropes 89

Chapter 9   Gun Drill 107

Chapter 10   Challenges 119

Chapter 11   Out of Discipline 129

Chapter 12   Questions Arise 139

Chapter 13	New Skills 147
Chapter 14	Antigua 163
Chapter 15	Goodbyes 173
Chapter 16	HMS Mermaid 187
Chapter 17	The Test 197
Chapter 18	The Auction 209
Chapter 19	Wheelin' & Dealin' 219
Chapter 20	Getting Even 225
Chapter 21	Canso 243
Chapter 22	Blockade 247
Chapter 23	Pursuit 259
Chapter 24	Louisbourg 273
Chapter 25	Night Action 281
Chapter 26	Lighthouse Point 291
Chapter 27	Aftermath 305

Historical Notes 309

About the Author 319

Chapter 1
Meat for the Table

The darkness of the night fluctuated. One moment, the quarter-moon wanly illuminated the ground, while in the next scattered clouds blocked any light. He had to be careful. It had been a very dry summer. The leaves on the trees and foliage on vegetation closer to ground were dry. It was so dry that his father was worried the crop harvest might not be enough to pay the rent for the farm, let alone provide enough food to last until next year. Without the game he hoped to bag tonight, the entire family would go hungry, if not immediately, then in the not-too-distant future.

Jonathan Swift carefully slid through the brush on the flank of the marsh. His progress was slow, measured, and cautious. Each step or movement was thought out. He avoided brushing against or treading on any dry vegetation that would provide a telltale crackle. Such a sound might give away his position. Worse, it might frighten away any game. He had to be worried about both. He needed meat for the table. Taking game, without permission, from someone else's property was poaching. Everyone in the district knew that. If caught, it would result in severe punishment.

He could imagine what any tenant farmer in the area would do if someone were caught taking game on that farmer's acreage. The poacher would be lucky to get away with his life. It was simple: the poacher was taking food off the farmer's table. That food could mean the difference between a farmer's family eating or going hungry for a day or two. Most of the surrounding property was long ago hunted out. Even marsh land was now rented, not because it was productive, but because the renter could legally hunt any game found on it. The only land not hunted out was the squire's property. There were a number of game wardens to ensure it stayed that way.

A few minutes before, he had heard a noise foreign to the natural environment. It was a warning that someone else was about. That other person might be a game warden from the squire, as it was his land. It might also be another individual like himself - someone who needed meat for the table. In either case, if he was spotted, it would be a fast, violent affair unlikely to turn out in his favour.

He kept these thoughts in the back of his mind. Of primary concern was eating. He needed food, and that meant trapping meat with snares or being able to shoot it. Snares worked better, he knew, but you had to set them and then go back to check them. In between, if they were spotted by a game warden, he could be waiting to ambush you. On the other hand, if they were seen by a competitor, the snare would be emptied if it held game. If there was no game in it, the snare or trap would be sprung or possibly broken.

No one like him had money for a firearm. Even if he did have a firearm, he couldn't use it as the noise would be his undoing. He therefore relied on a slingshot. He was accurate with it, having practised countless hours. There was one drawback; however, he had to be close to his quarry, and the quarry had to be rabbit-size or smaller for a clean kill.

He was near the edge of the marsh. There were usually ducks or even geese near the edge of the marsh. He savoured the taste of either.

Using all of his cunning, he soundlessly approached the tree line marking the edge of open water. After the darkness of the brush, the open area of the marsh was significantly brighter, even though there was just a quarter-moon.

He scanned the open water and glades nearest him, but saw no quarry. There! About one hundred yards to his right there were two ducks. They were motionless on the water and close against the glades. They were too far from his current position for any shot. He would need to get closer, but how?

He could go along the bank, but the ducks might see him, or even worse, a game warden. Alternatively, he could sink back into the brush, move to the right, and then come out directly opposite them. This is what he decided to do.

Quietly he backed into the brush, being careful not to make any noise that would disturb the ducks. The going was slow. He needed to feel every hand and foot location to ensure he was soundless. In this he succeeded, but at a cost in time. Ten minutes later he edged through the brush only to find no ducks. He hadn't heard or seen anything suspicious. Where did the ducks go, and why?

He eased back slightly into the brush. He stuck the index finger on his left hand into his mouth to wet it. Then he raised the finger slowly into the air. The wind was from the west, toward him. His scent wouldn't have been a factor. He was puzzled, and a bit apprehensive. What had made the ducks move position?

He slowly lowered his hand as motion is more rapidly spotted. He decided to back further into the brush. He instinctively knew something was not right. As he started moving, he sensed movement further to the right. He saw nothing. It was more of a sense. One shadow in a bunch of shadows didn't look quite right. Was it a branch or something else?

Caution was foremost on his mind. He looked to his left and to the front. He relied on his peripheral vision to determine if someone was, in fact, on his right. He knew from experience that when staring directly at something for awhile, the eye tends to imagine. Using peripheral vision, the eye tends to catch motion faster than when you look directly at the object. And he needed to spot motion as fast as possible. He was scared. Not scared as in terrified, but scared enough that every sense he had was working overtime.

He tried to control his breathing. All of a sudden, his breathing was abnormally loud in his opinion. In reality, it was so shallow it appeared that he was either dead or just another bush.

His eyes snapped to the suspicious shadow again. This time there was distinct movement. It looked like an arm or leg being moved slowly to work out a cramp. But who?

Jonathan decided not only did he not want to know, but he also did not want the other chap to know of his presence. It was time to pull back before being detected. Hungry as he was, he would rather be hungry than get caught.

He resumed crawling backward further into the brush, being even more silent if that was possible. He had gone but ten feet when a branch cracked. He froze. He was in trouble, and he knew it. He had not cracked the branch, nor had the shadow. The crack had come from further to his right. There was a third person in the vicinity.

As he watched, the closer shadow moved toward him. It appeared the closer shadow was circling toward the area from where the crack emanated. There was no motion, no noise in that area at the present - just total silence. Just the same, in another ten feet, the shadow would be tripping on Jonathan. He debated whether to remain motionless or run. Neither choice was encouraging. He decided to remain motionless.

The shadow moved closer and then stopped. Jonathan could see him clearly except for the face, which was only in profile. The shadow was still concentrating towards Jonathan's right where the noise had originated.

Seconds changed to minutes. No one moved. Then Jonathan saw silent movement from the shadow. He did not register the movement until he heard the click of the hammer being cocked. He dared not move or make a sound lest the musket be swivelled toward him.

Jonathan had to master the fear that was threatening to overcome him. He stopped breathing. He was motionless, but he was fearful his trembling might be spotted by the man with the musket.

After what seemed like an hour, the click of the hammer on the pan followed by the explosion of the musket's discharge nearly caused him to wet his pants. The shadow with the musket charged to Jonathan's right. Jonathan rose to a crouch and rapidly but near soundlessly skedaddled to his left in the opposite direction to where the shadow was heading. Whatever noise he was making was masked by the noise the shadow was making.

He put about a quarter-mile distance between himself and the shadow before slowing first to a walk and then to measured pace that was quiet and stealthy. He moved from one patch of darkness to another, always being careful to avoid branches or dry leaves that would notify anyone or anything of his presence.

He stopped and listened. There was some sound from behind but it was distant. This re-assured him that he was out of danger. Rather than head directly home, he decided to skirt the southwest side of the marsh. He figured that way was less traveled and unlikely to have any other of the squire's men. He was sure it was the squire's men who were out, as no one else in the district had the money for muskets. No poacher would fire a musket and advertise his presence.

He picked a good secluded spot and sat down. He needed a rest to calm down, to re-assess things, and to verify that he hadn't soiled his breeches. He also needed a stretch. He would never have believed how sore his muscles could get when remaining immobile for a period of time.

Jonathan sat on the ground and leaned against a tree. He sat there with his forearms resting on his knees. He opened his ears and listened to the night sounds. No sounds out of the ordinary were heard. He further relaxed. If only his belly would stop growling for food. He began to think about food. He could smell it, taste it. The image of a large meal was clear in his mind.

He slid his left hand down and touched the slingshot stuck in the waistband of his pants. He froze. There was motion to his front. He caught his breath. Not more than twenty feet away in the open area was a rabbit.

Ever so slowly, he pulled the slingshot clear of his waistband. He raised the slingshot, ready to shoot. He slid his right hand down from his knee very slowly. He had sat on a small stone when he first slumped down. He had brushed that stone aside. That stone was close and screened from the direct vision of the rabbit. Ever so slowly he searched with his hand. He found the stone, picked it up, and placed it in the sling. Now for the tough part - he had to draw back the sling and aim, without frightening the rabbit.

The rabbit stopped. It sat back on its hind legs and raised its head. It was sniffing the air. It turned its head away from Jonathan. That was all he needed. He drew back the sling, raised the slingshot, and let go in a fluid motion he had practised a thousand times. That practise paid off as the rabbit dropped.

To be sure, Jonathan quickly covered the distance to the rabbit. Swiftly drawing his knife he slit its throat. He then gutted it. He dug a shallow hole with his knife and tossed the entrails into the hole. There was no sense leaving evidence around that the squire's men might find.

He was preparing to leave when a sixth sense warned him that something was not right. He had not been paying attention while working on the rabbit. He ducked down and listened carefully.

There were sounds - movement - and that movement was close. What was worse was that the sound was coming from the southwest, the way he was heading. The sounds were metallic meaning that it was a man making the noise.

Jonathan was in a dilemma. Forward was movement to avoid. To his back, albeit at a distance, was a known squire's man who was armed.

He decided to move to his left. It was toward home. To his right was the swamp. If he made a noise, it was a sure thing that whoever it was would swing to their right - directly into his path. He therefore needed to ensure he did not make any noise.

There was another problem. Blood smells, and there was fresh blood on the rabbit and some on him. That would make tracking easier. If dogs were used, he was finished. He looked down at himself and the rabbit. He grabbed some dirt and rubbed it over any blood that he could see. Jonathan hoped that this would eliminate as much blood smell as possible. He was suddenly very grateful he had buried the rabbit's entrails. The person coming towards him was only yards away. If the entrails were found in that fresh of a state, whoever was coming would be aware of his proximity.

Whoever was coming was not very quiet. They were not making very much noise, but enough. Jonathan reasoned that the person was knowledgeable about the woods. Jonathan risked a look. Whoever was coming was using dark patches and staying away from patches of light. But the person was either tired or didn't care about the little noise that was generated by his movement. Jonathan knew that could change in an instant.

Just the same, Jonathan felt distance was warranted. He began to move silently and kept low. Never standing, never in any light patch, making sure he did not disturb vegetation at any level. He had covered one hundred yards before the noise behind him stopped.

Jonathan now knew he was the quarry. There were only two hundred or three hundred yards more of the woods. After that were open fields with no cover until the rise. He would be spotted in those open fields. He had three options for escape. One was to run for everything he was worth, directly for, and then across, those open fields. He was reasonably sure that he could outrun any of the squire's men. There were just two problems. One was if he was not fast enough. If his pursuer had a musket, he might still be in range. Worst yet, if the pursuer had a rifled weapon, the range was more than double that of a musket. But more worrisome was the possibility that he might be identified even if he could evade his pursuers. End result, he would be caught.

Another possibility was to circle back in the brush and hide. Unfortunately, the pursuer only had to wait until daylight, then he would be easier to find or identify.

The third option was to move to the edge of the woods, and then run for it along the tree line as far as possible. He would then duck back into the woods and keep going. The advantage of this would be putting significant distance between him and the pursuer without making much noise. If he could duck back into the trees again, before being spotted, it would take the pursuer time to track him. He would run to the next county if that's what it took. After that he could circle around to home. This was the course he decided on.

Now that he had made his decision it was time to put it into motion. Jonathan started moving rapidly from dark patch to dark patch. He wasn't sure how much noise was being generated by his movements, but he knew he was making some noise. All of a sudden he was at the tree line. He burst out into the open, turned right, and sprinted for all he was worth. He was young, in good shape, knew how to run, and fear added extra momentum. As his feet were bare, no appreciable noise was made on the open ground of the field. He held the rabbit in his right hand to keep it from slapping against his leg. He counted to two hundred and then darted into the tree line. The only sound he believed he had made was the sound of his breathing.

He only went in about ten yards, but that was enough to shield him from view. He broke into a walk at a fast pace, while he attempted to get his breath back. He kept his eyes on the ground, sweeping back and forth to avoid any entanglements or possible sources of noise. He kept going like this for some time. There was a slight rise to the west. He approached and ascended it. Only then did he consider looking back. He circled to his left and cautiously came to the tree line. What he saw wasn't encouraging. Two men were walking in the open field about ten yards out from the tree line. In this position, they had faster and easier walking. They also had a clear view of the tree line for some distance ahead. Their path effectively cut off his direct route home.

He now had a decision to make, and it had to be made even faster than the previous one. He could cut back into the brush and get behind these two. Alternatively, he could go flat out, in the hope of out pacing them to the road about three miles away. Then he would need to go at least a mile down the road to his left, before they got to it, in order to get away. And he only had an hour or so before dawn. Somehow he also had to ensure the rabbit was hidden, so that he was not seen carrying it.

Instinctively, he knew cutting back through the woods was very risky. He therefore decided to speed up through the woods, heading for the road. Fear is a reasonable motivator, so he was able to maintain a good pace despite his fatigue. After about twenty minutes he reached the road.

He took off his shirt and rolled it around the rabbit. He then slung his shirt over his shoulder, and started down the road at a steady run. He put his mind in neutral and just ran. He followed the road all the way home. When he got there, he was covered in sweat, despite being bare-chested. He was also exhausted.

But was he safe? Had he gotten away without being identified?

Chapter 2
A Warning

Just because he was home did not mean that he was safe. He was literally covered in evidence. His first concern was to get the rabbit in the pot and hide the bones and fur. This he started immediately.

Unfortunately, he made too much noise in the kitchen. The next thing he knew, his mother was looking over his shoulder. She immediately grasped the significance of what he was doing and took over the task.

"What happened, Jonathan?" she asked. She looked at her eldest child. He was a good looking youth of nearly seventeen years of age. His sweaty, lithe, muscular body glistened in the weak dawn light. His brown hair was matted to his forehead from sweat.

"Squire's men were out," Jonathan replied. "I'm not sure if I was spotted, or if I was, whether I was recognized. Regardless, I figured to get rid of the evidence as fast as possible."

"There's blood on your pants. You need to be gettin' cleaned up," she said. "Do that, and then get rid of these bones."

Since Jonathan only had two pants to his name, it was an easy decision on which pants to put on. He went out behind the house to the well and fetched a bucket of water. The first bucket he poured over himself. The second bucket he used to start washing his blood-covered shirt and pants.

Mother Swift came out with a small bundle of fur wrapped around the rabbit bones. "Get rid of these, and make sure it ain't too close to the house," she said.

While Jonathan trudged off with the bones, she continued preparing rabbit stew. After she set it to the side of the fire to simmer, she went out into the yard and finished scrubbing Jonathan's clothes.

Her husband Joseph, or Joe as he was called by everyone, came out into the yard heading for the outhouse. He was surprised to see her already at work washing clothes. Not surprised at the task, for Mother Swift was a hard worker, just at the hour. The days were long enough as it was without adding more hours of work.

As Joe came back after finishing his business, he looked again at his wife. She was a stout woman, who was aging prematurely. She was only an inch over five feet, had a will of iron, and a temper to match. But she was a good wife and mother to their children. Joe commented to her "You're up early!"

"We may have visitors this mornin' - the squire's men," replied Mother Swift. "Jonathan was out last night. He thinks they may have spotted him."

Joe shot back "He get anything?"

"In the pot"

"Well that's something at least," replied Joe. "And without evidence they have nothing."

The family, which included his mother, father, his fourteen year old sister Susan, and his nine year old brother Robbie, were just finishing a breakfast of porridge, when a horse was heard outside. Joe rose from the table and peered out the window.

"It's one of the squire's men, Martin Abercrombie," Joe said. "This doesn't look good. I'll see what he wants." Joe went to the door and hailed Abercrombie. "Morning Martin, what brings you out so early?"

Abercrombie replied "Just delivering an invitation for you and young Jonathan."

Abercrombie remained on his horse, a fact not lost on Joe. It was usually common courtesy for a rider to dismount while speaking to man on the ground in his own yard. Not only did Abercrombie not dismount, but he was also pompous and high-handed in his manner. This irked Joe.

"An invitation for what?" asked Joe.

"At noon the squire is holding court. Your attendance and that of young Jonathan is requested," replied Abercrombie.

"What could I or Jonathan possibly have to do with the squire's court?" questioned Joe.

"McMillan thought it would be highly educational for both of you," replied Abercrombie.

"I need to get work done in the south field," said Joe. "I don't have time to go to any court. What's this all about anyway?"

"You'll see when you get there," spat out Abercrombie. "Just make sure you're there."Abercrombie shifted his reins, and turned the horse. He spurred the horse out of the yard and cantered off down the road.

Joe turned and went back into the house. He passed Jonathan standing in the doorway. "You heard?"

"I heard, but it doesn't make sense," responded Jonathan. "If they had identified me, they would've come for me. So I don't understand what this is all about."

"Neither do I," replied his father. "That worries me. And I don't have time to attend any court. I got work to do."

"So whatcha goin' ta do?" asked Jonathan. Jonathan's father was a strong, steady, dark haired man. He was slightly taller than Jonathan at the present, but everyone figured it was only a matter of time until Jonathan stretched past him. He was a hard worker with lots of common sense. Jonathan, and the entire family, relied on his farming and general knowledge to guide them.

"I don't have much choice," replied his father. "I don't know if this request is McMillan's or the squire's. If it's the squire's I can't afford to get on his bad side, so we go."

※

After a hard morning's work, a scrap of bread, and a dipper of water, Joe and Jonathan left for the squire's court. They walked two miles to the hamlet where the court would be held. All the while, the apprehension that each felt, kept growing.

When they reached the hamlet, a few of their neighbours were already milling around the exterior of the building used for court trials. No one seemed to know what was happening, or who was on trial. They had all gotten word to be there, the same as Joe and Jonathan.

Speculation was rife. Someone was being evicted. Someone had been caught poaching. There had been a fight at the local tavern and the culprits were being brought before the squire. The more speculation, the more fear. Everyone was nervous. Virtually everyone in the hamlet was dependent to some degree on the squire. They rented farms from him, or he was the main consumer of their crops or product. In the case of the tavern and church, their clients were workers directly employed by the squire or the squire's tenants.

At 12:15 the door opened and McMillan, the squire's right-hand man, ushered everyone inside. There weren't enough seats for everyone, so Joe and Jonathan ended up standing on the right side of the court.

McMillan shouted "All rise," as the squire ambled in, taking his seat at the desk at the front of the court.

"Be seated," McMillan said. "The court is now in session."

"Bring in the prisoner," said McMillan.

Archie Cartwright was half carried, half dragged into the courtroom. His hands were shackled, and he had either limited use, or no use, of his bandaged legs. He was unceremoniously dumped in a chair. The man beside him, supposedly his counsel, was another squire's man - an Irishman called Murphy. At the table to the right of Cartwright was Buchanan, acting as the prosecutor. Buchanan was one of the more knowledgeable and literate individuals within the hamlet.

For all present, without knowing any of the circumstances, it was obvious that the deck was stacked against Cartwright.

The squire said "Mr. Prosecutor read the charges."

Buchanan rose and said "If it please the court, Archie Cartwright is charged with poaching. On the night of July 6th, in the year of our Lord 1744, he was observed by game warden Fitzgerald stalking fowl in the marsh on the squire's property. When told to stand up and give himself up, he threw a knife at game warden Fitzgerald, who then, in fear of his life, opened fire with his musket. Cartwright was wounded in the legs and apprehended on the spot, before he could get away."

The squire rotated toward Cartwright and said "Archie Cartwright, how do you plead - guilty or not guilty?"

It was obvious that Archie Cartwright was in pain, and not in much of a position to defend himself. Murphy stood on Cartwright's behalf, and stated "Guilty your Honour, but we pleads for the mercy of the court."

The squire said "Archie Cartwright, you have been found guilty of poaching. Before I sentence you, I would like to make the following comments to all present. The court will not tolerate poaching, or any other infringement upon the rights of landholders. This is seen as a very serious crime for which appropriate punishment must be awarded. Archie Cartwright I sentence you to ten years hard labour."

Deathly silence hung over the room. There was only one significant landholder in the area - the squire. He had just placed all on notice that severe penalties would be awarded for anyone caught poaching on his land. Not a movement, a cough, or any other sound was heard. Everyone present knew that Archie Cartwright had many mouths to feed. At last count there were eight kids in the family. They all knew, because they all were tenant farmers to the squire and neighbours of Archie. In a good year, after the squire's high rents were paid, there was usually enough food for a family of five, but in a bad year they could barely feed two. Last year had been a bad year. Archie had done the same thing that many of them had resorted to in the past - poaching to feed their family. The sentence imposed on Archie was a death sentence for his family. Archie would live - maybe - in prison. His family would be evicted because they could not work the farm. The family would be split up, as no one could support the entire family, and some would probably die of starvation.

The squire said "If there's no further business for the court, this court is adjourned. God save the King."

As the temporary court room emptied, the mood of the spectators was gloomy and negative. There was still plenty of daylight left so many spectators retreated back to their work. As Joe and Jonathan walked back toward the farm, they heard horses cantering behind them. Only the squire's men had horses other than draft animals, so it was a sure bet that these were the squire's men. However, the squire's homestead was in the opposite direction, so where were these men going?

The answer came quite quickly. As the horsemen cantered up to Jonathan and Joe, they slowed until the horses' pace matched that of Joe and Jonathan. McMillan, Abercrombie and Fitzgerald were the riders.

McMillan spoke "Did you learn anything from today?" It was not clear who he was addressing - one of the other riders, or Joe. Jonathan knew he would never lower himself to speak to Jonathan directly.

Joe replied "Nothing new." It was no good antagonizing the squire's men, because they were very vindictive. Joe knew this, so he carefully chose his words. Jonathan took the lead from his father and kept his mouth shut.

"You should take particular heed young Jonathan, because one night you will slip up and end up the same or even worse than Archie Cartwright. Don't think we don't know, because we do. Your time is coming."

A chill went down Jonathan's back.

Joe looked up at McMillan. There was anger in his eyes. This pompous, arrogant windbag was threatening his son. Yet there was little he could do about it. He knew that McMillan was a sneaky, conniving prick. McMillan had handpicked Abercrombie because he was the same. He wasn't sure about Fitzgerald, but he had his suspicions. Without doubt, any of these three, or all three, could make life for the whole family miserable - even a living hell. He thought the squire a reasonable man, but all of his decisions were based on the information that McMillan and his ilk fed him. It would be fighting an uphill battle just to get an even shake from the squire.

McMillan, seeing his taunts strike home, laughed and wheeled his horse around. He viciously spurred the poor animal and cantered off with his two cronies.

Jonathan and Joe continued walking in silence. They were both aware of the implications of those taunts. Joe looked at his son and said "It would appear they're out to get you. You'll have to watch your back."

"We're near out of food," replied Jonathan. "It will be another two or three months before the fall harvest. If we don't get food from some other means we're going to starve. You can't go out all night, and then work all day. The family needs you working the farm, or else we will be evicted."

"You're right," replied his father. "I don't trust McMillan or Abercrombie. I'm not sure about Fitzgerald. He may be reasonable, but I'm just not sure."

"I'm sure," stated Jonathan. "Last night, he stalked Archie Cartwright and waited for the right moment. Then, without any warning, he shot him. All that talk in court was just a bunch of lies. Archie Cartwright never had a chance. Was he guilty of poaching? Sure. But did he deserve to get shot and then get ten years of hard labour? That's cruelty. And Fitzgerald is as bad as, or worse than the other two."

"Then you had best be cautious," said Joe. "I'd rather go hungry than see you shot - or worse, in prison."

"Yeah," whispered Jonathan.

CHAPTER 3
The Setup

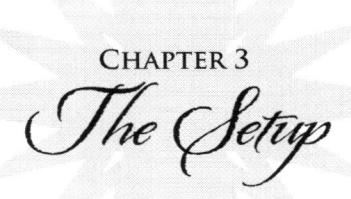

The days passed. The work continued. Starvation stalked the countryside. Everywhere it was evident, but no one spoke about it. It looked like there would be a bountiful harvest in the fall. If only they could survive until then. If only the squire's payment did not consume too much of the harvest. In the past, when bountiful harvests occurred, the price of the produce dropped. This meant a higher percentage of the crop had to be used to pay for the rent of the farm. The result was less of the crop for food and next year's seed. Additionally, a portion of the crop had to be sold in the market for cash. They needed this cash to pay for debts already incurred. Such debts included this year's seed, clothes, and other living essentials.

Three months was a long time to go without meat. Traps had been set on the farm but to no avail. All game had long since been consumed. On most neighbours' farms it was a similar situation. There was only one area with game - the squire's property. Not only was the property huge compared to their little rented farm, but it had a massive sanctuary area in which game sheltered.

Jonathan knew the risk, but had little choice. His only brother Robbie was eight and could not hunt. Neither could his sister Susan. If his father was caught, he would be sent to gaol. They would lose the farm. The family could be split up and possibly suffer the same fate as Archie Cartwright's family. It was too risky therefore, for his father to go out. He was the only option.

Jonathan had been poaching for over three years. He had learned a great deal about animal habits, tracking, shooting with a slingshot, and dressing game. More importantly, he had to excel in stealth to survive. He had an acceptable knowledge of camouflage, as he could blend into the environment without notice. He used this in the field, but was also able to use it occasionally in other areas. He had slid into the tavern and into the house on a number of occasions to eavesdrop on various conversations.

He was a master; however, when it came to silent movement. He was generally barefoot, which made less sound. It also meant he could feel branches under foot before putting too much weight on them, causing a snap. He could use shadows, avoid noisy foliage, and could crawl and crouch readily. He was extremely comfortable, confident, skilled, and wise in wood lore.

When Jonathan went out he rarely returned without something. His forays were less frequent, both because of the vigilance of the game wardens and because the game had more meat as winter approached. On those occasions when he did venture out, he was doubly cautious, knowing the squire's men were likely waiting. He avoided a number of traps that had been set for him. The complexity of these traps increased as time went on.

When he went to the hamlet, he avoided the tavern because the squire's men were often to be found there. Even so, each time a squire's man saw Jonathan, some comment such as, 'Just wait, we'll get you' was heard.

It became evident over time that the squire's men were increasingly frustrated by their inability to catch Jonathan. It was only a matter of time until some other trick or deed was used to trip Jonathan up. Jonathan was aware of this, and his father reinforced this awareness as often as he could. Unfortunately, the entire family depended upon Jonathan's skill to feed them. He had to go out, but each time he ventured out, the probability of his getting caught increased. Skill and caution, caution and skill - these were the hallmarks of his nightly forays.

Jonathan never left the Swift residence for a poaching foray in daylight. He never knew if any of the squire's men were watching the house. He occasionally had circled the farm in daylight to see if he could find any evidence of someone watching the house. He had seen indications more than once. He also knew that if someone was watching his house, there were likely to be fewer watchers in the marsh. He would probably have less risk when hunting, but greater risk approaching home. The watchers waiting near the house couldn't effectively cover all routes of entry to the Swift home, so all he had to do was determine which route was clear.

It was a hard life though. He had to spend the majority of the day helping his father in the fields. He spent the majority of darkness hunting. He had little time to sleep. And his mother scolded him for not keeping up his lessons. The only schools at the time were charity schools, but these were in the larger centres and not in the countryside. All the formal education Jonathan had so far attained had come primarily from his parents, and to a lesser extent, from the local pastor. Both his mother and his father had good capabilities in arithmetic that seemed to have been passed on genetically. Each had their own style for cultivating Jonathan's mathematical abilities. When working beside his father, his father would ask him questions like "It takes two bags of wheat to sow a quarter acre of land. The north field is six acres. In a good year, we can get a hundred thirty bags of wheat from the north field. The price of wheat is ten shillings a bag. How much profit will I get, if I sow wheat?"

Jonathan would have to figure out the answer in his head because he had nothing to use. If the correct answer of forty one pounds was not given fast enough, Jonathan would be penalized. Such a penalty might be a cuff, extra questions, or more work. Since he wished to avoid any of these penalties, Jonathan became very skilled in basic mathematics. Jonathan could also understand the reason for these types of questions. If the question was rephrased, as his father often did, to rye, barley, oats, or some other crop, then the answer of what crop provided the better potential profit for the farm could be determined.

His mother was gentler in her approach but just as hard a taskmaster. "How many navy beans are in a peck?" she would ask.

The first time Jonathan could honestly answer that he had no idea. His mother's approach was to take out a quart container, fill it with navy beans and then have Jonathan count them. He then had to multiply the number of beans by sixteen to come up with an approximate number of beans in a peck. It had two purposes. Jonathan never forgot having to count the number of beans, or cabbages in a bushel, tomatoes in a bushel, or other crops / products. Secondly, it set the stage for determining value in farming. For instance, how many beans had to be grown, in order to get the number of beans in a peck? If a bean plant produced ten bean strings per plant, and there were four beans in each string that could be used, how many bean plants needed to be planted? Her next level was to include the concept of wastage. A percentage of plants would die or not produce ten strings. Then would come the space needed to grow the plants, the labour costs for weeding, watering, and harvesting the various types of plants. Next, the cost for seed and sale of the harvested product was considered. The final level was the comparison of different crops, and the amount of space to be allocated to them in the garden.

The local Pastor had attempted to school the local youth who were sons and daughters of his congregation. Although studying only two mornings a week, Jonathan had learned his ABCs. He could print both his name and rudimentary information, such as the names of the various crops or items he might need to buy or sell. His reading was limited. He could at least read the names and labels on barrels and boxes in the local store.

※

One day in September, Malcolm Cartwright, a cousin of Archie's, came over to the Swift farm. He sat with Joe and outlined a proposition. The harvest was bountiful, but there was not much of a market in the hamlet. He proposed to take a wagon load to Rye, a distance of about twenty miles. At Rye there was a better market for their produce because it was a larger centre. There were also ships arriving in the port that needed provisions and sometimes agricultural cargo. The coastal ships were especially looking for fresh vegetables and fresh meat. Neither Malcolm nor the Swifts had any meat, but they did have vegetables. Malcolm proposed that he provide half a wagon load and that Joe Swift provide the other half. He also proposed that instead of Joe accompanying his produce, young Jonathan could go. That way Joe could continue working at the farm, and Jonathan could oversee the transactions on behalf of the Swift family. It was a good idea, and Joe liked it.

Joe knew that Malcolm Cartwright was having a tough go of it. He had taken in two of Archie's children after Archie was sent to gaol. This was an opportunity for Malcolm, and he had invited Joe as well. It looked to Joe that there was no downside to this proposition.

Joe agreed to the deal, and it was further agreed that the next day was as good a day as any. They had no idea when ships would be entering or leaving the port, so any day was as good as the next.

Joe called Jonathan over. He explained the proposition, and the part that Jonathan would have to play. They began preparing the produce for loading in the morning. After a break for supper, Joe took Jonathan aside and started explaining how much Jonathan should be getting for each quantity and type of vegetable. When he was satisfied that Jonathan fully understood the seriousness of the transactions to take place the next day, Joe said good night to him.

Jonathan had planned on a hunting excursion that evening, but he now cancelled it. He went to bed, but tossed and turned as he realized the responsibility that was being placed upon his shoulders. He would not let his family down.

In the morning, Jonathan was up early to get washed and make himself presentable for the trip to Rye. He even put on his only pair of shoes. As he finished breakfast, a horse and wagon pulled into the yard. It was Malcolm Cartwright driving an empty wagon. Although initially surprised at the empty wagon, Joe and Jonathan rapidly loaded the wagon with the Swift's produce. All the while Malcolm watched. Once loaded, Jonathan mounted the wagon, and Malcolm started the horse. They ended up going an extra two miles back to Malcolm's farm where they both loaded Malcolm's produce onto the wagon.

Two things were evident to Jonathan. The first was that Malcolm was lazy. The second was that there was considerably more produce from the Swift farm than there was from the Cartwright farm. Jonathan would have to be very cautious to ensure that the Swift's produce was actually sold as the Swift's produce. In other words, the money needed to end up in his pocket, not in Cartwright's pocket. He didn't know how far to trust Cartwright. His father had warned him never to trust another with your money - to always look after it yourself.

The trip to Rye was long and boring. Cartwright only mumbled a few words during the entire trip. Jonathan contented himself with observing the countryside; noting the crops, any game he could see, and the state of the various farms.

Rye was a bustling little community. There were a few small ships in the harbour. The fishing fleet was out. There was an open market not far from the wharves. It appeared to be very active. Jonathan hoped it would also be very lucrative.

What appeared to be very active from a distance was in fact deceptive. It was afternoon by the time they arrived in Rye, and the market was winding down.

Malcolm found a location toward one end of the market and rolled in. He unhitched the team, and led them away for water. In the meantime Jonathan started moving the various vegetables to improve the display, and make them more appealing to potential buyers.

Jonathan's efforts were well and immediately rewarded. No sooner had he positioned the first two rows when a nautical gentleman strolled up to him. The nautical gentlemen began inquiring about the prices for certain produce. Having been briefed by his father the night before about the minimum price, Jonathan set a price approximately twenty five percent higher than what his father had suggested. The nautical gentleman looked at him quizzically, and then closely examined the produce.

"It's not worth that much," he said.

Jonathan spotted the opening, and queried, "In your opinion, what do you think it is worth?"

The nautical gentleman replied with various figures for each produce, approximately thirty percent less than what Jonathan quoted. Jonathan said, "Well, I disagree with your figures, but I am prepared to meet you halfway." He then outlined various figures for the different produce that ranged between ten and fifteen percent higher than what his father had recommended he get for it.

The nautical gentleman mumbled to himself while trying to make a decision. He then quoted a lower price for each type of vegetable. Jonathan just looked at him, smiled, and said, "Thank you for your kind offer sir, but I met you halfway already. I think that's fair to both of us."

The nautical gentleman looked hard at Jonathan. He had completely misjudged the lad. He turned and walked away. As he strolled down through the market, he was carefully observing the remaining produce at other vendors stands while in his peripheral vision he was observing the body language that Jonathan was sending. He was dismayed. The quality of the vegetables remaining in the market was much lower than that of Jonathan's. These other vegetables had already been well picked over. Secondly he had expected to see Jonathan wringing his hands and bemoaning the fact that a buyer had walked away without purchasing. He was surprised because Jonathan displayed none of these telltale signs.

At the end of the first lane of the market, the nautical gentleman turned around and idled back toward Jonathan. He looked at the young man and shook his head. "All right young man, you have a deal."

Jonathan looked at him, and said, "Very good sir, and how much would you be having?"

The nautical gentleman approached the wagon, and counted the various containers of vegetables. "All of it - the entire wagon load. However, I expect it to be delivered to my ship, Sussex Lady. Payment will be made there. Do we have an agreement?"

Jonathan did not say anything immediately. He first tallied all the containers of each type of vegetable, and did the sums in his head as he had been taught. After tallying each produce type, he completed the sums, and stated the price to the nautical gentleman.

"Agreed"

"Then I will proceed directly to your ship. Where might I find her?" questioned Jonathan.

"She is docked, fourth ship down from this end," stated the nautical gentleman.

"I will need either payment now, or a paper indicating purchase, before I move, if you please sir."

The nautical gentleman blinked. "I have never heard of that," he said.

"It's protection for both of us," stated Jonathan. "You might not be at the ship when I arrive, and they would not know that you had purchased this produce. I could also possibly say that you purchased it, but for a higher price. With the paper, or the payment, you get exactly what you asked for at the price we agreed."

The nautical gentleman was dumbfounded. He had again totally underestimated this young lad. He was more astute than most of the sellers in this marketplace. Begrudgingly, he took out paper and a pencil. He wrote up a bill of sale, had Jonathan look at it, and he signed it.

Jonathan thanked him, and visually started searching for Malcolm. He saw Malcolm shuffling back toward him.

While waiting for Malcolm he started to reload the wagon with all the produce that he had shifted for presentation purposes. By the time Malcolm shambled back the wagon was reloaded.

Malcolm was obviously disgruntled. He saw many of the market vendors closing shop, and loading to go home. It was going to be a challenge selling a full load of produce, so they did not return home with most of the produce that they brought. Additionally, it looked like he was going to have to do all the work himself because this young lad had no sense of sales. The wagon hadn't even been unloaded for display as yet!

Malcolm shuffled up beside Jonathan and said, "I thought I'd mentioned for you to unload some of the product to present it better".

"You did," replied Jonathan.

"Well then why is it not done?" bemoaned a frustrated Malcolm.

"Because we have to move it," replied Jonathan.

"Move it? Move it to where?" responded Malcolm.

"I've sold some to a ship's agent, and he wants it delivered to the ship," countered Jonathan.

"Couldn't you have waited to deliver it until later, after we sold the rest?" whined Malcolm.

"No. He wants his purchases delivered immediately, so we have to go now," replied Jonathan respectfully.

Malcolm grumbled, turned around and went to fetch the horses. When he returned, he lackadaisically hitched up and mounted the wagon. He started the horse, and they slowly progressed toward the wharves.

Jonathan spotted the Sussex Lady, and they trundled over to it. "Ahoy, on the Sussex Lady," he yelled.

A figure appeared and leaned over the side. "Whatcha want?" hollered the figure.

"Load of fresh produce to be loaded aboard," replied Jonathan.

The figure backed up, walked over to the stairwell and called down. A couple of minutes later a husky man dropped over the side onto the wharf, and approached Jonathan.

Jonathan pulled out the bill of sale, jumped down, and met the man. "An agent for the ship agreed to purchase this entire wagon load of produce. A condition of sale was that it be delivered here to the ship."

The husky man said, "Fine, can you back that wagon down the wharf to near the entry port?"

"Sure," said Jonathan, "but before loading, I will require payment."

At this statement, both the husky man, and Malcolm perked up, and stared at Jonathan. The husky man disappeared back aboard ship. A few minutes later he reappeared with another man who appeared to be his superior. In fact, the other man was the vessel commander.

"What's this about payment?" asked the captain.

Jonathan approached the captain. "Good day sir. An agent for the ship agreed to purchase this entire wagon load of produce, for an agreed sum. A condition of the sale was that the produce be brought to the ship. We are also willing to assist in the loading, however, before loading, we will require payment. Here is the paper signed by the ship's agent."

The captain took the contract out of his hands, and read it. He checked the signature at the bottom of the contract to see if it was his agent. He swore under his breath, but loud enough for Jonathan to hear.

"Alright," said the captain. "I have to go get the funds. Miller, get a crew together. Prepare to sling this load aboard."

Malcolm grabbed the paper from Jonathan's hands. He quickly looked at the paper, but it was meaningless to him as he could not read. As he looked down at Jonathan his jaw dropped. Jonathan had sold the entire wagon load of produce. He could apparently read and write. And he appeared smart enough to make sure the captain of the Sussex Lady did not gyp them.

Malcolm whispered to Jonathan, "What did you sell them for?" As Jonathan whispered back some of the prices, Malcolm was further astounded. Jonathan had attained higher prices for his produce than he had believed possible. And he had done it all within minutes. Unbelievable!

The captain reappeared and doled out the money. Even though Malcolm was by far the senior person, the captain gave the money to Jonathan. He sensed that Jonathan was far more competent to look after it than Malcolm.

Malcolm and Jonathan assisted the ship's crew in loading each sling as it was lowered to them. The first one was difficult, and required a ship's crew member to show them how. Once they figured out how to do it, each time it became progressively easier. Within thirty minutes the wagon was empty, and they were on their way.

It was now around four in the afternoon. Jonathan was hot, tired and thirsty. He had missed lunch and hadn't had a drink of water since he left the Swift farm. Malcolm suggested that they stop somewhere for a bite and a drink. Given his state, Jonathan was quite agreeable.

One thing bothered him however. He was carrying a lot of money, some of it Cartwright's. He did not want that responsibility. Additionally, he didn't trust Cartwright. It was, in his opinion, very possible that Cartwright would order drink and a meal, and then claim he had no money. The no money part was likely true, but then he would expect Jonathan to pay out of the funds. Cartwright would then demand full payment of his share of the sale. This would leave Jonathan to foot the entire bill for food and drink. Jonathan wanted to avoid this. He was also concerned about showing any money in the tavern because who knew who, or what dangers were in there. They had a long way to go back home, and it would be easy to get waylaid en route.

Before entering the tavern, Jonathan excused himself, and went to the side of the tavern to relieve himself. In reality it was for another reason.

First he divided the money into Swift and Cartwright portions. Then, from the Swift portion, he took just enough for a meal. He would drink water, because he doubted that they would sell any beer to him anyway. Besides, he had never had beer, or any type of alcohol, because of his age, and the family couldn't afford it. The rest of the Swift money he tightly rolled in a bit of cloth so it would not clink or make any type of noise. He then tied each end of the cloth with twine, and wrapped the twine around his waistline, so that the money was tucked behind, and slightly below, his belt. He pocketed both his meal money and Cartwright's money.

Jonathan went inside. The tavern was L shaped. On the long side was the bar. At the back, at the base of the L, was a large fireplace covering the majority of the wall. There was a low fire burning, but the room was reasonably cool. Old wooden beams, that appeared to be oak, showed axe marks where they had been originally formed. It was hard to tell if the beams were oak, as they were blackened from years of soot emanating from the fireplace. There were a few crude tables and wooden benches. All of the furniture was heavy, and appropriate for rough handling. The floor was beaten earth with some straw and sawdust.

Behind the bar, the bartender was built like a barrel. He had thick arms, almost no neck, and a flattened nose. He was about five and a half feet tall, and looked like he could handle any type of problem in the tavern. As Jonathan entered, he saw Malcolm at the bar conversing with the bartender. No one else appeared to be in the tavern.

Jonathan walked over to Malcolm. As he approached, he heard Malcolm ask the bartender if it was possible to get anything to eat. The bartender replied, "Supper's in an hour, so you'll have to wait."

"What's the fare?" inquired Malcolm.

"The regular - ploughman's special," replied the bartender.

"Give me a beer and a ploughman's special," said Malcolm without even glancing at Jonathan.

The bartender replied, "That'll be five pence." He looked directly at Malcolm, taking in his clothing and mannerisms. "In advance, just so there's no misunderstanding."

Malcolm's hands were below the bar and out of sight of the bartender. Jonathan used this opportunity to pass the money owed to Cartwright over to Malcolm. There was a slight clink of coins as the transfer took place. It was evident the bartender heard the clink because the expression on his face changed. The bartender did not realize however that it was a transfer of money. He believed that Malcolm was just digging in his pocket.

Jonathan looked at the bartender and said, "Excuse me sir. How much for a ploughman's special only and a mug of water?" As he said this Jonathan displayed two pennies in his hand where the bartender could see them, but it appeared that he was attempting to hide the fact that he had little money.

The bartender replied, "Two pence."

Jonathan said, "I'll take one please." The bartender nodded.

As the bartender turned and walked back to the door to the kitchen, Jonathan said to Malcolm, "The money I gave you is for your portion of the vegetables we sold this afternoon. I therefore don't owe you any further money."

Malcolm became immediately suspicious. He walked away toward the window and turned his back toward the bar facing the window. He took the money, and counted it in his hand. It was accurate, less the money he had just paid for his meal. He was not happy however. Even though he had made more money than he had anticipated, having to deal with a youthful Jonathan, who at sixteen had more confidence and more smarts than he did, irked him.

Malcolm returned to the bar, picked up his beer, and walked over to a table. He lifted his legs over the bench and sat down. He placed both hands on his mug and bent over it. His eyes scanned the room. Nothing caught his attention, so he commenced emptying his mug.

Jonathan waited at the bar. When the bartender came back, he filled a mug of water and set it in front of Jonathan. "Thank you sir," said Jonathan. The bartender nodded. Jonathan drained the mug almost immediately, and set it back on the bar. The bartender smiled. "A little thirsty were we?" He refilled the mug, and moved further down the bar.

Time passed slowly. Jonathan left Malcolm alone. The man was not much of a conversationalist, and appeared to be moving further and further into a foul mood. Jonathan reckoned the ride home would be unpleasant.

Finally the bartender appeared with two large plates of food. He sat one in front of Malcolm, and the other directly across from him. There was a spoon with each plate. One look and one whiff from the plate were enough to make Jonathan's mouth water. He quickly sat down, and devoured everything on the plate.

He looked up and saw that Malcolm was slowly consuming his meal. He had purchased at least two additional mugs of beer, and appeared to be more focused on drinking his supper than eating.

Jonathan was impatient to be away. He spoke to Malcolm, "It's getting dark out and we have a long ways to go. We should be leaving. I can drive if you wish."

Malcolm replied, "All in good time."

There wasn't much that Jonathan could say or do at this point to speed Malcolm up. In fact, given Malcolm's mood, it was probably better not to say anything and just wait.

The minutes ticked by, and darkness descended. Little by little the tavern started to fill up. For the most part the patrons were trades people and residents of Rye. After a bit the locals drifted on. They were replaced by sailors, or what appeared to be either fishermen or others working on the sea.

By this time Jonathan was impatient. It was at least four hours to home. In the darkness anything could happen, and he was carrying what he considered a large sum of money. Given the current state of Malcolm's sobriety he doubted Malcolm would be of much use if something happened.

He rose to leave, and felt a hand grasp his jacket. Malcolm said, "What's your hurry?"

Jonathan replied, "I wanna get home."

Jonathan's caution turned to concern when he glanced up and saw Abercrombie and Fitzgerald in the door. They were looking around as if they were seeking someone. He did not have a good feeling about this.

As Abercrombie's eyes swivelled toward him, he saw recognition on Abercrombie's face. Abercrombie elbowed Fitzgerald and mumbled something to him. Fitzgerald then looked directly at Jonathan. A leering grin covered his face.

Abercrombie and Fitzgerald moved toward the bar. They ordered a mug of beer each, and leaned against the bar slowly sipping their respective drinks. From time to time they glanced over at Malcolm and Jonathan. The longer it occurred, the more nervous Jonathan became. Cartwright appeared to be drunk and only semi-responsive to any approaches by Jonathan.

As Jonathan saw it he had three possibilities. He could try and drag Malcolm out of here. That might be successful, but then he had a long way to go in the dark with Malcolm on a known route. If Abercrombie and Fitzgerald were after him they would have no difficulty finding him. Alternatively, he could leave immediately without Malcolm. If he took the wagon he could be accused of stealing, so that was out. That only left a long walk home. And if he was smart he would not use the road. But Abercrombie and Fitzgerald would know that. They would be hunting him. Then again he could be imagining all of this, but he didn't think so.

If he was going, he'd better get on with it. Waiting would not improve the situation.

Jonathan figured he might be able to get away by going out to relieve himself. Then he could slip down another alley and get to the countryside. He figured if he could get to the countryside he would have a reasonable chance because he knew his wood lore was good. There were a lot of open fields, but with enough fence lines to make it challenging for two people to find him when he was on the move.

He got up and started moving toward the door. In front of him the door opened, and a number of muscular men holding small wooden bats entered. All of them were dressed similarly in white duck trousers with blue jackets, although there was a wide variety of kerchiefs and different coloured shirts beneath the jackets.

The entire tavern went deadly silent. "The Press," someone yelled, "run for it". The entire tavern exploded into frantic activity as all the male patrons scrambled for a way out. Jonathan was shoved, and reeled to his left. He was just attempting to gain his balance when he was pushed again. He lost his balance and fell.

Around him furniture was crashing. Men were screaming and yelling. The small wooden bats were rising and falling on heads.

He lifted himself up, and felt a heavy blow on his head. Everything went black.

He was vaguely conscious of being dragged, but he did not know where. His head pulsated. He saw flashes of light, then darkness over and over again. He had no conscious memory of anything. He had no strength, no coordination, and no desire to move or do anything until this tremendous pain in his head ceased.

He came to with a start. He couldn't breathe. His face was submerged in water. In fact, his whole front was soaking wet. And there was a swaying motion. His head was still pulsating, but even with that, more pain of an acute nature happened, when someone grabbed and lifted him by his hair. He felt he was dragged a short distance and then unceremoniously dropped, so his face cracked against some wood. At least it was dry wood - although the rest of his body still remained in some water. The next thing he knew someone stepped on him. It wasn't the full weight, but there was still a foot on his leg and another on his back. This went on for some time until he lost consciousness again.

Chapter 4
Headaches

Jonathan regained some vague form of consciousness. He was lying heaped upon some form of wooden floor, his body bruised and battered. He ached all over, but it was nothing compared to the pulsating pain throbbing through his skull.

Jonathan attempted to focus his eyes but he could see nothing. There was blackness all around him, but he sensed movement - lots of movement. There was a malodorous smell like something rotten or foul. He could not quite identify it, but it was not pleasant. It reminded him of the barnyard, but it was different.

He felt cramped, but as he attempted to move, pain flashed through his body. Bright white light flashed across his eyes. The pounding in his head was sheer agony. He just closed his eyes, and sank back into oblivion.

At some point in time Jonathan felt hands grab him, and move him up. His feet dragged along the floor and then hit something solid. He moaned. Things shifted. The hands that had been grasping him on either side of the shoulder now shifted, and he felt himself being lifted. He felt a heavy pressure in the middle of his stomach as if someone had thrown him over his shoulder.

Jonathan attempted to open his eyes. With all the blood rushing to his head the throbbing inside intensified massively and he saw flashes. After considerable agony, he was able to see that darkness had changed into a dimmed light. As he was bumped and jostled further, the light increased until it was blinding.

He felt himself beginning to swing. The next thing he felt were hands, first upon his back, then shifting to his arms. He heard a shout from somewhere, "Stand in line, you useless toads".

Jonathan had no strength. He could not stand. He could not balance. He could not focus. He could not make sense of things. All he knew was the incredible pain in his skull. He sensed rather than knew that he was being held up on either side by other men.

He felt his hair being grabbed, and his face being lifted. Someone said, "What's wrong with this one?"

"Took a pretty hard crack on the skull, sir," replied a different voice. "Not sure when he will come out of it."

"Or if he will come out of it?" stated the sir. "Who hit him?"

"Not sure sir," replied the other voice. "There was a right ballyhoo for a few minutes as everyone in the tavern tried to scamper. When it was all over we found this one unconscious on the floor. None of my men admit to hitting him, and honestly sir, I don't believe we did. There were two suspicious characters around this lad and another man. They showed us protection papers, so we had to let them go."

"Where's the other man?" queried the sir. "Perhaps he can shed some light on this?"

"He's dead. We found him that way after the dust had settled, so to speak," replied the other voice. "It's also a funny thing, but the dead man's pockets and this lad's pockets were all pulled out or ripped as if they had been searched or robbed."

"So what you're telling me bosun is that this young lad is the victim of theft and attempted murder. That the press were responsible for saving him? Won't he be especially grateful when he recovers?" smiled the sir.

The bosun was not sure how to take that comment, so all he said was, "Aye, sir."

"Take this man down to the surgeon," ordered the sir. "Does anyone know this lad's name?"

No one spoke up.

"In that case we'll put him on the books as Jon Smith," stated the sir. "We will rate him 'Landsman'. We will worry about his watch when or if he recovers. Next man!"

Jonathan felt himself being lifted on someone's shoulder again. Again the throbbing in his head increased and he descended into darkness and that malodorous smell.

A short time later he felt himself dumped onto the floor, or at least some hard object.

He heard a new voice, "What's this?"

"Business for you Bones. You can thank the press gang for it. They really clobbered this guy," said another voice.

"Didn't the surgeon look at him on deck?" queried Bones.

"No, this poor bastard was too far gone. Jimmy the One ordered him down here before the surgeon could get to him," replied the other voice.

"Well then give me a hand, and put him up on the table. Let's see what's wrong with him," said Bones.

"Just look at his skull. There's blood. Nobody's lifted a finger to help this poor bastard. The press gang just dumped his carcass in the hold, and left him to fend for himself. Christ, he can't even lift himself up. What a bunch of heartless bastards," stated the other voice.

"Will you get me some water?" asked Bones.

Jonathan heard movement, and then sensed fewer people were present. A hand was placed on his head, and turned his head to one side. The hand was not gentle. It was firm. Another hand started working its way over his head. On the right side, as the hand touched his scalp above the hairline, pain shot through to his very core. He twisted his head to alleviate the pressure. Concurrently, he heard screaming. He did not realize it was his screaming. The pain was too much. He arched his back and collapsed. He had passed out.

When he next regained some form of consciousness he was lying in some contraption. He tried to lift his arm, but had difficulty. There appeared to be some weight on it. After some time, Jonathan realized it was some type of cover or blanket. He was lying on part of it, and it therefore was difficult to move. He worked his arm free of the blanket, and touched his face. It was sweaty. He continued to move his hand up his face. His hand encountered a bandage. His entire head was wrapped in some kind of wrapping or bandage. He gently started to feel all around his head. As he touched the right side of his head he winced. The pain was severe, but nothing like what he vaguely remembered from before.

It was dark. There was no movement to indicate that others were present. There was, however, a sensation of motion. He was terribly thirsty, and his bladder felt like it would explode.

"Water," he croaked, but the sound was very feeble. The effort left him exhausted. He passed back into unconsciousness.

He again woke. His mouth was dry, his pants were wet, and he felt terrible.

"Water," he croaked. This time a shadow appeared.

"What is it mate?" asked the shadow

"Water," he croaked again.

Jonathan felt something against his lips and felt water on his lips and face. He opened his mouth. A trickle of water flowed in. He swallowed, and continued swallowing until the water stopped.

He tried to focus on who had helped him, but he could only see shadows.

The pain in his head was still present, throbbing, but not the blinding flashes he had previously experienced. "Thanks," he croaked. It was not clear if anyone had heard him.

Jonathan drifted back to sleep. He dreamt of his family. Did they know what had become of him? Where he was? It was unlikely, because he had no idea where he was. All he knew was that it was not with his family. He had no knowledge of who was caring for him. Whoever it was, was not gentle like his mother, but was not rough either.

He tried to piece together what had happened. The last he could remember he was waiting upon Malcolm to leave the tavern. He remembered several men entering the tavern who appeared to be in some form of uniform. He also remembered someone saying something about 'the press'. The only press he knew was something he had heard about the Navy doing to abduct men.

But primarily he concentrated upon his family. He remembered suddenly that he was supposedly carrying money from the sale of vegetables at Rye. Where was that money? He felt along his pants. His pockets had been pulled out or ripped apart. It was obvious that someone had robbed him at some point. But then he remembered the money was not in his pocket. He slid his hand under his belt and searched for the cloth strip in which he had wrapped the coins. Surprisingly, it was still there.

He attempted to raise his head to peer around. There was significant pain, and he didn't see much. It was dark or semi-dark, and there were no windows that he could see. He was confused as to his location.

He had no idea of the time, how long he had been there, or how long it would take before he had full use of his senses. He did know that he was very, very hungry. It was if he had not eaten in days. He knew that feeling from the past.

He sensed a motion, and saw a shadow move. "Please," he croaked. The shadow stopped, turned, and moved toward him. "Please," he croaked, "where am I?"

The shadow chuckled and said, "Well, it looks like you're going to live, and I'll bet you're hungry?"

Jonathan croaked, "Yes, but where am I?"

"You're in your new home, His Majesty's Ship Winchester," replied the shadow. "Now just lie still and I'll go see if I can find some food for you." The shadow disappeared.

Jonathan sank back and closed his eyes. I'm on a ship he thought. I've never been on a ship in my life. And this ship's Royal Navy, so the press must have got me. They whacked me on the head, and dragged me back here, probably with other victims from the tavern. Just great!

Jonathan had heard stories about men taken by the press. Most had never returned. They went away to the far corners of the world, died, escaped and were hunted like criminals, or stayed in the Navy unable or unwilling to leave. He had heard stories of sailors from Rye. But he had also heard that farm labourers were exempt. If so, then why was he here? What of Malcolm? Was he here? He had lots of questions, but no answers. And something told him intuitively that he was unlikely to get many answers. He was feeling too poorly to worry about his status on board a navy ship at the present. That would come later once he regained his strength.

The shadow reappeared. He felt his head lifted, and something brushed his lips. He opened his mouth and ate something. It felt like a piece of wood. "What's this?" he mumbled.

"You'll get used to it. Wheeze calls it bread. Others call it hardtack, and yet others have some other fancy names for it. Generally, to eat it you need to soak it for a bit. Since I don't have anything for you to soak it in, you'll have to do without. It's the best I could do for you," said the shadow.

"I need to go," said Jonathan.

"No doubt," replied the shadow. "You've been laying there for three days. Do you think you can stand?"

"No idea," replied Jonathan.

"Well let's give it a try," said the shadow. He lifted Jonathan's legs, and rotated them. He then grasped Jonathan behind his shoulders, and gently lifted his body. He ensured his hand was on the back of Jonathan's neck so that his head was steadied. As Jonathan's body shifted into an upright position the pain in his head pulsed. Jonathan involuntarily groaned.

"I don't think so," croaked Jonathan.

"Well then, we'll do it the hard way," chuckled the shadow. He tipped Jonathan over his shoulder, and then started moving. Despite his throbbing pulsating head, Jonathan realized he was being taken up two different flights of stairs. The further up he went the lighter it became.

After the last flight of stairs, he got a whiff of fresh air. It was still dark, but a lighter dark. He was on the deck.

The shadow bent down, and Jonathan's feet touched the deck. "Now be very careful," said the shadow. "I'm going to set you down. You need to drop your pants, and shift backwards. You're going to be hanging over the edge of the ship, so you'll need to hold on because if you fall backwards you're gone. Do you understand?"

"Yes, I think so," replied Jonathan. "If I can only get my balance, I should be alright."

"All right, place your left hand here on this rope, and hold tightly," stated the shadow. "With your right hand lower your pants. There's another rope on your right side the same as the left. Once you drop your pants, grasp the rope on your right side, and sit down on the jakes. Then you can do your business."

Jonathan did as he was instructed, and collapsed on the jakes. Luckily when he dropped his pants his shirt dropped down, and covered his money strip.

When he was finished he reached down with his right hand, and pulled his pants back up. He managed to buckle his belt, but he was dizzy.

He fell forward, and was grabbed by the other man, who slung Jonathan over his shoulder. He was then carted back down to where he began.

After some difficulty, he was rearranged in what he now realized was a hammock. It was the first time he had ever slept in a hammock. He found it reasonably comfortable. The trip up to the deck had exhausted him, so he rapidly drifted off to sleep.

The next time he awoke it was still dark in the bowels of the ship, so he had no idea of the time. He did hear some sound like a whistle, and shortly thereafter the sound of many feet moving above him.

Shortly thereafter a shadow appeared over him.

"What time is it? Is it morning?" requested Jonathan.

"Morning watch," replied the shadow. But it was a different voice. "The captain has everybody stand by the guns at first light just in case."

"I don't know what that means," replied Jonathan.

"You'll find out matey," chuckled the shadow as he shuffled away.

Jonathan was left to himself again. He was still in pain. His head still throbbed, although it wasn't as bad as before. His stomach ached and growled from lack of food. And finally his intestines and bladder were again working properly. He needed to ease that pressure.

Jonathan decided to take matters into his own hands, so to speak. He lifted his legs, and started to rotate in the hammock, so that he could stand up. The next thing he knew he was on the floor. If his head had hurt before, now it was excruciating. He gasped at the pain. He stayed immobile for a few minutes, and gradually the pain subsided.

He got to his hands and knees, and prepared to lift himself up. It was a major struggle as he had little or no balance. He had lost some coordination. He was lacking any strength in his legs. He rose until he was resting on his knees. After the pain subsided he swung one foot out in front of him, and prepared to stand up. Since he was close to the wall, he grasped the hammock rope to steady himself. He sucked in a lungful of air, pulled with his hand, and used whatever strength he had left in his legs to stand.

He was standing. Fortunately, he was still bent over because his arm still grasped the hammock rope to steady himself. He stood up fully erect, and hammered his head into a low deck beam. The pain was so unbearable he passed out and collapsed on the floor.

That's the way they found him when the surgeon came down to examine him a short time later.

The surgeon and the surgeon's mate manoeuvred him back into the hammock. The surgeon's mate held a lantern over Jonathan's head as the surgeon examined him.

"Well, he had a concussion. Now it appears he has a second one," stated the surgeon, shaking his head. "At this rate he'll be here another month."

"Either that, or overboard," replied the surgeon's mate.

"Two days ago I would've said that's a distinct possibility," said the surgeon. "But now it appears he has some use of his faculties, or at least he had. I guess I better go report, as Mr. Wilkinson was inquiring about him this morning."

At that the surgeon turned and walked away. He hesitated. "By the way," he said. "Have some food down here in case he comes to. Gruel, or soup, I should think".

After another week Jonathan was steady enough to stand, and climb up the decks by himself. He was escorted by one of the surgeon's mate's each time he made the journey.

The surgeon felt he was ready for light duties. He reported this to Mr. Wilkinson, the first lieutenant. But he stipulated that Jonathan would have problems with balance and coordination for a period of time.

Chapter 5
HMS Winchester

Jonathan was called on deck. Up to this point his only interaction was with the surgeon's mates, and infrequently, the surgeon. One of the surgeon's mates - Chuckles he was called- was friendly enough, and a reasonably kind man. He was older, about 40 as far as Jonathan could tell. He also was short, about five and a half feet tall. The most remarkable thing about Chuckles was his nose. It was big and odd coloured in the shadow-like darkness of the sick bay.

The other surgeon's mate, called Sticks because of his peg leg, was a bitter, uncommunicative man. He seemed to enjoy, or at least be indifferent to, anyone else's plight or pain. He was compact and physically very strong. He had lifted Jonathan on more than one occasion without any apparent effort.

After having learned their names Jonathan was surprised when other men addressed them. They all seemed to address either Chuckles or Sticks as 'Bones'. Jonathan couldn't make any sense out of it.

Knowing that he would be taken before the first lieutenant, Chuckles provided some unsolicited advice. He told Jonathan, "Keep your mouth shut. Respond only to the questions you're asked by him. And say sir at the end of each response."

Jonathan asked him, "Why?"

Chuckles just laughed and said, "If you want to find out why, then just don't do what I told you."

As Jonathan rose out of the hatch onto the main deck he blinked at the sunlight. He stared around in awe at the number of men, the guns, and the height of the masts. For him it was overwhelming.

"Smith," bellowed a voice. "Get over here."

Jonathan stood dumb founded. He did not realize who was speaking, and that the individual was speaking to him. A rough hand grabbed him, and propelled him aft toward the quarter deck.

"Get your ass over here," bellowed the voice again.

Jonathan looked around trying to identify who belonged to the voice. He saw a big, balding man, with biceps as big as his thighs staring at him, and looking impatient.

He walked over to the man and said, "Are you looking for me sir?"

The big man just glared at him and said, "Come on."

They strode a few feet to the lee side of the ship and went up the stairs to the quarterdeck. The big man knuckled his forehead to a younger distinguished looking officer. "Jon Smith, sir."

"My name is Wilkinson. I am the first lieutenant of His Majesty's Ship Winchester," said the distinguished looking officer. "The last time I saw you, you were in no condition to state whether you wish to volunteer for His Majesty's Navy."

Jonathan was all of a sudden very aware of Chuckles' warning. He looked carefully at the first lieutenant.

"So would you like to volunteer?" asked the first lieutenant.

Jonathan replied, "Sir, I have no idea what that means. I have never even been on a ship."

The first lieutenant raised his hand and covered the lower half of his face. He shifted his gaze toward the bosun. Jonathan glanced at the big man who was rolling his eyes and shaking his head at what Jonathan had said. Jonathan felt foolish, but he truly did not know what he was being asked.

"If you volunteer, you get a signing bonus. If you do not volunteer, then you are entered on the books as being pressed," stated the first lieutenant.

Jonathan stared at the first lieutenant. He tried to analyze what had been said. It was not what had been said, but what hadn't been said that captured his attention. He was stuck here. He certainly couldn't physically challenge the men who had pressed him, as he would be crushed. The size of the bosun's bicep was the same size as his thigh. The only difference being offered to him was whether he got a signing bonus or not. What other negative things associated with being pressed were also not discussed. Given the limited information available to him, Jonathan made the only decision he figured would be beneficial to him.

"Sir, I believe I would like to volunteer, but I know of no skill that I have that might be useful to the Navy," stated Jonathan.

Again the first lieutenant raised his hand and covered the lower portion of his face. "I will mark you down in the books as a volunteer Smith. And don't worry about your skill level. I trust the bosun will be able to teach you something - won't you Bosun?"

"Aye, sir, that I will," growled the bosun. Jonathan cringed at the menace in those words.

"Now as to watch, we'll put him in the larboard watch in Mr. Galbraith's division," stated the first lieutenant. "Carry on Bosun".

The bosun grabbed Jonathan by the arm and spun him around. He pushed him toward the stairs on the lee side of the quarterdeck. Jonathan moved cautiously toward the stairs as he still did not have his full balance. He staggered, and felt another push on his back. It was clear the bosun had a low tolerance for anyone that was not a sailor.

The bosun spotted Mr. Galbraith in the waist, and headed toward him with Jonathan in tow.

"Lieutenant Galbraith, sir," said the bosun. When he had Mr. Galbraith's attention he further stated "Lieutenant Wilkinson has assigned this man to your division, larboard watch."

"Thank you, Bosun," replied Lieutenant Galbraith. "Name?"

"Jon Smith, landsman, sir," replied the bosun.

Lieutenant Galbraith looked at the bosun and arched his brow. He then turned, and looked at Jonathan.

"So Smith, what do you know about ships?" queried Lieutenant Galbraith.

"Sir, I have never even been on a ship before," replied Jonathan.

Galbraith sighed. He looked around, and spotted an older sailor from his division. "Pollard, come here."

Pollard looked up, and walked over to Lieutenant Galbraith. "Aye sir?" said Pollard as he knuckled his forehead.

"Pollard, this is Jon Smith. He's on the larboard watch same as you. I'd like you to take him under your wing, and teach him what he has to know," ordered Lieutenant Galbraith.

"Aye, sir"

"I'll give you the full details of his assignments after I figure them out," stated Lieutenant Galbraith.

"Com' on lad," said Pollard. Jonathan and Pollard withdrew from Galbraith's presence.

Pollard was an average sized man in his mid thirties with a slight limp. His dark hair was in a braid that extended half way down his back. There were a number of grey hairs that contrasted with the black.

"All right, before you get yourself into some trouble, let me explain a couple things to you," started Pollard. "When you are called or addressed by an officer the appropriate drill is to knuckle them, and say sir." Pollard then demonstrated the correct salute.

"When they give you an order, you acknowledge the order by saying "Aye, sir" or "Aye, aye sir,"" he continued. "Show them respect whether they have earned it or not, because if you don't, you could find yourself on the grates getting a striped back."

"Striped back, what is that?" asked Jonathan.

"Being flogged," responded Pollard. "There's little tolerance here for any mistake. If you don't know, ask me or one of your mates. Never ask an officer directly."

"We'll start with the layout of the ship," continued Pollard. "This is a ship-of-the-line. What they call a 4th rate. The Winchester's got fifty guns on two gun decks, the upper gun deck and the lower gun deck. Some people refer to a ship this size as a two-decker."

"What about the lower deck where the surgeon is?" inquired a curious Jonathan.

"That's called the orlop. It's the deck that covers the hold. The hold is where we store our ballast and heavy items like casks of water, beef, peas and such," replied Pollard.

"What's ballast?" asked Jonathan.

"Ballast is anything heavy used to keep the main weight of the ship at the bottom. You see the mast and guns are really heavy. If we get a big blow, it can cause the ship to lean way over. If the centre of gravity was too high, the whole ship would roll over on her side. We use ballast in the lowest part of the ship to prevent that. We can shift the ballast as well. If we were not carrying as much weight up top, then we could remove some of the ballast. There are other times when shifting the ballast forward or aft - that's to the back of the ship - can improve the ease of steering and handling. You can tell the difference once you're on the wheel," lectured Pollard.

"Alright, from the bottom or keel of the ship, tell me the names of decks," questioned Pollard.

Jonathan replied, "The hold, the orlop, the lower gun deck and the upper gun deck."

"Good," responded Pollard. "Now look foreward. We're standing on which deck?"

"The upper gun deck," quickly replied Jonathan.

"There are three masts on this ship; the foremast, the mainmast and the mizzen mast aft," said Pollard as he pointed them out. "Now look at the area between the foremast and the bow. That's called the forecastle or fo'c'sle. In this ship it is raised above the upper gun deck, but on others it may be the same deck. Now turn around and look aft. The area from the mizzen mast to the stern is called the quarterdeck. That's officer country, so you don't go there unless you have business there, understand."

"Yes," replied Jonathan.

"Now on this ship the quarterdeck is raised. It sits on top of what we call the poop deck," continued Pollard.

"Poop deck? How did it get that name?" asked Jonathan.

"In truth, I don't know where the name can from," replied Pollard. "I can tell you what sailors say. We all know what flows downhill, and from all the shit we get from them officers, well I think you get the picture. The officers live aft. The men who do the real work live foreward."

Pollard continued his discourse, "Now them masts are mighty heavy. When the wind blows you have to make sure that the mast remains in place. You lose a mast and you're in big trouble - at the mercy of the wind and waves. So each mast is secured or held in place with ropes." At this point, Pollard and Jonathan walked over to the nearest shrouds. "These here, are the shrouds that keep the main mast in position when the wind is from abeam - that means from the side - or from aft. Look up, and you will see that they are all attached to the masthead aft, and come down aft of the mast. In between the shrouds are ratlines. These are placed so the topmen can easily climb the shrouds in all weather. Now since the wind may not always come from abeam or aft - it may come from forward, we need other lines to secure the mast in place from the front. These are called stays. Notice that they are attached to the masthead foreward of centre and then run down toward the bow, as opposed to aft like the shrouds."

"You'll notice that the mast is split into different sections. You can't find a tree long enough for the whole mast. Even if you did, I doubt we could lift it into place. The different pieces also allow some more flex. Something that doesn't flex much is more prone to break, and when it breaks, it's usually nasty. Each section has a smaller masthead, and smaller shroud and stay lines. Remember that you have to keep the weight down low to keep the ship stable."

"Them pieces of wood that the sails are attached to - the ones that are horizontal. We calls 'em yards," Pollard explained. "Now them yards are suspended, see. We have to be able to adjust their position to catch the wind. You'll get to know all about that real well before long."

"Now the names of the sails are pretty much the same on all masts. From the bottom they are: the course, topsail, topgallant sail, and the little one at the very top is the royal sail, although we use it only in light wind. We use the name of the mast first, then the name of the sail to identify them - like main course, or main topsail. Get it?" Jonathan nodded.

"Now on this ship there are differences. For example, there is no mizzen course. If you look, you will see why. The course on the foremast and mainmast are square. If you look at the mizzen, you'll see the lower sail is different. We call that the lateen mizzen or mizzen lateen."

"Every once in a while you'll hear the officer of the deck say 'get the courses on or off her'. What he is saying is to either clew up or furl all the courses on each mast."

"What's the difference between clewing up and furling a sail?" asked Jonathan.

"Well in reality, clewing is the first stage of furling. If you look at that course - by the way, what's its name?" demanded Pollard

"That's the main course or mainmast course," replied Jonathan.

"Alright, now look at the bottom of the main course - that's called the 'foot'. The top of the sail is called the 'head', and the sides are called 'leeches'. Do you see the ropes there that go back up to the yard? Those ropes are normally called clewlines, but on the courses, they're called clew garnets. Don't ask me why the difference, I just learned the names. Anyway, when you pull on the clewlines it raises the sail or clews it. This reduces the amount of wind it can catch. We normally clew to different levels if there is blow coming on. The last thing we want is to blow the sticks out of her," commented Pollard.

"By sticks, do you mean the masts?" asked Jonathan. "Is that possible?"

"I've seen it happen," replied Pollard sombrely. There was a faraway look in Pollard's eyes. "If youze been around the sea long enough, sooner or later, you will see the power of the sea for yourself. Many a man's met his Maker when the sea unleashes her fury. Many a man's called upon his Maker for divine help - I know I have."

"Let's go foreward," said Pollard. He seemed to shake himself to get rid of the images he had conjured up in his mind.

Jonathan and Pollard went foreward up to the bow. As they were standing on fo'c'sle, Pollard began to explain the rigging at the front of the ship. "Alright, at the bow we have a different rigging setup than we use on the masts. First, you see that big length of wood jutting out forward - that's called the bowsprit. Think of it like the mast, only pointing forward. Like the mast, it's built in sections - two sections. The bottom section is the bowsprit; the further section is called the jib boom. Got that?"

"Got it - bowsprit here and the jib boom out further," replied Jonathan. "What's that piece sticking up vertically from the end of the bowsprit?"

"That's the jack staff," responded Pollard. "We mount the Union Jack on it while wheeze anchored."

"Why only when anchored?" questioned Jonathan.

"Don't really know," responded Pollard. "But when wheeze at sea, we fly the flag at the top of the main mast, so it can be seen. When the great guns are firing there's a lot of smoke, so it helps if you can see who you're shootin' at, and to make sure that you're not shootin' at your friends, or them at you."

"Now for sails, these sails are generally different shapes - triangular staysails. These sails may be called slightly differently on different rigged ships. You just need to concentrate on the names used on this ship. The one the furthest out you see right now is called the jib. The other is the staysail. We can add another sail further out called the outer jib. There is also a spritsail that can be added, but it is rarely used."

"Now since you're rated as landsman you don't have to go up top. You get to pull on a lot of ropes. We raise and lower yards. We constantly adjust the angle of the yards to improve the amount of wind we capture. We tack back and forth. We raise and lower boats, stores and other stuff, and you'll get to work the great guns. Right now you think a rope is a rope, but you'll find each one has a different name and different characteristic when you pull. The only thing they have in common is that they're all a bitch to pull and you have to work in a team with rhythm to get the job done" said Pollard.

"Pollard," hollered a voice. "What are you skylarking about for when you're supposed to be working in the waist?"

Pollard looked up startled. "Mr. Galbraith ordered me to familiarize this man with the ship."

The voice appeared. It was a lanky, foul looking man with a flattened nose. He looked Pollard up and down with his beady eyes. He then shifted his gaze to Jonathan. He took in Jonathan's ragged clothes, his youth and the bandage around his head. "Name," he bellowed.

"His name is Smith - Jon Smith, Mr. Hurley," replied Pollard before Jonathan could open his mouth.

Hurley gave Pollard a look of contempt, and then swivelled his head back toward Jonathan. "What's a matter boy - you as dumb as you look?"

Jonathan was furious. He had only been spoken to before in such a manner by the squire's men. This man was easily as vicious as Abercrombie, Fitzgerald or MacMillan. He bit his tongue. He glanced at Pollard. Pollard's face was blank, but he just perceptibility shook his head.

Jonathan looked back at Hurley. From his experience with the squire's men he knew if he back-talked he might feel good for standing up to this bully, but bullies always plot payback. So considering everything, Jonathan decided to swallow what he was thinking of saying.

"Aye, sir," said Jonathan.

Hurley looked quizzically at Jonathan. He had expected this newcomer to literally explode at being called a dummy. Most pressed men fought authority until it was beat into them. Hurley was therefore at a momentary loss as to what to make of Jonathan's response. "What do ya mean 'Aye, sir'," queried Hurley.

"No disrespect sir, but I don't know who you are, and I don't know anything about ships, other than what Mr. Pollard has explained to me. I guess that makes me appear dumb," stated Jonathan.

Hurley looked sharply at Jonathan. There were a dozen men within earshot who had likely heard the conversation. Was this man mocking him?

"My name's Hurley - MISTER HURLEY to you boy. I'm the bosun's mate for the larboard watch, and don't you forget it. You cross me and I'll have you before the master-at-arms before you can blink." With that Hurley pivoted and stormed off aft.

After Hurley was out of earshot, Pollard said very softly, "Watch yourself with that bastard. He's always on the prod for something. And if you get on the bad side of him he'll make your life a living hell."

Jonathan said, "I wasn't kidding when I spoke to Hurley. I realize I must look dumb because I don't know anything, and I'm asking a bunch of stupid questions."

Pollard replied, "How else are you going to learn if you don't ask questions? Let me explain something to you. When a man is pressed he has two choices. He can fight against his situation, but in that case he is like a nail sticking up from the deck planking. He'll get hammered down. And every time he gets hammered, he'll get more bitter and resentful. He'll end up doing more stupid things, and get hammered harder and harder each time. The first thing you know he'll have a striped back. Now if he doesn't learn after that, then he'll try and run. If he's lucky he'll get away. If not he'll probably get another striped back or dangle from the yardarm. The second choice is to go with the flow. It's not the easiest life, but it's not a bad life either. At least you have some place to sleep, food to eat, grog, and mates to share with."

Jonathan pondered that, and stuck it back in the recesses of his mind.

"Okay," he said "What is the master-at-arms?"

Pollard explained "The master-at-arms is responsible for keeping discipline on the ship. Think of him as the chief enforcer. The master-at-arms is also responsible for small arms instruction, and to train boarding parties. However, one of the officers may also have this responsibility. This is a new ship, so we're still working out the routine. Anyway, the master-at-arms, or any officer, can put you on report. In Hurley's case, he can assign you all the shit details, extra work and so forth, without having to take it to the officers. If he does take it to the officers - normally to the officer the watch - then you go in front of the captain. You will find out all about the articles of war. The articles of war are the rules that govern all ships in the Royal Navy."

"Now we haven't talked about the great guns yet," Pollard continued. "This ship is a 4th rate with fifty guns. It was built and launched earlier this year, so we have no real history. We were supposed to have over three hundred and fifty men, but we're short. That's why the press was out."

"Okay, explain to me the decks again," questioned Pollard.

"The hold, the orlop, the lower gun deck, the upper gun deck, the forecastle, and the poop," replied Jonathan.

"Good, you remembered them without any difficulty," said Pollard. "Now the great guns are located on upper and lower gun decks. Heavier guns are on the bottom, lighter guns are on upper decks. Why?"

"To keep the weight lower in the ship, so the ship is more stable," replied Jonathan.

"Good," said Pollard. "On the lower gun deck we have twenty two 24-pounders. On the upper gun deck we have twenty two 12-pounders. On the forecastle there are two 6-pounders pointed forward. We use these when we're chasing someone, so sometimes you hear them called chase guns. On the poop deck there are four more 6-pounders."

"The weight of iron that these guns can fire is what counts in a battle. When we go down to the lower gun deck, take a look at the thickness of the walls. It takes a lot of force to penetrate those walls, and the smaller 6-pounders can't penetrate the thick walls lower down on the side of the ship. What the 6-pounders can do is fire ball, and grape that cuts rigging, and cuts down men. Also, if you get a chance to look at the back of the ship, or directly to either side of the bow you will notice that the wall thickness is less. The ship is therefore more vulnerable at those points. If another ship crosses our bows, or our stern they can use all of their guns while we cannot point more than two guns at them. You can guess the results."

"You've told me about the ship, the guns, and the sails, but I still don't understand who's in charge," commented Jonathan.

"Well, the captain is in charge of the ship. The first lieutenant we sometimes call Jimmy the One, is the second in command. He's really responsible to ensure everything is all shipshape on board. Then there's the second lieutenant, the third lieutenant and the fourth lieutenant. Each of these has his own division. For example, Mr. Galbraith is the third lieutenant, and you're in his division on the larboard watch. Everyone on ship has different duties according to what we are doing. If we are sailing, then the duties involve sail handling. If we're cleared for action, then the duty stations change. If we are in harbour, then there are different stations yet again."

"The master, the purser and the surgeon are considered officers and share the officers' wardroom."

"There's midshipmen who are officers, but not commissioned officers. Theyze officers in training, so to speak. Some of them are younger than you, and don't know much more than you, but because they are officers we have to do what they say. You be real careful around them. Some of them are real pricks and bait you."

"Look aft. You see the guys dressed in red? Those are marines. They are separate from us sailors. They provide sentries for the captain, and the powder magazine. When cleared for action, they man the aft guns on the poop deck, and put sharpshooters in the tops. If we land a force on shore, they go. There's a captain and lieutenant of marines who are officers, and sergeants and corporals who control sections."

"The officers have their own mess aft. The midshipmen have a separate mess aft, beneath the officers' mess. Think of the quarter deck as officers' country. Beneath the quarter deck on the poop deck, is the captain's quarters. Underneath the captain's quarters on the upper gun deck is the officers' wardroom. Underneath that on the lower gun deck is the midshipmen's wardroom, and the warrant officers' wardroom."

Pollard continued, "The sailing master is responsible for navigation, and ship handling although the captain and officer of the watch are ultimately responsible. He has master's mates who stand watches for him. The boatswain or bosun is responsible for the boats, sails, rigging and such. He's the man that really runs the deck. He has mates for each watch. One of them is Hurley. The sailmaker and ropemaker report to him."

"For discipline of the ship, there's the master-at-arms and his corporals. Then there's the gunner and his mates, who's responsible for the guns, powder and ammunition. The armourer, who fixes the guns, reports to the gunner. There's a gun captain for each gun. The carpenter and his mates are responsible for patching and repairing the hull or anything wood. There is a caulker who reports to the carpenter."

"The purser is responsible for provisioning the ship, and is a miserly bastard who will screw you out of every penny he can. The cooper, who breaks down and assembles the barrels for water and food stored in the hold, also works for the purser. The cook and his crew prepare the grub - if you want to call it that."

"For us sailors there's the topmen. They have the most skill and go up the masts in all weather to handle the sails. There's a senior topman for each mast, but technically the captain of the top is a midshipman. There's also some odds and sods as we call them like the captains' clerk, and the surgeon's mates."

"Pollard, report to Lieutenant Galbraith," said another man.

"Aye, Aye," responded Pollard.

"Wait here," said Pollard as he departed aft to see Lieutenant Galbraith.

When Pollard reached Lieutenant Galbraith, he knuckled his forehead and said, "You sent for me, sir?"

"Yes," replied Galbraith. "Young Smith will be assigned to your mess. He will be assigned to a 24-pounder crew when we are cleared for action. Gun captain will be Morrison. As for sail drill, keep him close to you and show him what to do, until such time as you can re-join the topmen. I'll have a word with Mr. Hurley about him. In the meantime, take him down to the purser and get him some slops."

"Aye, sir," responded Pollard. He turned and left.

Pollard traversed the waist and beckoned Jonathan to follow him.

"What's up?" questioned Jonathan. "Where are we heading?"

"You're going to get your first introduction to the purser," replied Pollard.

They descended through the forward hatch from the waist. They came to the cook's refuge - the brick and copper oven. There was plenty of activity around the oven as the cook and his helpers prepared the noon meal called dinner on board ship. Jonathan was later to find out it was the only hot meal of the day.

Pollard inquired, "Has anyone seen the purser?"

"Last I saw, he was headed to the orlop," replied one of the cook's assistants. Pollard nodded his thanks and continued on.

They descended to the orlop deck, and began to work their way aft searching for the purser. About halfway aft they came upon him. He was a short, rotund man. He wore spectacles that had slid part way down his nose. He stared over top of these spectacles at Pollard.

"Excuse me, sir," said Pollard. "I have a new man with me and Mr. Galbraith ordered me to bring him down to you so's he could get outfitted."

The purser saw profit potential and immediately became more agreeable. "Let's go aft, and see what we can get for him."

They all moved aft past various stowed items to the steward's room where all provisions were counted out. The purser started rummaging around and pulled out slops - trousers, shirt, jacket, a piece of canvas, and a hat.

Pollard gave the purser the mess and hammock number for Jonathan. The purser pulled out a hammock, two blankets, a spoon, a crude wooden cup and wooden mess plate that he called a trencher. Jonathan looked at the trencher, because he had never seen one before. At home they had bowls and plates. This trencher was a square of wood that had the centre hollowed out somewhat. You could put porridge, stews and such in it without any liquid spilling out. You could equally use it for dry solids.

The purser looked at Jonathan and said, "Name?"

Jonathan looked at the purser who was waiting to write down his name in a ledger. "Jon... Smith," he said. He looked at Pollard when he said this. He wondered if he should provide his real name. He would ask later.

The purser said, "The hammock and mess kit are the property of the ship. The slops you pay for - one shilling. It will be deducted from you wages."

"One shilling for these? Why back home I could get three for the same price," said Jonathan.

The friendliness of the purser disappeared in an instant. "Maybe so," he said, "but you ain't there. And in future you show some respect to me or else."

Pollard said, "No disrespect was intended sir. The lad ain't right in the head. He took a nasty knock from the press gang, and he's lucky he's still alive."

The purser was not impressed. He said, "Grab your gear and get back to work." He shoo'd them out of the steward's room and locked up.

Jonathan and Pollard retreated back down the orlop toward the bow, retracing the way they had descended. Pollard assisted Jonathan by carrying his hammock.

They ascended to the lower gun deck and Pollard started looking at discs nailed in the beams above his head.

"What are you looking for?" inquired Jonathan.

Pollard pointed at the discs with numbers engraved upon them. "See these numbers?" he asked. "Each of these discs is above a hook. You hook the end of your hammock on this hook that has your number, and then on the corresponding hook on the other beam."

Jonathan looked up. "Okay that I can understand, but jeeze these hooks are damned close."

Pollard smiled, "Ten inches each side, so you get a whole twenty inches for yourself."

Jonathan looked aghast. "If I roll one way I get my neighbour's ass in my face, and if I roll the other way I get the other's ass in my face."

Pollard laughed. "Just pray they don't fart in their sleep." He continued to chuckle. "Normally, every other man sleeps the opposite way - head, foot, foot, head - against the same beam. That way there's a bit of room."

"Just great - instead of farts I get to look forward to smelly feet," replied Jonathan.

Pollard continued smiling "Well it's not quite that bad. If you look at the discs, you will see that they are L S L S with the number below the letter. The L means the larboard watch; the S means the starboard watch. Since one watch is on while the other is off, then you get a whole forty inches of room. The only time it tends to be a problem is when we are in port, or anchored, or for some other reason when both watches are off, or lightly manned."

Pollard continued, "We have a few minutes before dinner. Let's see if you can get into, and out of, a hammock without falling or making a lot of noise to wake up your neighbours".

Pollard then showed Jonathan the manner in which to rig his hammock, and the proper way of getting into the hammock without disturbing the neighbour or flipping over. A practised hand can make it look almost instantaneous. Jonathan took longer. He also realised that he had little of the strength or technique needed. After a few attempts he started to get the "hang of it".

Pollard said, "Now unhook your hammock, and I'll show you what has to be done with it each morning" continued Pollard.

Pollard took the hammock and placed it on the deck. He flipped the outer edges into the middle, and then rolled the hammock. "Once the hammock is rolled, youze take it on deck, and it's placed with the others in the netting. This way it gets aired out. When we clear for action, the hammocks are placed at strategic points around the upper deck to absorb bullets and wood fragments."

Jonathan said, "I guess that makes sense - only what happens if it is raining?"

"Well then the hammocks get washed, don't they?" responded Pollard.

"But aren't they wet when we go back to sleep?" asked Jonathan.

Pollard nodded. Jonathan started to get an appreciation for just how hard a sailor's life could be.

"What's this piece of canvas for?" asked Jonathan.

"That's for your ditty bag," replied Pollard. "You put all your personal effects in your ditty bag like your extra pants, shirt, shoes and such. It is then hung over on them hooks on the bulkhead. When we clear for action they are all gathered up and taken to the orlop."

"But what about theft?" asked Jonathan.

"Well none of us has much to start with," replied Pollard. "And everyone tends to do small things to their kit so it's personalized. If someone was to take something from someone else's kit, it would be noticed either when it was took, or by someone who recognizes it. There's no mercy for a thief foreward of the mast. All we have here lad is trust - we trust our lives to the next man, so if a man abuses that trust he does so at his own peril."

Just then they heard a type of whistle.

"I've heard that before," stated Jonathan "What is it?"

"About the sweetest music on a man 'o' war," replied Pollard with a smile. "That's the call for Up Spirits. Let's go."

"Roll your slops into the canvas and leave them until after the meal," said Pollard.

"Grab your hammock, trencher and spoon, and follow me," said Pollard as he scampered toward the stairs.

Chapter 6
Mess Mates

Pollard and Jonathan made their way to the deck, where Pollard showed Jonathan where and how to stow his hammock. Below, he had mentioned to Jonathan never to place any of his valuables, or personal kit into the hammock. This was because if it was raining it would get wet, and not likely be able to dry properly. Additionally, there was no guarantee that he would get the same hammock back at night, although it was accepted practise for men to mark their respective hammock, so they would get the same one back.

There was a crowd milling around the waist awaiting their turn for spirits. The purser was responsible for the issue of the rum ration and associated paperwork, however, in reality it was generally the master-at-arms who physically issued the drink, under the purser's watchful eye. Each man was entitled to a half pint of over-proof rum diluted with water, lime juice, or sugar. The dilution, Jonathan learned, had been ordered by Admiral Vernon in 1740. Prior to that rum had been issued neat. Sailors at the time had nicknamed the diluted product "grog" after Admiral Vernon's trademark grogram cloak, and the nickname had stuck. When the drink was issued it was issued to each specific man, so it took some time to work through the entire crew.

After getting their grog, Jonathan and Pollard headed down to the lower gun deck to the mess. Setting up the mess consisted of lowering the table from its raised position, and getting everyone's mugs, trenchers, dishes or bowls and spoons from the mess bag and placing them on the table. When whoever was selected to be mess 'cook' for the day arrived, with the wooden kid with their hot meal, all would observe the distribution to ensure each received the same amount. The rations were placed on each plate or bowl, or whatever the respective man had. When equal shares were issued to all, the men would begin to shovel it into their mouths.

The spirits were always distributed before the meal. It allowed the members of the mess to have a tot before eating, thereby making the meal somewhat more palatable. The longer the cruise away from fresh stores on shore; the more the sailors welcomed the spirit ration.

Having Jonathan join the mess for the first time resulted in a bit of turmoil. Only rations for eight men had been drawn. Now there were nine men. Seating around the mess table was another challenge, as the table configuration was for a maximum of eight men. If a ninth man were present, he would have to sit at the end of the mess table, in the aisle. This tended to obstruct normal movement in the aisle, and was not welcomed by other messes. It hindered the normal movement, and slowed down the speed at which the messes got their food. In any type of weather where footing was challenging, someone sitting in the aisle could trip the mess 'cook' carrying a mess's food. This would be disastrous if the food was spilled. Fights had been started for much less. Jonathan's new messmates were therefore not especially overjoyed to see him join the mess.

The immediate problem was to get him some food. Mullins, who was responsible for getting the food that day, was despondent. "Well he can get his own food. I've done my bit, and I ain't doing no more."

Pollard looked at Jonathan and said, "Well lad, if you want any food at this meal you'd better hustle over to the cook, and see if he's got anything left. Otherwise, you'll get no hot food until tomorrow."

Jonathan grabbed his trencher and departed. He moved foreward past multiple other messes distributing food just as his mess had. There were hundreds of noisy men engaged in a relaxed noon meal. He entered the cook's area, and found only one poor soul left.

Jonathan explained his problem, and the cook's helper just shrugged his shoulders.

Jonathan was furious. He'd had low points since he had come aboard, but this seemed to him to be about the worst. Here he was. He had been hit over the head, beaten and left for dead. He had been carted like a piece of dead meat, and thrown on board this ship without any say. He was no better than a slave, but at least they fed slaves. Here he was not even allowed to eat. And all his supposed mess 'mates' would do about it is point him in a direction and say, "Go shift for yourself."

What options did he have? If he spoke to an officer or someone like Hurley, then he would be in trouble, like with the squire's men. There was no telling what they would do, but he'd already heard of a striped shirt or back, which was flogging, and he had no wish for that. All the men in his mess were larger than he was, and stronger than he was. Fighting was not an option because he could not win.

The question was what did that leave him? The first thing was a fierce desire to get the hell out of here, but he was on a ship in the middle of the sea - there was nowhere to go. He had to live here until such time as he could get away. At this point, however, he had no idea how long would that be. And where would he go? What would he do when he got there?

Jonathan tightened his belt. It was not the first time he went without food. It probably wouldn't be the last. His mind began working overtime. He had to think his way through this. He wasn't scared, just very angry. He knew from past experience that his anger showed easily, and could be used against him.

Jonathan's first challenge therefore was to mask his anger. He strode back aft along the lower gun deck, down the aisle between the different messes. As he approached his mess he noticed there were no stools or benches or anything else he could sit on at the end of the mess table. His messmates had not even attempted to find him something to sit on. That, in itself, said a lot about his messmates, or at least his standing in their eyes. According to them he was worthless.

Well, if his mess mates did not want him, perhaps he could move to somewhere that did. He looked across the aisle and down one mess and saw a vacant position at the mess table. He looked hard at them, and considered his options. He walked over to the man at the table, and said, "Excuse me, I'm new on this ship, and I notice that there's an empty place at your mess. Would you agree to me joining your mess?"

All the men at the mess table eyed him carefully. They took in his clothes, his youth, his newness and his inexperience. One of the men, sitting on the opposite side of the table and two places down from where Jonathan was standing spoke, "Lad, looking at your clothes, you're rated 'landsman'. This mess is all topmen. So the short answer to your question is no, you'll not be joining our mess. You're only allowed to change messes on the first day of the month with the consent of the members of the mess. But lad, if you're so inclined to become a topman in the future, then we would consider having you join our mess."

"Thank you sir," said Jonathan.

The man nodded, and turned to converse with his other messmates. They had all fallen silent when Jonathan asked his question. Now they resumed their conversation.

As Jonathan turned and walked back toward his mess, it struck him that none of the topmen had laughed or snickered at him. He sensed there was a big difference between that mess, and the mess he was stuck in.

As he approached the mess table Pollard looked at him. His eyes were appraising Jonathan. The other members of the mess disregarded him.

It was obvious to him that he would have to fend for himself for everything. He might as well start right now. He looked down the aisle in both directions, and saw another man sitting on a stool in the aisle at the end of his mess table. Jonathan walked down the aisle to the man. The man was physically large and plain looking. He touched the man on his arm and said, "Excuse me, but I'm in the same situation as you. I'm the ninth member of a mess. Could you tell me where I could find a stool similar to yours that I might be able to use."

When he touched the man's arm, the man quickly turned in the seat. He had hostile eyes, and was ready to strike. All the men in the adjacent messes on both sides of the aisle froze. They gazed openly at Jonathan.

"Whoa Henry," quietly said another man sitting beside Henry. "The lad is only trying to find out some information."

"Whatcha want?" growled Henry.

"I apologize for disturbing you, but I'm in the same situation as you; I'm the ninth member of a mess. Could you tell me where I could find a stool similar to yours that I might be able to use," repeated Jonathan.

"Well, Henry," said the man sitting beside Henry. "The lad is being polite and asking for your help. Do you know where he can find another stool like yours?"

"There's another down in the carpenter's stores," replied Henry.

The quiet man said to Jonathan. "Come with me after the meal, and we'll get you the stool."

"Thank you, sir," he said to Henry, and then he nodded to the quiet man. He turned and walked back to his mess.

At his mess, the man sitting opposite Pollard said, "Don't value your life much do you?"

Jonathan replied, "What do you mean?"

"Henry Turnbull is about as mean as they get. Everyone here steers clear of him. And no one lays a hand on him if they wish to live."

"Well I guess I did startle him, but he seems a right enough fellow. So does the man sitting beside him," replied Jonathan.

Pollard looked at him, and said, "Well, I guess you should be introduced to the mess."

Pollard pointed to the man opposite him, "This is Bates. The ugly little fellow next to him is Kirk"

The entire table laughed at that because while Kirk was indeed smaller than the man on either side of him, he was an attractive looking blonde who had a jaunty disposition. Jonathan thought of him as a lady's man. Bates, by contrast, was a bigger man, although it was hard to tell while they were all seated. Bates had the look of a farmer used to handling a cantankerous plough. He had big hands and strong forearms.

As they continued down the opposite side of the mess table Pollard said, "Our resident woodcarver is Knobby, and next to him at the end is Joe Wright." Knobby was an older man, well past forty years of age as far as Jonathan could tell. He had braided hair that was mostly grey. His face was like dark leather, with a high forehead as his hairline was receding. Wright was somewhere between twenty and twenty-five, solid, dark haired and youthful looking. He had an honest, outgoing appearance and readily smiled.

"On this side at the end is Abe Sweeny, then Hatcher, who'll volunteer to look after your and anyone else's spirit ration, and Mullins." Abe Sweeny was cast in shadows. He was a very quiet man of average height and build. Hatcher was a brooding hulk. The width across his shoulders was very noticeable. But the most remarkable thing about him was the menace that he radiated. He looked like he was sour on life in general. Jonathan immediately worried that he might become the focus of Hatcher's displeasure. Mullins was another average looking man of average build. The most that Jonathan could say about Mullins was that there was nothing notable about him.

"Everyone, Jon Smith," said Pollard.

Judging by the reactions of the members of the mess, Jonathan could see indifference, or in a couple of cases contempt. The exceptions to this were Pollard and Knobby.

This mess were all currently rated "ordinary seamen or landsmen" according to Pollard. But Pollard admitted to having been a topmen before he was injured. Pollard was therefore more skilled than others at this mess table. It appeared that Knobby had a skill set that was greater than the others as well.

Jonathan wondered why these two regarded him differently than the others. He felt good that at least someone considered him somewhat worthy; because it was obvious the others did not. It made him think. What am I doing that is different than the others and might be considered worthy?

The meal was over. It was time to go back to work. Jonathan turned and went down two messes to find the quiet man. He stood respectfully waiting for the quiet man to finish his conversation, and acknowledge his presence.

The quiet man stood up, nodded at Jonathan, and turned to Henry and said something. Henry grunted, and left. The quiet man turned to Jonathan, and extended his hand, "Luke Guitard". Luke was older, and radiated a quiet confidence. He was about five foot eight and like almost everyone on a man-of-war was lean. He had a long hair braid and covered his head with a dark knitted watch cap.

Jonathan took his hand and shook it. "Jon Smith," he said.

"Let's go Jon Smith," said Luke. Jonathan followed him as he descended to the orlop. About halfway down the orlop, Luke stopped. He moved around some boxes and barrels that were stored there. He returned with a small stool. "Here you go," he said as he extended the stool to Jonathan.

"Many thanks," said Jonathan. "Just out of curiosity, where should I store this stool while the mess table is stowed away?"

"That's a good question," replied Luke. "It shows you are thinking like a sailor. I wish some of these others would think ahead. It would probably save everyone some time and effort."

"When you go back up to the lower gun deck look at our mess, and see how the stool is stowed. Then go down to your mess, and stow your stool the same way," said Luke.

"Thanks again for your help," said Jonathan. "I hope to speak to you again."

"I ain't going anyplace," responded Luke with a smile.

Jonathan turned, went aft to the stairs, and climbed back up to the lower gun deck. He went to where Henry had stowed his stool to see how it was done. Then he moved back to his mess, and stowed his stool in the same manner. Once this was accomplished, Jonathan went searching for Pollard. He was unsure what to do, but at least he felt better that he was accomplishing something.

He went forward, climbed up the steps, and exited through the hatch onto the main deck. He scanned the area for Pollard, but did not spot him. He stepped further onto the deck and looked over his head on the forecastle. He spotted Pollard. He climbed the steps up to the forecastle and approach Pollard.

"What am I supposed to do now?" demanded Jonathan.

Before Pollard could reply, a voice bellowed, "Smith". Jonathan recognized the voice.

"Mr. Hurley," responded Jonathan. "I am not sure what I'm supposed to do now."

"I'll find you some work," replied Mr. Hurley. "Come with me"

Jonathan followed Mr. Hurley down the forecastle, across the deck, up the stairs to the quarterdeck. As they approached, the officer of the watch ambled toward them. Mr. Hurley knuckled his forehead, and turned to check that Jonathan had as well. Jonathan had watched Mr. Hurley knuckle his forehead, and did the same. This action was enough to prevent Mr. Hurley jumping all over him.

There was a master's mate near the wheel. "Ferguson, this is Smith. He will polish your brass for ye, if you have a rag."

"Good enough," replied Ferguson.

Ferguson was a friendly enough fellow of about twelve stone in weight and five eight in height. He wore a navy jacket like all the officers. He pulled out a rag, and handed it to Jonathan.

Jonathan said, "Mr. Ferguson, I'm willing to do whatever task you assign me, but I need to understand how to do it. Could you show me what needs to be done, sir?"

The officer of the watch, Lieutenant Smithers, snapped his head around, and his left eyebrow arched. Ferguson's face was a picture of mild astonishment. It was their experience that a sailor tasked with polishing brass did so unwillingly and in silence, so that his discontent would not be heard. Here this young lad was doing just the opposite - he was willing to do the work, and wished to be shown how to do it so it would be done correctly. What a refreshing attitude.

"Smith is it?" queried Lieutenant Smithers.

Jonathan turned to the voice behind him. It registered on him that it was an officer. "Smith, sir," Jonathan replied, as he knuckled his forehead somewhat apprehensively.

"Carry-on," said Lieutenant Smithers.

Jonathan turned back to Ferguson. "Did I say or do something wrong, sir?" he inquired of Ferguson.

"No lad," responded Ferguson. Hoping not to dampen the lad's enthusiasm Ferguson immediately shifted the topic back to the work at hand. "Now lad, watch what I am doing."

Ferguson proceeded to give Jonathan a quick demonstration on how to polish the brass. The ship's bell, the compass, and several other fittings in the immediate area needed to be polished. After a couple of hours polishing Ferguson inspected his work, and approved it. There were no compliments.

While he was on the quarterdeck, Jonathan kept his ears open and his mouth shut. His mother had often told him, you have two ears and one mouth, so listen twice as much as you speak. He realized he needed to put that into practise on this ship. He heard numerous expressions that made no sense to him. He attempted to remember these expressions, so that he could ask someone to explain them to him at a later time.

The work kept his mind partially occupied. He was able to forget temporarily how hungry he was, although he did tighten his belt once to alleviate some of the rumbling in his stomach. He liked working on deck in the fresh air. It was far better than the funky smell below. There the smell of humanity reeked like smell of the farmyard, only worse because of the confinement.

Jonathan had never seen a compass before, although he had heard of them. He had to polish the compass from the side or front, never from the back, because that would obstruct the view of the compass from the man on the wheel. He learned this the hard way, when the man on the wheel scolded him for getting in his view of the compass.

After the polishing was completed to Mr. Ferguson's satisfaction, Jonathan was told to report back to Mr. Hurley.

Jonathan did not have a good feeling about Mr. Hurley. He did not trust him. He was to find later that he was not alone. Almost every man in the entire larboard watch detested Hurley.

As Jonathan was reporting to Mr. Hurley, he heard the bell he had just polished ring. Mr. Hurley looked at him and said, "Go below, and get something to eat. You're on the last dog watch."

Two things struck Jonathan. First, Mr. Hurley couldn't be all bad - he had just sent him to get something to eat. Secondly, he had no idea what the last dog watch was. He knew he was on the larboard watch, but what was this last dog watch?

He went below as instructed.

As he entered the lower gun deck, he noticed that the mess tables had been lowered and that mugs had been placed on the tables. No one was sitting yet, but that changed as he watched.

Jonathan noticed that his stool had been taken down, and placed at the end of the mess table. That was a good sign. He also noticed that his mug was with the others on the mess table. There was a wooden box on the table. It was called, according to Bates, a bread barge. There were a number of solid yellowish biscuits in the barge.

Jonathan looked at Bates, pointed to the biscuits, and asked, "What is that?"

Bates replied, "The yellowish stuff is bread - some call it hard tack. It's best to soak it before you eat it. I've seen some break their teeth on it."

"What do you soak it in?" asked Jonathan.

Bates responded, "Most people have a mug for water and just let it sit in that. At noon, some let it sit in their spirit ration - it changes the taste. In your case, I would advise leaving it in your mug and soaking it in water."

Jonathan placed the bread in his mug and added water from the pitcher on the table. The water was not fresh. It looked something like the stagnant water in a swamp. The bread was left to soak for approximately ten minutes. After that Jonathan's hunger was such that he attempted to eat. He was able to pulverize the bread to crumbs and then swallow it down. It was not appetizing, but it was some form of nutrition. Even after this 'meal', he was still not satisfied.

"Is there anymore," he asked, but he already knew the answer before asking the question.

"If you want anything else, then you have to purchase it from the purser at his prices," commented Knobby.

"How are you supposed to pay for any of this?" asked Jonathan.

Hatcher chimed in, "You get paid as a landsman fifteen shillings a month, as an ordinary seaman nineteen shillings a month, and as an able seaman twenty-four shillings a month."

Jonathan looked at him in surprise. "But even a farm labourer makes more than that," he exclaimed.

Hatcher replied sourly, "Yeah, well their Lordships haven't increased seaman's wages since 1660. Too busy fillin' their own pockets and bellies on the backs of us." There was a murmur of agreement on this last statement by most of the men in the mess.

Wright explained, "They don't pay ya for months at a time, but at least the purser allows credit. But when they do pay ya, the purser deducts all ye owe him from your pay and pockets that money. And since he sets the prices, ya can be assured that ya'll not be seeing much of your pay."

Jonathan shook his head and wondered about the injustice of it all.

After a time, he realized there was not much that he could do about any of it. He looked at Pollard who was watching his face.

Pollard said, "Don't you be frettin' about it lad. There are worse ways to make a living. And don't listen to these naysayers too much or you will sink as low as they are."

Hatcher heard the comment, and responded, "Who you callin' low, Pollard?"

Pollard ignored Hatcher's comment. "In the meantime, you have kit to get ready before we go on watch again."

"That's something I wanted to ask about," said Jonathan. "Mr. Hurley said that I was on the last dog watch. I thought I was on the larboard watch?"

Pollard smiled. "A little confusing, is it?"

Jonathan smiled in return, "I'll say."

Pollard began to explain. "We need to man the ship twenty four hours per day. Since no one can effectively work twenty four hours a day, the duties are split into two shifts or watches. These are called the larboard watch and the starboard watch. They're named after the sides of the ship. The larboard is the left side of the ship when you are facing the bow, and the starboard is the right side. The ship's crew is split between the two, so there's an equal number on duty at all times. Understand?"

Jonathan replied, "Makes sense."

Pollard continued, "Now you could have one watch on for twelve hours, and the other on for the other twelve hours. However, the navy has a different routine. You see, in the morning at first light, we stand by the guns in case an enemy approaches us in the dark. Then we are ready to fight if the enemy appears. You noticed today that no one was sleeping in the day - all the hammocks were stowed away. We're allowed only to sleep at night. If the same watch was on each night, all night, they would never get any sleep. So in the navy the watch on duty is split into different times. There are seven watches. I'll start with the morning watch - that's from four in the morning until eight in the morning. Then from eight to noon, it's the forenoon watch. From noon to four in the afternoon it's called the afternoon watch. From four in the afternoon to eight o'clock at night, it's called the dog watch. However, the dog watch is split in two. From four in the afternoon to six is the first dog watch, and from six to eight in the evening is called the last dog watch. From eight to midnight is called the first watch. The second watch covers from midnight to four in the morning. Understand so far?"

Jonathan replied uncertainly, "I think so."

Pollard continued, "Now each watch - larboard and starboard takes the next shift. For example, if the larboard watch takes the morning watch, then the starboard watch will have the forenoon watch. But if you count up the hours each watch has per day, you will see that one watch has fourteen hours, and the other only ten. By alternating the watches over two days however, each watch has the same amount of time on duty - twenty four hours every two days. It helps out for messing and sleep, because the duty watch is away from the gun deck, so things are less crowded."

"How in hell does anyone get a full night's sleep then?" asked Jonathan.

"You can never get more than four hours at a time, and you're lucky to get that. Most of the time, if you are off on the last dog watch, you sleep, and then get another four hours during the middle watch. Other nights, you get the first watch, and depending when first light occurs, you may get some of the morning watch. In the summer, you get what sleep you can, anytime you can get it," explained Pollard.

"So Hatcher has a point then," said Jonathan. "Underpaid, overworked, poorly fed, and charged high prices for anything that is outside the norm. And pressed, so a man does not have an option as to whether he wants to be here. Is that fair?"

Pollard looked at him hard. "You can look at it that way. Everything you said is true. What can you do about it? Nothing! Look lad, what I've been trying to tell you, and I thought you understood, was you can think poorly about the situation you and all of us are in, or you can make the best of it. If you dwell on all the bad things, you'll become bitter and malcontent like many of these men. You're never happy. You'll seek refuge in the bottle, or worse you'll try and run. That generally has a bad ending for you. But you also have the alternative to go with it - don't fight it."

Hatcher spoke up. "And you Pollard, what has 'going with it' gotten you? Here you sit with us, rated as an 'ordinary seaman', eating the same food, working the same hours. So tell me and our new lad here how much he can benefit from 'going with it' as you call it."

Pollard clenched his teeth. He was silent for a moment as he composed his thoughts. It was clear that he did not like Hatcher, but there was truth in what Hatcher was saying.

"It's true, that I am sitting here as an ordinary seaman. I was a topman on another ship, but I had an accident. When that ship was paid off, I was left on the beach. I needed a job. I can't work the tops anymore, so all I could get was an ordinary seaman position. It was either that or starve on the beach," explained Pollard "What I am saying to the lad is that if you look at the bad or evil in things, and only that, you end up going downhill. The joy of life is lost. You start to take solace in the bottle. Then you either continue sliding downhill or make a mistake that costs you. I know, I've seen it often enough with good men slowly souring on life. Sure you have your good moments, but these come further and further apart as time goes on."

"If, on the other hand, you try to look at the good in things, then there is more joy in life. You can learn - you can improve. I did it before I got hurt. I started as a landsman, then worked my way up to ordinary seaman. On a merchantman, I was able to raise myself to an able seaman. But it all came crashing down when I fell during a bad blow. I'm lucky to be alive after that fall."

"So all you got after all that effort was to land back where you started," smirked Hatcher. "And here you are - trying to say to this lad - follow me, I'll show you the way! What bollocks!"

Jonathan felt bad for Pollard. He could see that Hatcher's remarks were grating on Pollard, but he also understood there was some truth to them, so Pollard had little defence.

"We are but in the hands of God," mumbled Sweeny.

"Aye," mumbled two or three others.

This came as something of a surprise to Jonathan because he had not heard a single word up to that point in time that indicated that anyone here was religious.

Pollard looked dejected. As he looked up he expelled air in an audible sigh. "Well lad, can you sew?"

"Sew?" responded Jonathan with surprise. "Why would I need to sew? My mum looked after all of that back home."

"Well you're not home now, and you need to ensure your kit is up to par, or the mates will be on your back."

"Aye, that's true enough," said Kirk.

"What do I have to sew?" questioned Jonathan.

"Well, for one thing, a ditty bag. And you haven't tried on the slops that were issued to you, so you don't know if they will fit," said Pollard.

"I don't even know what I'd need except a needle and thread that I don't have," said Jonathan.

"The purser will be more than willing to sell you what you need," said someone. Jonathan thought it was Wright.

"But that still doesn't help me, because I still don't know how to sew," said Jonathan.

Mullins jumped in at this point. "I'll tell you what. I'll sew you a ditty bag and adjust your slops, if you give me your spirit ration for the next month."

Everyone looked at Jonathan. They all knew it was an outlandish offer, but Jonathan didn't, and they were interested in how the lad would handle it.

Jonathan looked at Mullins. "How good are you with a needle and thread?" he asked.

"Good," replied Mullins quickly anticipating that Jonathan would then accept the offer.

"Who's the best with needle and thread in this mess?" inquired Jonathan.

Well that sparked considerable discussion and debate amongst the mess members. After some back and forth, Jonathan decided to ask Bates who was sitting to his left.

Bates rubbed his chin and said, "Mullins can do a good job. Kirk can equal him. But for fancy work, Wright's your man." Down at the end of the table, Wright beamed.

Jonathan said, "My father forced me to go to Church every Sunday in the hamlet where I'm from. Every week I had to listen to whatever sermon the preacher droned on about. He once talked about a fisherman and charity. Since I liked to fish, and I didn't understand what the preacher was droning on about, I asked my father as we walked home. What he told me was if a man was hungry, and the fisherman saw it, then charity would be to give the hungry man a fish. But my pa said it was better to teach the hungry man to fish, because while the act of charity, in this case the fish, would only quench his hunger for a day or two. Teaching the man to fish would feed him from then on."

The whole mess had listened to Jonathan's story without making a sound. It was a trait that Jonathan noticed. A sailor likes to listen to a good story.

Hatcher as usual spoke up, "What the devil does fishing have to do with making a ditty bag?"

Jonathan smiled at Hatcher and responded, "Making a ditty bag and altering my clothes for a fee is like receiving a fish from a fisherman. It will help me today, but tomorrow I may need to alter my clothes again, just like a hungry man will want to eat again and again. If I'm going to have to pay for sewing, part of the fee should be for learning how to sew."

"Now my mother always told me to learn from the best around. Back on the farm when I was cutting and stacking hay, I would watch others doing it to see if they did it faster and easier, with less effort than I was using. If they did, I copied them, or asked them to show me. If I need to learn to sew, and it appears that I do, then I would like to learn from the best if possible," continued Jonathan.

"What I am asking, is for someone to sew me a ditty bag, and alter my slops tonight and teach me how to sew over the next month or two, however long it takes," countered Jonathan. "Do I hear any offers?"

Mullins spoke up, "Same offer, but I'll show you what I know about sewing."

Jonathan said, "Any other offers?"

Wright spoke up, "I'll do it."

"For what price?" asked Jonathan.

"I think two weeks spirit ration is fair, but I don't want the ration every day. Every other day would be better," replied Wright.

Jonathan summed up the offer, "Just so I get this straight - you want my spirit ration every other day fourteen times. For that ration, you will sew my ditty bag and alter my slops tonight, and teach me how to sew whenever we get some time over the next month or two?"

Wright nodded.

Everyone thought the deal was done. Jonathan surprised them all. "Any other offers?" he said.

The mess members at the table looked at each other. Then they looked at Mullins. No one said anything.

"Agreed," said Jonathan. He then rose and walked over to Wright and shook his hand to seal the agreement.

The group at the table started to migrate away from the table. Pollard and Bates stayed and raised the mess table back into its travelling position.

Wright approached Jonathan, and said, "Let's get started. If you want this done tonight, I need to be about it. I would like some sleep."

They went to the bulkhead where Jonathan had left his rolled up canvas. After some searching, he found the roll where someone had kicked it. Luckily everything was still there.

Wright said, "The ditty bag is straight forward. What I need for you to do is to put on the slops to see what alterations are needed. Bottoms first, then we'll see about the shirt."

This was the moment of truth for Jonathan. He still had the coins wrapped in the cloth strip secured around his waist with a piece of cord. He needed to hide this, so Wright did not spot it.

Jonathan took off his shirt. He turned to face the bulkhead. He untied the cord, and grasped with one hand the coins in the cloth strip, while with the other hand he unbuckled his belt. He pulled the cloth strip under his crunched up shirt, and tossed the shirt down on the deck. The coins, being tightly wrapped in cloth and surrounded by the cloth in his shirt did not make any noise when they hit the deck. He had dropped his pants at the same time, so his belt and buckle thudded onto the deck masking any possible noise from the coins.

Bare-assed he reached down, and pulled the slop bottoms up to his waist. They were huge on him. He could fit another half body into these pants. They were also long enough to cover his heels.

"Take your shoes off," commanded Wright. "You'll be working most of the time in bare feet, so you want the length of these pants to come down only to your ankles. I'll have to rip the seams out of both sides of the waist and take the waist in about 8 inches each side. Do you have a cord to hold up your pants?"

"No," replied Jonathan.

"Okay. Use your belt for now, but tomorrow we'll go see the purser together. You'll get cord, thread, chalk, a needle and some buttons," said Wright.

"What's the chalk for?" Jonathan asked.

"We use it to mark where the material is to be taken in, or let out. You'll see," responded Wright. "I'll be back in a minute."

Wright went over to his ditty bag, and pulled it off the hook. He brought it back, and fished out a smaller bag. In this wrap-a-round bag were needles, thread, buttons, chalk and a silver item that Wright called a thimble when asked by Jonathan.

Wright chalked the pants at the waist and cuff area. He looked at Jonathan and said, "OK, let's take a look at the shirt"

Jonathan donned the shirt. It was large, and felt more like a tent on his back than a shirt. Surprisingly, Wright said, "Not bad."

"Not bad - what do you mean not bad! This shirt is like a tent on me," said a shocked Jonathan.

"What you don't understand is this," replied Wright. "When you are on deck and it is cold, you can't go down below and get a jacket. The extra material helps keep you warm. When it is hot, there is lots of room for air to cool you, so you don't sweat as much. There is plenty of room for movement, and in your case growth. The only possible problem is wind. With the extra material it catches the wind. If you were a topman then wind catching it could kill you - but not down on the deck. However, we could take it in somewhat. Remember, that you have to pay purser prices for everything, so the longer you can use it the better off you will be."

"Okay," said Jonathan. "But it needs to be taken in some under the arms."

"Alright then, hold out your arms to your side," said Wright, as he started to chalk the adjustment.

"Alright, put on your other clothes and bring all your kit. We'll sew near the lanthorn where there is more light," stated Wright. He bent over and grabbed his ditty bag, carrying it with him to the lanthorn near their mess area.

"Now watch what I am doing," said Wright. "We'll start with the slop bottoms. First, you have to let out the existing seams. You'll need a good knife for that. That's another thing we'll have to get from the purser at some point, or from some other poor bastard".

"What do you mean by that?" asked Jonathan.

"When some poor bloke dies, it's custom that his kit is sold off to his shipmates for whatever they can pay. Whatever money they raise goes back to the poor bloke's family, if he has any left. If he doesn't, then the money is given to a sailor's home. If someone dies on this voyage, and you still need a knife - if he had a knife in his kit - then you could purchase it, probably cheaper than if you got one from the purser. Then again there is always another way of getting a knife - taking it off a man you kill during a boarding. You just relieve him of it after you kill him, and make like you're using it to kill another of the bastards. At the end you slip it into your belt and no one the wiser. Even if they were, no one's going to say anything after what you went through to get it."

"Now after you let the seams out, fold in the material to the chalk marks like so - see? Now thread the needle, and start at one end. I generally start down here at the bottom, because there is already a seam in place. I work my way up the pants and create the new seam. That way, if I make a mistake, it is easier to correct. Now there are different ways of doing a stitch - a straight stitch like this - or various other types of stitches that compress and anchor the new stitch. I prefer the straight stitch with a loop under the far end. That tightens the stitch, and it holds it better and longer. If somehow a thread breaks, then this stitching holds the seam in place longer. A straight stitch would easily slide out, and you don't want that happening to your britches when you need both hands to hang on," Wright smiled at the image.

Wright managed to do the pants, and was partially complete with the ditty bag when the bell rang announcing change of shift.

"We better shift our asses and get on deck," said Wright. Rapidly everything was stuffed into the respective ditty bags, and they rushed to the deck. Mr. Hurley was there counting heads.

Mr. Hurley turned and knuckled his forehead to the officer of the watch, Lieutenant Galbraith. "All present, sir"

"Very well, Mr. Hurley," replied Lieutenant Galbraith. "Stand the men easy in the waist."

The men on watch moved quietly to the bulkhead and in between the guns. They found comfortable sitting positions resting their backs against the solid wood. Jonathan watched others and selected a position against the forward bulkhead of the forecastle. There was sufficient light to see most everything between him and the quarterdeck.

He was seated all alone and wondered why few men were seated in this area. Another man got up and wandered over to where he was sitting. It was Knobby. He sat down beside Jonathan.

Jonathan could hear light whispering, but could not make out any of the words being spoken. "Evening Knobby," he said.

Knobby nodded, and spoke softly. "You handled yourself well at the mess today."

Jonathan waited silently for him to go on. He waited for the BUT...

Knobby continued, "What Pollard was saying is true. It is possible to move up through the ranks. Just look at Mr. Hurley. You may not like him, fact is most don't, but he was once a pressed man."

"So what are you suggesting?" responded Jonathan.

"Only that you keep an open mind, and try to not let it get you down. Fellows like Hatcher will always be with us. They make a bad situation worse, and dwell upon all the bad things. They never see the good things," continued Knobby.

Jonathan just sat there, and chewed on what Knobby was saying. It was a comfortable silence. After a bit Jonathan remarked to Knobby, "Just out of curiosity why are we the only ones sitting against the foreward bulkhead?"

Knobby replied. "Well lad, when the officer of the watch wants something done, who do you think either he or the bosun's mate will spot first? If you can see him, he can see you. Those that don't want to do anything stay in the shadows, so they can't be spotted."

"Makes sense," said Jonathan.

"In the long run, it really doesn't matter where you sit," said Knobby. "If we have to trim the sails then everybody is called. If it's only a task for one or two, then whoever's on the bosun's shit-list is usually called first."

"How long you been in the Navy?" inquired Jonathan.

"I've been at sea, since I was about your age," replied Knobby. "Sometimes on board his Majesty's vessels, and sometimes in merchantmen depending how lucky I was."

"If you had a choice wouldn't you rather be in a merchantman?" asked Jonathan.

"Surely," replied Knobby. "But it ain't easy to stay in a merchantman."

"Why's that?"

"When the navy's short of men, they stop inbound merchant vessels, and press the sailors off them. In many cases the captains of the merchant vessels are happy to comply because then they don't pay the pressed sailors. They make more money, especially if it's an East Indiamen that's been away for a couple of years," said Knobby.

"It appears that a sailor always seems to get the dirty end of the stick," said Jonathan.

"Not the good ones," said Knobby. "If you are a good topman, or a mate, everyone - Navy or merchantmen - protects you because you're hard to replace. This is something you need to understand - the key about being a sailor is to improve your skills to such an extent that you're considered valuable to the powers that be."

"So how does one go from being a landsman to a topman?" inquired Jonathan.

"I guess it's the same way in any profession - attitude and technical skill. The difference for a sailor is -if you don't have the technical skill - you're likely going to die. All it takes is one slip from the tops, and you're in Davy Jones's locker," stated Knobby.

At that point, the watch was called to trim sails. Not knowing where to go or what to do Jonathan followed Knobby. He mimicked Knobby's actions, and came through the sail trimming without anyone screaming at him.

One of the things that Jonathan noted was that as soon as the watch was called everyone became mute. Only the officer of the watch, and the bosun's mate said anything, and that was to give specific orders. The orders were loud so that everyone could hear them, but to Jonathan they might as well have been Greek for all he understood.

As they brought the courses around he had occasion to look foreward. Knobby and he were working the course on the mainmast. Another two men were heaving on the line for the foremast course. Although it appeared to him that everything was fine, apparently Mr. Hurley didn't think so. Hurley yelled at them, and flicked a rope that Jonathan learned was called a starter at the back of one of the men. It obviously hurt the man, although nothing was said, and the man pulled harder.

After the manoeuvre was completed the men stood by in their positions. Jonathan looked forward at the man who had been started, and saw him rubbing his back. When he turned his head Jonathan recognized Hatcher.

Jonathan thought - well that explains some of his bitterness. The second thing he thought - better him than me. A third thought popped through his mind. If I don't learn these commands, and what I'm supposed to do quickly, I'll be the next one being started. I sure want to avoid that.

It was at that point, Jonathan vowed to learn what he was supposed to do, and what others were supposed to do as fast as he could, and to do them as efficiently as he could. He reasoned that by doing this he would avoid being started. At the same time he would begin to make himself more valuable as Knobby had suggested.

A few minutes later they fell out, back to their sitting positions in the waist. Knobby was quiet, so Jonathan did not disturb him.

Jonathan's thoughts drifted. He was trying to gather together what he had learned through the day, and since coming aboard this vessel. He had learned much about the ship, but it didn't stop there. He was seeing things in a way he had never looked at things before.

He had always gotten on well with his father. His father was a hard man, but he had never beaten Jonathan. Instead he would scold Jonathan, or make some comment or remark that did not seem to make any sense to Jonathan. Jonathan was reminded of an incident about a year earlier. He had been down in the hamlet and was speaking to some of his friends. One of their fathers had shared a bit of gossip. He couldn't remember exactly who it was at this point. He'd gone home, and told the story at the supper table. He had thought it was quite humorous, but his father was not impressed. He scolded Jonathan, and then he made another one of his dumb comments. "Always be careful who you listen to," said his father.

"Always be careful who you listen to," didn't seem so dumb right now. All Jonathan had to do was think about his experiences in the last day. Pollard and Knobby were saying it was possible to get ahead. Hatcher was saying you can never get ahead. You're doomed to be at the shitty end of the stick so long as you're in the navy. Who was right?

Jonathan started to think a little bit deeper about this. All his life, his mother had made him go to church where the parson had droned on and on about good and evil. Well his situation was not that different. There was good if he went one direction; there was bad if he went the other direction. This was too much for his mind to consider at this point.

Unfortunately, thinking about the parson, his mother and his father made Jonathan homesick. He wondered what his family was doing at this very minute. His little brother and sister were probably in bed. His mother was likely sitting in the chair by the fireplace sewing or mending something. His father was probably staring at the fire, and thinking about what he had to do tomorrow.

Jonathan wondered if they gave any thought to him at all. Loneliness crept over him, and he wanted to cry. But with Knobby sitting beside him he dare not.

"Worst thing about sitting here when on watch is that you get to thinking. What about home? What if I had done something differently? What if? What if? What if?" suddenly said Knobby. "It can pull a man's spirits down if he doesn't watch it."

"What's the trick then?" asked Jonathan.

"That I don't have an answer for," replied Knobby. "Each man has to find his own path, his own way of dealing with it."

"But you're not alone," continued Knobby. "If you're feeling lonely, you just get up, and move over and talk to the next man. If you're feeling really low just go talk to Hatcher. He'll either make you feel lower, or you'll realize you're not as low as you thought."

They both chuckled.

The watch was called twice more during the last dog watch to trim sails. Overall, it was a short quiet watch. As the watch was relieved, Jonathan withdrew down to the lower gun deck. He found his hammock, and rigged it as Pollard had shown.

Before he could alight in his hammock, Wright handed him his new ditty bag. "You might want to leave your shoes in the bag, and grab your jacket for the middle watch."

"Thanks, I will," replied Jonathan.

He then raised himself up and into the hammock. Within seconds he had dropped off. Jonathan's first working day was finished.

Chapter 7
Adjusting

At midnight Jonathan was jostled from sleep. It was time for the middle watch.

He shifted his legs; half fell out of the hammock, and dropped to the deck. It was cool, and he remembered Wrights' suggestion that he wear his jacket. He looked around at the rest of the watch preparing to go on duty. They were all unhooking and taking down their hammocks, so he did likewise.

He stayed in his bare feet, and grasped his ditty bag. He pulled his jacket from the bag and donned it. He then followed the other men of the watch and stored his ditty bag on the bulkhead wall. Then he went up top.

As he reached the deck, mute silence from the men indicated either an officer or a mate present. He quickly fell in beside the next man for the headcount.

He heard "All present, sir," from a voice he recognized as Mr. Hurley's.

Even while standing in line waiting for the headcount to be finished, Jonathan could sense that the ship was livelier. There was a pronounced up-and-down motion, and from time to time a sideways motion. He looked overhead to see if he could spot anything. Although it was difficult in the darkness he could see that the masts were moving away from the vertical in almost a circular fashion.

He could not imagine being up on the mast in the dark with this type of motion. It must be scary.

"Very well Mr. Hurley. I'd like a reef in the topgallants and topsails," voiced the officer of the watch, who Jonathan thought was Mr. Galbraith.

"Topmen aloft," shouted Mr. Hurley. "A reef in the topgallants first, and then the topsails. Get a move on!"

The topmen raced for the shrouds, and scampered up the ratlines. Jonathan admired their dexterity and envied their skill as he watched them disappear into the darkness. He was moving toward the mainmast where he had been positioned during the previous watch. He joined Knobby, and awaited orders.

"Knobby, what's a reef?" inquired Jonathan.

"Shhh, I'll tell you later," whispered Knobby.

The deck remained silent as the action was all taking place overhead.

"Topgallant lines, take the strain," roared Hurley.

Jonathan and Knobby heaved on a line. They were now holding the topgallant yard steady.

"Ease," came the order. They slowly allowed the lines to move forward, lowering the yard until the order "Belay," was heard.

Jonathan noted that a number of things were likely to occur if this kept up much longer, and he could see no reason why it wouldn't. The ropes that he was pulling on were hemp and rough. He had not considered his hands delicate after working on the farm. If he was going to haul on these ropes on a continuing basis, his hands needed to be a lot tougher. He could now understand why bare feet were better on the deck than shoes. They allowed a better grip on the deck. It was worse for him in this area. At home, he had only worn shoes for Sunday meetings or special events. His feet were tender compared to the feet of the men around him. Jonathan knew his feet would have to be much rougher and tougher if he were to survive on this ship. He also wondered about the cold. As he held the rope steady he glanced above him. He could only barely see the topmen at work. He knew they were all bare footed. He imagined that their feet must be much tougher if they were to stand on those ropes and cling to them with their feet. Another thing he noticed was that the ropes were covered in tar and that this tar was coming off on his hands. He would need a rag or something to make sure he was able to remove as much of this tar as possible, or his clothes would be stained easily. He did not think they would last long. The last thing he wanted to do was pay for more clothes at the purser's prices.

The order "secure" was passed. Knobby started winding the excess rope around a belaying pin. "Watch here," he said. "All excess rope is to be left 'Bristol fashion' so we can easily get at it - there are no twists or kinks, and it is out of the way. This is how it is done." Knobby proceeded to show Jonathan the correct method of coiling the rope around the belaying pin. "You'll do the next one."

"Topsail clew lines take the strain," roared Hurley. Again Jonathan and Knobby eased the line, and kept it up until the order "Belay" was heard. They again kept tension on the line until "secure" was heard. Jonathan then coiled the rope around another belaying pin as he had been shown by Knobby.

He felt a hand go past his shoulder and grasp the rope around the belaying pin and give it a tug. "Too much slack, do it again," roared Hurley in his ear. Jonathan quickly unravelled the rope, and re-coiled his rope keeping more tension on it. As Jonathan was re-doing his work, he could hear Mr. Hurley at the foremast saying the same thing to the men stationed there.

Knobby whispered, "Don't let that worry you lad. It's just his way of showing everyone that he's in charge. But he's right. If the clew lines ever came loose in a blow and the reef didn't hold, it could rip the yard right off of her. Not something you'd want to have happen in a blow."

The topmen were now alighting on the deck, their work aloft for the moment complete.

"Mr. Hurley, stand the watch at ease," came the order from the quarterdeck.

"Aye, sir. Watch, stand easy," said Mr. Hurley in a normal voice.

The watch left their stations and migrated to various positions in the waist. Knobby and Jonathan hunkered down between two cannons on the larboard side just forward of the mainmast. After they settled and got comfortable Jonathan turned to Knobby and said, "Okay, now can you explain what a reef is?"

"A reef means that you're reducing the amount of sail available to the wind. It's mainly done to ease the pressure on the mast," replied Knobby.

"I don't understand," said Jonathan.

"Okay, when a sail is let loose and hangs from the yard, it captures the wind. One horizontal end of the sail, called the head, is attached to the yardarm. The other horizontal end, called the foot, is anchored by ropes. When the wind blows, it catches the sail, and forces it in the direction the wind is blowing. Because each horizontal end is anchored, the sail cannot blow away. All of that power or momentum from the wind is transferred to the yard. Because the yard is attached to the mast all the momentum is transferred to the mast. The wind pushes us through the water, but all that force comes down the masts. If there's too much force, the masts might not be able to handle it, and may break. If they break, then we cannot control the direction of the ship, and are at the mercy of the sea. To avoid that, we ensure that the pressure on the mast is not too great. One way to reduce the strain on the mast is to reduce the amount of sail area that the winds can catch," explained Knobby. "Are you with me so far?"

"I think so," responded Jonathan.

"Now imagine the sail divided into quarters horizontally. At the foot of the sail are the clews. These are attachments to the sails where the clew lines are anchored. The clew lines run up the front of the sail. Every quarter of the way up, there's other attachments to hold the sail in place on the yard. When the entire sail is pulled up to the yard, and anchored or tied to the yard, we call that furling the sail. If we bring the first quarter of the sail up, and furl it, that is called one reef. One reef leaves only three quarters of the sail available to catch the wind. If half the sail is furled, that's called two reefs. If three quarters of the sail is furled, that's called three reefs, but I have rarely seen three reefs," continued Knobby.

"Now not all ships' sails are the same. They all have some capability for reefing, but not necessarily as I have described it," stated Knobby.

"A good officer of the watch will put in a reef if the wind is too strong or if the ship is heeling over too much," continued Knobby.

"What is heeling?" inquired Jonathan.

"Heeling means the ship is leaning over in the direction the wind is blowing. The force of the wind is pushing the ship over sideways," stated Knobby.

"Pollard mentioned that the weight of the ship had to be low," said Jonathan.

"He's right; the heavier and lower down the weight, the less the ship will heel. To ensure we have enough weight at a low spot we add what's called ballast near the keel of the ship," Knobby remarked.

"Pollard told me that ballast is weight added at the bottom of the ship. But what's a keel?" inquired Jonathan.

"The keel is the lowest part of the ship. The easiest way to explain it is that a ship is like a man, or I guess to be more accurate you could say a woman, as we always call a ship her. When the ship is built imagine a man lying on his back. The first thing that's put down is the spine, or in the case of a ship the keel. The ribs are attached to the spine or keel. The ribs are cross braced and the decks are built on the cross braces. The skin or side of the ship is attached to the outside of the ribs. When the masts are put in, the bottom of the mast is notched so it fits over the keel," explained Knobby.

"Ballast can be anything, but generally we use some form of rock. When we are outfitted for a long voyage we don't need much. That's because the weight of the stores will provide the ballast. However, if we've been at sea for quite some time, and have consumed much of the stores, such as food and water, we may have to stop somewhere and add ballast. The way the ballast is positioned also impacts on how fast we can go. Sometimes the officers make us shift the ballast in order to improve the ship's speed and performance. Now that's back breaking work, but it doesn't happen often thank Christ!" exclaimed Knobby.

"There just seems so much that I need to learn," commented Jonathan.

"There's a lot to learn, but it's not difficult," responded Knobby. "There's a reason for everything, and if you understand the reason, learning is easy. And you don't have to learn everything at once. I like to think learning is like eating. You spread it out over every day."

"That I don't understand," responded Jonathan.

"Well when you eat, you don't sit down with all the food for a day and gobble it up at once. If you do, you might get sick. You're also likely to get hungry before your next meal the next day. You sit down for different meals, with different foods for each meal. Learning is like that. You can't gobble everything up, and understand and remember it all. You need to learn only a certain amount at a time, so you can understand and remember it. And it's best to concentrate on a specific area, at a certain time each day," explained Knobby.

"I guess that makes sense," suggested Jonathan, but his tone indicated he was not convinced.

Around them there was the occasional whisper, but as the night continued the whispers were slowly replaced by either silence or snores.

Jonathan drifted off, and the next thing he knew Knobby was shaking his shoulder. "End of watch," whispered Knobby.

"What happens now?" whispered Jonathan back, once he had his wits about him.

"Go get some sleep while we can," replied Knobby.

The watch descended to the lower gun deck. Jonathan was quickly adapting to the routine. He grabbed his hammock, rigged it, and levered himself in. Very shortly he was asleep.

He was dreaming of the farm, when he was rudely awakened.

"Let's go," said someone.

Jonathan dropped to the deck, and immediately unhooked his hammock. He went forward to the bulkhead and grabbed his jacket. He was proceeding toward the deck when someone said, "Where you going? It's break fast time."

"Oh!" said Jonathan. He went to the mess table. As he watched, other mess tables were lowered, so he did the same with his mess table. He grasped the mess bag, and started placing mugs on the table. Other messmates appeared, but only after he got the mess table ready.

Mullins looked at him and said, "Tomorrow it will be your turn to be mess 'cook.'"

"Okay," said Jonathan. "What do I have actually have to do?"

Mullins said, "It might be better if you follow Kirk this afternoon, so you understand what has to be done."

Jonathan nodded. He grasped his stool from the wall, and placed it at the end of the table but did not sit.

By this time all the members of the mess had arrived. They all took their places, and started some conversation. Jonathan still felt as an outcast to this mess. He was not comfortable expressing himself because he didn't know much. At this point he felt inferior to any of the individuals at his mess. Physically he was, and this also played upon his mind. He was very careful not to give offense to anyone, because he had no fighting ability compared to the other men present. If they meant to bully him there was little he could do about it, and he saw no indication that anyone would stand up for him.

He sat down and took a piece of bread. He watched other members of the mess tap the bread on the mess table. He wondered why they did this, but did not have the courage to ask. The bread was too hard to eat, so he poured some water into his mug, and laid the bread in it to soak and soften.

As Jonathan went to pick up this piece of bread he noticed something floating in the water. It appeared to be still alive as it was moving. Jonathan looked at it and was disgusted. It was some type of worm. But he couldn't figure out where it came from. He had not noticed anyone's hand near his mug, so either the worm fell off the ceiling, or it came out of the bread. He had a sickening feeling as he looked over his head that it had come out of the bread.

He closely watched as other members of the mess continued to absently tap their bread on the table before dunking it in their drinks. He noticed something moving on the table in front of Sweeney. It was another little worm similar to the one in his bowl. There was no doubt about it; the worm had come from inside the bread.

"Wheeze call 'em bread weevils," said Bates to his unspoken question. "That's why we tap the bread on the table before eating it, unless you want a little extra meat with your bread." There was no accompanying laughter - just the statement by Bates.

"And what if you don't want any extra meat?" inquired Jonathan.

"Then tap extra hard," chuckled Bates. "I hear tell that the young gentlemen collect the weevils and feed them to their chickens. Fattens them up."

"Who, the officers or the chickens?" asked Jonathan innocently.

Bates roared with laughter "That's a good one. You got a good sense of humour, lad. Don't lose it 'cause you'll likely need it around here."

Kirk rose, and started collecting the mugs. Jonathan helped him. "Can you show me what I need to do?" he asked. "Apparently, I'm supposed to do what you are doing tomorrow."

Kirk nodded. "Grab the rest of the mugs and stuff them in the bag. The only other thing we need to do is ensure the bread barge is put away." He was fortunate that Kirk was showing him his duties as the mess 'cook'. Kirk was more patient, more cheerful and willing to assist than some in the mess. Jonathan also felt less intimidated by Kirk because of his size. Jonathan was only about eleven stone and five foot six. Kirk was about the same height and only marginally heavier. He was more muscled than Jonathan however.

The bell signifying change of watch rang as they were ascending to the deck. They sped up a little to ensure they weren't late. Mr. Hurley was busy counting heads to ensure the entire watch was present. Another day had begun.

Chapter 8
Learning the Ropes

Jonathan looked out over the waist. All he could see was sea. He looked in all directions. To the front, to the sides, he could see nothing but sea, and the horizon in the distance. To the back, or aft of the ship, he could see nothing because of the poop. He had no idea where they were, but it did not matter all that much because he was stuck here. He needed to make the best of it.

He scratched his head, and felt the bandage that was still there. His scalp was itchy, and that was a good sign because it meant that he was healing.

Mr. Hurley bellowed, "You four, come here."

Jonathan looked around, and realized he was one of the four that Hurley was bellowing at.

Now Mr. Hurley was the kind of man that believed in work. If he had a motto it would be *idleness breeds discontent*. He apparently hated to see someone not working. While many men on the ship hated this philosophy, and secretly cursed Hurley under their breath, the result was to give them less time to gripe about their fortunes in life.

Jonathan rushed over to Mr. Hurley mainly to ensure that he avoided his wrath. Pollard, Knobby and Wright also appeared, albeit at a slower, more orderly pace. They were mindful of Hurley's wrath, but not over-awed by it, as was Jonathan at this point.

"There's rope to be worked on," Mr. Hurley said. "As you're working on it see if you can impart some of your knowledge on Smith here."

'Ayes' were heard from all, and Mr. Hurley walked away toward officer country.

As Mr. Hurley departed, Jonathan, Pollard, Wright and Knobby went foreward to the forecastle. There they found piles of rope lying scattered on the deck.

Pollard took Jonathan and went to one side of the pile. Knobby and Wright took the other side.

"Now the first thing you have to understand is there's lots of different maintenance that has to be done on any rope. New rope needs to be tarred so the water runs off it, and the sun doesn't damage it. This allows the rope to last longer. New rope always stretches, so we try and stretch it before it goes into use," explained Pollard.

"Used rope needs to be inspected for wear. The last thing you want is for a worn rope to break in the middle of a blow, and you have to go run another line at the worst possible time. As well, if the rope breaks, it could result in loose canvas. Loose canvas might put strain on the masts, the yards, or some other area of the ship that might cause problems. You could imagine what would happen if a rope broke and a 24-pounder started rolling from side to side. Not a healthy situation," continued Pollard.

"Now those tasks that I just mentioned are done routinely. There are other rope maintenance tasks that are done less frequently, and need some degree of skill - knowledge at least. These are splicing, and whipping the ends of rope. Of these two - whipping is straightforward - splicing can be a little bit more complicated."

"Okay, what kind of rope do we have in front of us?" inquired Pollard.

"Looks used to me," said Jonathan.

"Then let's start by inspecting this rope" said Pollard as he lifted the nearest rope. "Describe the rope to me."

"It's a rope," said Jonathan quizzically. Pollard gave him a dirty look.

"All right, it's a used rope," said Jonathan semi-apologetically.

Pollard looked at him and shook his head. "What I'm trying to get through that thick skull of yours is that each type of rope is different. In most cases the difference is in the thickness of the rope, but there may also be a difference in the fineness of the rope.

"Now describe the rope again for me," demanded Pollard.

"This is a thin, used rope," replied Jonathan.

"Gawd, don't you know anything? Didn't you learn anything on that farm you claimed you came from?" muttered Pollard.

"Obviously nothing that can be easily used on this ship," mumbled Jonathan.

"You guessed that right," shot back Pollard. Knobby and Wright both looked up but said nothing.

Pollard took the length of rope, and waved it under Jonathan's nose. "This here's hemp, boy. Almost all the rope on this ship is hemp. Why hemp? Because it's tougher and lasts longer than anything else I've seen so far."

"Now this here piece of rope can be easily identified by the number of strands. This is a strand." Pollard pointed to the end of the rope, and with his index finger pushed one braid out, so it was easily identifiable. "Now how many strands are there?"

"Three," sputtered Jonathan.

"Now ropes are generally three, four, five, or six strands but three-strand is the most common. It depends on the maker. Generally the more strands, the better the rope, because it tends to be stronger and lasts longer. For example, on a six strand rope if one strand breaks, there are still five left. But on a three-strand, if one breaks then one third of the strength of the rope is lost. The strands themselves can be different sizes, so we measure rope by its width - one inch, two inch, etc. When we get to four inch or higher we generally call them cables instead of ropes. A cable may be a number of ropes braided together. If you get the order to inspect all three-strand inch ropes, then every rope that has three strands and is an inch in width must be inspected. Got it?" Pollard demanded.

Pollard proceeded to hold the rope between his left and right hand. "To inspect it properly, hold a length between your hands like this. Look at it carefully. It's best to run your eyes over it right to left because you tend to go slower and miss less that way. After you go from one end to the other, roll the rope over and do the other side. If you really need to be thorough, on a really old rope, roll it only a third of the way, so you don't miss anything. Once you are finished, shift the rope from the right hand to the left."

"What am I supposed to look for?" inquired Jonathan.

"Look for wear, tears, fraying - any part of the strand that appears to be damaged. Look to see if the tar covers all of the rope and that there is no moisture or mildew in the seams between the strands."

"What if I find something like that?" asked Jonathan.

"Depends what you find," responded Pollard. "For example, if the rope needs more tar, get more tar and coat the rope. If the rope has bad wear, call the ropemaker and let him make a decision. If it is minor, ask me or a more experienced man, whether it is bad enough to warrant calling the ropemaker or the bosun," explained Pollard.

"What happens to any rope that has bad wear?" asked Jonathan.

"Again that depends where and when the wear is discovered," said Pollard. "If it is in harbour, then the rope might be condemned and replaced. If at sea, and there is more rope available, then it might be condemned. If there are no spares, then we continue using it. We might have to splice it. Like I say, it just depends."

"With the amount of rope that I see around, it looks like this maintenance is a never ending battle," commented Jonathan.

Wright quipped, "You got that right."

Knobby said, "I got a frayed end over here that needs whipping. Come here and I'll show you how it's done."

Jonathan moved over beside Knobby and sat on the forecastle deck.

Knobby pulled out a large needle and a cord. "Now this cord is made of cotton, so it is easier to handle for this type of work than hemp. You can use hemp, but the job is easier with cotton."

"To whip the end of a rope, there's a little trick I use," explained Knobby. "First you align the frayed end as best you can and get it as tight as you can. Then you make a little loop and tie it tight. This keeps the end of the rope from unravelling when you are working on it. Next, measure down about a thumb-length from your loop. This is where you'll start the whipping. Now take the needle and work it in behind one of the braids - it doesn't matter which one. Pull your cotton cord through. Make sure you have one end much longer than the other. Take the longest end and start wrapping it round and round the rope. Keep it tight, and each line tight against the other. When you get about ten to twelve turns round the rope, stop going round. Now take the end and pass it under a strand, down a groove, under another strand, up a groove, under another strand. Now take the shorter end and do the same under, up, under, up, under, up, in the reverse order around the rope. Now tie the two ends of the cord together using a reef knot."

Knobby showed Jonathan how to tie a reef knot, and then trimmed his cord. Next he cut off the frayed end of the rope to just above the whipping point with his knife. "Done," he said.

"Now you try," as he picked up another piece of rope with a frayed end. He handed Jonathan the rope, his needle, the cord and sat back watching Jonathan with a critical eye.

Jonathan followed the procedure that Knobby had shown him. As he started wrapping the twine around the rope, Knobby stopped him. "It's not tight enough. You need to ensure it's much tighter or it will fall apart." Jonathan was forced to take the whipping apart three times before he got it tight enough to satisfy Knobby.

Jonathan cut off the frayed end of the rope and handed it to Knobby for inspection. Knobby just nodded. "It'll do," he said. Wright chimed in, "Now try it in a blow while you're hanging on for dear life."

Jonathan looked at him and said, "You're joshing me." But he wasn't sure.

Pollard quipped, "Wish he was, but you need to be able to do this very fast, with one hand hanging on to something, so you're not slamming into something."

Knobby handed him another frayed rope end and indicated he was to do it without supervision. This went on for the entire watch. Little by little his skill developed, but he still was slow.

Mr. Hurley came round, as did the ropemaker, to check on their progress. The ropemaker inspected the whippings. He said nothing and tossed the completed ones back where he had found them. He then shuffled away.

Mr. Hurley stopped to observe the lad for a few minutes. His only comment was, "You'll need to be a lot faster that that lad" before he moved on.

Before Jonathan knew it, the watch was over.

The pipe 'Up Spirits' was made. Jonathan rushed down to see if he could find Kirk. He met him coming up from the mess. In his hands he had the mess bag with the mugs. He had a grin on his face as he met Jonathan. "Best part of the day."

After Kirk received his tot, he waited for Jonathan, and then they headed off toward the galley. Jonathan again fell in behind him. At the galley, Kirk stated the mess and the number of men. The cook annotated something in his book while cook's assistants doled out the noon meal into a container for food that he learned was called a kid. Then the cook's assistants carefully passed the kid to Kirk, ensuring that he had a firm grip on it before letting go.

Jonathan said as they departed from the galley, "That was nice of them to help you with the kid."

Kirk just chuckled. "That was self preservation at work. More than once a cook's assistant has been beaten because a mess didn't get their meal when a cook's assistant was too lazy to help the mess 'cook'. When an entire mess comes up in anger against a cook's assistant it generally ends up in a trip to the surgeon."

"Doesn't the mess get in trouble?" inquired Jonathan.

"Sure, but rarely does the cook's assistant do it again. And even if the mess doesn't come up, who's to say the guilty bastard doesn't trip going through a hatchway or down the stairs. We take a lot of shit, but messing around with our food - that something we don't stand for," shot back Kirk.

Jonathan took the kid from Kirk, and carried it back to the mess.

Kirk was responsible for the distribution of the food. Other members of the mess watched him like a hawk to ensure they were not short-changed and that shares were equal. Wright claimed Jonathan's spirit ration as was their agreement for sewing. Other members of the mess noted this.

As far as Jonathan was concerned he had a good deal. He had never had rum, and it was not necessary as far as he was concerned. To him, rum was a luxury. Now small beer was something else. He had consumed some while on the farm and was fond of it. After a few weeks at sea however, it was no better than the foul water that they received. If however, the spirit ration was replaced by beer while in harbour, he would be reluctant to forgo his ration.

Conversation at the table he noticed rarely altered. It was still about the same topics - the food, the drink, occasionally women, and lots of negative comments about officers and their lackeys.

Jonathan's eyes wandered over the table and the tables of other messes. He noticed a great difference in the mugs and bowls or dishes used by various men. Some were elaborately carved, others just a plain trencher like his. Likewise with the mugs - some were wood, some metal. Some were plain, as issued, others much more elaborate.

Jonathan had been a member of this mess for only a couple of days. Yet he felt somehow that he was now a member. He didn't feel the same as he did when he first joined the mess - like an outcast. While he didn't feel quite like a true intimate of the mess, he at least wasn't treated with the contempt he had earlier felt.

The meal was a porridge, but different than Jonathan was used to. This one had black dots in it. Jonathan started eating the porridge, but avoided the black dots. "What are these black things in the porridge?" he asked innocently.

Hatcher looked at him with a blank expression, and said, "You'll get use to them. The cook adds them as a bonus. Every time he finds a rat, he chops it up and adds it to the porridge for extra meat. Whatcha got?" He reached over and tilted Jonathan's trencher, so he could see more clearly. "Looks like little pieces of the tails," he said. "Them's the more appetizing parts, but there's no real meat in 'em."

Jonathan's jaw dropped, and he looked at Hatcher in amazement. "You must be kidding me. They expect us to eat this?"

The entire mess burst out laughing. It was a grand joke, and Jonathan had fallen for it totally. Hatcher looked at him, roaring with laughter, and gasped, "You should have seen your face."

Pollard, who was laughing as well, said, "It's all right lad, they're raisins."

"I've never even heard of a raisin. What is it?" asked a shocked Jonathan.

"It's like a currant, only dried. Go ahead. Try it," fired back Pollard in between breaths as he was still chuckling.

Jonathan took a spoon and cautiously moved one of the black dots onto the spoon. He put the spoon in his mouth and closed his eyes as he chewed. This caused the mess to burst out laughing again.

There was a bit of a sweet taste, but that was all. Jonathan spooned the remaining black dots into his mouth and ate them without fanfare. He scraped his trencher clean, and then reached for a piece of bread.

It took a while to soften, and during the entire time, the conversation revolved around pieces of rat in Jonathan's porridge. It would be a while before Jonathan got over that one, if ever.

He fuelled his body with whatever nourishment was in the food, for the concept of dining in this place was as foreign as he would be in the King's court. He mulled over things. After some time it came to him that what he was missing was any true friendship. He got along well with Knobby and passably with Pollard and Wright. But even with Knobby, the relationship was closer to father - son than true friendship. There didn't seem to be any issue between him and Kirk. Bates and Sweeny were mysteries to him, as he had rarely spoken to them, or they to him. Hatcher, he was cautious of - he sensed a negative, violent personality that was always ready to explode.

He scratched his head again, and realized that he still had the bandage on it. He should get it looked after. Well, he wasn't on watch after the meal, so it would be a good time.

All of these thoughts kept spinning around in his head. He focused back on the table, and shovelled more bread into his mouth. It suddenly hit him out of nowhere. He looked closely at the mugs and bowls on the table, and then at their owners. Was it really that simple? The mugs that were more elaborate were placed in front of the men that he most respected - Knobby and Pollard. Trenchers instead of bowls were in front of Hatcher and himself. The remainder of the bowls and mugs had some improvements over his, but were nowhere near the quality of Knobby's or Pollard's. Now why was that?

Jonathan's face tightened up as he started to think about it. He had never realized his expressions were so evident until Bates looked at him and asked him, "What's the matter?"

Bates's question caught him off guard. He shook his head and looked at Bates.

"What's the matter?" Jonathan parroted. "Why nothing's the matter. Why do you think something's the matter?"

Bates chuckled "Because your forehead was all scrunched up as if you were doing a powerful lot of thinkin', and the effort was foreign to ya."

"He's just schemin' how to get his rum ration back," jested Hatcher.

Jonathan was caught and he knew it. His facial expression had given him away. But he could not tell them what he had been thinking because they would ridicule him. Or worse, it might touch off Hatcher which is something he feared, especially if that violence was directed at him.

He grasped for an explanation, any explanation that would seem plausible. He had always had fast wits that had saved his bacon many times. He thought of numerous excuses. Then he realized that Hatcher had inadvertently given him one.

He looked up and stared at Hatcher and smiled. He had found in the past that a smile tended to disarm his oppressors, and he felt that he needed to disarm everyone now.

"Well Hatcher wasn't far off the mark," stated Jonathan. "I'm not trying to figure out how to get my rum ration back. I made a deal and I will honour that deal. But as I was looking around the table I realized that I didn't have a fancy mug, and that all youze did. I was trying to think of a way that I could get myself a better mug."

"Buy it or make it," quickly responded Bates.

"Ah yes," replied Jonathan soberly. "But that is the problem. If I go to the purser, he will charge me a price for a golden mug and give me the crummiest, poorest one that he has, and it will probably leak. At his rates I will leave this ship an old man and have to pay money just to leave."

Virtually everyone in the mess murmured agreement to this comment.

"Now about making one. Well I don't have wood. I don't have a knife. And I don't have the skill yet with a knife to make one. I think at this point I would have difficulty making a cup let alone a mug with a handle. That's what I was thinking about," continued Jonathan.

Everyone in the mess accepted Jonathan's comments at face value. Surprisingly, Hatcher was the first to comment. "I think I might be able to get you a piece of wood from the carpenter's stores. But it won't be a big piece, only enough for a small mug."

Sweeny jumped in, "I could loan you my knife. But you'll have to find a stone and sharpen it."

Jonathan was really surprised. It showed on his face. "Thank you," was all he could say.

"I think I can do the outside of a mug without any great problem," he said. "But how do I get the inside carved out?"

"Patience and time," said Knobby, who was probably the best wood carver in the mess.

"Thank you, I appreciate it," said Jonathan.

That problem solved, the mess resumed their normal discussions. Jonathan just sat there in a confused daze. He had solved a problem that he hadn't even considered a problem, just an inconvenience. But after the goodwill shown by Hatcher, he was at a loss. Apparently there was more to the relationship between elaborate mess items and their owners that he needed to understand.

As the mess broke up after the meal, Jonathan assisted Kirk. They went foreward to the galley where the cook had a tub prepared. They stood in line and waited their turn to wash the mess equipment. Once it was washed, and wiped, Kirk placed it back in the mess bag. Jonathan was preparing to leave when the cook said, "Not so fast, you've still got to wash these." He then pointed to a line of pots and kitchen utensils.

"Is this part of the job?" asked Jonathan.

"Unfortunately it is," replied Kirk.

For the next half hour, Kirk, Jonathan, and men from other messes washed, scrubbed, and cleaned the equipment used for making dinner. When it was completed to the satisfaction of the cook, they were allowed to leave. Kirk grabbed the mess bag and they went back to the mess. The mess bag was hung up. There was little time for anything else however, because it was watch change.

After the watch was over, Jonathan went looking for a surgeon's mate to have his head and bandage looked at. After some effort, he finally found a surgeon's mate, who examined his head. After poking and probing his head numerous times with his fingers, the surgeon's mate announced that his head appeared to be healing well. Henceforth, he would not need a bandage. The surgeon's mate did recommend a haircut.

"A haircut?" questioned Jonathan. "Why? Especially since winter is coming?"

"Easier to clean, less chance of lice, and will let that head heal properly," replied the surgeon's mate. "I also recommend you remain clean shaven." But the surgeon's mate looked closely at Jonathan. "I don't think that's going to be too difficult for you, lad."

"Thanks a lot," commented Jonathan and left.

When he got back to the lower gun deck, he was intercepted by Wright. "Here are your slop pants and shirt," he said. "Try them on. Let's see how well they fit."

Jonathan was suddenly very conscious of the money belt he carried. He wanted to make sure that Wright did not see it. He first took off his shirt and put on the other shirt. Sure enough, the slop shirt hung down enough to obscure the money belt. He next undid his belt and took off his pants. He put on the slop pants and then tucked in his shirt. He buttoned up the front of the pants. They fit nicely. He strapped on his belt.

"Stretch and bend," ordered Wright. "Make sure you've got the necessary give in the clothes."

As he stretched and bent in different ways, the practicality of the slops became very evident. They were much more suitable than the clothes he had just removed. "Feels fine," he said. "You did a good job."

Wright smiled. "Now all I have to do is to teach you to do it as well by yourself."

Jonathan took his old clothes over to his kit bag, opened it and placed them in. He closed the bag, and hung it back on the bulkhead wall. He turned back to Wright and inquired, "What now?"

"We're off watch at the moment. Why don't I show you some of the basics about sewing," said Wright.

For the next hour Wright and Jonathan huddled together and went through various stitches, and where they were used. Jonathan practised on a rag. He could sew, but it looked horrible. The lines weren't straight, and the spacing varied between stitches.

"Don't worry about it - it'll come with practise," Wright reassured him.

Jonathan leaned back and slumped against a 24-pounder. He was tired and drifted off.

The next thing he knew Kirk was shaking his shoulder. "Come on, we have to go see the purser," Kirk started to explain.

"On this ship there are forty messes for the men. Each mess is given a wooden stick with a metal tag on it indicating the mess number." Kirk showed Jonathan the stick. "Every day on this ship the purser issues a full day's rations to each mess during the dog watches. The assigned mess 'cook' for each mess has to go and get it. That's what we're doing."

"Now, from what I've heard, the rations haven't changed much in the past one hundred years. Most of the time I think we're eating stuff that was put into hogsheads that long ago," continued Kirk as they descended to the orlop deck to the purser's stores.

"It certainly isn't fresh," commented Jonathan.

"That's for sure," replied Kirk. "Anyway, there are only four different ration allotments. Every day we get a pound of bread and a gallon of beer, or its equivalent. On Sunday, for each man in the mess we get one pound of pork and one half pint of peas; Monday, one pint of oatmeal, two ounces of butter; Tuesday, two pounds of beef; Wednesday, one half pint of peas, one pint of oatmeal, two ounces of butter and four ounces of cheese. Thursday's the same as Sunday, Friday the same as Monday, and Saturday the same as Tuesday."

"Now don't get your hopes up too high, because you got to take into consideration the purser's eighth and substitutions," continued Kirk.

"What does that mean, the purser's eighth?" commented Jonathan.

"The bastards that run this oppressive navy gave the right to the purser to take one eighth of everything. That means instead of getting the sixteen ounces of the pound we only get fourteen, or only seven pints instead of eight. If the food is spoilt, we get it anyway because the bastard is too miserly to condemn it, especially as it might cut into his profit," explained Kirk.

Kirk continued, "Then there's the substitutions. For example, instead of beer, we get a substituted amount of rum that I won't complain about. But sometimes we get this crap called blackstrap."

"But what about fruits and greens?" demanded Jonathan.

"They don't keep at sea lad, so we rarely get them. Rarely get them in harbour either, because somebody's got to pay for them and the Royal Navy's too dam cheap," said Kirk bitterly.

"But what about the raisins we had in our porridge?" questioned Jonathan.

"You can thank the captain for that. He bought a barrel of them, and we have them once a week so long as the supply lasts," responded Kirk.

As they stood in line in front of the purser's stores, Jonathan learned more of the rations and sailor's perceptions of inequities related to food.

Once they reached the head of the line, Kirk provided the purser with the mess number and the number of men in the mess. The purser annotated this in his records, as his assistants counted out the required rations. The rations for today were simple - two pounds of beef and a pound of bread for each man. Each were placed in a separate bag and handed back to Kirk. The bag with the meat had the metal mess number attached to it.

Kirk and Jonathan headed for the galley. Once there, they handed over the bag of meat to the cook for cooking. They returned to the mess with the bread bag, and placed the contents in the bread barge.

They had been standing waiting for the purser for so long that the next thing he knew the call for the watch change was being made. He rushed to the deck and fell in for the head count. He had made it only by the skin of his teeth.

During the watch, he was placed with Pollard, Knobby and Wright again working on inspecting and maintenance of ropes on the forecastle. He now knew what to do and was concentrating on inspecting line when Pollard called him over.

"Tell me what you see," demanded Pollard.

"A 3-strand hemp rope that's one inch wide. A strand has been nearly worn through, and a second strand is worn to some extent," replied a wary Jonathan. He didn't think that he had missed anything when he inspected this rope. Although, by the way Pollard was acting, it was as if he was guilty of missing something as important and easily observable as this wear.

"So what do we do," demanded Pollard again.

"Since I know nothing, I'm to ask a more senior man to determine if we bring it to the attention of the ropemaker," responded Jonathan.

Pollard chuckled, and the seriousness of the moment disappeared. "OK, what do you think? Can we trust this rope?"

"I wouldn't," replied Jonathan.

"Neither would I," said Pollard. "So what do we do with it?"

"Get the ropemaker, and see if he will condemn it," responded Jonathan.

"Would you condemn it if it was yours?" asked Pollard.

It was a long rope. Only about a forearm's length was worn. It seemed a shame to Jonathan to waste that much rope. He said, "I guess you could cut the rope into two and whip each end. At least you'd be able to use most of the rope."

"Possible, but not the best solution," replied Pollard. "Ropes this long are needed for the clew lines. A shorter rope wouldn't reach. What we do in a situation like this is to splice the rope."

"What's splicing?" inquired Jonathan.

"In this case we cut the rope on each side of the worn part. This gets rid of the worn part. Then we take the two ends and splice them together. Now, you can accomplish the same thing by knotting the two rope ends together. The question is 'what happens if the rope has to run through a block?' The rope knot gets caught and you can't move it. Splicing is better because then you can get the rope through a block. There might be a bit of a bulge in the rope, but it is not big enough to interfere with the movement through the block."

"When you splice two ropes together, you need to understand what the rope will likely be used for. For instance, is it goin' to run through a block? Is it going to be wet most of the time like a line on the log? Are you depending upon the strength of the line? The type of splice will change somewhat based on the answers to these questions."

"In this case the rope will likely run through a block, and we're countin' on the line. We need to make sure the splice is narrow for the block. For strength, the shorter the splice, the less likely it is to fail. That's because for long splices, we cut two of the three strands from each rope, whereas for a short splice, we don't cut the strand. The short splice is stronger, but it is also much thicker and has difficulties goin' through a block. We therefore need a long splice that's tapered so that it will run through the block without jammin.'"

"OK, let's get started." Pollard cut the rope in two, cut the worn section out, and let it fall on the deck. "You take that end and do the same thing with that end that I am doing with this end."

"First you unravel the strands. It's easier and faster with a marlinspike." Pollard deftly used the marlinspike to unravel the rope. He then handed the marlinspike to Jonathan and guided him in its use while Jonathan unravelled the strands of his rope. Jonathan handed the marlinspike back to Pollard who quickly sheathed it.

Pollard showed him how to braid the two ends together. A lot of strength was needed to keep the size of the braid as small as possible. Once the braiding was completed, Pollard began to whip each end of the braid, so that the braid would not unravel. Using the whipping creatively, Pollard was able to put a bit of a taper on the rope on each end of the braiding to assist it through any blocks that it might encounter. To test the splice, he had Jonathan grab the rope on one end and he grabbed the other end. They each tugged to ensure the splice held. Jonathan was literally tugged off his feet.

Pollard laughed, "It seems the rope is stronger than you are."

Jonathan laughed with him. "I hope that won't always be the case."

Pollard replied, "No, probably not." He dropped the rope and resumed inspection of the rope past the point of the splice. Jonathan returned to the inspection of the rope he had previously been doing.

The watch continued. In each watch so far, Jonathan had learned something new. He realized that he needed practise to hone the skills that he had been shown. He just wondered what it would be like when he was not learning something new, when he reached a level of skill in the various arts of the sailor.

He had no idea how long it would be before he would feel comfortable as a sailor. He had not yet suffered the same as others he witnessed. He wasn't seasick. He was hungry most of the time, but in fact he was eating more often than at home. However, the quality of the food was below what he was used to, and there was never the feast that he occasionally enjoyed when he was able to place game on the table. He wondered about fishing. They were at sea, there had to be fish. But all his experience of fishing was standing on a bank with a pole. Here on the ship they were moving at a rate of knots - whatever that was. How did one fish like that? He had seen no one fish since he had been aboard. There had to be a reason for it. It was something to consider at least.

He realized he was daydreaming when a stinging snap hit him. He jumped and grabbed his ass with his right hand. Mr. Hurley bellowed at him, "Stop your lolly gaggin' and get to work."

"Aye sir," quickly replied Jonathan. He quickly began to inspect the rope he still held in his left hand. His right hand snapped back up to the rope and stretched the rope for inspection.

End of watch was called moments later. Jonathan's ass was still sore. He rubbed it as he was moving toward the hatch. He caught the smiles and snickers of more than one man as he descended to the lower gun deck.

Tiredness seemed to be his constant companion. His body still had not adapted to the watch routine. He went to his ditty bag and pulled out his jacket. It smelled worse than it had when he took it off. He realized that the smell had come from his older clothes that he had stuffed into the bag before the watch started. It was obvious that he needed to wash those clothes, and himself.

It could wait. He rigged his hammock and climbed in. He fell asleep almost at once.

He came awake aware that men were moving past him. Change of watch. He rose and moved to the deck. For once he was early. The quietness of the deck was soothing.

He formed up for the watch, and went through the ritual of the head count and reporting.

As usual Lieutenant Galbraith, as officer of the watch, wasn't satisfied with his predecessor's sail trim, so a short sail adjustment was called for. Then the watch was stood easy in the waist.

Jonathan found a shadowed area beside a 12-pounder and settled down. Soon another body settled down beside him.

"If I fall asleep, make sure to wake me if you see the bosun or anyone," whispered a voice he recognized as Mullins. Now sleeping on watch was not allowed. It happened all the time, but if you were caught there was sure to be some sort of punishment. Mullins had just dumped the problem into Jonathan's hands. He was counting on Jonathan covering for him. Jonathan thought about this as he kept searching for moving shadows that might indicate the bosun or Mr. Hurley was checking on the watch.

Luckily Jonathan spotted Mr. Hurley walking toward them, and grabbed Mullins by the arm and squeezed. Mullins was instantly awake, checking around. "Whatcha think of that," he asked as Mr. Hurley appeared directly in front of them. "Not much," replied Jonathan immediately catching on to the game. As long as they were whispering, they were alert and not asleep. Mr. Hurley was satisfied with that and slid away silently.

"Thanks kid. I'll do the same for you someday," whispered Mullins.

The watch continued on. Once more they were called for a slight adjustment to the trim, but it was more to ensure everyone was awake and alert than for any improvement to the sailing qualities of the ship.

As the watch ended, there were muted expressions of thanks. The watch tumbled to the lower gun deck, grabbed their hammocks and rapidly strung them and alighted into them. Within seconds, the sounds of snoring could be heard. But not by Jonathan, he was too busy adding his snores to the rest.

CHAPTER 9
Gun Drill

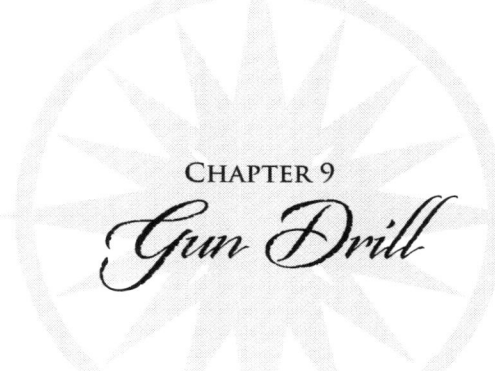

The morning watch started at four in the morning. On each watch Jonathan had learned something new. This watch was no different. However, what he learned wasn't any desired skill. Once the watch was underway they commenced to holystone the decks. The decks were wetted with water drawn in buckets from over the side. Then sand was sprinkled on the deck. Finally, a line of sailors rubbed a holystone that was essentially a brick back and forth across the deck. This sanded and cleaned the deck in one motion. It did not however, do much for a sailor's hands, knees, feet, or motivation. It did keep the decks clean, ship-shape, and kept the men occupied.

Jonathan was beginning to learn that unoccupied sailors greatly concerned the officers. It was as if the path to mutiny was idleness. While there is some truth in that, too much of a good thing in the form of useless or semi-useless work is not overly helpful either.

As it was his first taste of holystoning, Jonathan did as he was shown. Thereafter he would do his holystoning with his mind in neutral - not thinking, just shifting the holystone back and forth.

At the end of the watch, Jonathan realized it was his turn to gather the mess food, so as the next watch was piped he scurried down to the lower gun deck, and grabbed the mess jug. He filled the jug with water, and carefully navigated his way back to the mess.

When he reached the mess he found that his stool had been placed at the end of the table, and that the bread barge was on the table. He put the jug of water in the middle of the mess table.

His hands were sore from the holystoning - not blistered, but red and tender. He gingerly grabbed a piece of bread, and filled his mug with water to soak the bread. The conversation this morning was very restrained. Jonathan glanced around to see if there was any concern directed toward him. It did not appear so.

The meal was nearing completion when a faint shout was over-heard, "Land-ho".

That started off the conversation with a bang. Everyone was speculating where the land was, what country it was, and whether they would be anchoring. Since no one had a clue about the location of the ship it was total speculation. There were some "whoppers" about where they were.

Jonathan gathered the mugs, cleaned, and secured the mess table. After his chores were complete he ascended to the deck. It seemed that most of the crew were present on the deck attempting to determine their location. There were only low whispers on deck. But you could tell most ears were cocked to sounds on the quarterdeck to see if any officers, the master, or master's mates would let slip the identity of the sighted land.

Jonathan spotted the sailmaker, who had been pointed out to him the day before. He did not know him, but approached him carefully. He worked his way around in front of the older man. He turned and was face to face with the man. "Excuse me sir," spoke Jonathan "I wonder if you might have an old rag or two. I am learning to sew and I need something to practise on."

The sailmaker looked right through him. His eyes were steady and looked almost dead. Jonathan wondered if had made a serious breach by speaking to a superior without being spoken to first.

Around him, men started to edge away, fearing that any wrath from the sailmaker to the impudent lad addressing him would fall on them as well.

After a significant pause, the sailmaker spoke, "What's your name?"

"Smith, sir, Jon Smith, landsman, larboard watch."

The sailmaker half turned and strode away. He reached the bosun, and leaned over and spoke into his ear. The bosun turned his head and looked at Jonathan.

Jonathan felt like his name had just been painted on a gravestone. The feeling in his belly was nauseating. He glanced around. He noticed some men were staring at him. Others were avoiding his gaze on purpose. Not a good sign. His mother had always said his audacity would get him into trouble, and it had on a number of previous occasions. This appeared to be another of those occasions.

Still nothing happened. He edged back to the stairs and retreated back to the lower gun deck. He felt there was a storm cloud hovering over his head. As he was not on watch, he decided to make himself scarce for the moment.

No sooner had he made this decision, than he heard the bosun's pipe calling all hands on deck. He made his way back up to the deck. As he arrived he heard the order, "We will practise the great guns this morning".

The next instant, drums started, and men were scurrying in every direction. He realized that he had made a serious error. He had been given the name of his gun captain, but had not identified the man or the location of the gun. This was serious since he had no idea where to go. He needed to get moving. If he stood still, he was likely to get run over.

Since he had been told his cannon position was on a 24-pounder, he knew at least that it was on the lower gun deck. Therefore he hurried to the lower gun deck. The deck was in complete chaos.

His feet had barely hit the deck when he was grabbed by the arm and told to head aft and help break down the walls for the cabins aft. He dodged personnel as he moved aft. When he arrived, a midshipman ordered him, "You there, grab that chest and get it down to the orlop."

Jonathan mumbled "Aye sir," and grabbed the chest. He knew there was a set of stairs aft somewhere, but had never used them, so he frantically searched for the stairs. He felt a push on his back and was propelled forward. It happened to be toward the stairs.

He staggered down the stairs under the weight of the chest. At the bottom of the stairs he saw someone, but could not identify the man. "Where shall I put this?" he demanded.

The man just pointed forward. Jonathan turned and moved forward. It was awkward. The weight of the chest, his not knowing where to go, and the low headway were all concerns. He saw some men moving aft toward him, so he headed toward where they were coming from. In the middle of the orlop deck there was some space available. The carpenter and his mates were organizing the items coming from the decks above. Jonathan handed the chest to a carpenter's mate. He replied to the man that the chest was from the lower gun deck, but he was not sure from what mess it came.

He turned and retreated from the area, moving aft. He encountered others who were similarly tasked to bring down chests and other items from the lower gun deck. He made way for them as they were carrying the items. As they passed, he continued to move to the aft stairs. He ascended to the lower gun deck and looked aft. He was amazed, as there was a whole row of guns on each side of the ship of which he had previously not been aware. The entire ship was open all the way to the stern. He could see windows and some light cascading onto the deck through the windows. By this light he was able to see men standing by the cannons. He still did not know where to go.

A midshipman screamed at him in a voice that sounded like the young gentleman had not yet reached puberty. If Jonathan had not been so concerned about finding his gun crew, he would have laughed. "What the hell do you think you're doing just standing about?"

"Looking for Morrison's gun crew, sir," replied Jonathan, knuckling his forehead at the same time.

"Gun Four," came a quick reply. "Get moving."

Jonathan moved foreward, and counted from the bow back four guns. "Morrison, sir?"

"Get your ass over here! Where have you been?" replied Morrison, the gun captain.

As Jonathan got within reaching distance, Morrison grabbed him by the shirt, and shoved him into a position at the side of the 24-pounder. The gun captain then raised his arm. A different midshipman was promenading behind the foreward guns. He shouted, "Foremost quarter manned and ready."

Lieutenant Galbraith was the officer commanding this part of the lower gun deck. He motioned to the midshipman near the aft guns and said, "My respects to the Captain, lower gun deck cleared and ready". The midshipman bolted for the stairs and disappeared.

"Listen up. Gun captains, we have a number of new men who have never been involved in drill with the great guns. Instruct them on their duties now while we have a few moments," shouted Lieutenant Galbraith, so that his voice would carry the length of the gun deck.

Morrison looked directly at Jonathan. "What's your name idiot?" Morrison was a brute of a man, so there was never a thought in Jonathan's mind to upset him any further.

"Smith, sir"

"Your job, while you're in that position, is to be a strong back and pull on that tackle when we run the gun out. Your current position is 1st Train and tackle. Got that?"

"Aye, sir"

"I ain't any sir, I work for a living. I'm the captain for this gun," responded Morrison. The remainder of the gun crew snickered silently but noticeably.

"For all youze lazy slobs, if we do any firing, watch your feet. The last thing I need is for one of you dozy buggers to have his foot crushed."

The midshipman that had disappeared aft up the stairs re-appeared. He reported to Lieutenant Galbraith.

Lieutenant Galbraith shouted, "Gun Captains, we will begin mock loading and firing drills. Starboard side only. At your own speed, with simulated charge and simulated single shot, CAST LOOSE and PROVIDE."

Morrison decided to take his time, and explain the duties to all members of the crew, even if they had heard it before. "A 24-pounder usually has a twelve man crew. On the left side of the gun from muzzle proceeding inwards, Morrison indicated the positions as Rollins - 1st loader, Evert - 2nd loader, Mason - 2nd shot and wad, 2nd train and tackle position is empty, Berry - 2nd handspike train and tackle, and me as gun captain. On the right side from the muzzle proceeding inwards the positions are: Billings - 1st sponger / rammer, Nelson - 2nd sponger / rammer, Culbert - 1st shot and wad, Smith - 1st train and tackle, Rothman - 1st handspike train and tackle, and Jansen as 2nd gun captain. Our powder monkey, little Davy stays at the centreline of the deck behind the gun when he is not off to the magazine in search of powder. When running out the gun, all members of the gun crew will heave on the tackle. That's because a 24-pounder is between five and six thousand pounds. When the deck is canted downward to the bulwark, normally on the lee side of the ship, running out the gun is straightforward. When firing if the deck is canted upward, generally on the windward side of the ship, it takes everything a crew can muster to run the gun out, so put your backs into it. As you can see, at present the starboard bulwark is on the windward side of the ship, so we're goin' to have to fight the damn deck."

Jonathan counted the number of men in his gun crew. There were only eleven and that explained the empty space opposite him. He wondered what difference the extra man would make.

Morrison continued to explain "All number 2's will report to the larboard guns if we have to fight both sides at the same time. Number 1's will stay here at this gun. Got that?" Heads nodded.

Jonathan just had enough time to realise that if half the men went to the gun on the opposite side only six men would be left to run out the gun. He was shortly to find out just how difficult it was with eleven men shifting the gun upslope on a canting deck. He could only imagine the effort it would take for six men.

"Alright you dozy buggers, let's be at it," growled Morrison. "Cast loose."

"Now I have a system that has worked well for my crews. We'll use it. It is only slightly different from what the gunner will teach you in that we do things by the numbers because you simple buggars can't seem to remember what to do. Upon the command cast loose, will be ONE. Now I want each one of you dozy buggers to remember each step because some of you may have to depart for other tasks, like sail handling, boarding, to see the surgeon, or to meet your Maker. There's no guarantee all of you will be here."

"At ONE - CAST LOOSE, the 1st loader goes to the inside of the tackle and checks the port. If the port hasn't been opened before, he will make sure it's unbarred. He will pass the bar to the 2nd loader who will stow it amidships, where it's out of the way. If the officer has already given the order to open ports, he will open the port. If the order has not been given he will not open the port. The first time he will physically check the security of the breeching rope and tackle to the bulwark rings. Thereafter he will look at it, but not physically check it. He then places the hand swabs and chocking quoin against the bulwark where they can be easily reached. He aids the 1st sponger to take out the tompion from the muzzle. Rollins - demonstrate these actions."

"The 1st sponger / rammer will go on the inside of the tackle. At the onset of this drill he will physically check the security of the breeching rope and tackle to the bulwark rings. Thereafter he will look at it, but not physically check it. He will then take out the tompion from the muzzle with the assistance of the 1st loader. He will hand the tompion to the 2nd sponger, who will hang it amidships. Billings - demonstrate this action."

"The 2nd loader will check the side tackle to ensure it is properly hooked to the side training bolt on the left side of the gun. He will do this while the 1st loader is checking the bulwark rings and tackle connections. He will then take the port bar and carry it amidships and stow it out of the way. Evert - let's see you."

"The 2nd sponger will check the side tackle to ensure it is properly hooked to the side training bolt on the right side of the gun. He will take down the sponge and rammer. He will take off the sponge cap and hang it behind him. He will then place the sponge and rammer either on the deck or back in the overhead mounts, whichever he is more comfortable with. Heads will face inwards, so that when they are handed to the 1st sponger the heads will be pointed into the muzzle. He will then take the tompion from the 1st sponger and carry it amidships and hang it out of the way. Nelson - show everyone how it's done."

"Both shot and wad men will check the breech rope and the tackle to see if it is secured to the gun and ready for action. They will prepare wads and shot for loading. Mason, Culbert - let's see you perform."

"The tacklemen will look at and check the breech rope and the tackle to see if it is secured to the gun and ready for action. They will make sure the training tackle is connected at both ends. The 1st tackleman will assist the 2nd sponger and make damn sure the sponge is properly moistened. Not wet, not dry in any spot. It has to be just right so that it extinguishes any residue in the barrel, but not too wet that it causes a misfire, hang fire or anything else. You got that Smith? Nelson, show him how to do it."

"Both the 1st and 2nd handspike men will set their handspikes down on the deck parallel to the barrel, and out of the way when we run out. They will pick up the tackle lines, and stand by near the rear truck. They will leave enough slack that the loader and sponger can get past the lines. Berry, Rothman - let's see you do it."

"The 2nd gun captain will check the breeching rope, at the breeching ring on the gun, and look at the breeching rope and tackle on the left side of the gun to make sure it's okay. He will cast loose any additional breeching or rope placed on the gun for securing it in a blow. He will prepare the priming wires, priming powder, boring bitt, and linstock. Okay Jansen - show them."

"I will remove the vent cover, ensure the sight is set up, and check all vent tools. I will put on the thumbstall and place the powder horn over my shoulder. I will ensure the training tackle is hooked into the eye bolt at the rear of the cannon. I will then inspect the entire gun and crew to see if everything is done and correct. I will expect each of you to be wearing a waist belt ready to hold your boarding weapons. Okay, here's how it's done," growled Morrison. "Now for you virgins, I suggest you either get something to plug your ears, or wrap your shirt around your head, because the noise when these guns go off is something. After a good round of firing, I've known men to be deaf for near on a week."

"On TWO - SPONGE YOUR GUN, the 1st sponger will insert the wet end of the sponge into muzzle and push it all the way down the barrel. At the same time I will put my thumb over the touchhole to make a vacuum in the barrel as the sponge is withdrawn. This will ensure there is no burning residue left in the barrel that would ignite the charge when it is placed in the barrel. Let's see it Billings."

"On THREE - LOAD CARTRIDGE, the powder monkey will move forward and hand the charge to the 1st loader. He will place it in the muzzle and shove it in to the length of his elbow. The 2nd sponger will hand the rammer to the 1st sponger. Okay Davey, hand it off to Rollins." Little Davey surged forward and handed a cartridge case to Rollins. Rollins simulated taking the charge out of the cartridge case and mimicked putting it in the muzzle.

"On FOUR - RAM CARTRIDGE, the 1st sponger will then ram the charge all the way down the barrel. The 2nd shot and wad man grabs a ball and checks it. The 1st shot and wad man grabs two wads and checks them. Show them Billings." Billings hammered the end of the barrel with the rammer he had been handled by Nelson. Billings then pulled the rammer out of the muzzle and held it waiting.

"On FIVE - LOAD BALL, the 1st shot and wad man hands a wad to the 2nd loader, who then hands it to the 1st loader. The 1st loader places it in the muzzle and pushes it in far enough that the 1st sponger can properly stick the rammer in and rams it all the way to the charge. The 2nd shot and wad man will pass the ball or other load as the officer orders to 1st loader. He will then place the ball in the barrel. The 1st shot and wad man will pass the 2nd wad to the 2nd loader. He will pass it to the 1st loader. He will shove it as far down the barrel as he can. If any of you are wondering why I use a second wad; well I have seen a ball roll right out of a barrel and drop over the side when the ship rolled. And I can tell you that the Captain was not overly pleased when half the weight of his broadside disappeared. Okay let's see it." Culbert, Evert, and Rollins went through the motions.

"On SIX - RAM BALL, the 1st sponger will ram the ball and 2nd wad home. He will then pass the rammer to the 2nd sponger who will either lay it on the deck or place it back in the overhead - whatever he feels is easier for him. The 1st loader and 1st sponger will then get on the other side of the tackle. While they are doing that, I will insert the priming wire into the touchhole and make a hole in the charge bag. I will then fill the touchhole with priming powder from the Powder Horn. Okay Billings let's see that rammer in action." Billings, Nelson and Morrison mimicked the actions they would do to the satisfaction of Morrison.

"On SEVEN - RUN OUT, Everyone grabs the tackle and heaves. The gun is advanced all the way to the bulwark. Once there, I will sight the gun. I may ask for the barrel to be elevated or depressed. I may also ask for the gun to be moved from side to side so I can train forward to aft. This is the handspike men's job. To elevate or depress, they will lever the gun up and the quoin will be moved forward or backward. If we have to shift to the left or right, then both handspike men may be required on one side or the other. Right, get your backs into it." Everyone grabbed the tackle and on the command 'heave' started heaving and kept it up until the gun was against the bulwark. It took every ounce of strength Jonathan had to pull.

"On EIGHT - FIRE, the gun will be fired. There may be special orders so listen for them. The officer may shout "CLEAR THE GUN" which is his way of tellin' you to get out of the way because we're gonna' fire. He may also say "ON THE UPROLL" which means that we will wait until the ship is rising before firing. Anyway, when the order is given, I will touch the linstock to the touchhole. The priming powder will ignite and ignite the main charge. When that happens, the cannon will jump back. The breeching rope will stop it. We then start all over again. Is that clear?"

"Alright, enough explanation. We're goin' ta see if you can do it, do it right, and see how fast ya can do it," growled Morrison.

"Get on the training tackle and let's move this beauty to the rear," ordered Morrison. Everyone got on the training tackle and hauled. The ship was still on a tack that meant it was heeled to leeward. Thus the pull to move the gun back was aided by gravity, and was relatively easy compared to the run out.

"SILENCE" All talking and murmuring by the gun crew ceased. They all had a feeling they were going to need every breath that they could get.

"ONE - CAST LOOSE" Since they had already gone through these motions there was little to do for this step, but Jonathan just knew what was coming.

"TWO - SPONGE YOUR GUN"
"THREE - LOAD CARTRIDGE"
"FOUR - RAM CARTRIDGE"
"FIVE - LOAD BALL"
"SIX - RAM BALL"
"SEVEN - RUN OUT"
"EIGHT - FIRE"
"HEAVE HER BACK INTO POSITION"

The commands went on and on. Once, twice, twenty times, thirty times, after a while he lost count. He was bone tired. He was covered in sweat, even though it was cool with a chill wind drafting in through the gun ports.

Both the foremast midshipman and Lieutenant Galbraith had ambled over to watch the drill.

In fact Jonathan had little to do in the drills except heave on the tackles. He had watched the others diligently at first, but as the number of repetitions increased his powers of observation slackened, and finally became non-existent. As far as Jonathan was concerned there was little skill to be obtained by pulling on a rope. His arms ached, his back ached, the muscles in his legs ached. Even the soles of his feet were tender from trying to keep a grip on the deck as he was pulling. He had no idea how long it had been going on or was to likely to continue.

A quick glance around showed that he was not alone in his feelings. No one said anything. It wouldn't do any good anyway. In fact it would likely get the transgressor in trouble. Even the officers on this deck couldn't do anything, because it was the captain who had ordered the exercise. Everyone needed their strength to continue. Dissipating that strength by sounding off was futile.

Finally, the order came to secure the guns. With pleasure, Jonathan heaved on the tackle to move the gun into the correct position for securing. As the restraints were placed on the gun Jonathan heard the bell for noon and the "Up Spirits" pipe.

He now understood why so many of his messmates thought it was the best time of the day.

CHAPTER 10
Challenges

After the exhausting gun drill, all Jonathan wanted to do was collapse on the deck for a few minutes. He unfortunately did not have that luxury because he had the mess duty. He stumbled down the line of guns to find his mess. He hesitated because there was nothing there. All the mess kit had been moved to the orlop when the 'Clear for Action' order had been given.

He knew that if he was in the state he was in, then the other members of his mess would likely be little better. They would be in an ornery state if their food and spirit ration were to be delayed. He therefore got moving, and headed for the orlop deck.

It wasn't hard to figure out where everyone's gear was placed. All he had to do was follow the line of men grabbing kit and hauling it up to the lower gun deck. He grabbed bags in each hand and ascended to the lower gun deck. He deposited the bags there. He found the mess bags for his mess after some searching. He grabbed the bag of mugs and headed immediately for the deck. There he joined the line up for the spirit ration.

He passed out the mugs to the members of his mess. Since it was a day when Wright was due to get his tot, he pulled Wright into line ahead of him. Finally his turn came. He provided the master-at-arms his name and mess number. His ration was issued. He handed off his mug to Wright and then headed as fast as he could to the galley to get dinner for the mess.

"It's about time," grumbled Hatcher. As he was approaching the mess Jonathan had made a silent bet with himself. He bet that Hatcher would be the first to say something, and that something would be either negative or outright vulgar. He had won his bet.

The mess table had been lowered, the plates, bowls and trenchers were out, and the bread barge was on the table. Jonathan set the kid on the table. Before he could pick it up again to issue out the rations, Hatcher had grabbed it and was pulling out food into his trencher. The mess went silent. They were all waiting for dinner with some degree of anticipation, but it was bad form to usurp someone else's place to issue the ration. Knobby commented, "Hatcher, it's the lad's responsibility today to issue the ration. If it takes another minute, it's no big deal. You can wait."

Hatcher looked at his fellow mess mates, "I was just helpin'". He turned, moved the kid back to Jonathan, then sat and began to fill his face.

"I wouldn't if I were you," growled Pollard.

Hatcher's breach of mess etiquette had hardened virtually everyone in the mess against him. They had all seen what he was attempting to do. If there was a shortage in rations, the mess 'cook' on duty was responsible to make up the difference. Hence the requirement for the responsible mess 'cook' to issue out the rations. By usurping Jonathan's control, Hatcher had taken more than his allotment and Jonathan would have to make up the difference. While no one was overly concerned about Jonathan, the same thing could happen to any one of them, and this was of concern.

Hatcher stared at the faces looking at him and stopped chewing. He said not a word. Nothing was likely to go over well at this point.

Jonathan emptied out all the contents of the kid into the various trenchers, bowls and plates. There were equal shares of beef in everyone's except his and Hatcher's. This was the moment of decision.

If Jonathan touched Hatcher's trencher, Hatcher would become his enemy, if he wasn't already. If someone else touched Hatcher's trencher, then it would indicate that Jonathan needed protection. If Hatcher moved some of his ration onto Jonathan's trencher and they were equalled, then mess peace would be assured. If not, Hatcher would be asked to leave the mess. It would be hard for him to get into another mess, because everyone would know the reason for his being ejected and would not trust him in their mess.

Jonathan deftly made his move by doing nothing, but it was more by pure luck than skill or knowledge of men. In fact he was afraid to do anything against Hatcher. Hatcher could flatten him easily. The importance of what was happening did not sink in until later.

Hatcher reluctantly picked up his trencher and slid some of the contents into Jonathan's trencher until they were equal. He scowled at Jonathan but said nothing.

The mood in the mess was sombre. Jonathan knew that he had made an enemy of Hatcher, but he rationalized that it was bound to happen anyway. No matter how it had turned out, Hatcher would either hate him, despise him or loath him.

Jonathan was not sure how the remaining members of the mess had felt about it. None of them were looking at him or Hatcher - in fact most were looking at the table. Hands were placed around their respective food protecting it. Their body language reflected how they felt. Jonathan however, was not consciously aware of this.

"Toss a hunk of that bread down here, will you," said Bates. The mood was broken as the bread barge slid down the table.

Next, Jonathan's empty mug slid down from Wright. Jonathan rose. He took the pitcher over to the water butt and filled it. Jonathan added water to his now-empty mug and tossed a piece of bread in to soak it.

There was limited conversation. Jonathan crunched away at his bread. He swallowed some water to assist in getting the bread down.

The pipe for watch change was heard, and they all rushed. Contents of the mugs were rapidly drained down throats. Jonathan grabbed the mugs and placed them in the mess bag, which he hung on the wall. He grabbed the kid, trenchers, bowls and plates and headed to the galley to clean up. Other members of the mess hoisted the mess table back into place. Some, like Jonathan, stuffed a piece of bread in their pocket so they could gnaw away at it while on watch.

The afternoon watch was undertaken without Jonathan's conscious involvement. He was tasked again to the forecastle to work on ropes. He now had a feel for the job and he went about it without any concern. While he did not have a high skill level, he intuitively knew that the longer he worked on theses ropes, the better and faster he would get. He initially started with a fast pace, but was subtly approached by Wright and then Pollard. Wright hissed, "Slow down. The more you accomplish, the more they'll give us to do, and you're making the rest of us look lazy."

Pollard had a slightly different approach to say essentially the same thing. "Go slow at first. Get experience, and get the technique correct. Once you have the technique down correctly, then you can increase your speed. That's the sign of a good seaman. Another thing to remember is that speed is essential in an emergency. It's not as important right now. Let's say that we complete all the work that has to be done here in the next hour. That still leaves lots of time in the watch. Look around you. You see other groups doing their tasks. What do you think the officers will do if we are finished and just sitting around and all the others are working?"

Jonathan just shrugged his shoulder.

"They'll find something else for us to do. If there's nothin' else I know, this I do. The officers just hate to see an idle man when others is workin'," explained Pollard.

As the watch continued, Jonathan broke off a morsel of bread and stuck it in his mouth. He just let the bread moisten from his saliva. Finally when it was soft enough, he chewed on it and swallowed. He left the forecastle and descended to the main deck and got a dipper of water from the butt at the mainmast. As he was returning to his work at the forecastle, Mr. Hurley stopped him near the steps.

"Where do you think you're going?" he demanded.

Jonathan assumed a respectful posture. "I was just returning to the forecastle after getting a drink Mr. Hurley."

"Who said you could get a drink?" demanded Hurley.

"No one Mr. Hurley. I didn't realize there were any restrictions on getting a drink. I thought that was what the butt was there for," responded Jonathan.

"Don't get uppity with me lad," growled Hurley.

Jonathan recognized the signs instantly. He had similar warnings from the squire's men, and look how that had worked out - he was here. He needed to diffuse this situation immediately, or Hurley would be all over him. It was amazing how a little fear can focus the mind.

"Mr. Hurley, I respect the position you have and I meant no offence sir." By this time Jonathan's posture had changed from a relaxed position of respect to a ramrod straight position of attention. Sweat was breaking out on his forehead.

Mr. Hurley stepped closer to Jonathan so that his growl into Jonathan's ear could not be heard by other eavesdroppers standing nearby. "I've got my eye on you lad. You've got spirit. I could make a seaman out of you, or I could crush you like a cockroach."

Jonathan swallowed hard, not daring to make a sound. His fear was palatable.

"You spoke to the sailmaker without him addressing you. Why?"

Jonathan realized instantly that this was what it was all about. It had nothing to do with his getting a drink of water. "Sir, I want to learn to sew. A messmate is showing me how, but I have nothing to practise with. I was looking for a rag to use for practise, sir."

"So you would risk a striped back for a rag?" growled Hurley.

"Sir, I didn't realize........... I figured it was better to ask than to get caught stealing a rag," stammered Jonathan. He could see disdain or disbelief; he wasn't sure which, in Hurley's expression.

Hurley took a step back from Jonathan and spoke louder. "You daft bugger, report to the ropemaker for extra duties midway through the first dog watch today and for every dog watch until the ropemaker says you can stop."

"Aye, Mr. Hurley," Jonathan said to Hurley's back as Hurley sauntered aft. Jonathan needed another drink after all that sweating, but he did not have the courage to get it. Instead he went back to the forecastle. He was aware of the stares he was receiving.

No one dared go near the water butt for the remainder of the watch.

Wright whispered, "What's that bastard got against you? It ain't right! Imagine, not being able to get a drink from the water butt when on watch. I could see it if we were on water rations, but not now."

Jonathan just let Wright's comments pass. There was nothing he could say or do at the present, but he did wonder. His actions were against the sailmaker, so why the ropemaker? This he could not explain.

At the end of the watch Jonathan went over to the water butt and got a dipper of water. He was not the only one, as others were doing the same thing. A number of men nodded at him as he drank. Word spread quickly amongst the watch and ultimately the crew. There was a lot of resentment.

"Could have been anyone of us," mumbled one of the men. "It's not right."

From the quarterdeck came a command "You men at the water butt, get below if you're not part of the watch." Unfortunately, this only fuelled the resentment, but the men not on watch started disappearing back to their respective messes for the evening meal.

The talk at all of the messes during the evening meal was of the injustice of having to do extra work because of having a drink of water in the middle of the watch. Jonathan was silent. He didn't think the extra work was because of the drink, but he wasn't fully sure either.

He laboured through his meal. Since he had to give up much of the off time for the watch, he asked Wright if he could go through a couple of stitches before he had to depart for the extra duty. Wright was very accommodating. They retreated to the foreward bulkhead, out of the way of any of the messes, and went through a couple of things. In general Jonathan was silent. Wright only spoke about sewing, as neither wished to speak about the extra work.

Nearing the half way point of the watch Jonathan excused himself. He went below looking for the ropemaker. He found him near the bow end of the orlop deck.

"Mr. Jergens, I was told by Mr. Hurley to report to you for extra work at the mid way mark of the dog watch," said Jonathan.

"Come with me," said Mr. Jergens. He proceeded to the cable tier. The cable tier normally housed the anchor cable, but there were also other ropes. In fact, there were lots of ropes of all different sizes. Some were new, but most were older, worn ropes.

"Your job is to prepare these ropes for re-use."

Jonathan took one look and his heart sank. This wasn't a job; it was a lifetime's work!

"Before I go much further, I need to know your capabilities. Take that cable and whip the end of it." Mr. Jergens pointed to a three inch cable lying on the deck.

Jonathan picked up the cable and automatically started checking it for wear. As he moved it to the closest end, he said, "I don't have a marlinspike, knife, or whipping twine."

Wordlessly, the ropemaker handed Jonathan all three items. Jonathan went through the whipping process that he had been shown by Pollard. He was slow, but did a thorough job. He handed the whipped end to Mr. Jergens and said, "I'm not fast yet - I'm just learning the technique."

Mr. Jergens examined Jonathan's work. "Technique's good, but you'll need both speed and more dexterity, especially if you have to do this in an exposed position in a storm." He pointed to some one inch 3-strand rope. "Now let's see how well you can splice. Do a short splice to remove that worn area."

Again Jonathan did what Pollard had shown him.

Mr. Jergens took the splice and twisted and tugged it. "Acceptable. I've seen worse, and I've seen better. Same problem though - speed and dexterity."

"Okay, find me the next spot on this rope that needs work," ordered Mr. Jergens.

Jonathan took the rope and started checking it for wear. The rope was in poor overall shape. However, some spots were much worse than others. He selected a spot, and cut the rope twice to remove the heavily worn section. As he was completing a short splice, Mr. Jergens quietly said "Stop! Now do it this way, instead of the way you were doing it."

Jonathan repositioned his hands in the manner that Mr. Jergens demonstrated. The positioning was foreign to him, but after working on the rope for a couple of minutes he could easily see that it was, in fact, a better position.

Mr. Jergens went further. "Alright, imagine you are leaning out over the bowsprit having to do this with a severed line. The bow is dipping and then cresting with each wave. As it dips, the wave is going to wash over you in your exposed position. You're going to need to hang on till the waves pass. But if you let go of the splice, you'll lose both the ropes and may not get them back. The topmen have a saying - one hand for the King and one hand for yourself. Keep that in mind as you use this technique."

Jonathan held the splice with one hand, and using the other hand he reached over and grabbed the one inch line resting nearby.

"The trick, lad, is to get enough of the splice done, so one hand can hold it. The second part of the trick is to pin the one side between your arm and chest, and have sufficient slack on the other end of the rope that it will not be tugging all that much when the wave hits. If it tugs too hard, Hercules would not be able to hold that partial splice with one hand."

They went over the splice technique again. Then they both heard the jostle of feet.

"Watch change - get your ass up on deck," growled Mr. Jergens.

Jonathan pelted up the stairs. He was the last man to arrive on deck for the head count. He fully expected to be started, but nothing was said.

The watch was cool with a refreshing breeze. Winter was coming. Jonathan felt it more as he was clad only in his shirt. He had been hot in the cable tier. The breeze revived him after the reek of the cable tier. He only wished that he had his jacket. He vowed that he would not forget it again. He would take it with him for the extra duties in the next dog watch.

He shivered. To warm himself, he hugged his arms around his body. As he placed his hands on his waist, he felt metal. In his haste to get on deck for the watch change, he had forgotten to return the knife and marlinspike to the ropemaker. Now he was for it. What should he do? Should he wait until the end of watch and return them, or should he ask permission to go to the cable tier and return them immediately? He was in a dilemma.

He at last decided to wait. He rationalized that he did not know where the ropemaker would be at this time. It was possible that he might be in the cable tier, but unless he had to be why would he stay there? He might be in his mess. That was an area that Jonathan had no desire to visit because he might run into the bosun or Mr. Hurley. Lastly, he wished no one other than Mr. Jergens to know of his mistake. If Hurley found out about it, it was likely that he would receive additional punishment.

The wind was constantly changing throughout the watch resulting in their almost continuously heaving on the braces. It helped keep Jonathan warm to some extent, but it ensured that he was standing in a more exposed position to the wind, compared to having his back to the windward bulwark.

As he thought about his predicament, he considered that this was what the Royal Navy was truly about. Lack of sleep, continuous work, cold or wet most of the time, poor food, and wages so low that it near equalled slave labour. He snickered when he remembered someone back at the hamlet suggesting that navy seaman had it made. Everywhere they went they took their beds, always had their "three squares", and got paid to boot.

He had only been gone for a couple of weeks from home, but he seemed a world away. He was homesick in a way, but not in any way that he expected. That's one thing that these watches provided - time to think - maybe too much time. Maybe that was why it was better to be busy, so you didn't have time to be sorry for yourself since there was a lot to be sorry about.

Jonathan stood by the braces awaiting orders. He was listening with one ear, but mulling things over at the same time. Why was he not overcome by homesickness? He had seen others that had been pressed around the same time as he was. He remembered some faces from the tavern. Some were truly bitter. One or two had broke down and cried. Men shunned them.

He tried to assess himself, to see himself as others might see him, and how he thought of himself. He couldn't get a picture of himself. He knew he wasn't as bitter as some of the others. He wasn't like Hatcher, but he could see that he might be heading in that direction. This life could get a man down, or a small error could have him down and punished in a heartbeat. He idly wondered what his attitude would be like if he had a striped back. He reflected that he would likely be bitter too.

As Jonathan continued his musings, interspersed with brief spells of intense muscular activity when heaving on braces, he noticed another thing. When he was concentrating on one thing, he forgot about other things. While he was musing about what others thought about him, he forgot the cold. Only when he thought directly about the cold did he start to shiver, or at least notice that he was shivering. Again he thought about why the officers and the bosun were so interested in seeing that everyone was working all the time. Was it because the men's minds would be focused on the work and temporarily forget the bad aspects of their lives?

As the bell clanged, indicating a change of watch, Jonathan felt there was not likely to be anyone more thankful than he that the watch was over.

He made a beeline for the hatch and scampered down the stairs to the lower gun deck. He made a snap decision to see the ropemaker about the knife tomorrow.

Jonathan rigged his hammock, and was nested in it wrapped in his two blankets in short order. Sleep was not long in coming.

Standing the middle watch was far more pleasant with a jacket than the last dog watch had been without one. The wind was constantly changing, and the motion of the sea was considerably different.

Knobby looked at Jonathan, "Can you feel it?"

"Feel what?"

"That distinctive motion. There's only one place in the world that has that motion. We're in the English channel, lad."

Jonathan admitted the motion was different than any he had experienced since being on board, but he was sceptical that anyone could tell exactly where they were just by the motion of the ship.

"You keep your eyes open this morning lad and you'll see. We was heading south yesterday before last light, so when the sun comes up you check if we are still goin' south. If we are, then be watchin' for two things. On the starboard keep your eyes peeled for big white chalk cliffs - them's the White Cliffs of Dover. The second is to keep your eyes peeled for Frenchies. They like to hunt around here because there's rich pickin's. We might get lucky and get us a prize."

As the morning watch began, they were ordered to stand by their guns. They were not cleared for action, but were ready to clear for action instantly. As the light increased other ships became visible, mainly numerous merchantmen just starting to hoist sail for the day. There were no Frenchmen.

To Jonathan's surprise, on the starboard bow were large white cliffs.

Chapter 11
Out of Discipline

HMS Winchester cruised along, engaged in the daily routine. During the afternoon watch 'all hands on deck' was piped. After the hands were mustered, the Captain spoke from the quarterdeck to the assembled mass.

"Men, the Winchester will anchor at Portsmouth. There we will take on stores, and put out to sea within forty eight hours. Trusted men will be allowed ashore for the afternoon and first dog watch. Bumboats will be allowed alongside only after all stores are loaded. There will be a picket boat from the port ensuring no unauthorized vessel approaches, and there are no unauthorized departures. The boat will be from the port admiral, so if anyone has an idea to go swimming, be aware that your fate will be out of my hands, and that the port admiral is not fond of deserters. So be warned."

As the men were dismissed there was lively discussion. Spirits appeared to be the highest Jonathan had ever seen in his short stay on board.

Obviously, Jonathan was not one of the trusted men. In fact, few landsmen were trusted. Jonathan asked Pollard and Knobby if they were going to be able to get off the ship. Both indicated that they could request liberty if they wished, but had no desire. They knew no one in Portsmouth, and they hadn't seen any money in months. Without money the trip into town was worthless. Additionally, neither of them had any desire to put up with the way some Portsmouth residents resented navy sailors.

Jonathan was unsure what they meant by this. The explanation was that sailors were considered 'low-life' by townsfolk. The only people that liked sailors were those that wanted money the sailors were likely to have – namely taverns or sailor knickknack vendors. These people liked merchantmen sailors far better than navy seamen because they had deeper pockets. Knobby and Pollard were therefore going to stay on board.

Just after first light, HMS Winchester entered Portsmouth harbour and anchored. A guard boat raced out to the ship. Dispatches for the Captain were passed to the officer of the watch, and the guard boat began patrolling between ship and shore.

A number of bumboats came out, but were turned back by the guard boat. Most turned, but a couple of more daring ones ventured in. A musket shot quickly altered their intensions. They departed back to the docks.

Various hoys started out from the admiralty yards. Both watches were turned out for the loading of stores. Yards were rigged to hoist, hatches were opened to receive cargo, and the hold stowage was re-assessed. Empty casks and barrels were brought on deck. As full items were hoisted on board, the cooper was working furiously at cleaning some water casks and assembling others that had been broken down.

When the water hoy arrived alongside late in the day, Jonathan was dispatched to the hoy to pump. Of all the work that he had been doing that day, pumping water was the least enjoyable. It was repetitive, backbreaking work. After two hours he was replaced, and went back on board the Winchester. The evening meal was delayed by the storing process. The mood was ugly. Long, hard work, with no breaks and no food, does not make for a happy crew. The men could not see any need for such a rush. But no matter, the men were pushed hard.

Finally, the last hoy left. Not because all the stores had been loaded, but because the dockworkers' quitting time had been passed and they were unprepared to remain. Just another stab in the back for navy sailors.

Even though the Winchester was anchored in a major navy harbour, there were no fresh victuals. It was just another reason for the men to gripe.

A harbour watch was manned. Jonathan found that he was on the watch. He was bone tired and wanted desperately to get some sleep. Even if he had been off watch, with both watches having hammocks slung, there was little room. When he came off watch, he simply wrapped his blankets around himself and collapsed beside a 24-pounder.

The next morning, the routine started all over again, but at least it didn't start until 0600. Hoys never arrived before the forenoon watch, and Jonathan's shipmates, eager for a run ashore, were worried that provisioning would not be completed before noon. They therefore set about the task with an enthusiasm that had not been present the day before.

Surprisingly, the last hoy pulled away just before noon. Hatches were being closed as the pipe for "Up Spirits" was made. There was a significant lightening of spirits as the ship went out of discipline for the next few hours.

After the noon meal, Pollard and Knobby took Jonathan aside. "Come on up to the deck with us." The three of them ascended to the deck. Jonathan looked around and saw what appeared to be scores of bumboats heading toward the Winchester.

"Lad, you've never experienced a ship out of discipline," commenced Pollard. "There is no way to accurately describe the depravity you will see."

Knobby began, "Anything that moves will be stolen, so empty your ditty bag. You have shoes, wear 'em; else you won't have 'em tomorrow. I see you have a knife. Keep it on you. Wear your jacket. In fact, I would keep your ditty bag close at hand. If you sleep, use it as a pillow, but I advise you not to sleep."

"Your best bet is to stay on deck as close to the quarterdeck as needed, but as far away from the entry port as possible," explained Pollard.

"You'd be hard pressed to find a more scurvied lot than the wenches and haberdashers that will shortly descend on this ship. They'll cheat you and rob you blind to fill their purses," continued Knobby. "You'd be like a babe in the woods for these creatures."

"Let's head back below and grab our ditty bags," suggested Pollard.

As they descended to the lower gun deck there was more light than normal. Jonathan realized that some of the gun-ports had been opened. People were passing to and fro through the ports, as were baskets and boxes.

Jonathan approached the foreward bulkhead where his ditty bag hung. When he was less than ten feet away he saw a short fat man, or at least he thought it was a man, grab his bag, open it and start searching through it.

Rather than say anything, Jonathan stepped up behind the man, drew his knife, and stuck the point of the knife in the man's neck. He pressed the point in slightly through mounds of fat. The man froze. "Whatcha think you're doing?" demanded Jonathan.

The man started to turn. Jonathan pressed the point in harder. He heard a sound behind him. Pollard reached past him and hammered the fat man on the head with a piece of wood. The fat man collapsed. Jonathan had to jerk his knife back or else the fat man would be impaled on it. Jonathan had to jump back as well because the fat man had collapsed backward into him.

"See what I mean?" murmured Pollard.

They both looked at the fat man because he looked strange. As they bent over for a closer examination, it became obvious that the fat man was not a fat man, but a fat woman, and a formidable one at that.

Jonathan stuffed the items back into his ditty bag and turned. He gave Pollard a look that said, 'let's get the hell out of here'. Pollard nodded.

As Jonathan and Pollard headed back toward the stairs, the sights and debauchery caused Jonathan to stop several times. Women without clothes, or with few garments, were straddling sailors left and right. One looked at him, and said, "Be with you in a minute honey."

Pollard had to grab him repeatedly to get him moving, and finally fell in behind him and pushed him toward the stairs.

As Jonathan reached the upper deck, he was still trying to assess the images he had just seen. Being from a farm he had occasionally seen the cows and horses going at it, but he had never seen a man and woman going at it. He had thought that the act would be somewhat different than what he had just seen. Some of these women had stepped from one man to the next as if they were changing horses. Out of one saddle - on to the next, so to speak.

The entry port batten had been lowered on the leeward side of the ship, so Pollard and Jonathan headed to the windward side and slumped down between a couple of 12-pounders. On the forecastle, and even in the waist, there was much activity, but it was considerably tamer than what was happening down on the lower gun deck.

Jonathan watched some sailors and women dancing in the waist. The music was lively. Jonathan slid his jacket on, grasped his ditty bag and wandered over. He found an empty spot, dropped his ditty bag, and sat on top of it. During a break in the dancing while the musicians were wetting their whistle, Jonathan noted than most of the seated men were also sitting on their ditty bags, or that one man was guarding his mate's bag while his mate danced.

As the festivities continued Jonathan felt the tug of drowsiness. He ambled over to where he and Pollard had first squatted. Pollard and Knobby were there. He lay down beside them as they made room. Little was said, and after some time Jonathan drifted off to sleep with one hand on his knife, and his ditty bag under his head.

Jonathan awoke in darkness. He wasn't sure what woke him up. He then realized it was someone shaking him. "Come on, get your ass up, ya lazy bugger."

Jonathan got up, as did Pollard and Knobby.

"Get the yardarm rigged for hoisting," commanded an unknown shadow.

Half a dozen men moved toward the mainmast and commenced setting it up for hoisting. "You and you, over the side and get that motley bunch ready for hoisting." Jonathan was propelled to the lee side entry port. Looking over he saw a boat alongside. He turned and descended into the boat. Everywhere he stepped, he stepped on drunken bodies. He now understood what was happening. A cargo net was lowered to the aft of the boat. The oarsmen, Jonathan, and the other man who had come down dragged, shoved and threw the bodies into the cargo net.

"Stand clear below," shouted the voice, "Hoist away". The cargo net was hoisted up and then swung inboard. Jonathan clearly heard a number of thumps as the drunken men were unceremoniously dropped on the deck. After a short pause while the bodies were removed from the cargo net, the net re-appeared over the side and was lowered back down. Jonathan and the others commenced shifting unwilling bodies back onto the cargo net. After the last body was piled on, Jonathan again heard "Stand clear below," and then "Hoist away".

Jonathan and the other man scrambled up the battens to the entry port and came aboard in time to see the contents of the cargo net dumped, as one side of the net was unhooked and the entire net raised. There were several loud thuds, a few groans and grunts, and then an extremely loud fart.

"You disgusting piece of turd," growled the master-at-arms to whoever had released the fart.

Someone on the opposite side of the mainmast found either the fart or the master-at-arms' choice of words humorous. A voice in a drunken slur said, "He probably is, if anything accompanied that fart."

Well that was the crowning point for the evening, as everyone present broke into laughter.

"Be quiet," growled the master-at-arms, although you could hear the laughter in his voice, "or you'll have us all in shit." It was unfortunate that the master-at-arms had such a limited vocabulary, because all his words did was to fuel the laughter.

But the men were dispersing, and as they split and went their respective ways, the laughter began to tail off. In a short time, the only sound was snoring and the occasional fart as the crew of the Winchester slept it off.

※

The crew of the Winchester was roused for the morning watch at 0400. Many men were still camped out on the main deck, so these men made their way to the lower gun deck to stow ditty bags. Some kept on going to the orlop deck to see the surgeon.

Holystoning of the deck commenced shortly after the calling of the watch. It was a dismal affair with the bosun's mates and other supervisors in essentially the same condition as the men. The first lieutenant overlooked the shambles of what had been his pristine deck. He was in a foul mood for the captain would expect his ship to be 'Bristol fashion' before setting sail. It would take a small miracle, which by the look of the crew was beyond them.

As per the Captain's orders, bumboats had been ordered away after the last dog watch. However, there were still hangers-on and all the trusted men had not returned until much later. A head count was still needed to see if anyone was missing.

The Captain had permission to sleep ashore over night and was exercising that privilege. When he returned, which would be shortly, he would expect the ship to be tidy and ready to get underway. Lieutenant Wilkinson wanted a good efficiency report for promotion. He was willing to push the men to get it.

He turned to the other lieutenants, and said, "Gentlemen, keep the men working. I want this ship ready to get under way as soon as the Captain gets back. I also want a head count to make sure we have everyone, so check your men and report back to me in fifteen minutes."

Unfortunately, Lieutenant Wilkinson's wishes were to be deferred. A commotion was occurring at the foreward end of the waist.

"Silence on the deck," shouted the first lieutenant.

The noise continued. Lieutenant Wilkinson strode over to the stairs and shot down to the waist. He was in a furious mood. "What in the blazes is going on here?" The noise continued unabated.

"Silence," he screamed. He was looking at one of the ugliest, fattest individuals it had ever been his misfortune to gaze upon.

"You sir, what the devil do you think you're doing, and why are you here?"

The ugly person shot back, "Who the hell are you callin' sir? You been to sea for so long you don't even recognize a lady when you see one?" The men holystoning the deck were careful not to show it, but were enjoying the spectacle immensely. Jonathan was one of them.

"I have no problem when I see one," replied Lieutenant Wilkinson harshly. "Now why are you still here?"

"I was robbed," yelled the woman. "One of you'ze hit me over the head and robbed me."

"And what did you lose?" demanded Lieutenant Wilkinson.

"All the rings on my fingers, and ten quid," she replied.

"Guard boat approaching with an officer, sir," reported the signals midshipman.

Lieutenant Wilkinson nodded.

Knobby rose from where he was holystoning the deck. He turned to face the first lieutenant, and knuckled his forehead. Lieutenant Wilkinson looked at him. "You have something to say Knobby?"

"Sir, I went down to the lower gun deck to get Pollard's, Smith's and my ditty bag. I seen this.....person going through ditty bags."

"You saw this woman going through ditty bags? And what did you do?" asked Lieutenant Wilkinson. He was staring hard at the fat woman.

"Why I grabbed my bag, Pollard's, and Smith's before she could get to them, sir."

The simplistic reply caught Lieutenant Wilkinson off guard. He looked over at Knobby and stifled a chuckle. "Thank you Knobby."

It was a dismissal, and Knobby took it as one. "Aye, sir," he said as he knuckled his forehead and resumed his holystoning position.

"Show me your hands," demanded Lieutenant Wilkinson of the woman.

Two pudgy hands were thrust forward. Lieutenant Wilkinson took the hands and examined them palms down and then palms up. "I see no ring marks."

"Master-at-arms, escort her to the entry port. She leaves with the guard boat," ordered Lieutenant Wilkinson.

"Sir, do I rig a chair for her?" asked the master-at-arms.

"She got onboard without one, she can get off without one," replied Lieutenant Wilkinson.

"Aye, sir"

"You've no right to man-handle me. You and this thieving crew haven't heard the last of this," screamed the woman.

"Master-at-arms, I want silence on the ship. If you have any difficulty with any person on this ship keeping that silence, you have my permission to use whatever non-lethal means necessary to rid this ship of that noise," stated Lieutenant Wilkinson.

The noise ceased abruptly.

The flag lieutenant had been the officer on the guard boat. Lieutenant Wilkinson met him at the entry port. He explained the situation to him and motioned the master-at-arms to get rid of the woman.

The flag lieutenant had brought orders and dispatches to the vessel. The dispatch case was addressed to the Commodore at Antigua. It was an easy guess that the Winchester was heading to Antigua.

Chapter 12
Questions Arise

After the Captain arrived on board, very little time was wasted before the order to weigh anchor was given. Jonathan had the dubious privilege of manning the capstan. Never before had Jonathan come up against an object as stubborn to move as the capstan.

From the moment the bars were placed in the capstan and he took his place at the bar, Jonathan pushed with all of his strength as did all of the other men. Still there was no movement. Finally, more men were brought in to assist. Even the mates took a place at the bar for the effort. Finally, the capstan clicked. Once, twice, three times.

"Keep her moving lads," shouted the bosun hoarsely.

The slow movement suddenly gave way to a rapid turning. "She's broke loose - finally," said someone.

Half the men could now walk the cable up. Round and round Jonathan went. There was an occasional stop - then around once more. Finally the word "Belay".

After a few moments of holding the anchor in position while another team secured it, the order was given to take the bars back out of the capstan and stow them. Upon completion of this, Jonathan went up to the main deck and got a drink from the water butt with a number of other sweating men.

Jonathan looked astern. He gazed at the shoreline. It would be a long time before he would see England again.

✷

HMS Winchester headed south. According to Knobby, this was the preferred route to the West Indies as the winds were better. Knobby had sailed to the West Indies a number of times in a merchantman but never on a King's ship.

The daily routine did not vary all that much for Jonathan. Each day at dawn they stood by the guns. The decks were holystoned. Sails and rope were repaired. On average two hours per day they spent time going through the motions of loading and running out the great guns. The guns were not fired though, because the cost of powder and shot were so great. Jonathan commented on this once saying, "Geeze, you'd think the Captain was paying for this out of his own pocket."

The reply shocked Jonathan. The foremast midshipman commented, "He is. The Admiralty only provides a limited supply of shot and powder. If any captain wishes to train his crews, then he has to be prepared to fork out money for additional powder and shot."

In the afternoon, they did more sail drill, rope repair, sail repair and maintenance on the hull. Or for fun, the bosun's mate would take them into the hold and let them shift casks, pipes and other provisions.

After the evening meal, Jonathan was still obliged to report to the ropemaker or one of his mates for extra duties. In most cases, Jonathan reported and was shown what to do. Then either the ropemaker or one of his mates would come back to check before change of watch.

The day Winchester left port, Jonathan had reported back to the ropemaker at the appointed hour. He broached the subject of the knife and marlinspike. Mr. Jergens just chuckled and said, "They're yours. All you have to do is pay the purser." Jonathan didn't want to know how much that was going to cost him.

Despite the extra work, Jonathan was able to squeeze in a few minutes here, a few minutes there, with Wright to learn how to sew. Wright had shown him virtually all that he knew, but Jonathan needed a lot more practise before he would be as capable as Wright. So practise he did.

He managed to get a couple of rags on which to practise. He often wished he had just scrounged the rags instead of approaching the sailmaker. He would have been a better sewer by now, and would not have had to do all of this extra duty.

He did concede that he was far superior with all kinds of rope work than just about anyone else. Certainly he was better than anyone at his mess. He could match anyone with the intricacies of any splice or accoutrement, and he was nearly as fast as any of the ropemaker's assistants. He respected the ropemaker and occasionally was able to speak to him man to man, when no one else was around, in the cable tier where most of Jonathan's extra duties were performed.

Jonathan welcomed the open discussions, for he learned from the older man, and not just rope work. One night as he was working on some rope, as directed by one of the ropemaker's assistants, Mr. Jergens entered the cable tier. Jonathan had just finished a short splice and a number of other splices were laid out for inspection. He had just found another severely worn spot on another rope.

"Evening Mr. Jergens," said Jonathan respectfully. Mr. Jergens nodded and watched Jonathan. Jonathan cut the rope, spread the strands and started the splice like he had been doing it all of his life. Mr. Jergens looked up at Jonathan's face, and realized that Jonathan was doing the entire splice solely by feel. Jonathan was looking at Mr. Jergens. Mr. Jergens' eye glanced back and forth between Jonathan's face and the splice. Jonathan was already finished the splice, and was just preparing the whipping for one end. It was fast work. However, Mr. Jergens held off making any comment until he could actually check the completed work.

Upon completion of whipping both ends, Mr. Jergens extended his hand. Jonathan rightly interpreted that this was a request to inspect the completed splice. Mr. Jergens thoroughly tested the splice, going so far as to tie one end off and heave on the other end.

"You've improved somewhat from when you first came here," stated Mr. Jergens.

"Aye sir, those tips you gave me have proven valuable," responded Jonathan. He then added, "I'm grateful."

Mr. Jergens eyes flashed up to Jonathan's showing surprise and estimating whether Jonathan was mocking him. He found no hint that Jonathan was mocking him. He appraised Jonathan for awhile. All the time Jonathan was checking more rope for wear and damage.

Mr. Jergens said, "My father was a tinker. He used to take a barrow out and try and sell goods up and down the roads in Kent. It was a long way between farms, and even then the farmers were generally tenants with little or no money. You can probably relate to that a little."

"Anyway he had a tough time of it. Poor weather, few sales, sometimes local kids hassling him or trying to make off with his merchandise. I asked him why he continued to do it. Do you know what he said to me?"

Jonathan shook his head.

"It ain't much he said, but it keeps us out of the poor house."

"I asked him, well, why not just work in the city? There were more people, less travel; he'd probably make more in sales. He told me this story..."

"There once was a little swallow that was more interested in having a good time than keeping an eye on things. This swallow was so busy having a good time that he failed to head south with the rest of the swallows. Never mind, he said, I can just fly faster and catch up with the rest. Late in the season the swallow heads off south. But the weather was so cold that ice built up on his wings and he fell to the earth. Now, it just happened that a barnyard was below him when he fell. After he crashed in the barnyard, a cow walked over him and dropped a big load of shit directly on top of him. The shit thawed out the ice on the swallow's wings. The swallow was so happy that he began singing for joy. Now there were a number of cats that called that barnyard home. One of them heard the bird singing and went to investigate. The cat found the bird, dug him out and promptly ate him."

"Now what can you learn from this story?" asked Mr. Jergens.

"It seems the bird should have flown south earlier, so I guess the point is to be on time," replied Jonathan.

"Actually, there's more to it than just that," replied Mr. Jergens. "My father put it this way. First, there is a time in life for everything. You can be early, or on time, and there are no consequences. If you are late, you may pay a heavy price. Next, not everyone who shits on you is your enemy. Being in shit sometimes can be beneficial. Third, not everyone who gets you out of shit is your friend. Fourth, when you're in deep shit and want to get out of it unscathed, keep your mouth shut!"

Jonathan stopped working on the rope and looked up as he concentrated on what Mr. Jergens had said.

"Think over the past couple of months since you been on this ship. Can you relate to anything in that story?" inquired Mr. Jergens.

Jonathan considered this for a while. "I'm just a swallow," he replied. "If I had got out of that tavern earlier, I wouldn't be here at all. I seem to have fallen into a pile of shit since I'm here. And not everyone that shits on me is my enemy." At this point Jonathan looked at Mr. Jergens and nodded. "And finally, if I want to survive, and eventually get out of the pile of shit that I'm in, then I'd better learn to keep my mouth shut."

Mr. Jergens smiled. "Well I can see that you're a quick learner - course I already knew that from your work."

"The bad news is that you're not out of shit yet," said Mr. Jergens. "Tomorrow, instead of reporting to me, you're to report to the captain of the mainmast top to help him."

Jonathan was stunned by the news. Keeping in mind that Mr. Jergens had not made this decision, that in fact he had just said that Jonathan was a quick learner and had learned about all that Mr. Jergens could teach him with respect to rope work, Jonathan just nodded while gritting his teeth in frustration.

Jonathan finished up in the cable tier and went up stairs to fall in for watch. He was more dejected than he had been in some time. As usual, the first watch was not overly strenuous. This was especially so when running with the trade winds. For hours at a time, the sails did not need adjustment, so the watch relaxed on deck.

Jonathan was truly frustrated, but he knew he could not let his frustration show. If he allowed it to show, then Hatcher, or someone like Hatcher, would work on him. He did not think that he was such a tower of strength that he could withstand continuous negative comments in the mess, on watch from the mates, and on extra duties. They would ultimately grind him down. The speed at which it could happen was what really concerned him. Additionally, there was no place that he could withdraw to and be alone. Someone was always present.

When he was at home, around the farm, Jonathan had always been a bit of a loner. He was being forced into being a loner to a greater degree, by the actions on this ship. He was doing extra duties and the entire watch knew it. They avoided him. He wasn't sure exactly why; probably no one could tell him. However, it was like he had a jinx or an evil curse. Wherever he went he seemed to fall into trouble. The trouble was not serious, but enough to cause extra duties. At least that's what he perceived the others thought.

The loneliness bothered him. He had no true friends on this ship. The closest to him were Knobby and Pollard, but they were much older and were more like friendly uncles than friends. He was able to converse with Wright, but even he kept his distance. In fact, no one seemed to approach him. If he had a conversation with someone he had to initiate it.

The result was that Jonathan slowly withdrew into himself. He kept his thoughts and opinions to himself. If asked his opinion about something, which occasionally occurred at the mess table, he was neutral about the topic.

He didn't flash his newly acquired skills. Few people realized how competent he was with splicing and ropes. Thanks to Wright he was good at sewing. In fact, during his spare time, what little he had of it, he had retreated to a private area and sewed an extra double liner into his jacket. In the second, inner liner, he had sewn in all the coins he had carried. He was glad of this, because the twine had been irritating his waist in the heat from these southern latitudes. He realized that this was probably better as well since he would need balance in the tops, and the coins wouldn't help in that area.

As the watch continued, Jonathan reflected on these points and others. He had begun to spend more time trying to think things through. It was new to him, trying to figure out his actions well before they occurred. He had heard of a game that helped a person do that. It was called chess.

His big question was, 'What was the bosun or Mr. Hurley doing with respect to him?' He was very confident that the extra duties were not caused by his drink at the water butts. The only thing that he could assume was that it was because of his conversation with the sailmaker. He remembered that the sailmaker had spoken to the bosun afterwards, but Jonathan had knuckled his forehead and said 'sir' in the conversation, indicating that he was showing the required respect to the sailmaker. From all accounts, the sailmaker was not a harsh or vindictive man. No one he spoke to about the sailmaker had suggested that. Speaking first to a superior generally resulted in a harsh but short punishment: a shouting, a starter, or something similar, especially when no disrespect was shown or intended. This begged the question - 'Was there something else behind these punishments?'

Another thing was that the bosun had never shown up to hassle Jonathan. Jonathan knew he was relying on his subordinates to look after Jonathan's work assignments and supervision. These had been satisfactory, or at least he had been lead to believe they were by Mr. Jergens. If so, what was the purpose of the continuing punishments? And why the tops? The tops were manned by the most experienced seamen. Jonathan had been on this ship only a couple of months, so he certainly wasn't experienced.

But how does a seaman gain experience? According to everyone it is by practise: the repetitive nature of doing a job over and over again until one can do the job in his sleep.

Who says when a seaman is experienced? As best he could think, it would be the bosun and other senior members of the crew, such as the ropemaker, the sailmaker, and the captains of the tops. And what would they be looking for? What would they need to check to determine the ability of a seaman? For example, what was the difference between an ordinary seaman and an able seaman? It had to be skills, but was that all? There had to be more.

Jonathan started to think of Mr. Jergens, Pollard, Knobby, even Mr. Hurley. What made them different from others beside seaman skills such as rope work, sail handling and such? Well, they were more knowledgeable about the sea and they had a vast amount of experience. But so did Hatcher. And Wright had some experience. It couldn't be just experience. It had to be something else, although experience was important.

Jonathan pondered on this subject for the remainder of the watch. He realized it was a serious question that needed an answer.

Jonathan was troubled deeply by the thoughts that were passing through his mind. When he was on the farm he could never remember a single time when he had cause to think about such important things. He wondered if his father had ever had to think deeply about important matters. The more he thought about it, the more he realized that his father had to make important decisions all the time. Decisions like what to plant so he could pay the rents on the farm and still have enough left over to eat for the next year. He had made a serious decision to send Jonathan to Rye that fateful day.

As Jonathan thought about this his emotions seized him. His eyes began to tear. He could not let anyone else see those tears, or he would be mocked. His only defence was to retreat to an unoccupied area and turn his back to the world. How were his parents taking his absence? Did they wonder what became of him? How were they coping without the funds that he had failed to return with?

He was still considering these topics when the watch ended. Jonathan slung his hammock, and despite his mental dilemma, dropped off to sleep almost immediately. It indicated Jonathan's need for sleep.

Chapter 13
New Skills

The afternoon watch was progressing as normal. The spirit ration had been issued, and the meal had been consumed when the pipe "All Hands on Deck" was heard. Rapidly the mess table and accoutrements where secured. Hands rushed to the main deck. Jonathan didn't know what to expect, but whatever he was expecting he was wrong.

Lieutenant Smithers was in the waist. He raised his voice and said, "Every man on a gun crew may be called away from the gun to participate in a boarding action. Now the boarding party has a number of weapons, the cutlass, the pike, the boarding axe, the pistol, and a variety of other weapons such as knives, clubs and so forth. We are going to train you on four of these to start; the pistol, the pike, the boarding axe, and the cutlass. You need to be able to handle these weapons effectively if you are to defend this ship against an enemy who is attempting to board us, or to overpower an enemy and take their ship to get some prize money. It's in your interests to learn how to properly use these weapons as it might keep you alive, and it's in the entire ship's crew's interest because you might save them, and everyone wants some prize money to take home - right?"

The crew eagerly growled an affirmative to the thought of prize money.

"What we're going to do is divide the guns crews into four groups. Each group will have a different weapon. Captain de Clare and the Marines will provide instruction on the pistols. I will take the cutlass. Lieutenant Galbraith will take the boarding axe, and the master-at-arms will take the pike."

"Group ONE will be composed of 12-pounder crews from guns 1 to 6; 12-pounder crews from guns 7 to 11 and the forecastle guns will be group TWO; 24-pounder crews from guns 1 to 7 will be group THREE; and the remaining 24-pounder crews and quarterdeck crews, less the Marines, are group FOUR. Each crew will train solely on one weapon today. Once the group is reasonably proficient we will rotate, and continue this until you are reasonably proficient with each weapon. Once that occurs, we will see about developing more skill with each of your assigned weapons," continued Lieutenant Smithers.

Jonathan and the men of group THREE mustered on the forecastle and waited to see who would provide their instruction. It was Lieutenant Galbraith, so it was the boarding axe.

"The boarding axe is often called the tomahawk, but it's different from what the natives use in North America," explained Lieutenant Galbraith. "First, the head is metal and slightly curved. You can put a better edge on it. The back of the head is a spike so you can use it to hammer into the side of a ship to get a grip, or make steps if there are no hand-holds. A third difference is that on the base of the handle, there is a lanyard. This allows you to secure the axe to your arm. Then if you need to drop the axe for a second to grab something else, you don't lose the axe. All you have to do is flick it back up and then grab it again. Very handy when boarding, or when someone jabs a pike at you."

"Now there are three basic striking strokes: the overhead, sideways from either left or right, and the reverse from below. Each has its advantages and drawbacks. Let's start with the overhead stroke. This is clearly a killing stroke. You aim at either the head or the shoulders. If you hit the shoulders, then at the very least, you are going to break a collar bone and likely incapacitate the enemy. More likely, you are going to crush his skull in the case of a head strike, or cut major blood vessels in the case of a hit on the shoulders. There are two problems with the overhead stroke. The first is that it is one of the easiest to block. Let me show you what can happen if your blow is blocked." Lieutenant Galbraith had his demonstrator attempt an overhead stroke and blocked it. The other man was totally exposed from the face on down.

"You get the picture. Now, I'm not suggesting that the overhead blow is bad, just understand its limitations. The second limitation is that if you get a solid direct head strike, your opponent isn't going to be standing long. He's going to be falling in some direction, and your blade is still going to be in his head. It's hard enough trying to withdraw a blade from a stationary target; it's doubly hard when that target is falling and dragging your blade with it. Now if you have the boarding axe attached by the lanyard, this could pull you in the direction the body's falling. It could leave you off-balance. At the very least, until you can get the axe head loose, you are going to be exposed. Not a healthy situation in the middle of a close quarter battle when seconds count." Lieutenant Galbraith demonstrated by pulling on his assistant's axe, which was attached to his arm by a lanyard.

"The sideways stroke is highly effective in disabling an enemy. It rarely kills a man instantly, but it generally takes him out of action. Just imagine how you would feel if you got hammered by this blade in the side, or in the front of your chest. There are two drawbacks using this stroke, however. One is a major drawback. The other is only an occasional problem. The big drawback on the side stroke is space for your swing. In close-quarters action you are likely to be almost shoulder to shoulder. This doesn't give you much room to swing. You can't, therefore, normally get full force behind the swing. Additionally, because of the close-quarters, someone else may get in the way of the strike, so it might not even hit the intended target. The second problem that I mentioned is that the head of the axe sometimes gets trapped between the target's ribs. Although this doesn't happen very often, it has the same effect as when the blade is stuck in the head. You are exposed, and possibly pulled off balance." Again Lieutenant Galbraith and his assistant went through a variety of motions to demonstrate the stroke and possible problems.

"The reverse stroke is one of the hardest to do, primarily because it is foreign to the average man in the heat of battle. You have to use an underhand swing. That means that the axe is low, and not in the best position for blocking an opponent's attack if needed. A second problem is that the primary target area - the crotch - is small compared to the torso, or head and shoulders. Any hit, with any force, in that area is going to incapacitate the target. The target is also soft, so the possibility of getting the blade of the axe stuck or hung up is remote." Lieutenant Galbraith again demonstrated the stroke.

"The most important things in a boarding or close-quarter action are footing and balance. Lose either, and you're likely to have a trip to see the surgeon, or worst case, to see your Maker. There are rarely second chances, so you cannot afford to make a mistake. You need to be aggressive and relentless. Never give the enemy a chance to get set. Keep them off balance. This applies to all the weapons."

"Now there is a technique that can be used effectively with few drawbacks. It is best used against a pike, musket with bayonet, or a cutlass," Lieutenant Galbraith continued. He said to his assistant, "Reverse your axe and use it like a pike."

As the assistant lunged at Lieutenant Galbraith, the technique was demonstrated in slow motion while Galbraith explained it aloud. "When the enemy is using a thrusting weapon of any type, you need to either block the thrust, or turn inside of it. Now when the enemy thrusts, you see that one of his legs is extended in front of his body. Sometimes it is only a foot, sometimes further. The further his foot and leg are extended, the greater his vulnerability, assuming he didn't skewer you with his thrust. You go for his extended upper leg. Because of his thrust, he is not in a position to block your stroke, or if he is really quick he might get in a partial block. Since you're using a down stroke, you have the maximum power. If you hit his leg, or only graze it because of the partial block, it's going to hurt him, possibly badly. It may not incapacitate him, but the average man is going to grab the injured area with at least one hand, and the pain will distract him for an instant. In that instant, you use another downward stroke against his head and shoulders. He won't be able to put up an effective block, so you will get a strike. Given the energy you have in a close-quarters battle, I wager that the hit will be a killing stroke, or at the very least, totally incapacitate him."

Lieutenant Galbraith went on to demonstrate various blocks to lunges and strokes from enemy boarding axes.

"Now, if I know this, the enemy may also know how to do this. Concentrate as much on your balance and footing in practise, as you do for the actual strokes. You have to understand that he may be as prepared and determined as you are. Never under-estimate an enemy. Remember as well, in a close-quarters battle, there will be bodies under foot, blood, and probably piss where the enemy lost control of their bladders when they saw us coming. All of these may cause you to slip, so control your movements."

Everyone chuckled at Lieutenant Galbraith's image of a scared and terrified enemy. Jonathan was charged with enthusiasm. He couldn't wait to get his hands on a boarding axe.

"Go grab a practise boarding axe and pair up," said Lieutenant Galbraith.

There was a barrel with wooden boarding axes positioned at the foremast. Jonathan picked up one and was surprised that it was all wooden. The head was a blunt piece of wood.

"What do ya expect, ya dozy bugger. If we gave ya real tomahawks half of ya would be in t'see the surgeon before we finished the practise," said Lieutenant Galbraith's assistant, who was standing over the barrel of practise tomahawks.

Jonathan turned to find a partner. He spotted Rothman from his gun crew and paired up with him. Rothman was taller and heavier than Jonathan, but was slower, or so Jonathan thought. Within seconds of the commencement of practise, Jonathan was thankful these were practise boarding axes and not real ones. He even wished that the blades were padded, because Rothman had managed to hit him a number of times despite his best efforts to defend himself.

The practise concluded with a bruised and battered Jonathan. The child-like enthusiasm, with which he had started the practise, had been replaced by trepidation and extreme caution. He realized he was either going to have to get much better at this or he'd get himself killed in a real boarding action.

New activities were the order of the day for Jonathan. During the dog watch, he reported to the captain of the main top, a man called Graves. Other than hoping that his name wasn't an indication of Jonathan's future in the tops, there was little Jonathan knew about the captain of the main top. That was soon to change.

Graves was in his late twenties with ginger coloured hair that was braided in a two foot queue. He was slim, but muscular. He radiated self confidence, something that Jonathan was lacking when looking at the tops. Graves looked at him, "What do you know about the tops?"

Jonathan said, "I know nothing. I have never even been up the ratlines."

"There's no time like the present. Follow me," said Graves. He swiftly went to the side, grabbed a shroud line and hauled himself outboard and up. He went up a few ratlines and paused to make sure Jonathan was following, and to determine if he was encountering problems.

Jonathan was nervous. He had never been outboard. The ratlines were rough against his feet. Although his feet had hardened considerably since he had arrived on the Winchester, the ratlines were a rougher and a smaller surface than he was used to. He was game though, and continued upwards, albeit at a slow pace.

As he reached the top of the shrouds he was faced with a dilemma. How was he to get on to the top? There was a small hole that he could squeeze through, or he could go over the top like Graves. Graves solved the problem, however, by saying, "Come through the lubber's hole. You'll learn the other way soon enough."

"Sit down facing forward, with your back against the mast. Now tell me the names of the masts, the sails and the ropes," demanded Graves.

Jonathan started describing the required items as best he could. He had no problem with the masts and sails, but did not know the names of all the ropes. After he had finished to the best of his abilities, Graves started to explain each rope, what it was used for, and when it was likely to be used. At the end, he said, "All right, now you know the masts, sails and rigging. From now on, you're going to practise how to use them."

Jonathan wasn't worried about the practise. He was concerned he wouldn't remember the names and functions of each rope. However, he was literally saved by the bell - the bell for watch change.

HMS Winchester was not a fast vessel. Even though she was a new ship, less than a year old, she was only making an average five knots per hour on the trade winds. From England down to the Canaries she had been even slower.

Jonathan was in the tops with Graves, same as yesterday. He was feverishly trying to remember all the ropes. He knew most of them, but not all.

"We're going to learn something slightly different today. It may help you understand how the sails and ropes work," stated Graves. "I'm going to explain the points of sail, and the wind-rose. We use these terms to easily understand what way to set and trim the sails."

"Let's say the wind is blowing directly from the north. I realize this is not likely to happen, but it will make the understanding a little bit simpler. As you know, we can't sail directly into the wind. Different types of sail configurations can get closer to it, but a square-rigged vessel can only go so far into the wind. If we have to sail north, then we're going to have to zigzag back and forth."

"Now, let's say that we were sailing due south. The yards would be straight across. This is called running before the wind, but as you know the wind rarely blows directly from behind. It usually comes from one side or the other. In order to hold a specific course or direction, we have to offset the sails to catch the wind. This is called a tack. Now if we are on a starboard tack, the yards are set so that the starboard side is ahead of the larboard side. On a larboard tack, the larboard side of the yards are ahead of the starboard. Fairly simple once it's explained to you. Now there are different degrees or points of tack. That means, in some cases the yards are pulled over as far as they can go, in other cases, they are close to, but not quite, even."

"Since the larboard and starboard tacks points are the same, we'll just talk about the starboard tack points. South is running, SSW is fine on the quarter, SW is wind on the quarter or I have also heard it called broad reaching and large on the quarter, WSW is leading wind, W is reaching, or wind abeam and the farthest we can get in this ship is WNW called beating, close-hauled, or full and by. The larboard tack has the same terms; the only difference is the points of the compass and the fact that the yards are slanted larboard up, starboard back."

Jonathan was then given his most scary task since coming aboard the Winchester. He was told to go out and touch the end of the yardarm. His apprehension was very noticeable.

Graves took pity on him, and went out to the end of the yard first to show him how it was done. Then he pointed and cocked his head.

Jonathan searched for the foot rope frantically with his right foot. With his hands, he had a near death grip on the yard, or as tight as he could get. He finally got a foot-hold. He moved by shuffling his feet along the rope. His foot never lost contact with the foot-rope. He had been told that he always needed three points of contact. The motto 'one hand for the King, one hand for yourself' made a lot of sense when furling a sail or doing other work in the tops. He made the end, reached out and touched the end of the yardarm, and then worked his way back to the top. He could feel the tension in his body. He had really worked his muscles. He had thought that he had really increased his strength because of all the gun drill and heaving on various lines during sail drill. But it was nothing compared to what he would need as a topman.

Jonathan realized the most important thing that he needed right now was confidence. Graves had a sure fire cure for his lack of confidence. He ordered Jonathan to touch each end of each yard on each mast and to touch the very top of each mast. Graves then sat down and watched him.

Jonathan was slow, but he accomplished his task. Each night at the end of his extra duties, he was required to do the same task three times. Since he would be either late for the next watch, which could mean additional punishment, or he would miss sleep that he desperately wanted, Jonathan increased his speed. Within a couple of weeks he was scampering up and down. Within three weeks he was like a monkey.

Jonathan's skill and speed improved noticeably each week. After a few weeks, Jonathan was not yet an experienced topman. He did have the same ability as any average topman. The major difference in his skill was that he had no experience in furling or reefing sails during adverse weather conditions.

Although the food was not great, the exercise and strength required to furl sails, while holding on in a breeze one hundred feet above the deck, had an impact on Jonathan. His body changed. He still had not reached his full adult size, but he was lithe and muscular. He had developed a very strong and quiet self assurance in his abilities.

He noticed the change when doing gun drill. He found it easier to haul the 24-pounder. The gun hadn't gotten any lighter, but his increased strength made the task more fluid. The other members of the gun crew were grateful, because with the increase in his strength there was less strain on them.

These changes were most notable during boarding party drill. He had rotated through boarding axe, pike and cutlass. Over time he had become reasonably proficient with both the pike and cutlass. His real strength was in the boarding axe. His speed and coordination made him a formidable foe. It was a rare occasion when he was even touched by his opponent, while he constantly tapped his opponent. He was highly successful with the down stroke to the leg and second stroke to the head.

In the fifth week at sea en route to Antigua, Jonathan's group was rotated to the pistols. Jonathan had never even held a pistol or musket in his life, so he welcomed the opportunity.

Captain de Clare was a dashing officer in his red uniform. He was good looking with fine blond hair. He wore his hair loose instead of using a wig like some of the other officers wore. He walked up in front of the group. "This is the service sea pistol. It is approximately twelve inches in length, and fires a .56 inch ball. The accuracy of the weapon is questionable depending upon who fires it. If it was one of my marines, I'd say ten to twenty feet, although they say pistol shot is thirty yards. One of you, I'd say stick it in his gut and pull the trigger and you might hit him. That's why the pistol has a metal base that we affectionately call a skull crusher so you can use it more effectively as a club once you have fired it. There is no time in a boarding to re-load a pistol."

"Sergeant Claridge is going to demonstrate how to properly load a pistol. Each of you will do that first without powder or shot. Once we are satisfied that you won't shoot yourself, or the man beside you, then Sergeant Claridge will demonstrate the correct manner for aiming and firing. Again you will practise this without a load. We call this dry firing. If, and only if, you are competent in loading and dry firing, then one of my marines will take you foreward to load and live fire a pistol at a target. If anyone happens to hit the target, then he will be considered for further pistol and possibly musket training."

"We will not train you on how to use the sea pistol as a club. You have already had training on the use of the boarding axe. You can use the pistol using the same strokes as you would use for a boarding axe, only you don't have to worry about having the blade stick, because there is no blade."

"When you're ready, Sergeant Claridge."

"Sir," snapped Sergeant Claridge, a ramrod stiff man devoid of humour. "To load the service pistol you'll need the pistol, a rammer, a ball, a powder horn, and a wad. To load, tip up the barrel. From the powder horn, pour in a measure of powder. Drop in the ball, place in a wad and ram. Put the rammer away. Now I know that you're all members of a gun crew and you place a wad between the powder and the ball. You can do it here, but it takes extra time. You can do it for the first shot, but for subsequent shots forget it, you haven't got the time. You do need a well rammed wad to hold in the ball and powder."

"Now once you get the shot rammed in place and the rammer put away, you need to prime the pistol. Take the powder horn again, and put a little powder on the pan, so when the flint strikes it will spark and a flame will go down the touchhole, the same as it does on the cannon. There is a short hesitation, and then the pistol will fire. As the captain said, then just flip the pistol around, grab it by the barrel and you have a perfectly good club. Questions?"

After some further explanations about the flint, Sergeant Claridge detailed off members of the group to various Marines tasked with training the fledgling marksmen. The Marines took the men and went repeatedly through the loading drills. They then proceeded to aiming and dry firing.

Both Sergeant Claridge and Captain de Clare observed various men, and when they were satisfied sent them foreward to Corporal Finney who was considered a Marine marksman. Jonathan was finally sent foreward.

While waiting on the forecastle until the men before him finished, Jonathan was able to chat to another Marine about the best way to aim. The

Marine was very forthcoming about the difficulties of hitting anything past ten paces accurately with a pistol shot.

Finally Jonathan's turn for firing came. He loaded the pistol as per the instructions, and was checked at each stage of loading by another Marine. When the Marine was satisfied, Jonathan was allowed to take position for firing.

The target was a small wooden square about the same size as a trencher. It was hanging by a rope from the end of the foremast course yardarm, well below the sail, so a miss would not hit the sail. The wind was steady and they were on a starboard tack. This meant the target was more forward than if they were running before the wind. The target still bobbed up and down as the ship crested waves, and rolled into the troughs.

According to what the Marine had said, so far only about two shooters per group had hit the target. Jonathan could now understand why.

Before he had loaded, he had watched the target carefully using his knowledge acquired shooting the slingshot he had carried. He had noticed that although the target was almost continuously moving, there was a moment when the ship hung on the top of a crest when the target seemed to pause in movement. That was fine, but the slight hesitation between pulling the trigger and firing, meant that he would have to lead the target, and fire where he expected the target to be stationary. He extended his arm and stuck his thumb up, using it as a sight. He practised for a couple of waves, until he was able to better estimate the final location of the target when stationary at the top of the crest.

He then took the pistol, cocked it, and waited for the ship to rise into the crest. Because of the delay, the men behind him were cajoling him in a good natured way.

"Open your eyes, you'll never hit the target if you can't see it", "He ain't gonna shoot it, he's gonna starve it to death", "Ain't gonna make any difference matey, officer says ya gotta ram it into the chest and then pull the trigger if you want to hit it," could be heard from the men behind.

Jonathan ignored them all, and patiently waited. He noticed that the Marine beside him said absolutely nothing. As the ship neared the top of the crest, Jonathan brought up the pistol. The pistol was heavy when extended at arm's length and he knew the longer he held it in that position the more likely it would be to shake. By waiting, he had all but eliminated this possible cause of poor aim.

He found the target in the crude sights and started to lead it slightly. He felt the ship steady under his feet as it hit the crest. He squeezed the trigger, but kept his eye and sights on the imaginary location he expected the target to move to in an instant. He heard the flint strike the pan, saw the flash in his peripheral vision, and felt the recoil as the pistol fired. A small piece of wood flew off the side of the target. He had timed the shot perfectly as far as he was concerned, and still nearly missed it.

The Marine at his side quietly said, "Good shot. That was no fluke. You've had experience shooting before, haven't you?"

The Corporal in charge of the firing came up to Jonathan. "Good shot. What's yer name?"

"Smith, Corporal, Jon Smith."

The hecklers waiting behind him were silent. Jonathan received a couple of nods, as he relinquished the pistol to a Marine and withdrew from the firing point.

"Smith, report to Sergeant Claridge," came the order.

Jonathan looked and spotted Sergeant Claridge near the starboard stairs to the quarterdeck. He had about half a dozen other seamen in front of him.

"You're all here because you hit the target," started Sergeant Claridge. "What we're going to do now is see if it was a lucky hit, or if you can repeat it. If you can repeat it, then we're gonna give you some additional training on muskets."

For the next couple of days at boarding party practise, Jonathan was shown and practised, loading and firing, of both pistols and muskets. Although he was nowhere near as proficient as the top Marine marksmen, he could hold his own with some of them. He earned the grudging respect of Sergeant Claridge, just as those Marines who couldn't better Jonathan felt Sergeant Claridge's ire.

✹

That night on the middle watch the wind had remained steady. There was little for the watch to do and they were stood easy in the waist.

Even though he was sitting beside another sailor, Jonathan withdrew into his own little world. Rumour had it that they would be seeing land in the next day or two.

He was bone tired, but he knew he couldn't sleep on watch. Instead, Jonathan fell into a habit he was developing, thinking about his life. From time to time he had heard others discuss the topic either at the mess or quietly, like this, when standing easy on watch.

What he remembered most about all of those conversations was that the older hands continuously said to forget about planning your life, or that your destiny was in the King's hands. They said the more you think about it, the more you realize that you have no control. That just gets you down or angry, neither of which is good for you, because you tend to sink lower and lower. Keeping your spirits up was important, because the opposite just meant it got worse and worse.

Jonathan didn't want to believe that. If it were true, then as far as he was concerned, he'd be no better than a ship without a rudder. You would only go where the prevailing wind pushed you. Yet that was exactly what seemed to be happening to him. He certainly had no say in whether he came aboard. Since being aboard he had almost continuously been given extra duties - punishment if you will. He had no say in where he would work, what tasks he would complete during any given day, even when he could eat or sleep. He was even told what he could eat on any particular day!

Jonathan mulled over the question of how to keep your spirits up. If he thought about his situation, it seemed depressing, so he had to look for something else to raise his spirits. He thought about all the men in his mess. None of them seemed to be overly cheerful on a continuing basis. There were sparks of cheerfulness, but they didn't last. On the other hand, there were good examples of negativity and depression. Hatcher was a fine example of that. He was bitter and morose. Jonathan knew he did not want to end up like that, so there had to be something that could turn it around.

He kept thinking about it as the watch progressed. He kept coming back to the phrase 'turning it around'. After considerable thought, he figured life was like his knife. There was a 'good' end, the end with the handle, and a 'bad' end, the point of the blade. Situations were like trying to grab the knife when it dropped. You had to grab the knife because if you didn't, you lost it, or it fell and hurt someone else. If you grabbed the blade or point, you got hurt. If you grabbed the handle, then things would work out. He thought he would have to always try for the handle, the 'good' in the situation. It reminded him of a saying he had heard before a few times, but had never understood. Look for the silver lining in the cloud.

Jonathan thought about the good since he had come aboard. He tried to add it all up. He had come aboard unconscious. He had healed. He had consistent food. Maybe the food didn't provide as much nourishment as he wanted, or wasn't of the quality he wanted, but it was at least fuel for the body. He remembered many times on the farm going hungry. He had learned a host of new skills, such as knots and rope work, sewing, shooting firearms, and how to defend himself with cutlass, pike and boarding axe. He had learned how to be a topman. He had learned how a ship operated, so much so that he figured he could do most jobs on board a ship, except navigate and steer. He had put on a lot of muscle. He had self confidence in himself and his abilities as a seaman. Supposedly, he had also earned some money, but he discounted this, as he had never seen any since arriving on the ship.

He countered this against what he had lost. His freedom for sure was gone. He had received significant extra duties, so he had lost a lot of sleep. Comparing his knowledge and abilities against those of some of the others who had been on the ship longer than he had, he could easily say that his skill levels were much better than theirs. In fact, he was the only one of the men pressed from the Rye area that was a topman. Now he wasn't rated as such, but he had the skill. Few could equal him with knots or rope work. In the area of sewing, his skill was good. In fact it was far better than most of his mess mates. In musket shooting he was equal to some of the Marines.

He thought of where he would be compared to this, if he was back on the farm. He knew instinctively that he would be not much better off than he was before. Surprisingly, Jonathan came to realize the navy had been very good to him personally, albeit at a cost in sleep and personal freedom.

Another thing Jonathan thought about was his spare time. If he had more spare time, and hadn't had the punishments, what would he have used that time to accomplish? He didn't really know, so the loss, such as it was, was not as important as the skills he had learned.

One area that did bother him however, was the lack of any real friends. Now this was not appreciably different than his situation on the farm. On a ship with men living side by side, the lack of friendship was not common. He had felt this lack of friendship from time to time. He needed someone to talk to and discuss things with. Most men either tolerated him, or avoided him because of all the extra duties he continued to receive. The ones who tolerated him were generally older and somewhat sympathetic. The ones who avoided him were generally worried they would attract unwanted attention to themselves.

Jonathan knew that he would need to spend time on building relationships. With who and when he did not know. He was either on watch, on extra duty, or sleeping. He had virtually no free time. He also didn't have much skill in this area. He had never developed any skill like this at home. Since he'd been onboard he had developed a skill to keep silent, so as not to attract further trouble. It was odd that despite the fact that he was silent, a great deal of trouble had still found him.

Chapter 14

Antigua

The day commenced the same as had each previous day for the past few weeks. The crew stood by the guns until they were allowed to resume the daily maintenance routine. Jonathan holystoned the deck as usual. As the watch changed to the forenoon watch, they exercised the great guns.

There was a difference this day, however. They were actually going to fire the guns. Some targets were prepared by the carpenter and his assistants. They were towed out to a range on the larboard side and let drift.

Each gun crew was to fire a single shot. For any gun that hit the target, the captain had offered an extra spirit ration. This was a significant incentive, so each gun crew was concentrating in earnest. Of all the gun crew drills, Jonathan knew the least about how to actually aim the cannon. While he had an idea based upon his experience with his slingshot, and his more recent experience with pistol and musket, he knew there were significant differences. Leading the target was different, because you had to manoeuvre over five thousand pounds of cannon to the left or right. The position of the ship relative to the waves and the wave action would seriously impact range. Where you wished to strike the ship would dictate what load was rammed. Roundshot was used for hull shots; canister or grapeshot against personnel or softer targets, bar or chain shot for rigging and masts. The gun was currently loaded with roundshot.

Morrison was standing well back of the cannon, and looking down the barrel at the target. The 2nd gun captain, Jansen, was holding the linstock with its smouldering slow match. Everyone stood back from the gun to ensure they were clear of any recoil.

There was dead silence. Jonathan could feel the action of the sea through the deck. The ship was on the uproll as it neared the crest of a wave.

"Number four gun, Fire," shouted the officer. Morrison touched the slow match he had taken from Jansen to the touchhole. A brief flash occurred, followed by a monstrous roar as the cannon discharged.

Jonathan had been warned repeatedly about the violence of the recoil, but he was amazed when he experienced it firsthand. The breeching rope contained the monster. The noise made him half deaf.

"Sponge out."

Each gun port was crowded with spectators eager to see where the shot had gone. A midshipman with a telescope said in his squeaky voice, "High, directly in line with the target, but a foot or two high."

The orders came for the next gun. Jonathan craned to see out of the gun port, but other members of the gun crew, with the same idea, blocked his view. He was slightly off balance and placed his hand on the cannon barrel to regain his balance. He jerked his hand away. The barrel was hot. Not burning hot, but hot. He could image how hot it would become after a few more rounds had been fired.

He noticed that Morrison had not joined the spectators. He moved over toward him. "Good shooting. A near miss. How did you get that close?"

Morrison was visibly disappointed. He had already tasted the extra spirit ration, and now it would not happen. To top it off, this young upstart was rubbing it in.

Morrison scowled and prepared to let Jonathan have it.

Jonathan saw the look on Morrison's face. It was apparent that Morrison was upset about missing the shot. Jonathan was about to take the brunt of Morrison's displeasure, unless......

"I'm real interested in how you aim. At that distance, you were only a foot or so off. If you were aiming for a ship's gun port you would have likely hit the top of the opening, just below the deck. That would have taken out the entire gun and crew. It was a far better shot than the first couple of guns."

"You waited until we crested, and fired while we were stable on the pause. What else did you do?" inquired Jonathan.

Morrison looked at him dumbfounded. He had never explained the finer points of aiming to any of the crew. That's why he was there. Morrison was shaken that Jonathan was explaining some of the techniques to him in a language that any gunner could understand. What was most surprising was that less than three months ago Jonathan had joined his gun crew, never having been on a ship before, let alone ever firing a cannon. Morrison was surprised that Jonathan had acquired so much information so fast. It was information that he himself had taken years to acquire.

Morrison, at that moment, totally re-assessed Jonathan. "How old are you lad?"

"Sixteen," replied Jonathan.

"Silence on the deck," shouted Lieutenant Smithers, who had wandered down to watch the action.

"Number five gun, Fire."

The gun captain at the number five gun touched the linstock to the touchhole. The 24-pounder roared and violently recoiled. It went on and on, as each gun crew tried their luck in turn. Occasionally the men could hear the 12-pounders above being fired.

Without a doubt Jonathan needed to get something better to block the noise. His head was ringing, and they had only fired a single round per gun. Based on conversations he had with other older shipmates, some battles went on for hours. If he didn't have better hearing protection, he wouldn't even be able to think for the pounding in his head.

After the firing was completed, the order to secure the guns was given. Morrison took Jonathan aside and described the technique he had used, or at least described it to the best of his ability. Jonathan thanked him.

'All hands on deck' was piped. Everyone crowded onto the deck. The captain announced the results of the shooting competition. Only four guns had actually hit the target, but another fifteen were close. The captain called the shooting adequate. From him that appeared to be high praise.

After dismissal the crew slowly moved off. It was only a few minutes to change of watch, so no new activities were started. Everyone was anticipating "Up Spirits", with the fortunate four gun crews relishing it even more.

The call from the top caught everyone by surprise, "Deck there, sail ho, off larboard quarter."

"Can you make her out?" called the officer of the watch.

"Only her royals are showing at present, but she looks like she's heading toward us," was the reply.

After some time, the call came down again from the tops, "Deck there, sails appear to be a frigate, possibly French, but no flag visible."

Then very shortly, "Deck there, she's turning away, showing us her heels. She's heading south."

The disappointment on the quarterdeck as well the main deck was palpable, but everyone was aware that a five knot ship that might be able to make eight knots with a good wind could not outrun a frigate that might be able to do ten to twelve knots in the same good wind. There was no surprise when the order, "Maintain your course" was heard.

Westward they continued.

✺

A day later, the lookout's cry of, "Land Ho" caught everyone's attention. It was in the dog watch, so Jonathan was able to climb up to see what was visible. The land was "hull down" for those on the deck. Jonathan had a slight advantage in that he could at least see the land. But where the land was located he had no idea. He realized it was somewhere in the West Indies, but was it Antigua?

As the ship slowly approached the land mass, the officers used their telescopes and discussed the features of the land. The master of the ship came on deck and took a look. He then spoke to the officer of the watch and ordered a change of course to the northwest.

Jonathan helped alter the sails as a topman. There was little to do, as most of the work was completed by the deck crew below pulling on the braces, and increasing the cant of the sails to a reaching starboard tack.

When Jonathan had finished his extra duties and descended to the deck, he overheard someone say that the land mass that he had seen was Guadeloupe, although that meant little to him.

Most of the crew had never been to the West Indies. There were a few souls on board who had some service in the West Indies, Knobby being one. When standing easy on watch, these men were asked repeatedly to speak about what they had seen, and what they knew of the women and the area.

Jonathan lost his usual sitting place beside Knobby as the others crowded around to hear the tales. Knobby knew how to tell a story, and he knew what sailors liked to hear. He fashioned his stories accordingly.

Knobby told of the dark skinned beauties that could be had in St. John's, although he doubted that any of us would get liberty there. He explained that the harbour normally used for the navy was English Harbour on the opposite side of the island from St. John's. Being on a merchantman when he was last in Antigua, they had set anchor on the eastern side at St. John's. English Harbour was on the southwest corner of the island. He mentioned that the locals, merchant and gentry, were all white, but there were a lot of blacks on the island. Most of the willing girls were coloured. He mentioned that there were all shades of darkies, and that the locals even had some system to tell them apart.

The island was not that big, about twelve miles wide and a bit more in length, but it was big enough if you had to walk it.

Knobby mentioned the wind, as it was something with which sailors were familiar. He commented that the wind, the trades, were from the northeast. English Harbour on the navy side of the island was generally leeward. More than once he had heard of a King's ship being only a ways offshore, but not able to beat into harbour for lack of wind, or because the wind was dead against them. There generally was no trouble in leaving harbour. The same didn't apply to St. John's because the wind was most often abeam. The temperature didn't vary all that much between seasons. It always seemed to be warm, or hot if there was no breeze.

There was a problem in the summer and fall, between June and November. Sometimes they got powerful strong storms called hurricanes. Knobby had never been in one, but the tales he heard said that everyone should respect them.

Toward the end of his tales, he became sombre. All through the Indies he stated there was sickness and strange creatures. He spoke of pesky little bugs that flew in clouds and bit anywhere skin was exposed. They were enough to drive a man crazy. They rarely stopped, and in most cases were worse at night. He had seen men go to sleep and wake up in the morning covered in small little bites. They were worse around swamps. You never saw them when at sea. He talked about sharks. Since coming to warmer waters, most men had seen more sharks. Most seamen had a loathing for sharks. According to Knobby there was plenty of opportunity to loath them in the West Indies. He had heard about big snakes and some big reptiles, big enough to eat a man, but he had not seen any.

Like most tale-telling sailors he saved the worst for the grand finale. He spoke about the sickness - swamp fever, yellow jack, dysentery, and malaria. There were others he supposed, but he didn't know their names. They were lethal he said, and had killed more men than all the battles put together. He mentioned one of his mates from an earlier cruise on a merchantman. They had gone into town for a wet one night. They had both gotten a load on, and never made it back to the ship. They had turned down some alleyway and slept there. In the morning, they had made their way back to the ship. Knobby had been wearing a long sleeved shirt, and had covered his face with his arm as he was sleeping. Even so, he had dozens of itchy bites on his ankles and neck. His mate was covered. He had bites on his arms, neck, face, chest where his shirt was open, and ankles. By the morning after they got back to the ship, he was in a fever. The captain was so scared that they had been ordered to carry his mate to the town hospital. They heard later that he died three days after being admitted.

"It's scary," said Knobby. "They don't know what causes it, so how can you protect yourself? Once you get it, it spreads like wildfire. On a ship, bunched up like we are, the whole deck can come down with it. Sometimes, depending upon what you get, you might live - like malaria. I know'd a fella on a ship that said he had it. He got it in the Indies, but got over it. Every once in a while he'd get another attack. He'd get the fever, and then he'd get the chills. I seen him once shakin' like a leaf in a big wind. Weren't nothin' we could do for him. Went on like that for three days, and then it broke. Took him a week to get his strength back, but after that he was alright. But the others with yellow jack! I wouldn't wish that on my worst enemy. It takes a strong man down with fever. After a couple of days he's vomiting black guts over everything. Ain't nothin' you can do to stop it. When he starts that ya can count the hours before he's off to see his Maker."

After hearing that, the little group broke up. There was not much conversation from then until end of watch.

※

In the morning, they got their first sight of Antigua. After being at sea for weeks and coming from England in the fall, it was strange to see the green of the island.

"Looks inviting," said Pollard.

"After what Knobby spoke about last night, I'm not so sure," replied Jonathan.

"Well what I meant, it being only a couple of weeks until Christmas, it's more pleasant to have warm temperatures and green trees than snow or cold rain back home," responded Pollard. "I hate the winter in the North Atlantic."

"I guess we better enjoy it while we got it," replied Jonathan. "Supposedly we're heading for the North America Station. I heard either Boston or New York."

"I heard that as well," Pollard muttered. "I wonder how long we're going to be here."

"Who knows?"

As the Winchester headed for the harbour entrance, crews of the foremost quarter 12-pounders were called to their station for saluting the commodore on Antigua.

But saluting was going to have to wait, for the closer they got to the harbour, the more the wind dropped off. Their sails were limp. To add injury to the situation, they were drifting ever so slightly.

The captain had a decision to make, and it did not take long for him to make it.

"Lower the boats, and tow her in," he ordered disgustedly. Instead of a fine grand entrance into the harbour as befitting a post captain, he was forced to tow his ship in - in front of numerous other King's ships. In fact, there were so many King's ships in the harbour; it looked like the entire squadron was present, instead of out on patrol.

Jonathan aided in hoisting out the boats. He was then directed to join the long boat crew. He jumped down into the boat, found a place and grabbed an oar. He then started rowing in stroke with the rest of the crew. First they rowed to the bow of the ship where they received a tow rope, then to larboard of the jolly boat for actual towing.

"Put your backs into it," squeaked the little midshipman who commanded the long boat. Jonathan rolled his eyes. The little pipsqueak was a tyrant. The commissioned officers had him in check, but Jonathan suspected that he would be a right bastard if he ever made lieutenant.

They rowed for five hours to get the ship to its assigned anchorage location. By the time they arrived, every man in the long boat and every other boat was exhausted, de-hydrated, sore, and most had blistered or raw hands. There was considerable hostility in the longboat's crew. The little midshipman had been all too willing to use a starter on all those that he could reach. Normally, only the mates carried starters as it was not proper for officers or officers in training to physically touch a man. Midshipman Pipsqueak had no such reservations.

The boats were secured alongside rather than being hoisted up on deck. As the weary men climbed the battens you could hear the muttered threats against Midshipman Pipsqueak. Jonathan sensed that they were not idle threats.

When Jonathan reached the deck he noticed an ominous silence. Sailors develop a sixth sense, able to 'feel' approaching bad weather, or changes in the men around them. Jonathan had sensed this, but he could not ascertain the source or the reason why.

"What's up?" Jonathan whispered to a man.

"Look at them ships," the man replied. Jonathan looked at the ships anchored on the other side of the harbour. He could see nothing that caused him any curiosity.

"What about 'em?" Jonathan whispered. "The yards are crossed properly, sails are furled alright. I don't see anything that indicates they aren't shipshape."

"Look at the flags man! They're all flying the yellow flag. Means there's yellow jack aboard," replied the other man.

Now flags and signals were one of the things that Jonathan had not yet learned, so this came as a bit of a surprise to him. After Knobby's tales last night, shock might have been a better word.

Jonathan looked from ship to ship. Every ship anchored on the far side of the harbour was showing the yellow flag. Unfortunately, all the big ships were anchored on that side. Jonathan looked aft to the quarterdeck. He could instantly see that he was not the only one who was concerned.

The captain's voice could be clearly heard in the silence. "Call away my gig. I must deliver these dispatches to the commodore in charge." He turned to the first lieutenant. "Make sure that you keep her upwind or at least out of their lee while I am gone, even if you have to move anchor. And keep anyone away from this ship."

"Aye, aye, sir," said a clearly relieved first lieutenant.

The captain departed from between the side party and over the side. Shortly his gig was spotted headed for shore in the opposite direction to the yellow flagged ships.

Jonathan went below. They had been in the boats for dinner, and had missed "Up Spirits". The "Up Spirits" was now piped. There would be a long evening meal routine. The crew needed a break. Jonathan went looking for some salve to put on his raw hands. It was not great but it did reduce the stinging to a tolerable level. He was glad that he had not traded his spirit ration, because he could sure use it today.

The mess was subdued. There were some comments, but every man was aware of the yellow jack and all were nervous. The gun ports were open, but the heat on the lower gun deck was noticeable. It was worse on the main deck. There, although the breeze was more noticeable, the sun beat down mercilessly, and with the sails furled, there was little to block it.

Jonathan had never noticed the sun much while they were sailing. That's because the breeze was constant and refreshing. At anchor with the majority of the breeze gone, the heat was a weight upon you. Additionally, you had to watch where you placed your hands and feet. Any metal soaked up the sun and could burn you if you placed your hand on it. The 12-pounders radiated heat like a brazier loaded with coals.

On the deck, the tar in the seams heated up and became sticky, as did the Stockholm tar on the rigging. If you stepped on a seam, and it was almost impossible not to, tar stuck to your foot and then you tracked it across the once pristine deck. All this meant that the first lieutenant and his underlings would be fanatic about holystoning tomorrow morning.

Touching the ropes would transfer tar to your hands and that would be transferred to anything else you touched. A wise sailor would have a rag stuck into his waist, and rub his hands after touching any rigging, and before touching anything else other than rigging. Unfortunately, tar still somehow managed to get onto your clothes.

Jonathan already knew he was going to need new, warmer clothes for the North America station. He had not yet purchased them. He had decided to wait until they were heading north before acquiring them. While he was in harbour, he was going to attempt to use only one set of slops, his oldest, because he suspected they would be shortly so soiled that he would be forced to get rid of them.

There was one blessing about the tar on the hands. It did tend to seal up the blisters and raw wounds on Jonathan's hands.

Jonathan was on deck when the captain arrived back on board. Although it was dark, Jonathan could still see his face, and its grim expression. Jonathan heard the order for the first lieutenant. He sensed this didn't bode well for the ship and crew.

Chapter 15
Goodbyes

The harbour watch was limited, and Jonathan managed to get eight hours of needed sleep. The crew was rousted from their hammocks before the forenoon watch. They were given time to break fast and clean themselves up. Ship's routine would commence at 0800 they were informed.

At 0800 Jonathan's watch reported for holystoning. The officers and senior mates were noticeably absent. As a result the holystoning was less constrained. Jokes were hurled as the men went about their tasks.

With a lot of effort, the tar marks from the day before were erased. Everyone knew it was just a matter of hours before their efforts were undone. The holystoning was just finished, and they were in the process of cleaning up and stowing their equipment, when the officers appeared on the quarterdeck.

The pipe for all hands was made. Jonathan didn't have to move. He just stood near the bulwark between two 12-pounders and waited for whatever was coming.

The captain came forward on the poop and addressed the crew. "Men, you can see for yourselves that things in Antigua are not good at the present. The yellow flag is flying on all the major ships here. The smaller schooners and brigs are alright, but the ships of the line and those frigates present cannot sail. Most of the ships you see have lost a third of the crews to yellow jack."

"Two days ago we saw what I believe was a French frigate. As soon as she saw us, she turned tail and ran," the captain continued. At his mention of the French frigate turning tail, there was distinct growl and muted catcalls from the crew. The captain smiled and let this pass. "Obviously, she didn't want to become our prize."

"But the commodore is worried. The longer the ships on this station remain in harbour, the more time the Frenchman has to cause havoc to our merchantmen. You can understand that the commodore wants to get his ships out of harbour as soon as possible."

"According to the commodore's surgeon, the worst of the yellow jack outbreak is over. From what I am led to believe, in another three days the last cases will be resolved - one way or the other," continued the captain. The crew knew that one way or the other was either the poor devil lived, or was dead.

"The commodore then proposes to sortie those ships that he can. He will strip the Superb and transfer some of her men to the other ships. Unfortunately, he has ordered the Winchester to supply a specific levy of men as well. While we are part of the North America Station, and not under the direct command of this commodore, due to the contingencies of the situation we have no alternative but to comply. The commodore felt we would have access to more men at our new station than he does here."

"The Winchester will stay here for three days. During that time we will re-provision. We will then depart for our station in Boston. Before we leave a number of you will be transferred to other ships. The first lieutenant will handle the details, and also align the revised watches, as we will be even further short-handed after we leave."

There was utter silence on deck.

Sailors are by nature superstitious. Some of them were being transferred to ships where an unseen death awaited. The captain had just stated that a third of those crews had already been taken, and more would likely go within the next three days. To say that there was rapid praying to God, or whatever lucky tokens the respective seaman held in esteem, would have been an understatement.

When they broke for dinner there was rampant speculation about who would go, and how those being sent would be selected. The majority opinion was that those men who were valuable to the Winchester would remain, and others considered less valuable would be sent. It was expected that most of those sent would be landsmen. No topmen were likely to go as they were considered the cream of the ship.

Jonathan looked at his mess mates. "I guess I should prepare my goodbyes. I'm a landsman, and I don't think there is a person on this ship that has had more extra duties than I have. I have to be the number one candidate for transfer."

Hatcher looked at him and grinned in a most malevolent manner, "Those ain't likely to be the only goodbyes you're likely to make, goin' to them ships." He laughed outright.

Jonathan shot back, "Maybe so, but what makes you think that you won't be goin' too."

Hatcher's smile disappeared instantly, "They wouldn't. I'm too valuable to this ship. Besides, I got over five years in the King's service."

Jonathan was tired of receiving all the crap from Hatcher. Since he was pretty sure he would be one of the ones transferred, he figured he had little to lose. He egged on Hatcher. "After five years, I would have thought that you would have realized that you're just a pawn to be pushed around. The King, the Admiralty, and the officers in this ship never gave a shit about you, or anyone else for that matter, other than to ensure that you did the work you were ordered to do. What makes you think that they will all of a sudden say 'Oh Hatcher? We need him! He's the best seaman we have!'" With this last comment, the sarcasm was dripping from Jonathan's voice.

Hatcher was ready to explode.

But around him the rest of the members of the mess were nodding in agreement with Jonathan. Hatcher therefore had to hold his fury in check.

It wasn't long before they had answers as to who was going. The bosun called the larboard watch to the deck.

All afternoon men were individually called aft to a table the first lieutenant had set up. The routine was simple. Lieutenant Wilkinson would mention a name to the bosun, who would then shout the man's name. The individual would go forward to the table. He would knuckle his forehead and report. Lieutenant Wilkinson would then tell the man where he was going. If the man was being transferred you could see the shoulders drop as if the man had a large heavy weight dropped on him. If the man was staying, he was told his new watch positions. As Lieutenant Wilkinson verbally informed the man of his new position, Lieutenant Galbraith, who was the officer in charge of the larboard watch, scribbled down the information. Then the man was dismissed. The man knuckled his forehead, turned and left. Those transferred tended to shuffle away, as if under sentence of death. Those remaining on board had a quick step, rapidly beating a retreat in case the first lieutenant realized he had made a mistake and would change his mind.

Jonathan was finally called.

After he reported, Lieutenant Wilkinson stated, "Smith, you're being transferred." Jonathan thought he was prepared, but the news was still like a punch in the guts. He tried not to show it. "You're probably not aware of it, but we have been levied to provide some topmen as the other ships have been hit pretty hard in that department. You are being sent as an ordinary seaman slated as a topman. Now I know you are currently rated as a landsman, and this is a leap of a level for you, but the bosun spoke on your behalf. He says you're as good as any topmen that we have, so I'm giving you the benefit of the doubt. You will undoubtedly be tested once you get to your ship; at least I would test you, if I were captain, just to ensure that you're the correct bill of goods, so to speak. You understand that? What I want you to remember is that you are representing this ship when you go over there. Now if you don't measure up, then you will probably be knocked down a level. If that happens, you let down this ship and the bosun who spoke up for you. Questions?"

Jonathan looked at Lieutenant Wilkinson, "Sir, what ship am I being transferred to, and when?"

"HMS Mermaid," replied Lieutenant Wilkinson. "As to when, we are not quite sure, but probably tomorrow or the next day."

"What about my pay and the amount I owe the purser? I also wondered about new slops before I left, sir."

"As far as slops, I would imagine there would be plenty to be had on the Mermaid. As for your pay and debts, a ledger will accompany the contingent to the Mermaid. On this ledger, will be the pay due you less the amount you owe our purser."

Lieutenant Wilkinson then caught him by surprise. He offered Jonathan his hand and said, "Good luck, Smith. You have progressed far on this ship. Let's hope you can do equally well on the Mermaid."

"Thank you sir," replied Jonathan as he shook Lieutenant Wilkinson's hand. He then knuckled his forehead, turned and departed in a state of shock. The shock was not from the transfer, but from the fact that Lieutenant Wilkinson had offered his hand, and about his statement that he had progressed well.

The bosun was busy. It was not the appropriate time to approach him. It would have to happen later. But Jonathan vowed to say thanks. He now realized that he had completely misjudged the bosun, and he expected the sailmaker as well.

He had a day or so before transfer. In that time he needed to say thanks to those who had taken the time to teach him, notably Mr. Jergens and Graves. He also had to say goodbye to his mess mates. As for Hatcher, it would be a pleasure to see the back of him, for most - a mixed remorse to be parting, for Wright and Pollard - regret, for Knobby - a deep sense of loss.

The remainder of the afternoon was a blur to him. He reckoned that the best time to say good bye to everyone was at the evening mess. Later he could speak to Wright, Pollard and Knobby separately.

When the evening meal rolled around, Jonathan assumed his usual place on the stool at the end of the table. All the messes were quieter than normal this evening. Jonathan asked, "Anybody know how many in total are being transferred?"

No one knew, so no one responded. Bates said, "What ship are you headin' to?"

"Mermaid 40," said Jonathan. "Anyone else?"

Sweeny replied, "Mermaid as well."

Bates winked at Jonathan and said, "Hatcher was just informed that His Majesty needs his valuable services elsewhere."

It was hard to make out Hatcher's expression. There was an element of loathing for Bates, or perhaps for the powers that had transferred him. There was also an element of fear. Fear of the unknown, fear of the yellow jack, or possibly something else, but Jonathan could not ascertain what.

"In what ship is your valuable presence being requested Mr. Hatcher?" mocked Bates.

"Shove it up your pipehole and smoke it," burst out Hatcher, no longer able to hold back. All Bates did was laugh. He wanted to taunt Hatcher, and he was enjoying the experience.

Mullins gently placed his hand on Hatcher's arm. The act was meant in friendship. Hatcher rebuked the effort by shrugging his arm and throwing off Mullins's hand. "Easy mate," said Mullins quietly.

"So what ship?" asked Kirk. "So I know which one to avoid." There was no trace of sympathy in his voice.

Jonathan was getting an eye opener this evening. Feelings that had been masked to keep peace in the mess were being allowed to show. He had thought that Bates and Kirk had got along alright with Hatcher. But it was now apparent that they did not care for him, and were not afraid of him.

Hatcher did not like to be baited or mocked. He had done this countless times to others in the mess. Now he was reaping his reward. Despite the situation, and having borne the brunt of many of Hatcher's mocking attacks, Jonathan felt sorry for him. Well maybe sorry was too strong a word. Pity might be a better word. Hatcher was scared of the unknown, hurt because he had been rejected by the powers that commanded the Winchester, and wounded by the indifference of his mess mates to his plight.

"What ship, Hatcher?" demanded Bates.

"Superb 60," muttered Hatcher. "At least while you pukes are freezin' your asses off in Boston, I'll be warm and cozy, sittin' in harbour here cause the Superb ain't going anywhere without a full crew."

Just to needle him some more Kirk decided to fire a parting shot. "Maybe so, but I'll take a cold wind before yellow jack any day."

That comment kind of ended any further conversation. Those remaining on the Winchester had serious suspicions that they would never see their departing messmates alive again.

The mess broke up with each man headed his own way. Jonathan went back up on deck. He kept his eye out for Wright and Pollard. He found each in turn and said his thanks for their help, and offered his best wishes.

After finishing speaking to Pollard, he spied the bosun speaking to the master. Jonathan knew that to get back to his mess, the bosun would have to use the stairs just forward of the quarterdeck, so he waited there to see if he might be able to say thank you to the bosun.

The wait was longer than Jonathan anticipated. Jonathan got sidetracked thinking about the changes about to happen. When the bosun appeared, Jonathan almost missed him. He took a step toward the bosun but said nothing. He had learnt his lesson with the sailmaker. The step toward the bosun was his indication that he wished to address the bosun.

"You want to speak to me, Smith?" asked the bosun.

"I wanted to say thank you, for speaking on my behalf with the first lieutenant," said Jonathan. "I'd also like to say that I think I now understand the reason for all the extra duties. I didn't at the time. Truth is, I was kind of put out at the time. It does seem much clearer now."

The bosun chuckled, "Yeah, I can see where you might feel a little 'put out' as you call it."

"Can I ask you, why me?" inquired Jonathan. "I mean, you don't do this for everyone, so why me?"

"You're young, willing to learn, eager to learn actually, learn fast and according to everyone, rarely have to be told anything twice. You've got a good attitude. According to Mr. Jergens, you never griped about the duties. You can see for yourself that your skills are as good as most and better than some. You've made mistakes, but they were honest mistakes. In short lad, you have potential. What you make of it is up to you. As you go on, you will face challenges, many of them will be new and you will be unprepared for them, like when you were pressed. If you can maintain the same attitude, you should be able to work your way through them when many others can't. That's why I decided to give you a chance. It's up to you to earn it," replied the bosun.

Jonathan drank in his words. He had never heard anything like this since being dragged aboard. It was foreign to him. Did the bosun and others of his rank assess people and rate them? He had never thought of it like that before. But of course they did!

"Can I ask you something else?" requested Jonathan.

The bosun nodded.

"What do you think is going to happen to me next?" asked Jonathan.

The bosun laughed out loud. "How the hell would I know? Do I look like a soothsayer?"

"No, that's not what I mean," quickly responded Jonathan. "What I mean is that you sent me to the ropemaker to develop my rope work. Then you sent me to the tops to develop my sail handling abilities. So where do I need to go next? What abilities do I need to develop to meet these challenges that you think I'm going to face?"

The bosun looked seriously at Jonathan, and rubbed his face as if he was in deep thought, which in fact, he was.

"If the Mermaid is as short of topmen as they claim, then you will probably get used as a lookout. You'll have to learn to tell the type of ship by her sails, and the origin, by her design and layout. You'll need to be able to read signals. You still need some time with the sailmaker. You get all that, and you might have enough to be a mate," replied the bosun.

Jonathan contemplated what the bosun was saying. What he was suggesting wasn't difficult. It would just take some time and the right opportunities to come true. The knowledge was one thing, as he had discovered. It was totally another thing to apply that knowledge or skill when needed. Up to now, the bosun had provided the opportunity for both. It was likely that he would have to make his own opportunity on the Mermaid and in situations where there would be little forgiveness for errors.

"You've given me a lot to think about bosun. Thank you again. Will you accept my hand?" said Jonathan.

"Good luck, lad. I hope you survive over there," replied the bosun sombrely as he shook Jonathan's hand.

Jonathan turned and headed foreward. He had his head down, mulling over what the bosun had said.

Jonathan's arm was grabbed savagely, and he was jerked around. Hatcher growled at him, the spit splattering on his face. "Whatcha talkin' to the bosun for?"

Jonathan was upset and past caring. "Since when does who I speak to concern you? Now take your hand off me."

"Not until you say why you were talking to the bosun."

"If I didn't make it clear before, let me! It's none of your business," responded Jonathan harshly.

"You've been snitchin' for the bosun. That's why I'm being transferred."

Other men who had been idling on deck, now edged in closer. Jonathan noticed that they were actively listening. This ugly incident could turn fatal if he wasn't careful.

"I'm no snitch Hatcher, and you're too dumb to realize it. If I was a snitch, then why would I be transferred out? Don't you think the bosun would protect his favourites?" said Jonathan. He was looking at the other men edging in closer. The looks on their faces seemed to indicate that they had accepted Jonathan's story. "Do you think I'm the bosun's friend after all the extra duties he's given me?"

Jonathan could see the nods of several men who knew that Jonathan had the misfortune to have endless extra duties. One or two of the men grabbed Hatcher and pulled him away; not because they liked Hatcher, but because they noticed the midshipman of the watch taking an interest.

Once his arm was released, Jonathan quickly disappeared below.

Jonathan retrieved his ditty bag, and pulled out its contents. He might as well prepare his effects for transfer. He pulled out his shoes and tried them on. They were far tighter than he remembered. He also tried on his pants and shirt that he had been wearing when pressed. He couldn't get either of them on. He had not realized that he had grown so much. Arms, legs and chest were all much bigger than before. It seemed that only his waist was approximately the same size. He needed to figure out what was he going to do about these clothes?

He gathered up the clothes and went in search of the purser. He finally located him and inquired about selling his old clothes and shoes. The offer that the purser made was so ridiculously low that rags were worth more. Jonathan politely declined the offer when the purser said, "take it or leave it".

Jonathan went back to his mess. Many of his mess mates were there, as the harbour watch duties were limited. There wasn't even a requirement for a guard boat. No one was deserting to an area with yellow jack.

Jonathan mentioned he had shoes and clothes for sale. He knew that it was unlikely that anyone in the mess would take them off his hands, but they may have some ideas.

"Trade 'em for something from a bumboat," said Mullins. It seemed like a practical suggestion. At least he could probably get more than the purser was offering. The big question was whether any bumboats would approach.

In the early evening, Jonathan was able to speak to Knobby privately to say goodbye. Knobby had been the person to whom Jonathan had voiced his concerns on many a watch. He had kept Jonathan from falling into the pit of despair on more than one occasion. Because of his age, Knobby had been a surrogate father for Jonathan, although Jonathan would not admit to that. Still there was a deep bond between the two, or at least on Jonathan's part. Therefore, when he came to speak to Knobby there was a lot of emotion.

"I reckon that I'll be shiftin' ships tomorrow," said Jonathan.

"Reckon so," responded Knobby quietly.

"What does a man say to a true friend when he must go?" asked Jonathan sincerely.

"Over the years, I have seen many men come and go," replied Knobby. "Some have gone quickly, without any opportunity for goodbyes. Others have lingered over death. Still others have gone to other ships, or have run. Yours will not be the last."

"Yes, but what did you say to those who left when you had the opportunity?" asked Jonathan politely.

"I wished them Godspeed," responded Knobby, not making it any easier for Jonathan. A faint expression of amusement was on his features.

"That's just not good enough for me," replied Jonathan. "Knobby, when I was down and struggling to keep my wits about me, you gave me sound council. When I was given extra punishment day after day, you provided a joke or some tale to lift my spirits. When I was so tired on watch that I drifted off, you watched my back. How can I ever repay you for all that?"

"No one's askin' for payment lad."

"I still feel that I owe you," said Jonathan.

"That's what friends are for lad. We watch each other's back. We keep each other's spirit up."

"Yes, but I don't think I've put out my side of the bargain," responded a chagrined Jonathan. "That's why I still feel that I owe you so much more."

"Lad, it has been an eye opener watching you," stated Knobby. "I been at sea nigh on thirty-five years. In all that time, I don't recall anyone comin' in and learnin' and doin' what you can do as fast as you have. You can do rope work with your eyes closed better than most men with years of practise. You've learned to be a topman already. It took me three years to get to the level you're at now."

"But that's me. That's not giving back to you; you've given me much more."

"I disagree, lad. You've given as much as I have. It's just that each of us has accepted different 'gifts' if you will, from the other. You took what you needed; a laugh, a snooze, someone to listen. I took what I needed; someone that would listen to what I had to say, laugh at my old jokes and get enjoyment out of them, and give me the odd wet. To me that's a fair trade. As a bonus, I watched you put Hatcher in his place many a time with a word, something that I've never been able to do," replied Knobby.

Jonathan smiled. He felt more at ease, but this was how he always felt with Knobby. He couldn't ever remember a harsh word between them. He didn't always agree with Knobby, but he respected his point of view. He wondered if it would be possible to find a friend on board his new ship.

"Well, just so you know," ventured Jonathan. "I think you got short changed."

Knobby chuckled silently, "I don't."

Knobby bent over and pulled something out from a cloth beneath his feet. "I made this for you. I was going to give it to you later, but there doesn't look like there will be any later, as you're movin' ship shortly. I just wished that we had the opportunity to hoist a few wets before it happened."

The item that Knobby pulled out was an intricately carved wooden mug. It was slightly over-sized. It had a rugged handle with room for a large hand. On the front, there was a carved J S encased within a ring of leaves. The insides had been smoothed out. For a carving made by hand it was a thing of beauty. Jonathan had only seen better mugs of pewter, never anything better of wood.

"Knobby, it's a thing of beauty," declared Jonathan.

Knobby beamed. "Every dog watch while you were workin' I was whittlin' away. That's why you never seen it before. I always made sure it was away before end of watch, and never took it out before you left for the extra duties."

"There's only one thing left to do with it," said Jonathan.

"What's that?" said Knobby, uncertain as to what he might have missed.

"Why to christen it," said Jonathan. "We need to have a wet together."

Knobby grinned, "I'm all for that."

Since the mid day "Up Spirits" had long since passed, they either had to wait until tomorrow, or see if they could find someone with a hoarded ration who could be convinced to part with it. They decided to try the second option first. It was not hard to do, because in each mess, if anyone was hoarding liquor the entire mess knew about it. Finding their man was not difficult. Convincing him to part with it was the challenge. In normal situations it would be easy to offer their rations over the next few days - coinciding with whatever price the man wanted. Since Jonathan was leaving, this was not possible. Jonathan therefore had to find a better way.

The man in question was Wright. After some back and forth, Wright agreed to depart with his hoard on the following conditions. First, he would allow only two-thirds of his hoard to Jonathan, as he wished the last one-third for himself. The second condition was that he would join them in their celebrations. He agreed to take Jonathan's clothes for trade. He figured that he could get something from a bumboat. Rum was cheap here and for the clothes he could probably get triple what he was giving up. In everyone's opinion, it was a good trade.

Wright filled Knobby's mug, Jonathan's new mug and then his own. They all hoisted their respective mugs. "To friendship," said Jonathan.

"To friendship," the others echoed. Jonathan took a large gulp, as did the others.

"To a fine mug, made by a worthy craftsman," toasted Jonathan. Again they all took a drink. Jonathan felt the warmth of the alcohol spread from the pit of his stomach.

The alcohol didn't last very long, but the comradeship would be remembered for a long time. Finally a consensus was silently reached, and they each headed off to rig their respective hammocks.

✸

In the morning, the bumboats appeared. They brought all manner of goods, some of which Jonathan was familiar with, such as rum and trade goods. There were many items that Jonathan had never seen before, such as coconuts, bananas, mangos, oranges, lemons and other fruits and vegetables.

Wright lost no time bargaining for Jonathan's old shirt and pants. He was correct about the price of rum, getting a large container in return for the clothes.

Jonathan wanted to get something for Knobby to repay him for the mug, but he didn't know what to get him. No one from the bumboats was allowed aboard. All the trading was done by hanging out the gun ports, preferably out of sight of the officers on deck.

After a prolonged search, Jonathan finally spotted a nice looking bag. He inquired on the cost of this bag filled with tobacco. The price was acceptable. He wondered if he could trade his shoes for it. He felt his shoes were worth far more than the bag, so he wondered what else he could get to make an even trade.

He moved to other traders and offered the shoes for trade. The price that he was initially quoted for the shoes was fair, but being the trader he was, he wanted to strike an even better deal. Jonathan spent the better part of the next hour moving from gun port to gun port, bartering with different bumboat traders. He finally reached a deal where in exchange for his shoes; he got a bag full of tobacco for Knobby, various fruits for himself and his mess mates, and a small silver pendant with some shiny stones on a silver chain. He put the pendant around his neck, gave the bag and tobacco to a grateful Knobby and then hosted a lively noon meal with the fresh fruit and raw veggies with his mess mates. Some of the veggies he did not care for, but in general he enjoyed the fruits.

But all good things must come to an end, and during the afternoon watch came the order to board the jolly boat to go to his new ship.

Before boarding, he shook hands with all of his mess mates, even Hatcher, and mumbled a goodbye.

With both anticipation and trepidation in his heart, he scampered down the battens into the jolly boat with his ditty bag, in which were the sum total of all of his belongings.

The jolly boat shoved off. For once he was not rowing. He was just a passenger. The jolly boat went half-way to the yellow flagged ships on the far side of the harbour and sat there. Shortly a boat from the Mermaid proceeded out to meet them.

The crew in the boat looked worn, beaten down in both body and spirit. This was not lost on anyone in the Winchester's jolly boat. Eight men were being transferred. As the jolly boat came alongside, the midshipman from the Winchester handled a bundle of papers to the coxswain of the Mermaid's boat. The eight men tossed their ditty bags across and then gingerly moved from boat to boat.

As Jonathan found a position, he looked over to the man rowing. He looked spent. Jonathan just motioned with his head and took his place. He looked up at the coxswain, who just nodded at him.

"Cast off. Give way," said the coxswain.

Jonathan was now a crew member of the Mermaid.

Chapter 16
HMS Mermaid

Jonathan scrambled up the side of HMS Mermaid grasping his ditty bag in his left hand. As he entered the main deck area through the entry port he saw an officer. He knuckled his forehead. The officer pointed forward, and awaited the arrival of the coxswain.

The coxswain momentarily appeared and handed the officer the bundle of papers he had received from the Winchester's midshipman. The officer sauntered over to a small table set up in front of the poop deck and sat down. He perused the papers in front of him. He called over another officer and called for the bosun. The Mermaid's bosun was a small wiry man almost half the size of the Winchester's bosun. He had a full set of hair. He reminded Jonathan of a puffed-up rooster they once had on the Swift farm.

One by one the six new landsmen including Abe Sweeny, were called in front of the officer. It was not necessary to check the basic qualifications of a landsman. It was assumed that they knew the basics after having been at sea for months transiting from England. They were entered into the books and given their respective assignments. They were then dismissed and sent below to draw hammocks and mess needs from the purser.

"Williams, Smith," called the bosun.

Williams had been a topman in the starboard watch. Jonathan knew him to see him, but didn't know anything else about the man. It was obvious by calling Williams and himself that the officer was now starting with the topmen.

Jonathan carried over his ditty bag, dropped it to his side and knuckled his forehead. "Smith, sir." Williams did the same.

Jonathan took a good look at the officer. He was a rugged looking man of about thirty five. He was of average size, but there was something about him that made him appear bigger. He had brown hair, covered in a regulation hat. His eyes were piercing blue. They seemed to look right through you.

The officers and the bosun looked over Williams, and then shifted their gaze to Jonathan. The seated officer said, "You're both rated as ordinary seaman and topman. You look a little young to be rated that high."

Jonathan didn't know whether to respond or not, so he said nothing.

"Before we enter you in the books with that rating, I want to assure myself that each of you are actually qualified, or if the Winchester is just trying to pawn you off on us," said the seated officer. Jonathan suspected that this was the first lieutenant of the Mermaid.

The officer then did something that Jonathan had never seen before. He had some type of apparatus that was in a wooden box, which he placed on the table and opened. The apparatus was shiny brass with something that appeared to be round with some lettering or marking. It was not a compass, as Jonathan had polished one often enough on the Winchester.

"I want each of you to touch the top of each mast. Williams you will start at the bowsprit and work your way aft. Smith, you will start at the mizzen and work forward. You will be timed," said the seated officer. "You will commence when I say Mark. Ready! MARK!"

Jonathan took the steps to the quarterdeck three at a time and then vaulted over the bulwark and grappled the shrouds to the mizzen. He was already climbing over the top before Williams had reached the bowsprit. He rapidly climbed the mizzen and touched the top. He grabbed a line and slid down to the deck at a speed he could handle, although there was a slight burning sensation even in his hardened hands. He landed on deck almost beside the shrouds for the mainmast. He was rapidly on them and scrambled his way up the main. When he reached the top, he decided to use the lines between the tops to more rapidly move between the masts. He didn't want to chance the lighter line for the royals, so he went down to the topsails and swung across. Then he scampered up to the top of the foremast and touched it. Williams was still on the foremast when he got there and was astonished that Jonathan had moved so quickly. On his way down from the foremast, Jonathan grabbed a stay and lowered himself to the forecastle. He then darted over to the bowsprit and edged his way up its length. After touching the end, he reversed his movements and regained the forecastle. The rest was an easy trot back to the desk.

Jonathan was breathing heavily as he reported. The bosun acknowledged that he had indeed touched all the tops of the masts as directed. The bosun then looked at Jonathan, seriously examining him.

It was another three minutes before Williams arrived out of breath and with raw hands from sliding down a rope from the mizzen.

But it was not over. While Jonathan and Williams had been racing around in the tops, worn rope sections had been brought on deck. Jonathan and Williams were asked to perform a variety of obscure knots, whips and splices. Jonathan completed these without thought. In fact, he looked around while he was doing them to observe his speed compared to Williams. The first lieutenant, the bosun, and the ropemaker who were assessing him, all observed this.

"Enough! Williams, I will enter you on the books as an ordinary seaman rated topman on the starboard watch," declared the first lieutenant. He then assigned Williams a mess number, hammock location and stations. "Williams, you are dismissed."

A man detached himself from the bulwarks after the first lieutenant had dismissed Williams, approached, and accompanied Williams below.

"Now Smith, what am I to do with you?" remarked the first lieutenant as he leaned back in his chair. "The ropemaker has commented on your skill, as has the bosun. Yet you are young to have such skill. Why is that?"

Jonathan was nervous. Anything he said could be taken the wrong way and come back on him. "Sir, I was taught by good men who knew their craft well. I believe that my ability as a topman would be put to good use on the Mermaid."

"Hmmmm," murmured the first lieutenant. "What I don't understand is why you were sent?"

Jonathan didn't know how to reply. He knew he couldn't say that he'd been in trouble since arriving on the Winchester. That would likely put him in the same spot on the Mermaid. He needed a viable excuse, so he said what popped into his head. "I was the most junior topman, sir."

"Do you mean to say that Williams was senior to you?" asked a surprised first lieutenant.

"Williams was on a different watch, sir. I only know him to see him. I suspect he was the most junior on the other watch. I believe that he has been performing topman duties longer than I have."

"I don't understand. Your rope work and ability to move in the tops is much better. How do you account for that?" asked the first lieutenant.

"It was the way I was taught sir - by the best. Mr. Jergens is the ropemaker on the Winchester. He instructed me in rope work. He showed me different techniques and made me practise over and over again until I could do each of them with my eyes closed. Same when I became a topman. I was trained by the captain of the top. Once he was satisfied that I was capable of doing a task, he forced me to do it in a hurry. My speed improved because of that."

"Do you think that you could teach others to the same level as you are?" inquired the first lieutenant.

"Aye sir, I believe I could, providing the others were willing to learn," replied Jonathan.

"Well that's always a challenge, isn't it?" commented the first lieutenant. "Alright, I'm going to take a chance on you because we are so short-handed. I'm going to rate you as an able seaman, captain of the mizzen top. You will be on the larboard watch. I will provide you a mess number, hammock location and stations, before evening meal. Smith, you're dismissed. Bosun, inform the purser and cook that there will be eight new hands joining us, and to ensure rations are available for their evening meal."

"Aye, aye, sir," replied the bosun.

Another man detached himself from the bulwarks and approached Jonathan after the first lieutenant had dismissed him.

"Cecil West," said the man who approached Jonathan. "I'm a topman on the larboard watch. Thought you might like to have someone show you the way. Follow me."

Cecil was a slim twenty-two year old. He was about Jonathan's height, had curly brown hair and an infectious grin. He was talkative and outgoing.

Jonathan fell in behind Cecil and followed him down to the gun deck. They took the aft stairs. As they hit the lower gun deck, Jonathan immediately saw there was something completely different. There were the normal cabins aft for the officers, but halfway down the deck, the deck was closed off. Canvas had been rigged from the upper beams to the deck.

"They're usin' the foreward half for the sick ones," commented Cecil. If that were the case, then half the crew were sick, because half the normal men's portion of the deck was blocked off.

"There's four topmen messes," explained Cecil. "Right now they're split; two for starboard and two for larboard. I reckon that you will be assigned to one or the other larboard mess."

"Seems likely," replied Jonathan for something to say.

"There's only twelve of us topmen on the larboard watch. You'll make thirteen," continued Cecil. Jonathan stopped dead in his tracks.

"Then why'd the first lieutenant go through all those tests? If you're that short of topmen, I would have thought that he would be glad to have any topmen he could lay his hands on," commented Jonathan.

"No doubt he is," replied Cecil. The problem is that a number of the topmen are only recently rated ordinary. They are new and don't know much. With you being an able seaman, and with the skill you just showed the first lieutenant, he's gotta be thinkin' about trainin' the new men."

"Jesus," said Jonathan. He thought to himself: 'I got no problem with the sail or rope work, but I've never trained anyone else on anything. How the hell am I going to accomplish this?'

Cecil looked at him. "You had better be prepared to teach all the others working on the same mast as you, because they ain't likely to have even half the skill that you got, and that includes me."

Jonathan looked at Cecil after that last comment. "What are the young gentlemen like?"

"Well there we caught a break," smiled Cecil. "We had a right nasty bugger, but he was transferred - permanent you might say. There's one we don't have to worry about him no more. At the present there are only two midshipmen up in the tops. One is young Mr. Farley. He's younger than you. Seems a good sort. Don't know nothin'. The other is Mr. Elkhorne. He's older. Tried once to pass his lieutenant's exams and failed, so he's keen on makin' it the next time. That probably ain't going to be too long from now, 'cause I heard that a number of lieutenants have joined their Maker in the last couple of months. That yellow jack, it don't care where you was born, as a blueblood or in the gutter. It'll take you regardless."

The two of them moved over to stand between two mess tables. The tables were dropped, and Jonathan realized that there was a make and mend watch occurring - at least by the looks of it. It was an appropriate time to get acquainted with his new shipmates.

Cecil started the introductions, "Mess mates, this here's our new mess mate Jon Smith. Jon, this here's Mannion, Liliput, Young, Peters, Hale, Langtry, Rosewood, Abbot, and Johnson. Somewhere else around here is a short fella called Beck. There's also another fellow called Harry Smith - no relation likely." The others laughed at that comment.

Jonathan's first impression was that all the topmen were cast in the same mould. They were all young fit men of average size and height. The shoulders and arms were all well muscled. They looked healthy until you looked at their faces. Each face except Cecil's seemed to have some level of despair, only momentarily altered by the laugh they just had.

Jonathan shook hands with each in turn, trying to memorize the face and name to go with it. A closer examination while shaking hands caused him to re-evaluate his initial impression. Liliput, Peters, Rosewood and Abbot could have been brothers. Mannion, Young and Langtry were older; in the case of Langtry, much older.

Cecil continued to monopolize the conversation. "Lieutenant Davis rated him 'able' after the little display he put on touching the tops of all masts."

Jonathan thought that it would appear that Cecil West was an admirer. Still, it would be best to be humble, as he did not know these men, nor did they know him. He didn't want to get off on the wrong foot. He decided to say nothing, as he had not mentioned it himself.

"I take it that we have a make and mend afternoon, or at least what's left of it?" inquired Jonathan.

A couple of the men muttered an acknowledgement.

"I'm in need of some extra slops. What's the going rate; or is it cheaper just to get canvas and sew them yourself?"

"Depends if you have any objections to dead man's clothes," quipped Langtry. "There seems to be a surplus of them at the moment."

"On my last ship, if a man died, we auctioned off his effects, and sent the raised money back to his next of kin," spoke Jonathan quietly. "Does that happen here?"

"In some respects," responded Langtry. He was in his mid thirties, with a powerful set of shoulders. He had a quiet way about him. When he spoke, others deferred to him. "Except if the man died of yellow jack, the surgeon checks his ditty bag to make sure everything was clean. If not, the ditty bag and all its contents are burned, same as the man's hammock, and clothes he was wearing. There were a number of men who never got the chance to even get to anything in their ditty bag."

"Let me understand this. What you're saying is that the stuff in the ditty bags may be alright, but it may also contain the yellow jack?' asked Jonathan.

"That's what everyone's worried about," responded Rosewood. "I won't touch one of them bags. They should have just burned the lot, but the purser figured he could make a profit out of them so he held on to them. Just for safety's sake, the captain had the surgeon go through them and burn anything questionable in the surgeon's mind."

"How good is the surgeon?" asked Jonathan.

"Not very good in my opinion. Most of the men put into his care with yellow jack were carried out and burned, not even buried," chipped in Hale. Hale was a hard looking man with black eyes. He was the type of man you would want on your side in a knife fight, and the type to avoid at all costs if you were walking alone down a dark alley.

Peters said, "That's not fair George. You know as well as anyone, once you come down with yellow jack, there ain't much that you can do about it. It's between you and your Maker whether you spend any more time on watch in this world."

"If a fella was gonna bid on some of these dead man's clothes, how would he go about it?" asked Jonathan. The trader in him saw an opportunity.

Silence descended on the two mess tables.

Langtry ventured, "I'd go and see the purser. He has them stored."

"He has them stored?" asked Jonathan. "If this purser is like the purser on my last ship, he'd have them 'stored' in with the rest of the stores, and would issue them to the next unfortunate that had to cough up his prices. More profit for him."

Jonathan could see that his words were having an impact. Others at the tables were cocking their heads or looking at other mess mates to assess whether they thought Jonathan had a valuable point. The consensus was that Jonathan had a point. They needed to verify it, if only to make sure that the purser wasn't making more money off their backs.

Langtry, Liliput, and Peters showed Jonathan the way down to the purser's storage on the orlop. It was in the same general location as on the Winchester.

"We'd like to bid on some of the effects of our mess mates and have the money sent back to their next of kin," stated Langtry to the purser, Mr. Bilbo, using the respect due to the purser's office. Bilbo was a typical purser. He was pasty-faced, overweight, and very secure in his position; hence somewhat arrogant.

"That requires an auction, and only Mr. Davis or the captain has the authority to order such an auction. You should realize there is little that wasn't destroyed," stated Mr. Bilbo.

The four of them departed. Once out of earshot of the purser, Peters tapped Jonathan on the shoulder. "You called that one right. That bastard intends to cheat the next of kin out of their rightful money."

"And make double his money selling back the same clothes and articles to us at purser's prices," voiced Liliput.

"We'll see about that," said Langtry.

Jonathan was about to find out that Langtry was well respected on the Mermaid. Langtry approached the bosun respectfully by himself, but with the others within hearing distance.

"Mr. Mason, could you tell me when we are going to auction off the effects of our departed shipmates. I'm thinkin' some of their kin could probably use what little funds we can scrape together for 'em."

Mr. Mason looked at Langtry. "I'll ask. Seriously though, do you really think anyone wants those items? I mean with the possibility of yellow jack?"

"It was my understanding that the surgeon had looked at all the items, took out anything even remotely questionable, and then ensured that everything else was washed in vinegar. Am I mistaken in that?" asked Langtry politely.

"No, you're right. I detailed the men for washing myself. And what you're asking has been common practise in any ship I've ever sailed in. Like I say, I'll ask," stated Mr. Mason.

"Thank you, Mr. Mason," said Langtry and withdrew.

When they had returned to the mess, Beck was present. He was a short man just shy of thirty years of age. He was reserved, but appeared to interact well with others in the mess. When introduced to Jonathan, he mentioned that he had been recently promoted to ordinary seaman.

Harry Smith was something else. He was as black as a dark night without a moon. When he smiled his entire face lit up. He was lanky and well muscled. He had short, very curly hair that was as dark as his skin. When Jonathan was introduced, he was surprised when Harry spoke. It was in some tongue with a splattering of English words. Jonathan had to concentrate very hard on what the man was trying to say, to understand even a small fraction of the conversation. He was thankful that Harry seemed very friendly; otherwise he would probably be terrified of this man. Once Harry got going though, he continued to make noise. It might have been conversation to another who could speak his language, but to the men in the mess it was noise. Jonathan smiled and was amused. This seemed to warm Harry to him. It was an experience!

CHAPTER 17
The Test

During his first watch, Jonathan met young Mr. Farley. Jonathan's watch position had made him the senior man on the mizzen. Mr. Farley was deemed to be the captain of the top, but with only two midshipmen left it was expected that Mr. Farley would be the sole midshipman on any given watch. Hence supervision on any given watch was likely to be limited. The flip side of this was that Jonathan would have to ensure that the men were kept busy. But as Jonathan had learned, there was work to accomplish a specific objective, there was work to learn something, and there was make work. Jonathan would need to ensure that anything he asked these men to do would not be considered in the last category. He had experienced make work jobs before and detested them.

His initial perception of Mr. Farley was mixed. He was young, only about fourteen, and had not gone through puberty yet. He was nimble in the tops, but not completely at home there. He was well dressed, even compared to other midshipmen. He always wore shoes, even in the tops. He had a rosy complexion. His light brown hair was reasonably short, and had bleached somewhat in the sun of the West Indies.

He appeared fair, but at the same time he was throwing his weight around too much. It was likely a lack of self-confidence. He was interesting to watch when he was around Langtry. Langtry had an air of competence and confidence about him. It was something that Mr. Farley did not have, and in some respects neither did Jonathan. When he was about Langtry, Mr. Farley told him what he needed done and left. Langtry then assigned the men and issued the orders.

Since it was a harbour watch, and the ship was not going anywhere, Jonathan spent most of the time getting to know the men on his top. He led them up to the mizzen top and kept them there, away from the eyes and ears on the deck. He periodically ran a drill like sending men out to the end of the yardarms, so no one would send them to other duties.

Jonathan had picked up some valuable lessons on the Winchester, even if he did not realize it at the time. When work to accomplish something had to be done, you gave orders clearly, so that there was no mistake as to what had to be done. When doing work to learn something, you explained what you wanted the individual to do, demonstrated the task, and then checked the work. This he used as a guide. It seemed to work very well. Of course in order to accomplish the task, the instruction had to have been completed at least to some level of competency.

What Jonathan was unsure of after that first watch was what did the men working on the mizzen know? Additionally, he needed to determine how competent were they to actually do it? His next concern was how was he to go about finding out the competency and knowledge levels of these men? This was something that he would need to speak to the other senior topmen about in the morning.

Jonathan slung his hammock and got some sleep. He felt that he was going to need it.

The morning harbour routine as a senior topman was relaxed compared to what he was used to when underway on the Winchester. First of all, because there was still the presence of fever on board, there was a restrained silence. No boat ventured near the anchorage. The lack of a large portion of the crew due to sickness meant that others were being assigned to complete work that usually was accomplished by others. As Jonathan had learned previously on Winchester, it was necessary to pump ship for a few minutes each day. Landsmen normally were given this necessary but unpleasant task. However some of the topmen were called to do this task due to the lack of landsmen.

This left Jonathan somewhat free to discuss with the other senior topmen how best to assess the skills and knowledge of those men working on the mizzen with Jonathan. Langtry had the main. Liliput the fore and Peters was the most senior man on the bowsprit, although he answered to Liliput. Jonathan asked each of them how they would assess their men.

Everyone stated that he would have them demonstrate the required knots, whips, sail handling and other skills as individuals or teams, as required. Jonathan had already come to this conclusion. This approach would cover all aspects but one. Jonathan was concerned about taking down the tops. He knew the sequence for striking the tops, but the correct orders eluded him. It was also a job that required strict control, because a falling top, or yard, could do a lot of damage to the deck and people below if it fell.

The good news was that they were in harbour. There wouldn't be any better time to practise than when there was no movement on the ship.

Jonathan needed to approach Mr. Farley, not only to get his permission but also to get the permission of the officer of the watch, and possibly even the captain's permission. He went to Langtry to ask him about how to approach Mr. Farley. He also asked Langtry to observe the work and assess his people, as he would be able to see things from a different perspective.

Surprisingly, Langtry was all for it. He interceded with Mr. Farley. A plan was then formed by the officers and Jonathan was directed to execute the plan.

The plan was for Jonathan to assess his people's skills and knowledge. If there were any deficiencies, then he would have to establish some plan to get them up to speed. Part of the assessment would be the speed at which the mizzen top was taken down and then put back up again. Jonathan was a bit concerned about the speed aspect of taking down and putting the mizzen top back in place. He would have much preferred doing this task at a slower pace, so that he could more readily spot errors and correct them on the spot.

Unfortunately it was not to be. He was directed to do the assessment the next day.

The assessment started well. The ropemaker had provided lots of worn rope so that the assessment not only accomplished the assessment; it also had the added benefit of checking and repairing some of the worn rope in stores.

Jonathan was underwhelmed at the capabilities in rope work, knots and whipping shown by his men. He could see that significant work would be required. In some instances complete retraining was warranted, so the individual could work while clinging to the rigging.

Sail handling was adequate. Practise would be the only thing needed to improve it. The technical skills were there.

Finally, they came to taking down the mizzen top. Things started to go wrong shortly after the operation commenced. Other topmen started to jeer and taunt the mizzen crew about how slow they were. Instead of concentrating on the techniques and safety, the men tried for speed. They cut some corners that an inexperienced Jonathan did not notice.

The top was stricken in a reasonable amount of time, but still the taunts continued in a good natured competitive fashion. The top now had to be put back up. This is where things went from bad to worse.

Safety in these manoeuvres was paramount. There was an assigned officer of the watch - Lieutenant Rylett, the third lieutenant, even though in most cases the lieutenants did not stand harbour watches. The captain had assigned him for safety reasons. Lieutenant Rylett was a bit peckish. He still had a hangover from last evening, had not been able to stomach his dinner, and was looking forward to getting out of the hot Antigua sun.

As a result, he berated Mr. Farley to, "Get a move on. This is taking far too long."

Mr. Farley then berated the mizzen crew. They all knew they were being watched and assessed. The additional berating, however, blew all prudence aside. In a rush to complete the whipping, Beck broke a cardinal rule. He used both hands on his task, instead of one hand for the King and one for himself.

Jonathan saw it happening, and shouted at him to grab hold. In slow motion, Beck started to slide and that momentum worked against him. Instantly he was in free-fall. He fell, hit a lower yard and bounced out board, never making a sound on the way down.

The splash was minimized because he hit the water feet first. Almost immediately, "Man Overboard" was shouted by someone, followed by a scrambling on deck.

The boats were all in the water at the stern, with only the captain's gig alongside. Half a dozen men were piling into the gig immediately. The gig shot out, but still had to traverse the ship and then find Beck.

Jonathan turned his gaze back to the rest of the men on the mizzen. "Continue with your work. There's nothing you can do from up here that's going to help Beck at the moment. Now I want you to slow down and do things right. I realize that there are officers screamin' at you to hurry up, but we need to do the job and do it right. Let's get at it."

The job was completed. Jonathan inspected it and was satisfied that it was in the same or possibly even better condition than when they had started. He ordered everyone down from the top. He went last.

The gig had picked up Beck, more like fished him aboard, because it appeared that Beck either could not or did not swim. Already the surgeon was on deck to examine him, as soon as he was brought aboard.

Jonathan braced himself for what was coming. First there was Beck. Then there would be the recriminations from the rest of the topmen. Finally, there would be the officers on his back.

By the time Jonathan reached the deck the captain was on the quarterdeck. Beck was coming over the side. He was apparently still alive, but in some pain.

Before Jonathan could venture over to see Beck, he was ordered to stand still. All the officers were on deck at the present. It appeared that there would be a public inquiry immediately, for all to see.

It was the first time Jonathan saw Captain Douglas. He was a man of average height, average build and receding hair that was greying on the fringes. He had taken off his hat to wipe away the sweat, and was reluctant to put it back on. He was not wearing a wig at the present.

"Mr. Rylett, you had the watch. What happened here?" asked the captain.

"Sir, the mizzen top had been struck to my satisfaction. I then ordered it to be put back in place. This was going slowly, and without proper consideration of safety when one of the topmen slipped and fell. He hit the yard on the way down and bounced out board. Your coxswain was on deck and he grabbed some men, jumped into your gig that was alongside, and rowed around the ship. He fished the man out of the water and brought him back here. The man is presently below with the surgeon. He is alive."

"Mr. Farley, let's hear your version of what happened."

"Sir, I saw what Lieutenant Rylett saw," responded Mr. Farley.

"Who was the senior topman on the mizzen?"

"Smith, sir. That's him there," Mr. Rylett responded and pointed at Jonathan.

After Mr. Rylett's comments, Jonathan felt that he was directly in the sights of the captain. He knew that the captain would take what his officers had to say into consideration before any one of the men.

The captain turned and faced Jonathan. "Smith eh, I don't recall seeing your face before."

Jonathan knuckled his forehead. He had never addressed a captain before and to say that he was nervous would have been a wild understatement - he was scared.

"No sir, I was transferred from the Winchester the day before yesterday."

"What's your version of what happened?"

Jonathan was between a rock and a hard place. If he agreed with Lieutenant Rylett's version, which he didn't, then he was guilty of either incompetence or not caring about the safety of his men. Either of which would mean that the men would be reluctant to follow him and would never trust him. If he went the other way, and said what he thought, then Lieutenant Rylett would be an enemy. That was equally unappetizing. He didn't know what to do and he was shaking like a leaf.

"Sir, I just joined this ship two days ago. I had never seen the men perform any drills, so I did not know where to start training them. I approached Mr. Farley with a request to do some drills while in harbour so I could assess the mizzen topmen. All the drills are safer in harbour because there's no motion and the mast is about as stable as it ever gets."

"You see sir, when I was trained on the great guns, my gun captain told me a good captain, pardon me sir, a good gun captain always conserves his shot." At this point Jonathan was mortified and near speechless.

"Well out with it man, what does any of this have to do with the mizzen top drill?" growled an angry captain.

"Sir, topmen are like the shot the gunner taught me to conserve; only they're more valuable. When I joined this ship, I realized that with trained topmen so scarce, every drill would have to be done really slowly until I was sure everyone knew what they were doing. After that, we could increase the speed."

As the captain said nothing, Jonathan went on.

"When the orders came last night that the drill was to be timed, I was worried. If the times were used as a starting point from which we could improve later with practise that would be fine. My concern was if the men considered the drill a race, then they would rush. Men that are not properly trained make mistakes or take chances when they are rushed. As we were striking, and again as we were putting the top back up, we were ordered to speed up."

"Beck made a mistake because he was rushing to comply with the order. He failed to ensure he was properly balanced when we were whipping the mast. He lost his balance, slipped, and fell."

The captain looked at Lieutenant Rylett.

"Sir, those men were trained. They were all topmen on this ship for our last cruise. The only new man is Smith here, and from his youth, I doubt that he has as much experience as other men on the mizzen," commented Lieutenant Rylett.

"Fair enough. You do look awful young to be rated able seaman, Smith."

Lieutenant Davis stepped in, as his judgement was being put into question by Lieutenant Rylett's comments. "Sir, you will remember that you recommended we check anyone at the ordinary or able level that was sent over to make sure the Winchester wasn't unloading their undesirables on us to comply with the Commodore's order?"

Captain Douglas nodded.

"Sir, I evaluated Smith and another man, Williams. The bosun was standing by during the evaluation and can verify the results. I found Smith more than competent. In fact, he was the fastest man I have ever seen moving from top to top. His performance in the tops and rope work were excellent."

The captain turned back to Jonathan. Although he was not trembling as hard, he was still slightly shaky and sweating profusely, and not just because it was hot.

"What's your opinion of the men on the mizzen, Smith?"

"Sir, after going through the drills today, their rope work and knots need improvement. Sail handling is average. I would say we could hold our own with any other ship. The basic knowledge for bigger jobs like striking the top is there. We need time to improve the skill some more, then pick up the speed. There are also other skills that I will need to check and possibly train. For example, every topman needs to be a good lookout. He needs to understand what a brig or schooner, or square-rigged vessel looks like from a distance."

Captain Douglas looked seriously at Smith. "Why were you sent here, Smith? Normally a captain hangs on to his best men, to 'conserve your shot' as you put it earlier."

"Don't know sir, but I think it was because I was junior."

"Gentlemen, let's retire below and discuss this. Smith, you're dismissed," said Captain Douglas.

Jonathan knuckled his forehead, and withdrew from the quarterdeck in a shaken condition. He went below and asked, "Where's Beck? How is he?"

"Down below still with the surgeon," replied Liliput.

Everyone avoided Jonathan. He walked away, back to the deck. He walked to the water butt and drank deeply. After he had quenched his thirst, he made his way down to the orlop deck and to the surgeon's area. He could hear Beck before he could see him. Since he was moaning in pain he was at least alive. Jonathan followed the sound of the moaning. He could see the surgeon working on Beck's legs.

Jonathan watched in fascination. He had never seen anything of the surgeon operations, although he had memories of the sick area from when he had been brought aboard the Winchester. He had heard the horror stories about the surgeon's operations, however. He watched as boards were placed on either side of Becks legs, and the legs and board were bound tight in gauze. He winced when a surgeon's mate pulled on the bottom of Beck's legs before the gauze was wound round. As the surgeon's mate continued to wind the gauze, the surgeon turned around.

"What are you doing here?"

"Beck is one of my topmen. I came down here to find out how he is," replied Jonathan.

The surgeon looked at him. He hesitated, and then decided, "Your friend will be all right. He has two fractured legs, a fractured arm, and maybe a broken rib or two. He will likely be out of action for two months, maybe longer before he can go back into the tops. "

The surgeon brushed past him on his way to report to the captain.

Jonathan hung around, knowing it was possible to get more information from the surgeon's mate than from the surgeon if he could find a starting point.

There were two surgeon's mates, both older men who were likely former sailors who had some injuries that had removed them from active duty. They had likely become surgeon's mates rather than starve on the outside world.

Jonathan approached one of them to see if he could speak to Beck. The surgeon's mate beckoned him in. Beck was to be kept at the orlop level, and not moved one deck above with those suffering from yellow jack. He had been placed in a slung hammock.

Jonathan bent over him. Beck was still conscious, but obviously in great pain. Beck could not focus on anything, so Jonathan took control. "Beck, its Jon Smith. You're going to recover. You've broken both legs and your arm. You probably broke some ribs when you hit the yardarm on the way down. All you have to do now is lie still and let time heal your bones. In a couple of months we'll have you up and working in the tops again. Just hang in there."

Beck whispered through pain clenched teeth, "Slipped. Heard you call, but it was too late. Gawd, it hurts."

Jonathan remembered the pain from his head. He turned to the surgeon's mates, "Is there anything we can give him to ease the pain?"

"Normally I'd give him some rum, but I don't know what his insides are like. Maybe in a day or so if we don't see any blood in his piss or bowel movements."

Jonathan nodded. There was nothing he could do. "Can I come down and see him again?"

The surgeon's mate nodded. "Just see me. I'll let you know if it's alright." Jonathan nodded. What the surgeon's mate had meant was the surgeon didn't believe in visitors, but the surgeon's mate would know when he could safely let a friend in to see his mate.

Jonathan headed back up to the mess. He needed time to think. He knew any trust that had developed between him and the mizzen topmen had been erased. Now he had to work doubly hard to rebuild that trust, assuming he was still in charge after the officers had their discussion.

Evening meal was in progress when he arrived back at the mess. He reported to both messes on Beck's condition and prognosis. He sat down to munch on some bread.

He needed time to think. No one disturbed him. In fact the mess was quiet. Everyone was disturbed by what had occurred to Beck, as they all knew that it could just as easily happen to them.

He felt a hand on his shoulder. He looked up. It was Langtry. "Could I speak to you Jon?"

Jonathan nodded. He drained his mug, left it on the table and stood. He followed Langtry up to the deck. They moved to the base of the main where there was no one who would overhear what was said. Jonathan waited for Langtry to begin.

Langtry took a moment to compose his thoughts. "Jon, I'm sorry for what happened this afternoon. I knew what you were trying to do, and there was no need to rush. I should have had a word with my guys, but you know how the competitive spirit is. It was just as important that I keep that alive for my guys, so I let them egg you on."

Jonathan looked at him but said nothing.

"I was watching, like you asked. I saw Beck at the same time you did. I know you shouted a warning, but it was too late. It was an accident. Beck should have kept one hand for himself."

Jonathan continued to stare at Langtry. "It was a preventable accident, and you know it. There was absolutely no reason to rush, nothing to gain, and something to lose, and we lost it. And I'm not only taking about Beck. You know those men won't trust me up there again - I wouldn't. You know that I didn't have any say. We were ordered to speed up. I never said anything to the men, but they heard the order from the quarterdeck as well as I did and responded. They're good men, but they aren't that skilled yet."

Jonathan continued, "Now I'm between a rock and a hard place. The men don't trust me. Lieutenant Rylett accused me of reckless action and incompetence in front of the captain. He was just voicing what the men probably think. I'm the new man. I'm the prick that made them do all these drills in harbour instead of standing relaxed harbour duties like their mates. When Rylett accused me, I had to stand up for myself, or I'd be at the grate with a striped back in two blinks. I had to defend myself, so I told the captain what happened. He went back to his cabin with the other officers 'to discuss the incident' I think were his words. What they were really doing was discussing what to do with me. I expect to be called shortly."

Langtry looked at Jonathan. "You're right about the men. They didn't trust you much before, even less now. You still might be able to gain their trust yet. It'll take time. Rylett however is a worse problem. He's an arrogant prick. If he thinks you crossed him, he'll make your life a nightmare. If he does that, that means anyone with you will suffer too. The result will be that you'll get no love from your men. Rylett will see to that."

Jonathan shook his head. "You know, being a sailor isn't such a bad life if it wasn't for all the bastards you run into." He turned and went back below.

Langtry chuckled to his turned back, "Ain't that the truth."

Chapter 18
The Auction

The bosun's mates moved through the messes and on deck. They were passing the word that there would be an auction of the effects from departed shipmates, during the last dog watch the next night.

By noon, Jonathan was surprised that he had heard nothing more about the mishap yesterday from the quarterdeck. He felt like a pariah. No one associated with him, but he was used to it from the Winchester. On the Winchester it was because he was always getting extra duties. Anyone near him thought that they would be tagged with extra duties as well. He now knew the real story behind all the duties on the Winchester. In this situation, he sensed that the others figured it was just a matter of time before he landed in shit, so it was best to avoid him. If what Langtry had said about Rylett was true, then they were wise to avoid him unless absolutely necessary.

During the afternoon watch Jonathan gathered the mizzen topmen, and started going through ropes. The ropemaker was delighted. He had extra help to check and restore his ropes. The men were not happy however. Jonathan started teaching them the basics. Since all of these men knew the basics, they looked at the afternoon as a make work exercise and scorned both it and Jonathan. Jonathan persisted however. When a man used a technique that Jonathan did not approve of, he was corrected. Patiently,

Jonathan would explain the technique over and over, the reason why it was better than the one the man was using, and demonstrate it. After a while even the ropemaker was paying attention to what Jonathan was saying. Others migrated to Jonathan's group in the waist. Cecil West and Peters both joined the group and had Jonathan show them his techniques. There was only a subtle difference in some techniques, none in others. The show catcher happened when Jonathan roped a line to the mainmast, and then asked a man to secure the line taut. He then grasped the line with both feet and one hand. He drew a line up and held it under the arm grasping the rope. With the other he grasped a swinging rope and proceeded to splice the two together with one hand in a long splice. It was an incredible feat that showed professional skill. With the splice near completion, Jonathan coiled himself around the taut line and held himself with his arms while whipping each end of the splice.

"This is why I'm teaching you to splice this way. Hopefully you will never need it, but in the event that you do, you'll need it bad," said Jonathan after he had alighted back to the deck.

Unbeknownst to him, his little instruction class had attracted the attention of those on the quarterdeck. The bosun, both midshipmen, the master and Lieutenant Caharty, the 2nd lieutenant, were actively watching this final demonstration.

The group broke up as the first dog watch began. Everyone retreated to the mess for evening meal. Things remained quiet until the second dog watch. Everyone moved to the deck. The purser and bosun had set up items on the forecastle.

The auction started, and there were no takers for any items. No one had any money. Then the purser offered a half pound for everything.

The bosun announced, "Look men, we have 60 ditty bags. Up to now, you haven't shown much interest. Do we continue, or is no one other than the purser going to buy anything?"

Jonathan spoke up, "Two pounds for the whole lot." Heads turned, voices gasped.

"That's cash on the barrelhead, Smith, no IOUs," said the bosun. "Any other takers?"

"So be it. Sold to Smith providing you can come up with the money," stated the bosun.

Jonathan had secretly removed two pounds from his jacket lining. He moved forward to the forecastle and laid down the coins. The bosun counted it out. He acknowledged that it was the full amount.

"What are you planning to do, become the new purser?" asked the bosun. At this comment the look on the purser's face turned even sourer than it was. "It's not likely that you will get any customers on this ship."

If he had been a pariah before, Jonathan had just elevated his status to the biggest pariah on this ship.

Jonathan now had a number of concerns. He needed to find out what he had just acquired. Also he needed to get it stored in a single location, probably on the orlop. He would have to make arrangements for that. Unfortunately, he had just announced that he had cash, so he would have to take precautions that the remainder of his money was not stolen. As time went on, and he was able to exchange some of these newly acquired items for cash, he would be even a larger target for thieves. He would have to figure out a way to protect himself and his money.

He started with the easiest task first. He moved amongst the ditty bags piled on the forecastle. The first thing he looked for was a sewing kit. He would need to separate the items, and prepare bags for each type of item.

He grabbed a couple of bags and dumped their contents on the deck. He rapidly separated pants into a pile, shirts into another pile, jackets into a third pile, shoes into a fourth, blankets into a fifth, plates, mugs and utensils into another, empty ditty bags into a separate pile, and other items into a final pile. He emptied a further number of ditty bags and sorted the contents. He finally spotted a needle and heavy thread.

He took his knife and cut the threads on a number of ditty bags. Then he started sewing the canvas from the bags into larger bags - one for each pile. He continued this by himself in silence for the next few hours, through the remainder of the dog watch and the first watch. Once all was sorted, everything was deposited into the respective bags. He then dragged these bags into the orlop. He collapsed into his hammock for a short sleep before starting another day. He had picked out a nicely carved plate, bowl, and spoon for himself. He placed these in the mess bag after morning breakfast.

He had replaced his knife with a beautiful bone handled knife and sheath. He had seen another knife that was very well balanced for throwing, and added both to his belt.

He had a number of items that he had placed in his own ditty bag for further investigation.

Over the next few days, he made his own sewing kit, which had different sized needles, buttons, and a number of different colours and thickness of threads for working with fabric, canvas, and leather. He made his own money belt using leather and fabric. He selected a number of shirts and pants for his own use. He washed them thoroughly, and altered them to fit his frame.

He checked all the various shoes that he had found, although in truth there were not many - only ten. He had found a pair that did fit him, and were in reasonable condition. He pulled out a jacket and started working on it. He used a blanket to make a doubly thick lining, as he had heard that in summer, the fleet may move north to stay out of the tropics during hurricane season.

He did this in his spare time, while continuing to train the topmen of the mizzen, and others, in various rope work and knots. He had inquired around and found the most experienced lookouts left on the ship. From them he started to acquire knowledge on how to identify various types of ships, and countries of origin of ships by their design. He sought out the men working the flags. From these he started to learn about signals.

Slowly, things changed aboard the Mermaid. The number of men in the foreward portion of the gun deck decreased. Either they were returned to light duty or were carried off to be buried or burned.

Mermaid's normal complement was supposed to be around two hundred eighty five according to what Jonathan had heard. Also from what he had heard, there were fewer than two hundred men still living on this ship. Some of these men were still either in sick bay, or just out of it, and weak as babies. It came as a surprise then in mid January, when it was announced that the Mermaid would go out on patrol.

Stores were replenished, and preparations were made. During all of this time they still flew the yellow flag. When stores boats were sent out with stores, they were accompanied by another boat. The crew of the stores hoys disembarked to the second boat. Mermaid personnel then boarded and finished the moving the hoys to the Mermaid. The stores were off-loaded. The hoy was then moved to shore, but not to the docks. Mermaid personnel were taken back to the ship. No one would approach the hoy for a week, by which time the surgeon believed that any contagious item would have lost its power.

※

The Mermaid had a challenge when preparing to sail. There were barely enough men to unfurl all the sails at the same time. A larger challenge was having enough men to man the capstan. The Mermaid had been at anchor for some time, and the anchors were well embedded in the harbour mud.

Jonathan waited patiently for orders on the mizzen topsail. He knew they were having challenges with the capstan just by how long it took. Finally after some time a shout was heard, "Free and Clear".

The order came almost at once. He released the gasket that he had loosened earlier. The yard was raised and the sail caught the wind. There was not much wind, but it was enough to get way on her. The rudder bit and they had steerageway.

The Mermaid slowly eased her way out of port. Jonathan looked back at the harbour entrance. He truly hoped that there was enough wind at the right angle to support sailing back into harbour at the end of this cruise. He remembered the row into harbour towing the Winchester, and was not keen on having to do that again. With the reduced crew, it would be a tough pull.

Once clear of the harbour entrance, the ship headed southwest, out into the Atlantic. It felt good to feel the steady rise and fall of the ship as she caught the motion of the Atlantic swells. Based on his past sailing knowledge, they were heading toward Guadeloupe, probably to look for that French ship the Winchester had spotted while coming to Antigua.

The sun, the wind, and the constant routine over the next few days seemed to put life back into the crew. Each man had a job to do. They were short-handed so extra work was added to everyone, but no one seemed to mind. After a week at sea, the yellow flag was taken down. The lower gun deck was finally opened up, and every able man was returned to active duty. There were still a number of men that needed light duties while their strength was built up, but all in all, there was a sense of relief by the entire ship's company.

With the ship opened up, two additional things happened. Because there was such a change in crew disposition, the first lieutenant authorized a change in mess. As soon as he heard this, Jonathan figured that he would find himself in a mess by himself. He was surprised however, when only Liliput and Peters changed mess. There had only been four at the other larboard topmen mess while Beck was still in sick bay, while there had been eight in Jonathan's mess. Evening it out to six and six allowed everyone more room.

The announcement that the Captain would daily exercise the great guns was the second occurrence. Jonathan had been placed on a gun crew as the second gun captain. He understood that he would not be a primary gun captain because he might be called away for sail handling.

Jonathan had missed the exercise he got from working the great guns. Even more, he missed the drills for the boarders. It was with some anticipation therefore, that he went to his assigned gun position. With a limited number of men, it required extra effort on everyone's part to run out the guns. Although tired after exercising at the guns for nearly two hours, Jonathan was content that men working his gun knew what they were about.

Completing boarding exercises was something totally different. Jonathan's skill with a pike, boarding axe and pistol or musket was confirmed. He did not fare as well with the cutlass. When cutlass drills were undertaken, Jonathan was holding his own.

During a session in the afternoon watch Lieutenant Rylett took over the class. It was clear that Rylett had not forgotten Jonathan. It was also clear that Rylett was an expert with the blade. Cutlass fighting and fencing were not the same, Jonathan well knew. Fencing was an art, while cutlass work in a boarding was brutal and anything but artful. But there were a lot of the fencing elements that could be used with a cutlass. Anyone having extensive fencing training was apt to do very well in a boarding action, and better than anyone without fencing training. It was obvious that Rylett had extensive fencing experience. To prove it he requested Jonathan as his training aid (read target) for the instruction that he gave. As his training aid, Jonathan was subjected to multiple strikes, slashes and pokes. If the demonstration weapon had been metal instead of wood, Jonathan felt he would not be still standing.

Lieutenant Rylett was slightly larger than Jonathan. He was much older, being in his late twenties or early thirties, and therefore stronger. His reach was slightly longer than Jonathan's. He was very agile and fast. The most infuriating aspect about Lieutenant Rylett was his air of superiority. He simply looked down on Jonathan, or any man who was in a position subordinate to him. He reminded everyone of this on a continuing basis.

Every day boarding drill was conducted, Rylett called on and used Jonathan as his personal pin cushion. Despite Jonathan's valiant efforts to counter Rylett's attacks, he was constantly foiled. Jonathan sensed his skill was slowly improving. It was a toss-up whether his skill would improve fast enough, or whether the bruises from his clumsy attempts to defend himself would ultimately do him in. To add insult to injury, with every additional strike upon Jonathan, the smile on Rylett's face grew bigger.

Finally one afternoon, after repeated strikes on his body, Jonathan lost his temper. He screamed at Rylett, and flailed away with everything he had. Rylett was pressed back and back, but he managed always to counter. Jonathan was drained. He visibly slowed, and that's when Rylett countered and struck him again and again. Jonathan went down in pain from a strike in his diaphragm. As he groaned on the deck, Rylett said in a cheerful voice and pointed at Jonathan, "That is why you never lose your temper when fighting a superior opponent. You will open yourself up to counter strokes."

Jonathan had learned one of the most valuable lessons he would learn in his life, and at the hands of his enemy. Never, ever, lose your temper in a fight. Be cool. Counter your opponent's attack. Wait for the opportunity to strike. That opportunity will always appear. You just had to be standing, and ready for it, to win.

Rylett turned to Jonathan and smiled, "Get up Smith. You expect to lie around all day? What would your mates think about you?"

Rylett's actions during boarding exercises were having the opposite effect that Rylett expected. Rather than seeing Jonathan as someone who couldn't take it, and someone who was in Rylett's sights, there was a certain amount of sympathy for him. Everyone could well see that Rylett's skill far exceeded Jonathan's. They could also see that Rylett was picking on him. Everyone could also see that Rylett did not pull his strikes, so that the full force was usually hitting Jonathan. The fact that Jonathan didn't complain, even when his torso and thighs were a mass of bruises from the repeated strikes was another point in his favour.

Just the same, most men avoided Jonathan. When shit is thrown at someone and hits, it often splatters. Most men didn't want to be splattered.

※

The cruise went on for about six weeks. They checked on most of the Leeward Islands; Guadeloupe, Dominica, Martinique, St Lucia and over to Barbados. All the time they were looking for French cruisers. Numerous smaller vessels were stopped, information was exchanged, but there was no sign of French cruisers.

They turned and headed back for Antigua without much to show for the cruise. They had shown the flag, the crew had come back to health, and they had increased their respective skills.

Jonathan had gone over numerous knots and rope work, instructing his own team and anyone who was interested. He had taken his turn as lookout and rapidly improved his vessel identification skills. He had learned all the flags, but without a signal book, he would not know how to interpret the flags.

As they neared Antigua, Beck appeared. He was able to move around with sticks, but was missing the strength for unassisted walking. He was grateful that he had remained on ship. Being at sea did more good for him, or so he said, than sitting in the yellow jack infested hospital at the port. He was welcomed back to his mess. All his mess mates and those from Jonathan's mess willingly assisted him as he regained his strength.

But all cruises must end, and on the first of March they reappeared at the harbour entrance to English Harbour on Antigua. The wind gods must have been with them, for there was enough wind to allow the Mermaid to ghost in to the harbour.

As they came up the harbour entrance, Jonathan noticed that most of the ships had moved across to the near side of the harbour. The yellow flags had also disappeared.

Chapter 19
Wheelin' & Dealin'

The anchor had barely dropped in English Harbour when the bumboats appeared. It was as if they had lost business during the yellow jack outbreak, and needed to make it up. That was probably true, reflected Jonathan.

Jonathan sensed urgency throughout the harbour. There was activity everywhere. Boats were moving freely between the shore and various vessels.

The captain's gig was lowered and manned. Captain Douglas went ashore to submit his report on their cruise.

Jonathan pondered what to do. It appeared that the fleet was outfitting to sail. He would have to determine what to do about all the items he had stored in the orlop. It was very likely that the space would be needed for the new stores that would come aboard.

The clothing would not fetch much on shore or with the traders on the bumboats. The shoes would. Some of the carved plates and bowls might fetch something. The knives and marlin spikes were smaller and would be better sold to sailors who would know their value. He would start with the shoes.

Jonathan's biggest problem was not finding buyers. It was finding cash. If he found seamen willing to acquire the items he had for sale, these same sailors were like his shipmates - poor, not having been paid in months. Any vendors doing business with navy sailors knew about the lack of funds. They had therefore devised means of exchange by barter. This was fine with Jonathan, but the only goods likely to be bartered were consumables such as rum, fruits, or human flesh. Jonathan needed something small, easy to carry, and readily transferrable such as cash, small amounts of precious metals or gems. He knew nothing of gems, so he would never know if he was getting a good deal or not. Cash was the ideal.

He started looking at the merchandise carried out in the bumboats. He recognized the dealer from whom he had acquired the small silver necklace and pendant that he wore around his neck. He hailed him over and asked him about exchanging shoes for cash, gold, or silver. Jonathan showed him a pair of shoes and mentioned a price. The bumboat dealer did not have cash, or was not prepared to use what cash he had. He did know of another dealer who might be interested.

Jonathan suggested that the other dealer bring some cash tomorrow and they could make a deal. He also mentioned that he had additional merchandise that might be of interest to the mysterious dealer.

The captain arrived back with the news that the Mermaid was going north to attack the French on some island. He also said that a new draft from England had arrived. The Mermaid would get some men from this draft to help fill the vacant positions. Only landsmen would be received from the draft. To make up the shortage in topmen, any current members of the crew who wished to become topmen were to put their names forward. Jonathan knew that the existing able seamen, such as himself, would be responsible to train any of these potential topmen. The new draft was to arrive tomorrow in the forenoon watch. Stores were to come aboard starting in the forenoon watch as well.

Jonathan decided to go to sleep and get as much rest as possible. He knew he was unlikely to get much sleep in the next few days until the new provisions were aboard and stowed correctly.

The morning started slow thanks to the harbour watch routine. The water hoys and stores barges were observed being rowed out to the Mermaid as break fast was completed and the forenoon watch started.

Jonathan and his crew worked with the topmen of the main to rig additional hoists for the incoming stores. He then disappeared into the orlop and moved his bags temporarily to the lower gun deck before they became an issue.

Upon his return to the deck, he spied a number of bumboats coming out. In one he recognized the dealer from yesterday. As space alongside was limited due to the provisioning, the bumboats were well foreward. Jonathan opened a gun port and hailed the dealer. Just as soon as he nudged against the Mermaid's side the negotiations began. Over a few minutes Jonathan was able to exchange all nine pairs of shoes, a pile of ditty bags, and a number of carvings, bowls, plates, and similar items, for two and a half pounds in cash, and enough fruit and vegetables to feed his mess for a week.

By this time his trading skills had netted Jonathan a half pound profit in cash, fruits and vegetables for a week for his mess, new knives, shirts, pants, jackets and blankets for himself, and he still had dozens of slops for trade. He had tried to sell the slops, but was offered a price so low that it was insulting.

He needed to understand what the costs were for the island dealers. That was his competition. He asked around the bumboats, inquiring about the cost of canvass and fabrics on the island. Surprisingly, one of the dealers had told him, and it was twice the price he was offered for his slops.

Jonathan retreated back to the tops where others had been covering for him. He let them know that there were fresh fruits and veggies for dinner, and thanked them for covering for him.

The topmen were called to spell the landsmen while the landsmen went for dinner. The loading of provisions was to be carried on without stop. The new draft arrived just before dinner. They looked in better condition than many men on the Mermaid. No time was lost in putting them to work. They were told to drop their ditty bags and led to hoisting ropes, or to the hold, for moving and stowage duties.

From the new draft, as was expected, there were no topmen, and therefore no new members for Jonathan's mess. Jonathan, recognizing the advantages of keeping on the good side of the larboard topmen, shared some fruit and veggies with the other mess. He especially ensured that Beck was looked after because he needed to regain his strength.

Once the hoys and provisioning vessels had departed for the day, the crew stood down to a relaxed harbour routine for the evening. Jonathan sought out the new men. As expected none of them had money, and were at the purser's mercy.

The next couple of days were essentially repeats of the day before, with various provisioning occurring all day long. By Jonathan's reckoning they had at least five months provisions packed away. Even finding room to stow his extra slops was a challenge. He could imagine the problems when they had to clear for action.

He was sitting between two 12-pounders on the main deck on a sultry evening after supper when he was disturbed. A man he did not recognize told him to report to the purser. Jonathan had half expected it. He figured that he was going to be told to get rid of his extra slops as they needed the room for stores. He also expected the purser to make a ridiculously low offer to take them off his hands.

He went down to the purser's stores where he was told he could find the purser. There was another man with the purser. Jonathan knuckled his forehead to the purser, "You wanted to see me Mr. Bilbo?"

"Ah yes, Smith. This is Mr. Freckin. He is the purser from the Launceston."

"Sir," nodded Jonathan.

"Mr. Freckin has just received a draft of new men from England the same as we did. He has a requirement for more slops. He came over here to see if I would part with any of mine. I suggested that it might be possible to make a deal with you, as you had some available."

"I might be so disposed sir, if the price was right," said a smiling Jonathan.

"I told you that he has the trader's knack, didn't I?" snickered Mr. Bilbo.

Mr. Freckin began, "What have you got and how much do you expect to get for it?"

Jonathan outlined the number of pants, shirts, jackets, blankets and extra ditty bags that he still had available. Mr. Freckin was surprised at the number. He had expected that Jonathan had maybe half a dozen, at most a dozen.

Jonathan continued, "I also wish to point out that the items are already sewn, so you can charge your higher 'finished' rate."

Mr. Freckin offered an amount that was slightly higher than what the dealer had offered a couple of days ago. However, Jonathan was in a totally different position now. He had found out much more information in the past two days. He also had a plan. The plan was challenging and time consuming. It had its risks, but had the potential to be a great money generator. Jonathan was therefore in a better negotiating position.

Jonathan easily replied, "You can do much, much better than that offer, and still make a tidy profit."

Mr. Bilbo had leaned back on a barrel head and was watching the negotiation with a professional interest.

Mr. Freckin doubled his offer.

Jonathan smiled and said, "Mr. Freckin, I know the cost of canvas on the island. If you purchased canvas, you still would have to purchase thread and hire someone to sew the slops for you to match the condition that mine are in already. You have not considered the spoilage, or your time finding the canvas and the people to sew. Your offer is far below what I would expect. If you double your offer again, and then some, you will still make a tidy profit."

Mr. Freckin was taken back. Not only had he underestimated Jonathan's local market knowledge and trading ability, he had also failed to intimidate him.

Jonathan could wait out Freckin, but he decided on a more aggressive tactic. "I'll make it easy for you. Give me fifteen pounds for the items I just described, and we can put them in the boat that takes you back to the Launceston tonight. No trouble, no further fuss, assuming you have the money with you."

Mr. Bilbo's eyebrows rose in surprise at Jonathan's bold move. That surprise was reinforced as Freckin was considering the deal. This was where Jonathan knew he needed to wait.

After some deliberation, Mr. Freckin said, "You have a deal. I was not expecting to get this much, however, so I haven't enough money with me."

Jonathan smiled and offered his hand to close the deal. Mr. Freckin shook on the deal. "The items will be here awaiting your payment, sir." Jonathan turned to Mr. Bilbo, "Is there anything else sir?"

"No, that's all Smith," replied Mr. Bilbo. Jonathan turned and went back up to the deck. He was ecstatic. He had spent two pounds, and now had fifteen and half pounds clear, additional personal kit, and still had some knives and small stuff for trading.

Jonathan knew that he should be a trader. This deal just reinforced his belief. Unfortunately, he was stuck for the present time being a sailor.

Chapter 20
Getting Even

They sailed from Antigua on the 13th of March. The course was north northwest. Jonathan heard they were headed to Nova Scotia. He had no idea where that was, but heard it was north of Boston. They were the third ship in column, behind the Launceston that was trailing the Superb.

The second day out from Antigua, they commenced exercising the great guns in the morning and boarding drills in the afternoon. It wasn't long before Jonathan was sporting a number of new bruises, courtesy of Lieutenant Rylett.

Over six months had passed since Jonathan was pressed. He had filled out significantly since then. He was taller by a good six inches, heavier by a couple of stone, and muscled compared to when he came aboard. He was still lithe and wiry in stature as opposed to having bulky muscles. There were many others on board ship who were stronger, but few faster. He was poised, self confident, and aware of his strengths.

Jonathan did not hate the navy, but he was not enamoured of it either. It was a living, albeit not one of his choosing. He was grateful; however, for the opportunities that had presented themselves. He now had strengths that were unknown to him six months previously. He had new skills such as rope work, hoists, pulleys, sail handling, recognition of vessels by their sail configuration, recognition of vessel design, fighting with pike, boarding axe, cutlass, pistol and musket. In fact, he could do most tasks on board any ship except navigation. He had been introduced to supervising men, and now understood some of the challenges supervision posed. He had learned a lot about his fellow man. He had learned how to assess their strengths, weaknesses, their morale, and motivation. He had learned to give orders and train men.

He was richer in all respects: physically, mentally, financially and emotionally. He had known moments of despair. He now understood that a positive attitude was the greatest of all assets. To maintain one's spirits when being beaten down, such as he was daily in cutlass drill, required more strength, more guts, than he had ever imagined.

He was still surprised at finding gaps in his armour. The first of these was identified the third day out of Antigua. Mr. Farley came to him to check on rosters. He showed Jonathan a written list of the revised roster as suggested by Lieutenant Davis. He asked Jonathan if he had any concerns. Jonathan knew he was being consulted because Mr. Farley did not have sufficient experience to understand all the skill sets required. Just the same, he was grateful to be consulted. Jonathan was more ashamed that he could not assist Mr. Farley. He had to inform Mr. Farley that he could not read at the level needed.

Since joining the Mermaid, Jonathan had some additional time. He did not have to undertake extra duties as 'punishment' like he had on the Winchester. In his spare time Jonathan had begun to think about his life. There were things more important to him than just staying out of trouble or out of the sights of his superiors. He had been taking inventory of his skills and desires - thinking of what he wanted out of life. The Royal Navy didn't fit into the picture. While he enjoyed being a seaman, he would much prefer being a seaman on a merchantman. He also thought about trading, as he really enjoyed it. For that reading and writing would be a great asset.

He approached Mr. Farley with his desire to learn to read and write. Mr. Farley thought he should gain the skill as soon as possible, as lack of reading and writing would limit him to further promotion in the navy. While Jonathan wasn't really thinking about staying in the navy, he realized that he was stuck in it for some time. Promotion meant additional opportunity to learn and develop new skills.

He asked around to see if anyone on the larboard watch knew how to read and write, and would be interested in teaching him. He found one of the new men who claimed to know how to read and write. The first obstacle thrown in Jonathan's path was the negotiation for services. Everyone on board knew Jonathan was rich. Jonathan wasn't rich, but he was rich compared to every other man foreward of the mast. Therefore no man did anything for Jonathan for free. The price was as high as a man could negotiate.

The second problem was that there were no books foreward of the mast. Any books that might be on board were the property of the officers or mates. Jonathan was not in possession of any materials with which he could practise reading. The third problem was similar. There was a scarcity of paper and pencils with which he could practise writing. It was going to cost something to overcome each one of these obstacles.

On the afternoon watch Jonathan was in the tops. Mr. Farley ascended to check on the topmen. When checking, he rarely checked on Langtry. He generally checked the foremast first, skipped the main, and came back to the mizzen. Jonathan had the opportunity to discuss things with Mr. Farley out of earshot of anyone. He outlined his desires related to reading.

"Sir, what I really need is a book to practise reading, and something I can use to practise writing. Any help you could provide, I would be grateful for," said Jonathan.

"I might be able to come up with paper and a pencil. I'm not sure about a book," responded Mr. Farley. "They don't grow on trees you know."

"Sir, I would be willing to exchange something. I don't expect anything for nothin'," stated Jonathan. "It all depends on what I got, that is of interest to you."

"Let me think about it," responded Mr. Farley. He descended apparently deep in thought.

The next watch they had, Mr. Farley approached Jonathan. "I can provide you a pencil and two sheets of paper. I can borrow a book on seamanship, and loan it to you for a while. It's not the easiest book to read or understand, but it is something."

"Does the owner of the book know that I will have it instead of you, sir?" inquired Jonathan. Jonathan had a healthy respect for addressing senior positions after all the extra punishment he had been given for speaking to the sailmaker on the Winchester without permission. As a result he always used the proper form of address, regardless of situation.

"He's not likely to complain," stated Mr. Farley. At that comment, Jonathan suspected that the book was once the property of a now dead midshipman.

"And what will you be wantin' from me in exchange, sir?"

"I've given that some thought," said Mr. Farley. "I have to improve my seamanship if I ever hope to pass my exams for Lieutenant. I still have to serve another two years before I can even attempt the exams. I know the navigation is going to take a lot of time. I would like to get the basic seamanship now, so I can concentrate on the navigation and book-work later. That's where you come in. You know more seamanship than most seamen on board, except maybe Langtry, and your rope work is equal to the ropemaker. I want you to teach me everything you know."

Jonathan thought this was a good deal. It cost him nothing but time. He would have to do it anyway to some extent, but to teach one more was no imposition. There were two potential drawbacks however. When would the training happen? What would others think about it?

"When would this training occur, sir? What I mean sir, would it be during the watch, or during my off watch periods?" inquired Jonathan.

"We'll attempt to do as much as possible during the watch, but some off-watch training might be required," responded Mr. Farley.

"Tonight's dog watch then, sir?" inquired Jonathan.

"Yes, we may as well begin while we have the time. There's no telling what will happen once we get north," responded Mr. Farley.

Jonathan arranged for his reading and writing lessons with Jason, the new man who claimed to know how to read and write. The deal called for Jonathan to give up his rum ration every second day. By now Jonathan enjoyed his rum, the same as any sailor, but he was to forgo any rum for approximately the next month. Half the ration went to Jason. The other half he managed to place in some bottles and cork. He was careful about this because it was hoarding and not allowed. It put him at the mercy of his fellow messmates, and that he did not like.

Jonathan had listened to countless stories as a youngster, about the warmth of a nip of drink when out hunting. He figured that would apply to fighting. Had he not heard from others on both the Winchester and Mermaid, about the need for a drink before a boarding to fortify one's courage? Although it was nominally against regulations to hoard liquor, he considered his actions differently. He wasn't going to drink it himself in one night and get blinding drunk as he had seen others do. Instead he was going to set it aside and sell it. He figured there would be bumboats around wherever they were anchored in the upcoming fight against the French. He knew as well that what he was doing would be easiest while the water was fresh after they left port. After a few weeks in the water casks, there would be a greenish slime on the water and foul taste. The rum and lime mixture cut the taste and made it more palatable. He would miss the rum more at that point.

Jonathan's days became a hard, busy schedule. Sail duty, maintenance work and instruction of Mr. Farley when on watch duties. Gun drill was in the morning - cutlass, pike, and boarding axe drill in the afternoon. Every fourth day, there would be pistol drill. In the evenings he would spend an hour with Jason on whichever dog watch he did not stand, and if necessary, another fifteen minutes or more with Mr. Farley.

Working with Jason was challenging in many ways. Jason had been pressed in London. He had been a clerk for some business. He had been in a pub near the waterfront when the press had arrived. There was something that didn't seem right with him, or at least his story. It was obvious that Jason liked his bottle. He was an older man in his mid thirties. He was still out of shape even after months at sea transiting the Atlantic. He had a drinker's ruddy complexion. Normally Jonathan would never have associated himself with someone like Jason, but unfortunately there were few alternatives at the present.

The reading and writing were more difficult than Jonathan would have imagined. It didn't take long for Jonathan to refresh his previously acquired basic skills such as ability to read and print his ABCs. Trying to put the letters together to form words was where he encountered difficulty.

Jason as a teacher was another hurdle. It became apparent within the first week that Jason was intent solely on getting extra drink, rather than attempting to provide any teaching service.

Using the book on seamanship provided by Mr. Farley, Jonathan found there were dozens of words he could not pronounce, nor understand. He obviously had a limited vocabulary. He didn't even know what a vocabulary was until Mr. Farley explained.

It was a struggle. He attempted to read a page of the book each night with Jason. By the end of the page, if they even got that far, his patience and Jason's were stretched beyond belief. In spare moments he attempted to re-read pages they had previously covered. There was a slow improvement.

He had attempted writing simple sentences like, "The rope was frayed." He had used both pieces of paper, multiple times, until it was almost useless to attempt any further writing on the paper. For him, it was a challenge to put together a simple sentence. He could say what he wanted, but not get the same thing on paper. If he did, no one would recognize it.

On top of it all, there were snide remarks about his familiarity with Mr. Farley. He spoke to Langtry about this one night after the evening meal, before he had to rush to find Jason.

"There's an old sea practise called the sea daddy," explained Langtry. "There's always boys on board a ship, and someone has to keep an eye out for them. Some older men generally look after the powder monkeys. It's different when young gentlemen are involved. Generally the captain or first lieutenant will talk to a seaman and ask if they would be the sea daddy for a certain young gentleman. This way, if you speak in a more familiar tone to the young gentleman, it's not seen as crossing the line. The young gentleman gets better instruction, and his position is upheld."

"I guess I could be called a sea daddy then," said Jonathan.

"No. Because you are almost the same age as young Mr. Farley, you would not even be considered for a sea daddy. Most important, no commissioned officer has approached you to become a sea daddy. You're running a risk there. All it will take is for one of the officers to make a formal complaint. I'm surprised that Rylett hasn't made one already."

"What are you saying?" asked Jonathan.

"What's the sailor's unofficial motto?" demanded Langtry.

"You mean keep your head down, head for the shadows, out of sight is out of mind, and never volunteer for anything?" said Jonathan hesitantly.

"Yes."

"But what does that have to do with this situation?" queried Jonathan.

"Your head is up; in fact, your neck is stuck way out. You're not in the shadows. Just the opposite, everyone sees you speaking to Mr. Farley all the time, and it can't be orders all the time. The question is familiarity. The captain or any of the commissioned officers can make that call at any time, and not in your favour. Guess what happens to your neck then?" explained Langtry.

"What do you suggest I do?" asked a shaken Jonathan.

"What do you think will happen if on top of this familiarity with Farley, they also find out about your rum stash? There'd be a lot of people that'd like to see you fall. Then you'd be a target for every man with a grudge. You'd probably be wearing a striped back, and be on defaulter's parade on a daily basis," continued Langtry.

"Where do I stand with the rest of the mess?" asked Jonathan. He needed to see if he had any defenders.

"They're still not over Beck's fall. I know that Beck doesn't fault you, and you tried to prevent the fall, but you were still in charge. There are also some that think you should have done more for your mates. You made a healthy profit buying up those items from them that died of yellow jack. A few fresh meals of fruits and vegetables don't seem much. There's a few that thinks you are getting a bit too big for your britches."

Jonathan had a suspicion that Langtry was speaking of himself, for all but Beck's fall. He was a major influence in the mess, and the way he steered others would follow.

Jonathan wished he had a true friend. He had never had a close friend. He could trust some men, mess mates to a certain degree, but he could not confide in them. He wished he had that ability now.

Jonathan went off to find Jason and do his writing and reading instruction, such as it was. His heart wasn't in it. Neither was Jason's, but that had been the case almost from the beginning. Jason was in it solely for extra rum. He couldn't care if Jonathan succeeded or failed. Jason was out to milk the last ounce of rum from Jonathan that he could.

When Jonathan asked him, toward the end of their evening session, how he was doing - Jason's first comment was that they had a long ways to go. Jonathan was sure he still had a ways to go, but whether he could get there with Jason's assistance wasn't clear to him. He reckoned he needed three things. He needed help with his vocabulary, now that he understood what that was. He needed help to pronounce words in the book with which he was unfamiliar. Lastly, he needed help putting his words into writing. Words in a sentence were to him like the braids on a rope. Either they were spliced together correctly, or the thing fell apart. For this he needed a real teacher - someone that cared whether he was successful. Such a thing was not to be found foreward of the mast on this ship.

Mr. Farley seemed to care, but he would have to immediately distance himself if Langtry was correct in his reading of the situation. Mr. Farley could not protect him from more senior officers. In fact, Mr. Farley would most likely have to run for cover himself. If that occurred Jonathan would not blame him.

It may be true that Langtry was jealous of his success so far. Jonathan's 'luck' that Langtry and the others had so often made remarks about was nothing more than hard work and planning.

However, Jonathan felt there was something of merit in what Langtry had said. He had been heavily punished for his familiarity with the sailmaker on the Winchester. That had turned out to be advantageous in a way that he never thought - a silver lining - as his mother had used to say. This time however, the familiarity was more prolonged and more noticeable. If punishment was forthcoming, it would be much more harsh and brutal. The officers would use him to set the example. A striped back seemed very real in such circumstances. The offence would likely be for some other reason, but the real reason, his familiarity with his superiors, would be understood by all.

He thought this all out during the watch. In mid watch Mr. Farley approached him. He quietly discussed all of his concerns with Mr. Farley.

"Sir, I really want to learn to read and write. I would be beholden to you if you could allow me to keep the book on loan I mean. I would still do everything I could to teach you what I was going to anyway. The difference, sir, is you need to order me to do it. That way both of us are covered. No one can claim familiarity if there was orders and I complied with them," explained Jonathan.

"I understand the situation. There has been talk. Comments by Lieutenant Rylett that others are starting to listen to. From here on, it will be orders. I agree and thank you Smith," said Mr. Farley.

Later in the watch Jonathan sought out Jason. "Jason, I've decided to quit our sessions together. I'd like to thank you for your help."

"But you're nowhere near finished," cried Jason, in despair at seeing his extra rum ration disappear.

"I realize that I am just like a newborn when it comes to writing. I don't see where writings going to help me here foreward of the mast. I am just going to stop. Maybe at a later time we might resume. Besides we're not likely to have much time for the next while. We're nearing this French island we're supposed to be attacking. It's likely that things will get a bit lively around here."

Jason sputtered but there was little he could say or do if Jonathan decided he no longer had use for his services.

Things on board the ship started to change. They left the Gulf Stream and the weather got colder. It was mid April. The North Atlantic was a cold body of water in any weather, but especially in later winter and early spring. Jonathan was well prepared with his lined jackets and extra blankets. He even had a warm watch cap that he rarely took off. He was also lucky when it came to clothes. With his extra sets he could wash two or three sets on make and mend days. Drying was very challenging in colder wet weather. Other men had to put on their partially dried clothes to dry them and suffered accordingly. Jonathan did not.

The relationship between Jonathan and Mr. Farley changed, or at least the outward appearance of it changed. Orders were given and Jonathan complied. Jonathan felt an easing of the tension around him. Instead of familiarity, and its taint of favouritism, there was now strict obedience to orders. This the other members of the mess could understand. Some of their reserve began to melt.

Jonathan continued to read during half of the dog watch, albeit with difficulty, and depending upon the light. Very slowly he began to improve. He found a chapter that dealt with rope splicing and had pictures. Since he already knew the subject he made a major leap forward with this chapter.

Another change was occurring, although Jonathan was consciously unaware of it. His skill at the tasks for which he was responsible had reached a very high level. He was unconsciously able to splice, knot, check rope, move throughout the tops, furl and trim sails, as required. He never even gave it a thought. He therefore had additional time, sometimes in longer periods, sometimes in seconds, when he could observe his surroundings and those in the surroundings.

He could anticipate a change in the wind, or the upcoming roll of the ship. He could also read the people around him better. They way they moved, stood, or held themselves. The expressions on their faces, and tone of voice told him more about those around him than he had previously understood. And the more that he observed or studied the man, the better he got at reading him. The skill was valuable not only for the men working on the tops with him, but also with the officers, mates and others he could observe.

He started observing traits or habits in others, such as the scratching of the nose or stroking of the chin when in thought, the forward tilting or leaning when in anticipation, and dozens of other little telltale signals. He wondered if he had any. He was positive he had some, but was not aware of them.

One afternoon during boarding drills, it hit him. If he had traits, so did Lieutenant Rylett. What he needed to do was figure out what his telltale signals were, and what Rylett's were. Once he had discovered them, he would have to mask his intent, and use Rylett's against him. Perhaps by doing that he could get the best of Rylett, or at least reduce the number of bruises. He was sure if he didn't; it would be just a matter of time before it went beyond bruises and became broken bones or deeper cuts.

Jonathan started observing every other man he was paired-off with for any specific traits. He was looking for any traits. It was a skill that he needed to learn. He had already been doing some of it subconsciously, but now he needed to do it consciously. He needed to figure out what to check, and the appropriate counter measures or tactics to use.

He began to see the telltale signals such as a drop of the shoulder before a thrust, a glance of the eyes at the deck to ensure footing before a move of the foot in either a lunge or move to the side, or a move of the eyes to the area his adversary wished to strike. Even the breathing sometimes was a signal. A deep breath in many cases advertised a forthcoming attack. Jonathan had been subconsciously reading all of these. And subconsciously, he had a standard set of moves to counter them. If he was going to defeat Rylett, then he needed to read Rylett's telltale signals, if any, and make new defences. To survive, he also needed to learn his telltale signals and use them to deceive Rylett, or others.

Learning Lieutenant Rylett's telltale traits was not easy. It required many more bruises. The man was fast - lightening fast. The man controlled his eyes better than anyone that Jonathan had so far encountered. And his shoulder never announced anything that Jonathan could discern. Jonathan did notice a number of very minor things. Firstly, Rylett was a true fencer. He was not a brawler. Secondly, he never fought in close proximity to anyone else. Thirdly, the deck where he fought was always clear and Rylett usually checked it before engaging. Fourthly, his strength was in his wrists, not his arms like most of the men. Rylett generally used a sword rather than a cutlass. The sword was lighter, and potentially more brittle, although since they were using wooden training swords that difference was not evident. Fifthly, Rylett knew he was damned good. He was perhaps overconfident. In these practise contests that was alright. It might not be in the real thing.

In one practise session, Jonathan glanced down at the deck himself before he lunged. As he lunged he saw a smile on Rylett's face. Jonathan realized, as he was struck solidly in the solar plexus, that he had telegraphed his move, and Rylett had read it correctly.

Jonathan went down on one knee with the strike. He stayed there for a bit longer while regaining his wind. Jonathan noticed that every time he had made a lunge, Rylett took a step backward, and moved his sword to a point in front of his left shoulder. Since Rylett was right handed, this covered his entire front. All he had to do with Jonathan's lunge was sweep back to his right to deflect the blade to the right of his body. Once this deflection occurred, he was inside Jonathan's guard. A simple lunge and Jonathan was defeated.

Jonathan wondered what would happen if he lunged, but pulled his lunge. If Rylett was to sweep right, Jonathan could then engage his sweep from Rylett's left. He would be inside his guard. Once inside Rylett's guard what strike could he achieve? He would have to extend his left leg for the initial lunge. There wasn't enough time to back up, and lunge again. He didn't think he would have the balance and reach needed to strike the torso, but what about Rylett's right leg? It would be forward because of his step back and preparation for the left leg lunge. What about going for the area just above the knee? A lunge was risky, so it was safer to slash the inside of Rylett's right leg just at or above the knee.

Jonathan had his plan. He regained his feet. He shook his head. He looked at the smiling Rylett. With a grim determination he went to the on-guard position. They commenced parrying. No opportunity presented itself before Jonathan was subjected to yet another hit, this time on his upper left arm. They started again. After a few strokes, Jonathan took a deep breath and started an attack. Since he had telegraphed it, he received the counters that he expected. But he still had the initiative. He deliberately glanced to the deck and back at Rylett. He then stamped forward in a classic lunge. But just as soon as he extended his sword, he pulled it back. Rylett saw the forward motion of the foot and sword, and having just seen Jonathan glance at the deck, swept his sword to the right, across his front to deflect the expected lunge. Jonathan then extended his sword again and helped Rylett's sweep along. When he determined he had deflected Rylett's sword sufficiently, he moved his own sword in a quick vicious slash that connected with the inside of Rylett's right leg just very slightly above the knee. The effect was immediate. Rylett collapsed to the deck in a howl of pain. He dropped his wooden sword and grasped his knee.

Jonathan dropped his sword to his side. "Are you alright, sir?" asked Jonathan. It was all he could do to contain himself; to not jump up and down and shout with joy. After all those bruises, to see Rylett howling in pain was sweet revenge.

All training activity around them had ceased. Everyone was looking at Rylett. There was no sympathy. They had all seen the pain he had inflicted on Jonathan. Many had seen the bruises that Jonathan carried.

Lieutenant Caharty came forward from the quarterdeck to see what was happening. As soon as he saw it was an officer on the deck he ordered, "Everyone stand fast." He quickly went and bent over Rylett.

Jonathan had a suspicion of what was coming. He was already in his shirt, as he had been sweating heavily from the practise. He decided that if Rylett wanted to charge him with striking an officer, then he would fight with everything he had. Jonathan rapidly took off his shirt. His chest and arms were a solid mass of yellow, blue, and purple bruises.

Caharty was about to shout at him to remain immobile. When he saw the sword on the deck at Rylett's side, the sword Jonathan still held, and all Jonathan's bruises, he held his command.

"Lieutenant Rylett, were you engaged in cutlass drill with Smith here?" asked Lieutenant Caharty.

"Yes, he struck me. He was supposed to check his strike, but intentionally didn't," cried Rylett. "I want him charged with striking a superior officer."

At this point the captain appeared on deck. He immediately saw one of his officers on the deck in obvious pain. "Call the surgeon."

"Mr. Caharty, I believe you have the deck. Can you tell me what has occurred here?"

Lieutenant Caharty replied, "Sir, boarding drill was being conducted as per you orders. Lieutenant Rylett was engaged in cutlass training with Smith here. It appears that Smith got inside his guard and struck him on the inside of his right knee. Lieutenant Rylett claims that Smith intentionally did not pull his strike."

"Smith, what do you have to say for yourself?" demanded Captain Douglas.

"Sir, I was engaged in cutlass training with Lieutenant Rylett. Sir, Lieutenant Rylett is an exceptional swordsman. I finally got inside his guard today. My strike was no harder than any I received. My sole intent sir was to defend myself from Lieutenant Rylett's offence and hopefully improve my capabilities," said Jonathan. The last time he had spoken directly to the captain, he had been shaking like a leaf. Now he was scared, but pissed that Rylett was trying again to drop him in shit. He held himself at attention, showing off his bruises like a badge of honour.

All the while this was going on the surgeon had arrived, and was examining Lieutenant Rylett. He checked the bones for breaks, and manipulated the knee.

"Mr. Longstreet, what is the prognosis?" demanded Captain Douglas.

"Sir, the skin is not broken, there are no bones broken, and there is full mobility in the knee. Lieutenant Rylett will have a bruise I'm thinking, but that is all. I'll need to take a look at Smith to see if he has any broken ribs," replied the surgeon.

"That will have to wait. Master-at-arms, I'll see Smith in my cabin," stated Captain Douglas.

There was a murmur from the deck as the crew mutedly expressed their displeasure.

Jonathan had been watching Rylett. As soon as the captain had mentioned that he would see Jonathan in his cabin, a sly smile broke out across Rylett's face. When he realized what the captain said, his jaw dropped in amazement as he shifted his gaze to the captain. Captain Douglas however, was looking where Jonathan had just been looking - at Lieutenant Rylett's face.

The master-at-arms approached Jonathan. Jonathan looked at him with resignation in his expression. He grasped the wooden sword by the blade and handed the butt to the master-at-arms.

When Jonathan entered the captain's quarters, he immediately saw the captain seated behind a table. The captain's face was somewhat in shadow due to the light coming through the aft windows. It was difficult to read his expression.

Jonathan was still without his shirt, so he was getting a chill, especially with the drying sweat. Add the fear from being brought to the captain's quarters by the master-at-arms, and it was all he could do to mask his trembling.

Captain Douglas sat there contemplating Jonathan, and possibly what he was going to say. The longer he kept silent, the greater the fear rose in Jonathan. Lieutenant Caharty was announced by the marine sentry at the door.

"Sorry I'm late sir, it took longer to hand over the duty to Lieutenant Dunkin than I thought," stated Lieutenant Caharty.

Still the captain did not say anything. The tension in the room was palpable.

Finally, the captain said, "Smith this is the third time you have been brought to my attention since you joined this ship, just before Christmas, as I recollect. That's as often as some of my most notable defaulters." He paused at this point, and then continued. "And each time, it appears that Lieutenant Rylett has been the officer who has brought my attention to you."

"First it was negligence. Next it was familiarity with a superior. Now it is striking a superior, commissioned officer. It would appear that your actions are increasingly more threatening to my command and authority. What do you have to say for yourself?"

"Sir, with respect to the first incident, ordinary seaman Beck fell because he was rushing in compliance with an order from Lieutenant Rylett. It was not negligence on my part. We were complying with the order to speed up, even if I disagreed with the order. As for the second, this is the first that I even was aware that there was an accusation against me. I don't even know who I was supposed to be familiar with sir. As for the third incident sir, Lieutenant Rylett and I were completing cutlass drill. Every time we have cutlass drill, Lieutenant Rylett chooses me to be his adversary. Today, I managed to get inside his guard for the first time. I struck him no harder than he has struck me in any other practise. I wish Lieutenant Rylett no harm, sir," explained Jonathan.

"Lieutenant Caharty, what do you have to say in this man's defence?" asked Captain Douglas.

"Sir, able seaman Smith is one of the best topmen we have. His work is excellent. I have him instructing other members of his watch in rope work and sail handling. Even the ropemaker respects his work. With respect to the incident of Beck falling from the tops, I spoke with Beck and he admits that it was his fault for not properly ensuring his grip. He also says that Smith tried to warn him, but he heard him too late. With respect to the second issue about familiarization, I did see Smith work on a number of occasions with Mr. Farley. On each occasion he was showing Mr. Farley some point of seamanship. I did overhear Mr. Farley order Smith to show him the correct method to splice a rope. There was also a direct question from Mr. Farley about the location of some ropes. Smith responded to these as any sailor would. With respect to this incident, most of the deck saw Smith and Lieutenant Rylett in cutlass drill. Several men saw Lieutenant Rylett strike Smith so hard that he was floored. Smith did strike Lieutenant Rylett on the inside of the knee, but as no bones were broken, and the skin wasn't even broken, I would venture that the strike was no harder than the strikes borne by Smith. I must also point out that there are more strikes for a long period of time against Smith, and not once has he complained, or gone to the surgeon. I regret having to say this sir, but it would appear that Lieutenant Rylett has a grudge against Smith for some reason."

Captain Douglas stroked his chin as he pondered what action to take.

"Mr. Pearly, take Smith down to the surgeon, and have him looked at. Then report back to me with Smith at the end of the first dog watch," said Captain Douglas.

"Sir," barked Mr. Pearly.

"About face, forward March!" snapped Mr. Pearly at Jonathan.

"Mr. Caharty, my respects to Mr. Rylett. Would you ask him to present himself, instantly, sir?" snapped Captain Douglas at Lieutenant Caharty. Lieutenant Caharty paid his respects and rapidly departed. He found Rylett in his cabin on the deck below and conveyed Captain Douglas's orders.

Lieutenant Rylett went into the captain's quarters after being announced. He hobbled in. It was unclear whether he truly was injured or if he was playing on the captain's and others' sympathy. If he was playing on sympathy, he had sorely misjudged everyone. Every officer knew that he had struck Jonathan repeatedly much harder than normal practise. He had gotten his just rewards as far as the officers were concerned. As far as the men were concerned, what he had received from Jonathan today was just a down payment.

What was said between the captain and Lieutenant Rylett was unknown, despite the eavesdropping of numerous individuals. What was known was that Lieutenant Rylett came out of the captain's quarters as white as a ghost. He also had nothing to say to anyone about his discussions with the captain.

As the end of the first dog watch approached, Jonathan got a twisting, tight feeling in the pit of his stomach. He ventured up on deck. He had spruced himself up as best he could under the circumstances. He had clean slops, and was wearing his elaborately sewn jacket. He had washed his hair, face and body as well as possible.

As the bell for the end of the first dog watch rang, Mr. Pearly marched Jonathan back into the captain's quarters accompanied by Lieutenant Caharty.

The captain was seated as he was before, but this time, his face was more visible.

"Smith, after investigating this afternoon's incident, I am inclined to say that it was simply a training injury that Lieutenant Rylett received. I will caution you; however, that there will be no future similar strikes against any of my officers. Is that clear?"

"Yes sir."

"You've been aboard the Mermaid for about four months. In that time, you have become known to virtually every man and officer aboard this ship. That's not common, unless you are a troublemaker. That has me worried. What surprises me is what you have made of yourself and others. According to officers and men alike you have good seamanship skills. You have used these to train others. From what I hear, you're not a drinker, you don't shirk work, and you're the richest man aboard. I don't want to see you in front of me again for the remainder of this cruise. If I do, I will ensure that you are no longer the richest man, and I'll put some markings on your back that will put those bruises to shame. Do I make myself clear?"

"Very clear sir."

"Dismissed."

Jonathan about turned and fled from the captain's quarters.

Chapter 21
Canso

On the 23rd of April during the morning watch, the ships arrived at Canso. Although he had no idea exactly where Canso was at the time, Jonathan later learned that Canso was on the mainland of Nova Scotia, at the furthest north-eastern point. It was apparently close to the French-held port of Louisbourg.

From what he had gathered, Canso was a transhipment place. It had been established years before by New England merchants operating fishing fleets to the Grand Banks. Fishing fleets from New England went out in the spring and summer to fish on the Grand Banks. Once they had a full load, it was faster to stop in Canso and off load the fish. They could then head back out to get more. About fifty years before, they had used Louisbourg for this. That was no longer possible, as Louisbourg had been given to the French in some treaty agreement along with the entire island of Ile Royale. Since that treaty, the New England fishing fleets had been using Canso.

Jonathan was in the tops. A spectacle like he'd never seen presented itself before him. Lying quietly were dozens, perhaps scores, of ships of all descriptions anchored offshore of the land mass to their larboard side.

Canso itself, or what Jonathan could see of it, was a number of scattered homes or cottages near the shore. There appeared to be a crude dock facility for smaller vessels. On the shore, were what appeared to be extensive fixtures or racks for drying fish. Also near the shore there were a few larger buildings, presumably warehouses or storage facilities for items prepared for shipping.

On the slopes well back from the water were rows of tents. Groups of men were in various stages of drilling on the flattest parts of the land. There were hundreds of them. As far as Jonathan could tell, few of them were in any uniform that Jonathan could readily identify, and certainly not the lobster red of the British regular army.

This was the invasion army from the colonies south of here, about which he had heard rumours. There were a great number of them, but he didn't see any horses or oxen to pull wagons or carts. For that matter, he didn't see carts or wagons. He didn't see any cannons although he assumed they were present somewhere.

Jonathan continued his scan. A cooper's facility was there; at least, he supposed it was a cooper's hut based on the number of barrels and casks nearby. Jonathan speculated on the process. The fishing vessel stopped here, and offloaded their catch. Then the vessel would either head back out, or perhaps give the crew a day or so of rest before heading back out. The fish would be cleaned and dried on the racks located along the shoreline. When dried, the fish were salted and placed in barrels or casks. Then they were likely hoisted on board coastal traders for shipment down to Boston or other points. That would explain some of the smaller vessels.

Those fishing vessels working the Grand Banks or other fishing locations would return to Canso once they had a reasonable size catch. The residents on shore would be responsible for handling the cleaning, drying, salting and packing processes. The smaller coastal traders would haul away the fish, and bring in needed supplies such as salt, metal for cooper's hoops, food and drink for the crews and residents.

The rest of the ships in the anchorage were transport ships for the troops, cargo ships for their supplies, and armed sloops to protect them.

On the other side of the anchorage was an island with what appeared to be a fort. According to comments he heard from the quarterdeck, the name of the island was Grassy Island. Since there was a lot of grass and few trees on the island, the name seemed appropriate.

Although there appeared to be heavy forests well back from the coast, Canso looked bleak. Snow was still visible near the tree line. Jonathan couldn't imagine what it would be like living in this place over the winter.

They had barely arrived and hadn't yet dropped an anchor, when a longboat headed out from the shore of Grassy Island to the Superb.

Jonathan kept his observation a full 360 degrees, although he had to admit the more interesting view was what he could see toward both shores. He remained in the tops as lookout mainly because he was interested in the view. He could have had another man stay there, but he was dressed with a warm jacket, so there was little discomfort.

About half an hour after they arrived, Jonathan observed a sail to the southeast headed directly toward them. He hailed the deck and let them know of the sail. After some minutes he was able to identify the sail configuration as a square rigged vessel, probably a fifth or fourth rate in size. At this point he could not see any flag or identification marks.

Slowly over the next few minutes the ship came hull up. He had been correct in both the configuration and size. The vessel was a design that was British in origin, but not quite the same as the Winchester or Mermaid. It appeared marginally bigger. He observed a British flag, but could not identify any other markings.

The ship turned a couple of points to the north before tacking into the anchorage area. When she turned Jonathan saw her numbers and called them out to the deck. She was HMS Eltham (44).

It turned out that the Eltham was from Boston where the Winchester was supposedly stationed. Jonathan idly wondered if any of her crew knew anyone from the Winchester that Jonathan might know. He was interested to find out how his old shipmates were doing.

After the Eltham arrived, all the captains were called to the Superb for a conference. The ships were still moving as the signal to drop anchor had not yet been received from the flagship. After the captain left, Jonathan dropped down to the deck. Ever since receiving the captain's threat, Jonathan vowed to stay away from him as far as possible. He had succeeded so far and intended on keeping it up.

As he moved from the mizzen toward the waist he nodded to Dickerson, a master's mate. He had spoken to him a couple of times, and found him friendly. It was from Dickerson that he had received much of the information about Canso's location.

For the moment, the quarterdeck was virtually deserted as everyone was at dinner. A man was watching for signals. All the commissioned officers and the master had disappeared below decks. Dickerson waved him over. He quickly showed him a chart and pointed out Nova Scotia, and where Canso was located. He then pointed out Ile Royale, which was French territory. Then he pointed to a small indentation in the coast toward the northeast corner of Ile Royale. "That's Louisbourg, their main port and military base. That's where we're heading."

Jonathan said thanks and scampered away before anyone took him to task for being on the quarterdeck.

The captain returned after a few minutes. He barely made it aboard when the flags were raised on the Superb to prepare to get under way. The captain's gig was rapidly hoisted on board. Jonathan returned to the mizzen tops with his topmen.

Sails were let loose, sheeted home, and they were underway. Next stop was Louisbourg.

Chapter 22
Blockade

Dawn on April 24th, year of our Lord 1745. After a night of easy sailing the crew of HMS Mermaid stood by their guns as per the captain's standing orders. As night changed to day the nearest ships in line could be seen. HMS Launceston was forward and HMS Eltham aft. Then the Superb, forward of the Launceston, came into view.

Jonathan was called away to the tops with his men. As he reached the tops he noted the land mass to their larboard side. He guessed that somewhere to larboard and ahead was Louisbourg.

Jonathan finished the work he had been sent aloft to complete. He then took a seat in the tops to see what he could discern of the land.

He used an observation technique taught to him by Pollard on the Winchester. He started in the far distance looking from right to left. This was opposite to the way he read. It meant that his eye movements across the landscape were slower with the result that he could pick out differences more readily. After he completed his sweep of the far distance, he shifted closer to the middle distance. After that sweep, he changed to the immediate front. He did this at each major point of the compass, starting with directly in front, then to starboard, then aft, and finally larboard. Each sweep had some overlap with the previous sweep, so the observation ensured that nothing within sight was missed.

After his 360^0 sweep was completed, Jonathan concentrated on the larboard area to see what he could make of the land.

There was white in the forests, so all the snow had still not melted. There was no apparent snow in open areas. Obviously the sun had melted all areas except those areas in shadow. Given the lateness of year, it indicated that either the sun was very weak in strength, or that there had been a heavy snowfall during the past winter. It struck Jonathan that perhaps it was a combination of both. There was a chill in the air. He imagined that it was probably worse on shore.

In the middle distance, he could see sheets of ice between the ship and shore. These sheets of ice looked dangerous. It appeared that sheets of ice had broken apart, drifted inshore, and crashed together. This left gaps in some spots, and ridges of upturned ice in others spots. For a wooden ship ice was a danger, so Jonathan was glad that the Mermaid was well seaward of it.

Jonathan was so intent on his observations shoreward that he failed to see the signal flags raised on the Superb. Although it was not his responsibility, he was chagrined, because he prided himself on spotting and understanding these signals as well as the signals team.

All four ships were continuing on to the north. Jonathan looked to the trim of the sails. They looked fine to him. He remained in the tops observing. They had been moving only a few minutes when Jonathan saw the coastline change. The coast seemed to pull back into a small bay. As they got closer, Jonathan saw some small islands. On the far side of the islands, he observed more water. The space between the islands looked shallow and very narrow, except for the two islands that were more seaward.

Over the next few minutes, they came abreast of these islands, and Jonathan could see a good passageway into the bay beyond. The bay would provide excellent shelter from wind from any direction. The bay was clear of any ice that he could see, but the entrance appeared blocked by sheet ice.

On the farthest point of land into the passage on the northeast side was a stone lighthouse. On the southwest side, there were the roofs of buildings visible. Some of these were very large buildings. Other fortifications were apparent, but at this distance Jonathan could not get a clear look. This was Louisbourg!

Other signal flags were raised on the Superb. Although Jonathan did not know the codes being used presently, he could guess. His guess was that Mermaid would be blockading the harbour. It was a good guess.

Jonathan had heard from others that blockading was one of the more boring duties that a King's ship could be engaged in. Days or weeks without any change in routine were the norm, perhaps interspaced by moments of extreme activity when someone attempted to break the blockade. The worst part was the blockade had to be maintained in all weather. In this case, if there was a storm and the wind shifted to the east, they would be sailing on a lee shore. In Jonathan's opinion, not a very exciting prospect. He could also imagine working the tops in this colder weather while in a storm.

Today started a trend that was to change very little over the next few days and weeks. The four large ships were to cruise back and forth across the mouth of the Louisbourg harbour entrance. They needed to be close enough to catch anything coming out of the harbour, but had to be far enough away to be outside the range of the coastal cannon.

As they cruised in closer to the harbour entrance passage, Jonathan was able to see a number of French positions.

As far as Jonathan was concerned, the French had chosen well for a harbour to defend. From what he could see, the shores all around were rock right down to the water. Further back between the sea and the forests, it looked marshy.

On the finger of land that extended from the southwest side of the harbour mouth was a battery of cannons. A further group of underwater rocks extended out from this finger, past Battery Island, blocking over two thirds of the harbour mouth. Battery Island was well named, because the French also had cannons in placements facing directly seawards and additional cannons facing the harbour passageway. There were two islands seaward of Battery Island. The farthest out was called Green Island. A smaller island between Green Island and Battery Island was called Rocky Island. Both Green and Rocky Islands were surrounded by offshore rock formations.

On the other side of the harbour entrance passage, was the stone lighthouse. Since there were no roads to Battery Island, Jonathan supposed that the troops were stationed there on a semipermanent basis and all transportation was completed by longboat. While he didn't know their daily routine, he reckoned the life of those men stationed on Battery Island was probably more miserable than duty on blockade.

He had no love for any Frenchmen. He'd never even seen one up close. He could however, relate to being penned up in a small confined area for months at a time with only work to look forward to. Jonathan at least was moving, and the work was more challenging. Just imagine only having to work a cannon, with nothing else to do! And to have a port within viewing distance, but not able to get to it! At least a farmer or a fisherman could come and go. His rewards would be the direct result of his toils. The harder he worked, hopefully, the more he would be rewarded, although Jonathan knew that was not always true.

The blockade had to cover the entire width of the harbour entrance. If a vessel master knew the waters around the harbour entrance, he could avoid the main channel, run between the islands, and shoot out to sea to the south.

The blockade was intended to keep all vessels in Louisbourg. This meant that even fishing vessels attempting to come out to fish were to be intercepted and taken. The reason for this was to limit the food supply and reduce the morale of the garrison and residents.

The blockade also had a second purpose. That was to keep any outside vessels from getting into Louisbourg. It was rumoured that French vessels sailing from France could be expected to bring supplies into the colony. These supplies could be very harmful to British purposes if they included shot, powder, or additional troops.

For the first few days they had ice working for them, as it prevented any ship entering or exiting the harbour, even though the harbour was ice free all year round.

Every time the Mermaid was in the southern portion of the blockade sweep, Jonathan tried to make out as much as he could about the fortress and town of Louisbourg. From the distance, he couldn't make out if the town was inside the fortress walls, or if it were separate from it. It looked like the walls were all around. On the seaward side these walls started just at the back of the beach. There were a number of angles or outward projections of the walls. From these angled portions fire would cut into the sides of any attackers. Jonathan could imagine trying to get over those walls while being subjected to fire from three sides concurrently. When he considered this, Jonathan was grateful he was a sailor, and not a soldier ordered to storm those walls.

What looked like a church steeple was visible. It was on a long building. The building appeared to be of some masonry construction. He would have figured wood would be more plentiful, but after looking again at the number of rocks on shore, maybe stones were more plentiful. He didn't think the steeple was actually a church, primarily because of the length of the building. The steeple also seemed to be sited toward the west side of the town. He figured a church would more likely be in the centre of the town.

It was obvious that the French had built strong fortifications, and permanent buildings. They were not interested in leaving. This meant a good fight.

Jonathan wondered how many troops the French had, and what numbers had come up from the colonies to oppose them. It was something to think about as he disappeared below.

The next morning, as per the captain's instructions, everyone stood by the guns. There was a heavy fog this morning. Extra lookouts were sent aloft. Captain Douglas was worried that it was excellent cover for a vessel attempting to break the blockade.

Unfortunately, the fog was thick and extended to heights greater than the mastheads. The masthead lookouts therefore were no better off than those at deck level. Extra lookouts were sent to the bow to warn if Mermaid was in danger of ramming anything. These were typical precautions in a fog.

As long as the fog continued, the crew remained standing at the guns. Captain Douglas did not take chances. At any time a vessel could appear through the fog, and the Mermaid would be defenceless unless the guns were manned.

Shortly before two bells in the morning watch the unexpected happened. An unknown ship ghosted out of the fog on the starboard side. She was a brig, pierced for seven guns on her starboard side, as she was coming towards the Mermaid. No flags were visible. The bodies that could be seen wore civilian clothing, the same as any merchantman. The only indications that she was not part of the blockade force were the quick orders shouted at the helmsman, which were distinctly French.

Captain Douglas screamed to open fire, but the guns were not loaded. Even before the order to load could be completed, the brig had tacked out of sight in the fog. The order to fire the forequarter of guns was given anyway to alert other vessels in the blockade that a blockade runner was about.

No observation of the vessel was again made by the Mermaid, although it can be readily stated that every man on board was certainly looking for her. The fog did not dissipate as the day continued. Captain Douglas stood the gun crews down, but had two guns loaded on each side for signals, and in case another opportunity presented itself.

The comments in the mess at the noon meal were largely concerning the loss of prize money. During the afternoon watch, cannon fire was heard to the south, or at least it was believed to be the south, as sound in fog is very difficult to locate.

From the sound of the fire it sounded like two ships were exchanging fire. This turned out to be the case, although Jonathan did not learn of it for another two days. The sloop Massachusetts spotted the same French ship sighted by the Mermaid. Because of the warning by the Mermaid, they were better prepared. They opened fire and scored some hits on the French brig. The French brig returned fire. The Massachusetts lost a man. The French brig managed to slip past them into Louisbourg.

The disappointment and boredom began to mount. Several smaller cruisers had accompanied Commodore Warren from Canso. These ships were fast and had a shallower draft than the Mermaid or the other larger vessels. They were able to work closer inshore. As a consequence, they were able to spot any fishing vessel or blockade runner before the larger ships working further out. A couple of smaller French vessels were captured as a result.

Jonathan and all others of the Mermaid's crew could feel nothing but jealousy and disappointment when they watched one of the smaller Colonial vessels pass shepherding a captured vessel. It wasn't loss of the prize money so much, for the captured vessel would not amount to much. It was the excitement, the sense of doing something important.

April ended and May began. The ice surrounding the coast had melted or drifted off. The pattern for the blockade was repetitive. One or two larger ships would stand in closer to the harbour entrance. The other two larger ships would stand out to sea and range along the coast to deter any ships potentially coming from France. There were no known French cruisers on this side of the Atlantic, as Louisbourg was the only ice free port the French had in Canada.

Captain Douglas ordered the Mermaid in closer to the harbour entrance. It was a tempting target for the French gunners, and they engaged.

Jonathan was in the tops. He heard a whistling rushing sound he had never heard before. He had no idea what it was. Then he saw water splashes on the Louisbourg side of the ship. Shortly afterward he heard the distant boom of cannon. He investigated by looking at Battery Island. He saw a number of small red flashes and smoke around the red flashes.

The rushing sound was much louder this time. He saw a brace line part and a black orb pass through the topsail below him. 'Christ!' he thought, 'they're firing at us. Those are cannon balls, and big ones!'

Jonathan had been in the navy almost eight months and this was the first time he had come under fire. It was a revelation. His thought process was short-lived however, as the orders were shouted from below to restore the shot-away brace.

Jonathan sent Abbot down to fetch rope. He pulled the parted line up from above. He took a good look at the line. It was faster to repair the line by splicing the two separated parts together than attempting to run a complete new line. When Abbot returned with the line, Jonathan completed a splice. He then ensured the repaired line was rigged properly. He barely noticed that more shots had passed around him as he completed his work. He was more interested in getting the job done, and holding on so that he did not fall.

After the Mermaid pulled out of range, further work was required. The holes in the topsail had to be repaired, and other lines needed to be checked. A ball had passed between the mizzen shrouds and cut a ratline that now needed to be repaired. There was some work foreward as well for the other tops.

Jonathan saw the irony in that action. He had wanted some action, some excitement. He had got it for a brief second. As a result he then had a lot of additional work. He wondered if it was always like this.

Jonathan reflected on his being under fire. He had not been scared. In fact he had been more surprised that anyone would even want to shoot at him. After the initial surprise, he had been too busy to even be scared or worry about things. Odd!

As the days wore on, it was their turn to hand over the inshore duties to the Launceston. She did not show up as expected, so the Mermaid stayed on station. A day later she showed up. As she came close, Jonathan could see her grinning crew. Virtually everyone could hear the communication passed between the captains.

"Ahoy, Mermaid. My apologies for being tardy," shouted the captain of the Launceston. "A French sloop was sighted and we gave chase."

"Any luck?" shouted Captain Douglas.

"Molineux, Fame and the Eltham were involved as well. We were finally able to box her in. Molineux was able to engage, and took her. She was the Marie de Grace (14) out of Granville destined for Louisbourg with supplies. A nice prize, but she won't amount to much for the Molineux with so many of us present."

"Something's always better than nothing!" replied Captain Douglas.

"Anything happening at Louisbourg?"

"Been quiet since you been away. Only activity was Battery Island taking pot-shots at us," joked Captain Douglas.

"Any word when the rest are coming?"

"Nothing yet," shouted Captain Douglas. By this time the ships had passed each other and further conversation was impossible.

Mermaid stood out to sea to the north. They spent the remainder of that day and the next patrolling far off shore.

The morning of the second day standing out to sea, they were heading toward Louisbourg from the south. It was first light, and they were standing to the guns. The wind was fluctuating, so Jonathan was called away into the tops.

As the light increased he had a great view seaward to the east. The light silhouetted anything in the east while the Mermaid was still in the darkness. Unfortunately, the horizon was empty. As they closed on Louisbourg and the sun lighted the distant coast, Jonathan saw something different. He called to the deck at the same time as the main lookout. He let the lookout give his report. There were many ships at Louisbourg. The reason it had looked different was that the sails were furled, and masts only were present.

The spectacle slowly became visible over the horizon where it could be seen from the deck.

Below him, he could hear muted comments from the gun crews, even though they were still standing by the guns, and silence was supposed to be maintained. No one it appeared, including the officers, had seen the likes of this armada before, at least not on this side of the Atlantic.

On shore, in the far distance some movement was observable, but not readily identifiable. There were tents set up. It appeared that large bodies of troops were ashore, at least by the number of tents that Jonathan observed. Some longboats were discharging cargo at shore's edge.

In the middle distance, the invasion fleet was anchored. Jonathan could see land on two sides of the fleet. There was some kind of bay, but there was no harbour. The wind at present was from the west, coming directly from the land, so the anchorage was currently very sheltered. In a storm there would only be minimum protection. It would be especially dangerous if the wind shifted and came from the east. It would put the fleet on a lee shore, the worst of all possible conditions.

He spent time looking at the various ships. There was nothing like a little practical experience to help differentiate between different ship types and sail configurations. If they stayed in this general area for a while, he might be better able to train his men on ship recognition. Unfortunately since the fleet was anchored, the sails were furled and he could not achieve the same training level on sail configuration.

The vessels themselves were a mixed lot. There were full rigged ships, brigs, schooners, snows, brigantines of all sizes. There were a few fishing boats. Jonathan could not understand why they might be here, except perhaps to fish for food for the troops on shore.

It appeared that virtually every vessel had some type of gun mounted. The cargo vessels appeared to have just swivels, while there were others that were fully outfitted as cruisers. He could see one vessel, a snow, pierced for seven guns on her starboard side, and another ship pierced for twelve on the visible side. All of the heavier armed vessels were situated on the periphery of the anchorage, while cargo ships were closer to shore. From those ships that he could see clearly, he was surprised by the number of swivels that were mounted.

From Jonathan's limited knowledge of maritime warfare, it would appear that the outer ring of armed ships was situated to ward off any threats from the sea, rather than worry about shore bombardment. Of course with troops already ashore, there should be no need to fire shoreward.

One good thing about the arrival of the fleet was that additional stores for the blockading ships were now available. Mermaid resupplied from a cargo vessel. It was the only change in the routine for the entire week.

The harbour blockade was being accomplished using layers or rings. The inner ring closest to the Louisbourg harbour entrance was maintained by colonial vessels. These vessels were faster, had shallow draft, and had equivalent armament to most French ships trapped in the harbour. Further out, the inner ring was supported by Royal Navy line-of-battle ships. And finally, at significant distance off shore were the patrols.

The Eltham was sent off to raid other French settlements to the north. Some of the colonial armed sloops were dispatched to ensure any French settlements to the south were taken. These armed sloops also had the task of protecting the respective northern and southern flanks. There were still a number of French sloops and schooners about.

While the Eltham was absent, the three remaining heavy ships, the Mermaid, Superb and Launceston maintained the blockade with two ships on the inner blockade and one ship providing the outer patrol.

Finally, Mermaid was ordered to stand out to sea to assume the outer patrol. Rumours were that a French fleet from France was due any day. Mermaid was to scout for this fleet. If a fleet was coming, then larger French battleships might be encountered. That was the reason for sending the Mermaid, as opposed to smaller colonial vessels.

To Jonathan, the only difference in being on the outer patrol, compared to being closer to the harbour, was that there was less to see. They could not hear the news or see any captured vessel if it was brought in.

May dragged on. The monotony continued with little relief in sight.

Chapter 23
Pursuit

Dinner was piped on 30 May. Jonathan was sitting with the rest of the mess nursing his rum, having just finished his dinner. There was little conversation. There was no news, so there was nothing new to discuss.

There was patchy fog with a light breeze from the west. The ship was on a starboard tack heading south. There was limited motion and everyone was relaxed. They were bored.

In the quietness, they heard the call from the masthead lookout, "Deck there, sail on the horizon, off the larboard quarter."

Jonathan got up. He knew the officer of the watch would be reporting to the captain. If the orders were given to investigate, then the watch would be called away. He was on the afternoon watch. He rapidly drank his remaining rum, jammed his mug into the mess bag and started moving toward the deck. Jonathan was not alone, for his actions had telegraphed his intentions to the other members of his mess who were on the same watch.

He had no sooner reached the deck when the orders, "Call the watch," were given by the officer of the watch.

Jonathan increased his pace and swung up onto the mizzen shrouds. He climbed all the way to the masthead.

He looked for the sail on the larboard quarter while listening for orders from below. Finally he saw it. The sails looked big, even at this distance.

"Deck there, French warship, larboard quarter," shouted Jonathan before the mainmast lookout could report.

Jonathan's report galvanized the quarterdeck. The order to investigate was given and further orders to alter the course and the trim of the sails were passed. At the present, most of the work was accomplished by slacking the braces on the starboard tack and running before the wind. Jonathan therefore took a long look at the sails, before they changed their angle and his sight line was obscured by the main or more fog.

"Deck there, by the look of her sails, I'd venture she's a large vessel, 4th maybe even a 3rd rate," shouted Jonathan. He noted that Mr. Farley was now at the main masthead with a glass.

Both ships closed on each other. The drifting patches of fog hindered observation. The fog was low. The mastheads were generally clear.

Captain Douglas was taking no chances. He ordered the topmen to remain in the tops and the rest of the crew cleared for action.

Finally both ships entered a clear patch. They were hull down to each other. There was no doubt of the intruder's identity. She was a French man-of-war. She was a lot bigger than the Mermaid. She made clear her intensions when her bow-chasers fired at the Mermaid.

Captain Douglas ordered a change in course to west southwest - back toward Louisbourg. Jonathan thought it made sense. This Frenchman was too big for the Mermaid alone, but there was plenty of help at Louisbourg.

As the Mermaid tacked, Jonathan realized that he was being given a front row seat, as the mizzen was now the closest mast to the Frenchman. He rotated to get a better view of their pursuer. He was able to count the gun ports on their starboard side as the Mermaid swung around. There were thirty including those on the poop. That made her either a sixty two or sixty four gun ship because there were at least two bow-chasers. He wasn't sure if there were stern guns or others that he hadn't seen. "Deck there, I count sixty two guns, although she may have more," shouted Jonathan.

Jonathan saw the flash. Momentarily he felt the air move as a cannonball whipped past him. He had been told by gunners that the French tried for the rigging of vessels. They tried to dismast or cut enough rigging to knock their adversary out of control. Then they would come in to rake the ship prior to boarding.

Given that the balls were passing him, he wondered about getting behind the mast. At least he would have the mast between him and the ball. He started to shift his position. Then he thought about it. If the ball hit the mast it would possibly go right through the mast. The mast wasn't as thick at this height as it was near the base. Even if it didn't go through, it might cause the mast to snap and fling him off the top. Even if he missed the deck and hit the water, the Mermaid wasn't going to stop to pick him up. If the ball hit the mast and it didn't break, it might splinter and still fling him off the top. Then he would still have the fall, only with one or more splinters in him. After some consideration, he figured it would be better to go fast with a direct hit, so he stayed where he was, to the side of the mast.

The French ship continued to fire their bow-chasers. They always shot high. They hit sail, and occasionally a rope. Jonathan kept his men checking ropes after each salvo had passed. When a rope had to be repaired, he forgot about the balls being fired at him. He was more concerned about hanging on and getting the rope repaired.

Over time the rate of fire from the French ship slacked off, but did not stop. The trajectory of the balls was lower. Either the Mermaid was increasing the distance between the two ships or they had lowered their sights. After a good look, Jonathan figured it was both. The distance between the two ships had increased marginally. It was as if Captain Douglas didn't want to lose them, and was drawing them in - but not close enough to harm the Mermaid.

The chase went on for over four hours. Jonathan could see the coast in the far distance. He could not see directly ahead, so he had no idea if the anchored fleet could be seen. There were still patches of fog, so possibly this obscured the fleet.

The course was altered. The Frenchman's bow-chasers fired again, but this time the mark was off slightly, possibly because of the subtle alteration in Mermaid's course. The Mermaid barrelled into a more dense fog patch. When she popped out the other side, the anchored fleet was hull up. The flags 'Enemy in sight" were hoisted. The Shirley, which was on the periphery of the anchorage, was the first to respond. She headed for the Mermaid.

"Bring her about," ordered Captain Douglas. "Stand by your guns."

The Mermaid came about, and headed directly for where the Frenchman was expected to appear. Once the sails were trimmed, Jonathan and his mizzen topmen rushed to their guns.

Popping out of the fog, the Frenchman took one look at the number of ships anchored there, and then a second look at the number of ships heading for them. The Superb, Launceston, Massachusetts and Eltham were now responding as well. The odds had distinctly changed for the worse, so the Frenchman turned tail and ran.

Captain Douglas had been expecting this. He manoeuvred the Mermaid as best he could and got in one broadside before the Frenchman disappeared totally into the fog. The Frenchman fired a partial broadside at the Mermaid, but had little success. The shots went through the rigging, not hitting anything important.

Jonathan worked the guns after firing, helping to reload and run out the 24-pounder again. He was then called back to the tops.

They were through the fog patch and back to clear sky. The Frenchman was within range to their front. Captain Douglas ordered the bow-chasers to engage. The Shirley came barrelling through the fog. She was running well, but the larger vessels had more legs.

At this time of year, daylight lasted until almost two bells in the first watch. That left about three hours to take the Frenchman before darkness.

The Superb and Launceston were coming up well. The Eltham was coming up as well, but was some distance to the rear. The Eltham had been farther away to the north when the Frenchman had come upon the fleet.

Somewhere between midway and the end of the last dog watch, the Massachusetts and Shirley dropped so far behind they could not be seen through the fog patches.

The Mermaid's bow-chasers kept pounding away. The transom of the Frenchman was heavily battered.

"Elevate your sights. An extra spirit ration if you can knock out her mizzen," said the captain. The entire crew was energized. After hours of having balls fired at them, they were keen on returning the favour to the Frenchman. They could smell prize money in the wind.

The bow-chasers fired again. They didn't hit the mizzen, but they did kill the men on the wheel. The Frenchman slewed to the larboard as the Frenchman fought to regain control.

The Mermaid surged ahead, not varying her course. Jonathan raced from the tops to man the guns.

"Rake her," shouted Captain Douglas.

The larboard guns were already loaded, and run out. As each gun came in line with her stern, the gun captains heard "Fire". The majority of the stern of the Frenchman disappeared in smoke and splinters as ball after ball smashed into her from eight 24-pounders on the lower gun deck, eight 12-pounders on the main deck, and three 6-pounders on the quarterdeck.

"Bring her about to starboard. We'll try to rake her again from starboard. Double-shot the guns," ordered Captain Douglas.

Jonathan rushed over to the starboard guns. As he was the second gun captain, he was in charge of the opposite side guns when both sides were in operation. Since they were still working the larboard guns, his was the responsibility for the starboard at the present.

It was quite a task to load the guns with double-shot with only half the crew. The training and eagerness of Jonathan's reduced gun crew overcame any potential problem that might have occurred.

They had barely run out by the time the Mermaid was around and heading back toward the Frenchman. The Frenchman could see it coming and was attempting to come around so they could bring their broadside to bear on the Mermaid. They had to be hurting after the broadside Mermaid had fired into their stern.

The Frenchman got part way around. Their stern was protected, but they could only bring some of the rear guns to bear as the angle was too great on the forward guns. Only a couple of these rear guns fired.

Jonathan felt the hits against the Mermaid. He couldn't tell exactly where the hits were, but they sounded and felt higher up, possibly on the upper gun deck.

The lower gun deck was silent, waiting for the order to fire. Jonathan's ears were ringing from the discharge of the last broadside. He sighted the gun, using a lower gun port on the Frenchman's side as an aiming point. He motioned for the gun to be traversed as the angles changed as the Mermaid steadily advanced.

"Fire," screamed Lieutenant Caharty.

Jonathan touched the slow-match to the touchhole. He jumped back and arched his back to get out of the way of the recoil. This was the first time he had ever commanded a gun in action.

The recoil was arrested by the ropes. Jonathan pressed his thumb over the touchhole and the wet sponge was inserted. The gun hissed. Jonathan was glad he had the leather over his thumb, because he could still feel heat. He hadn't heard the load order, so he turned and shouted, "What's the load sir?"

"Wait," shouted back Lieutenant Caharty.

Since he was waiting, Jonathan ventured a look at the Frenchman to see if he could see where his shot hit. The Frenchman was not visible through the gun port, only open water.

Jonathan, even though his ears were ringing, could hear the thunder of another broadside. Obviously someone else was firing, but who? He felt no strikes against the Mermaid's hull, so it was doubtful if Mermaid was the target.

"Standby to board," screamed Lieutenant Caharty.

Jonathan ran to the weapons barrels. He grabbed a tomahawk and pistol. He stuck the tomahawk in his belt. He checked the pistol, loaded it and lowered the flintlock so it wouldn't discharge accidentally.

"Boarders to the main deck!" came the order, but it was not clear who had given it.

"Upper gun deck larboard 12-pounders only, load canister over grape. Boarders standby larboard," shouted Lieutenant Davis.

Jonathan looked to larboard. The Mermaid was coming up to the aft starboard quarter of the Frenchman. He saw what was left of her name 'Vi__lant_' as they closed. One by one, the 12-pounders were fired to clear the deck area of any Frenchman. To Jonathan's eyes, they looked terribly effective.

"Grapples away," shouted Lieutenant Davis.

"Heave!"

The two ships nudged together, then, "Boarders Away!"

With the pistol in his right hand and his left hand used for grabbing a handhold to lever himself over onto the Frenchman's higher deck, Jonathan boarded his first French vessel. At first there was little resistance. As Jonathan scanned the area in front of him, a number of men came charging from the waist toward him and the other Mermaid boarders.

Jonathan cocked his pistol, levelled it at the second man who had a pistol, and pulled the trigger. The man was thrown backward by the force of the ball hitting his upper chest. A second and then third pistol shot was heard. Another two men within the group dropped. They impeded the rest of the charging group.

Jonathan screamed, "Ahhhhhhhhhhhhhh," as the battle lust descended upon him. He grabbed his pistol by the barrel in his left hand, and dropped his right hand to the tomahawk in his belt. He pulled the tomahawk out and flipped it up so his hand grasped it near the base of the handle. All the while he was moving toward the Frenchmen. A pike was jabbed toward him. With the pistol he knocked it to his left, and stroked downward and sideways with the tomahawk into the exposed right knee of his opponent. It wasn't a hard blow, but it was enough to lay the leg open to the bone. The Frenchman screamed and dropped the pike as he grabbed the knee with his hands. It was the last move the Frenchman ever made, because the next stroke of the tomahawk caught him on the side of the neck. He dropped in a spray of blood.

Jonathan screamed again, "Ahhhhhhhhhhhhhh". The next face he saw took one look at him and visibly cringed. He backed up and this probably saved his life. The blow Jonathan had aimed at his head with the butt of the pistol dropped him instantly in his tracks. Another pike lunged toward Jonathan. He barely had any room to move, but was able to get the tomahawk on the inside of the pike and deflect it to the right. It still grazed him as it went past. Jonathan thrust the pistol butt forward and hit the pike-holder in the nose. The pike-holder lost his focus when hit. Jonathan dropped his pistol and grabbed the pike with his left hand. He had to turn sideways to do this. He lowered the tomahawk, and swung underhanded with everything he had. The tomahawk entered the man's chest below the breastbone, and continued upwards where it stuck.

Rather than waste time trying to extract the tomahawk, Jonathan just stepped into the man. He screamed, "Ahhhhhhhhhhhhhh," and pushed the dying man backward with all his strength. The men behind were unable to move forward. In fact they were off-balance and were driven back. The dying man fell, face upward.

Looking at their shipmate with blood spraying from a chest with an embedded tomahawk, and looking at a demented, screaming, blood-soaked apparition in front of them, first one man then the remainder dropped their weapons and shouted for quarter.

In the meantime Jonathan had placed his foot on the dead man and levered the tomahawk loose. He looked up for his next victim.

Jonathan felt a hand on his shoulder. "Steady mate, they're surrendering."

Jonathan looked around trying to focus. The hand on his shoulder steered him over a few steps and pressed him down. He sat on an overturned gun carriage. Others were passing him as they rounded up the Frenchmen.

"I think you should go see the surgeon," said the voice. "Here, put your hand here and press." Jonathan's tomahawk was pulled from his hand and his hand was moved to his side. He felt blood flowing from his side. There was pain, but he had felt worse pain.

"Put your arm around my shoulder," said the voice. Jonathan complied. He was assisted to his feet. Slowly they made their way to the ship's side, and then over to the Mermaid. Extra hands assisted him all the way to the surgeon.

There were others already there. He didn't have to wait long before he was lifted to the surgeon's table. His shirt had been cut off. He looked down. His right side had a straight cut where the head of the pike had passed too close.

A surgeon's assistant mumbled, "Bite on this." A piece of leather covered wood was jammed into his mouth.

The surgeon pushed him to his side. He was none too gentle. He then started probing the cut. With each probe, the pain shot through Jonathan like a searing poker. Finally the surgeon said, "Looks clean enough. Sew him up." One of the surgeon's assistants then started sewing him like he was just another seam to stitch in a jacket.

Once finished, he was pushed and pulled back to a sitting position. A bandage was wound around him. He was pulled off the table to make room for the next unfortunate. He was led over to the side of the ship and assisted in lying in an elevated position. A blanket was draped over him. As he waited for the pain to subside he dropped off to sleep.

He woke up shivering. He moved his left hand up to his forehead. He was not sweating, so it was not a fever; at least, he didn't think so. He was just cold. He called out. After some time, a surgeon's assistant showed up. Jonathan said he was cold, wanted a couple of blankets, and he was hungry.

Within the next thirty minutes, he received blankets and a piece of bread. When he finished his bread he got a ration of rum. Wrapped in blankets, fed, and with rum-induced warmth flowing through his chest, he dropped off to sleep again.

When he woke again, he had no idea of the time. He knew he had to void his bladder in the worst way. That was probably what woke him up. He shakily rose to his feet. He was weak, probably from the loss of blood. He was mobile, however, and slowly climbed from the orlop to the jakes to relieve himself.

As he passed through the lower gun deck, he noticed that hammocks were slung and men were asleep. Once on deck, he saw that they were in the anchorage. He could see little evidence of battle damage. Then he realised that it was sunlight and no watch was on deck. He wondered why.

He was cold without a shirt or jacket, so he kept the blanket wound tight around his upper body. He decided to head back down and get some more sleep.

Jonathan awoke again in time for dinner. He rose and started to move to the stairs, but was intercepted by the surgeon's mate.

"Where you goin' mate?" asked the surgeon's mate.

"First, I'm goin' to use the jakes. After that, I'm goin' to find myself a new shirt. Then I'm going to see about something to eat," replied Jonathan.

"Best wait for the surgeon, mate," replied the surgeon's mate.

"When is he likely to be here?" asked Jonathan.

"After he finishes his dinner more 'n likely," replied the surgeon's mate.

"So he can eat while I miss my meal. Doesn't sound too fair to me," said Jonathan as he brushed past the surgeon's mate and headed up the stairs.

After hitting the jakes, and pulling another shirt from his ditty bag, Jonathan joined his mess mates. His rations had already been drawn the day before. He therefore claimed back his portion from everyone, because they had already divided up his ration.

Jonathan was very hungry. He ate his dinner portion, and took additional bread from the bread barge, soaked it in his rum, and consumed that as well.

"Who's on the afternoon watch?" inquired Jonathan.

"Starboard."

"Good, I have to go back down and see the surgeon."

"When are you likely to be fit for duty?" asked Beck.

"I'll wait and hear what the surgeon has to say about that. They sewed up my side like a seam on some sail. No fine stitches like Hale can do," joked Jonathan.

That drew a chuckle from all of them because they knew that Hale was the worst at sewing in the mess. Jonathan departed back to the orlop and the surgeon's sick bay.

Jonathan managed to arrive back in sick bay before the surgeon reappeared. When the surgeon did arrive, he found Jonathan sitting up and being examined by the surgeon's mate. The dressing around his wound had been removed. The wound was closed, the stitches working correctly, and there didn't appear to be any infection. The surgeon checked Jonathan's temperature. No sign of fever was present.

"You'll return to light duties forthwith," said the surgeon.

"Aye, sir," replied Jonathan. He had no desire to be in the surgeon's care for a second longer than necessary.

The surgeon's mate wound a new dressing around his wound. Jonathan pulled on his shirt. He recovered his ripped shirt and left.

Once Jonathan returned to the lower gun deck, he went to his ditty bag. He pulled out his sewing kit and a clean pair of slop pants. He sewed the shirt back as best he could, considering its condition. He went to the main deck and dipped a bucket over the side for seawater. He washed his blood-soaked clothes as best he could, using what soap he had. Others on his watch were doing the same. When his clothes were washed, he placed them on a 12 pounder to dry. The heat from the metal was the fastest dryer that he knew, even faster than wind.

Before the first dog watch began, he reported to Mr. Farley, and told him he was ready for light duties. He was informed that he would be temporarily going over to the Vigilant to assist in her repairs. Since he was on light duties, he could repair rope and sails on deck.

Jonathan went below, grabbed his jacket, and stuffed some hardtack into his pockets, as he figured he would miss the evening meal on board.

Jonathan helped row over to the Vigilant. As he neared the side of the ship, he looked down to see if he could identify the gun port that was his point of aim. He wasn't sure but it looked like the fifth port down from the bow. If it was, there was a large open area between it and the sixth gun port.

He was the second last man to climb up from the longboat. He had asked another to stay behind him in case he had any difficulty getting up the side. It was a slow ascent, but by taking his time he did not strain any stitches.

Once on deck, he was directed to an area near the forecastle to work on ropes. Most of the ropes he was working on were parted by shot. He sat and spliced rope after rope throughout the watch.

He requested, and was given permission, to go to the lower gun deck to check the damage that he had wrought. After checking, he wished he had not gone.

When he got to the lower gun deck there were still blood splatters everywhere - evidence of the destructive nature of the broadsides. On closer inspection of the hole between the fifth and sixth gun port, he found that the interior of the entire bulwark was compromised. There were in fact two holes, overlapping. These balls had torn the interior wall apart and sent splinters everywhere. Some splinters were embedded in the deck, the overhead beams, even in the trucks on the overturned gun carriages. He didn't even want to think of what impact they had on the men that serviced these guns. The blood pools on the deck and the blood splatters overhead were sufficient evidence.

A man he had never seen before approached him. The man had a grim face. "Not a pleasant sight, is it?"

"No, I'm glad that I wasn't standing here when those shots hit," replied Jonathan.

The other man looked at him, "While I don't wish any good for any Frenchman, they deserve everything they get; I pity the men that stood here."

Jonathan nodded, "I don't recognize you, are you from the Mermaid?"

The other man offered his hand, "Jubal McCain, out of the Fame."

"Jon Smith, Mermaid. You're the first colonial that I've spoken with. Where are you from?" asked Jonathan as he grasped the other man's hand.

"I'm from a little place in Massachusetts you've likely never heard of. I signed on with the Fame in Boston."

"What's Massachusetts like? What did you do before this?" asked a very interested Jonathan.

"I'm a farmer. My wife and son are workin' the land while I'm here," replied Jubal.

"I don't understand," responded Jonathan. "If you have a farm, why go to sea?"

"The farm's not that big and real money's scarce outside of Boston. They're paying wages for the crews of the armed vessels with the prospect of prize money as well. That's something that I can use. Maybe I can get me a team of horses and a better plough."

"Sounds like my folks, always one step away from starvation. The difference is that at least you own your land, or so I have been led to believe?" inquired Jonathan.

"Sure, I own the land. Had to clear it. Still need to clear a lot more. To clear it I need either horses or oxen, and that's where the cash comes in. Once it is cleared, then I need to plough and seed it. That takes a better plough and money for it. You gettin' the idea why I'm here?" grinned Jubal.

"Yeah."

"If you're from the Mermaid, were you in on this?"

Jonathan nodded. He was both ashamed of what he had done to the Frenchmen, and proud of what his ship had accomplished. The pride won out. "We out-sailed her, our gunnery was better, and when we boarded her they couldn't stop us."

"So you got some prize money comin'," suggested Jubal.

"More 'n likely," responded Jonathan, "but with Superb and the others within sight, the prize money will have to be divided up between everyone. I doubt that I'll see much from it." It was the first time that Jonathan had even considered the prospect of prize money. It was something he could talk about when he got back to the mess.

They were about to start a further discussion of Massachusetts when someone apparently in command shouted over at them, "What the 'ell do you think this is. You're supposed to be workin' not flapping your lips."

Jonathan nodded to Jubal and returned to the upper deck.

Chapter 24
Louisbourg

The repairs on the Vigilant for which Jonathan was responsible were finished after a couple of days. A crew comprised of men from the Fame, Caesar, and Molineaux went on board and continued other repair work. French prisoners from the Vigilant were loaded into the empty berth spaces on the Fame, Caesar and Molineaux. Once loaded, these three vessels set sail for Boston.

Captain Douglas was gone, promoted to command the Vigilant. A new captain, Captain Montague, read himself in and Mermaid continued cruising off shore.

After a few days of light duties, Jonathan attempted work in the tops. He was very careful of his side, and made no sudden moves. He did some stretching that he was surprised to find greatly assisted his ability to move and work freely.

As he came down from the tops on the afternoon watch on June 5th, he was called over by Mr. Farley.

"Smith, collect your kit. You're going ashore for a few days," said Mr. Farley.

"Sir?"

"Apparently, the colonials need some help with longboats. Each ship has been ordered to provide two men experienced in longboats. You're one of the two selected."

"Who else is going, sir?" asked Jonathan.

"Wilson from the starboard watch," replied Mr. Farley.

"Just what am I supposed to be doing once I'm there, sir?" asked Jonathan.

"I don't know. What I do know, is that your name was put forward to the captain by Lieutenant Rylett. Just watch yourself," responded Mr. Farley.

"Thanks for the information, sir. When are Wilson and I supposed to leave, and how are we supposed to get to wherever we're supposed to be goin'?" asked Jonathan.

"A boat will be by presently to pick you up. Go get your kit and stand by."

"Aye, sir." Jonathan headed down to the lower gun deck, grabbed his ditty bag, then went to the bread barge and grabbed some bread that he stuffed in his pockets. He then headed back on deck to wait.

After some time an approaching boat was hailed. It came alongside and picked up Wilson and Jonathan.

The boat had also picked up a number of men from various ships. It threaded its way through the shipping anchored in the bay south of Louisbourg. Finally it headed to shore.

The surf was present, but negotiable as they came in to the shoreline. The shore itself was rocky, and Jonathan thought it a lousy place for an amphibious landing. It had one good point. It was close to Louisbourg, so they didn't have far to walk.

After being on a ship for the previous few months, Jonathan encountered difficulties walking on land. The land seemed to be rolling, and his balance was 'off' accordingly. He noticed that he wasn't the only one. Wilson was having the same challenges, as were some other men from other ships.

A man beckoned them, and they followed him up the slope, through some woods, and then into a camp area. As it was getting dark, Jonathan did not gain a very great appreciation of the land. His orientation was also off somewhat due to his time at sea.

All the men gathered around. The man they had been following pointed out the latrines, the cook tent and some tents in a row. "Those tents you can use tonight. In the morning, get your grub at the cook's tent and meet back here at seven. I'll explain what's happening then."

Jonathan, having been at sea for an extended period was used to short hours for sleep. Rather than sleep, he decided to make the best use of the night. He and Wilson found a tent and prepared for the night. Jonathan was far ahead of most of the seamen. He had blankets in his oversized ditty bag. Most seamen had nothing.

It wasn't too long before Jonathan became aware of the greatest enemy he was likely to encounter that night - the relentless mosquitoes. "Close the flap and keep it closed," someone muttered. "It'll keep most of them out."

The first men had grabbed the first places near the entrance. They were to regret that. Jonathan and Wilson were about two thirds down the length of the tent, so the mosquitoes that did enter had ample targets before them.

Jonathan took a couple of bottles of rum from his ditty bag and put them in his jacket pocket. He then put the jacket on, as it offered good protection from the mosquitoes, and left the tent. Being reasonably at home in the woods, he marked the location of the tent, so that he could find it again. He began his search for customers. He wasn't too long in finding them. A couple of rows of tents away a group of men were sitting around a fire. He joined the group. "I'm new here, what's the situation?"

"Where you from?" asked a man.

"Just came in off a man-of-war. I haven't set foot on land for months, so I'm a little out of touch. That is why I'm asking," responded Jonathan.

"We got the Frenchmen bottled up in Louisbourg. Built us some breastworks on them low hills overlookin' the place. Got our cannon in place and bombarding them. Them Frenchmen are stubborn, and haven't quit yet, but I expect they will."

"I saw the walls from seaward. They look formidable," ventured Jonathan.

"That they are. I, for one, ain't in any rush to be goin' over them. But be a trustin', we'll take 'em," replied another.

"Just out of curiosity, what does a man do for drink in this place?" ventured Jonathan.

"We've been here for over a month. If you had come earlier, you might have had a little taste of corn, but for the last while, water's all we got. I figured that you navy fellas had lots of rum, and maybe you could share a little," quipped another.

"I don't know of any rum that's for sharing, but I might know where a little might be gotten a hold of for a price," ventured Jonathan.

"And what price might that be?" ventured another.

"What's the going price for a spiced rum in a tavern where you come from?" idly asked Jonathan. That got a good discussion going, because the prices differed somewhat depending upon the size of the mug, and the place from where the men originated.

A couple of prices were quoted, but one man said, "It don't matter what the prices are; no one here has two pennies to rub together."

Jonathan had considered this. It still was a let-down. He had taken a number of risks. If it didn't pay off, then he would consider himself foolish.

"What about something to trade? Something that could be turned into cash?"

Several offers of knives, and tomahawks were made. Jonathan already had a number of knives, so he was not interested. The tomahawks were of a local manufacture. The boarding axes he had used were better. A set of buckskins was intriguing, but he had no idea where he would wear such clothes. It looked like he had the same problem as on board the ship. High and willing demand but no means of payment that was suitable.

An older man approached Jonathan. "I got something that would probably interest you, but I ain't gonna trade it for no drink of rum."

"What are you offerin'?" demanded Jonathan.

"Come with me," said the older man. They disappeared into the tent lines. After passing a number of tents, the man stopped and entered a tent. He lit a candle and beckoned Jonathan inside.

Jonathan was very cautious entering the tent, in case there was an ambush awaiting him. He found the tent empty, but for the older man.

"This here's what I got," said the older man. The man pulled out a metal orb with a chain attached.

"What is it?" asked Jonathan. He had never seen anything like it. He had seen something similar on the Mermaid when he had arrived, when he was timed. But that orb was in a wooden box and was considerably larger that this object.

"It's called a pocket watch," replied the older man. It ain't workin' at present. Maybe you know someone that might be able to fix it."

"That's an officer's watch. Where did you get it?" demanded Jonathan. The last thing he wanted was to trade for some stolen item that, if found in his possession, would result in his being charged with theft.

"When we took the Frenchman's Royal Battery, we were able to liberate some things. I took this off a dead French officer so's you don't have to worry about the owner comin' lookin' for it," chuckled the older man.

"What are you willing to trade for?" asked Jonathan.

Jonathan took the watch in his hands and turned it over. It was a nice looking piece, but not working, as indicated by the older man. He pulled out a bottle of rum and handed it to the older man. The older man pulled the cork and took a small taste.

"That's good stuff," he said, as he returned the bottle to Jonathan. "But I ain't gonna part with that pocket watch for no bottle of rum."

"What about three bottles?" asked Jonathan.

"Not by half," replied the older man.

"So you're saying that for six bottles like this one, you'd be willing to part with that watch?" said Jonathan. He could sense the deal.

There was no sound from the other for a long period. Jonathan was trader enough to wait until the other man either agreed or counter offered. "Agreed," said the other man.

Jonathan and the older man shook hands to seal the deal. "Alright, I need to find my way back to where the rum is protected then I'll be back."

Jonathan opened the tent flap and checked around. He saw no one, so he exited and slipped through the tent lines back to his own tent. He went to his place, found his ditty bag, and put five additional bottles in his pockets and beneath his belt. This would leave one bottle in his ditty bag and another in his pocket after he had traded for the watch.

He exited his tent being careful to observe the surrounding area, and looking for anything suspicious. He used his woodcraft knowledge from his poaching days to ensure his safety. He even took a different route back to the older man's tent, and waited outside in the rear of the tent listening for any suspicious sounds. After a few minutes of hearing nothing, he went to the front and whispered. The older man opened the flap. They exchanged items, shook hands, and Jonathan slipped out again.

Although he chose a different route back to his tent, they were waiting for him. He had taken the time to place the watch in his money belt and put a rock covered in cloth in his pants pocket.

He wasn't sure how many actually jumped him. He saw three, but there may have been a fourth. He sensed them before they rose around him. His senses gave him a split second to prepare. His preparation was to draw his throwing knife in his right hand and his regular knife in his left hand.

What he hadn't reckoned on was the fact that at least two of them were holding sizable sticks. He ducked the one on the right, and slashed with his knife against an exposed arm. He felt the knife strike, and heard a gasp. The man with the second piece of wood was able to hammer him high in the forehead. The force of the blow knocked him over backward.

A leg appeared on his left. He slashed with his knife and struck flesh and bone. He rolled to his right, and just missed getting struck by another person attacking from the rear. As he continued to roll right, he rolled directly into the man on the right. He jabbed at the man's thighs and felt the knife graze cloth and possibly flesh. The man fell over the top of Jonathan as he kept rolling to his right.

Jonathan was acting on instinct. Stars were still flashing intermittently in his eyes from the blow to his forehead, so he was having a challenge clearly gaining any detail.

He raised himself to his hands and knees and prepared to lunge. He saw or sensed movement to his right, and lunged in a crouched motion toward the shadow. He collided head on with someone. Since he was crouched, the contact point was at the waist level.

When he hit the body, he simultaneously drove inwards with both hands. Since each hand was holding a knife, both ripped into soft flesh.

The body grunted, first when Jonathan struck him, and then as the knives ripped a muted scream tumbled from his mouth.

Both of them crashed to the ground, Jonathan on top. He rolled left this time, twice to make sure he was away from the man he had just dropped. He found himself beside a large tree, rose to a squatting position, and scanned the area to determine where the next attack was forming.

The attackers were withdrawing or limping away. Jonathan saw or sensed no immediate threat.

Jonathan drove the blade of his regular knife into the ground, left it there, and used his left hand to check his body for cuts. He also checked to make sure he had not dropped or lost anything. The only wound was a scrape and tender area on his forehead. Everything else was as it should be. His wound from the Vigilant battle was hurting, but not bleeding. He was even surprised that after rolling on the ground, the pint of rum still in his jacket pocket was unbroken.

As there appeared to be no further movement toward him, Jonathan grabbed the knife stuck in the ground, rose and retreated back behind the tree. He then turned and ran through a number of tent lines. When he considered himself reasonably safe, he turned and walked cautiously up a tent line until the end.

After some orientation, he finally made his way back to his tent. He went back to his kit, pulled out blankets and a kerchief. He bound the kerchief over his head, ensuring his forehead was covered. He took the rum out of his pocket. He took a good pull from the bottle, rolled the blankets around him and fell asleep.

It was a long and blessedly peaceful sleep. He rose in the morning, completed his ablutions, and reported to the cook's tent before seven to eat. He was one of a very few sailors who had any kit with which to eat. As sailors, they were normally issued a mug, bowl and utensils. These were property of the ship, so most sailors never carried their own. When the sailors arrived at the cook tent, they had nothing in which to put their food or drink. Jonathan was well prepared in this regard, as he had his engraved wooden mug, a pewter plate and bowl. He therefore dined in style. He loaned Wilson one of his spare bowls, for which Wilson was grateful.

The topic of conversation around the cook tent was about a fight that had occurred the night before. Three men were wounded in the fight, one seriously. Jonathan innocently asked what the fight was about, and who the men involved were. All anyone seemed to know was that the wounded men were from Boston, and known troublemakers. As to the cause of the fight, no one had heard.

After eating, they cleaned and stored the plates and utensils. They were ready for whatever was coming. They didn't have long to wait.

Chapter 25
Night Action

An officer in a red uniform appeared. Jonathan wasn't sure what rank he was because it wasn't evident from any markings on his uniform. Another individual mustered the sailors together.

"You are here because you are seaman experienced in handling small boats," stated the officer in red. "We have lots of men willing to row, but not many know how to steer in the dark and land on shores through this surf."

"What's going to happen is that we are going to split you into boat crews. You will, I believe the term is coxswain the boat. There will be an officer in the boat to lead the men once ashore, but you will be responsible to get the boat to the location in the dark, and land the men without capsizing. You may be under fire when this occurs."

"This morning, and this afternoon if necessary, you will practise your boat crews so they can row and follow your commands. Late this afternoon we will show you where you are going tonight. After dark we will launch you on your way. Any questions?"

"Sir, it is common practise in boat action to have at least one boat carrying a small cannon or swivel. This provides extra firepower, or fire suppression to keep the enemies' heads down while we're assaulting, or to give us cover between the time we disembark from the boat and the time it takes to reach the objective. Will there be any swivels or cannon on any of the small boats?" asked Jonathan.

"No. We hope to take them by surprise."

A boat crew was detailed for Jonathan. They were all men from Massachusetts, and a willing lot. Their officer was one of them, only he had been elected as their officer. This was very novel, and Jonathan relished the opportunity to discuss things with these men. Given the task ahead however, those discussion would have to wait.

Once they had been assigned a boat, the first chore for Jonathan was to determine their relative strengths. Each man rows at a different rhythm. This rhythm needs to be harmonized to work as a team. Jonathan's assessment would result in each man being assigned to the most appropriate position in the boat. Unfortunately, to determine their strengths he had to assess their rowing ability, and that meant they had to be afloat. That meant that they first had to get through the surf. Not an easy task for a crew that had never rowed together before.

They man-handled the boat around, so the bow was facing seaward. Next, Jonathan assigned men to various rowing positions. With the boat still firmly stuck on the shoreline, he assumed a position and showed the men how to go through the complete rowing motions. While this seemed silly, he had seen that if the proper instruction is first given there could be no excuses if someone didn't perform correctly.

He also explained the two most challenging evolutions in rowing a small boat - getting through the surf inbound and outbound.

With basic instruction complete, he aligned them and they heaved the longboat out into the surf. They then scrambled in, with the first two pairs of rowers holding the boat steady, while the remainder scrambled onboard.

They then headed out to sea. The surf was moderate, and they were able to keep the boat steady on the way out.

Jonathan deviated once at sea, and headed to a larger merchant vessel. As he approached the vessel, he called out to see if he could get a piece of oiled canvas, or oilskins as they were commonly called. That was about as waterproof a substance as could be found on a ship. Since the requested piece was small, the merchantman was willing to oblige.

While the crew was rowing, Jonathan took out his watch and wrapped it carefully in the oilskin. He then put the small bundle back in his money belt.

As the morning progressed, he made a number of changes in the alignment of the boat crew and had them rowing easily. He made multiple inbound and outbound journeys through the surf. Both his confidence in the crew and the crew's confidence grew. At about two bells in the afternoon watch he headed in for the last time. He broke the crew for dinner, and proclaimed that they were ready for the work this evening.

After eating, he reported to the officer who had mustered them. He stated his crew was as ready as could be expected given the amount of training that they had. He was told to stand down until called. Jonathan proceeded to his tent and snoozed as it was likely to be a long night.

At the end of the first dog watch, Jonathan and the other boat commanders were called. The objective for tonight was Battery Island. The crews were being told separately.

Jonathan was under no illusions. Battery Island had fired on the Mermaid. They had lots of guns, and although their shooting had not been overly spectacular, the closer you got the more accurate they were likely to be. They were going to be heading directly at the island. If there was no surprise, and the French were ready, it would be hot work indeed.

Discussions about the best place to land, and the route to Battery Island were discussed. The best place to land was on the southwest side closest to Louisbourg. The French had a landing jetty installed at that location. Unfortunately the jetty was out of the question. It was under observation and covered by direct fire.

Likewise, the northern and southern coasts had cannons sited. In the case of the northern side, the guns covered the harbour entrance passage. In the case of the southern coast, the guns faced seaward. These were the ones that had fired on the Mermaid. That left the eastern side. This side was not covered by direct fire, but that was because there were numerous rocks and heavy surf. The surf on the southern and eastern side was always heavy because the waves rolled in directly from the North Atlantic.

The best place to land, given the surf, was from the northeast. Other issues needed to be considered as well, including the position and state of the moon.

The weather was near perfect. With little wind, the seas were barely running. This was great for the movement to the island. As for the moon, it was in the second quarter, with some cloud cover.

Fog was a double edged sword. While it would cover the attackers, it would make finding Battery Island nearly impossible. The boats weren't issued with compasses, so some visibility would be needed. No one knew if fog would be present.

It was finally decided to row in two stages. The first stage would be from the anchorage to Lighthouse Point. The second stage would be the attack from Lighthouse Point to Battery Island. The landing place would be on the north northeast coast of the island.

At dark, they mustered at the boat. They all had their weapons. Jonathan had a musket issued to him with powder horn and a bag with two dozen balls and wads.

On his command the boat shoved off, and they began the attack.

The first stage went well. The crew stroked easily. Jonathan did not need to say much as they crossed to Lighthouse Point. They drifted at Lighthouse Point until all the boats were accounted for.

The command finally came to move. This was it.

The first boats played follow the leader. While this ensured that few were lost, it also meant that only one boat would hit Battery Island at a time. If the enemy was waiting, each boat would be targeted as it came in, with deadly results. Jonathan urged his crew on a track parallel to the lead boat.

He took a glance behind him and saw that other boats had fallen in behind his boat.

His ears picked it up first - the crash of surf on the larboard quarter. That would be the rocks he had seen while on blockade duty. He continued on the same course. Finally he saw the white of the surf. They were well to the north of the rocks. He had a true course. Off to the starboard, he could see the other boat moving steadily. He eased the stroke, trying to spot the Battery Island shore. He could hear more surf, but could not see the shore.

They continued forward, but more warily. Finally, surf appeared to their front. Jonathan was not sure if this was the shoreline, or just more rocks. They cautiously continued forward. The other boats behind had now caught up.

He increased the stroke forward, but put the tiller over slightly to run a bit more to starboard. They pulled ahead of the other boats again because of the stronger stroke. Then he sensed the shadow of the island. Stroke after stroke, the shadow turned into land. With each stroke the tension mounted. This was Battery Island, but where on the island, and where could a boat be put ashore? The surf was significant. It wouldn't be easy getting in. When they got in, they would be greeted by rocks that would have to be overcome before they could form to attack. If the enemy was alert, they would be decimated as they went in.

It slowly became obvious that they were in the spot planned for the landing. That spot was far from ideal however. In fact, it was a very challenging place to land. Regardless, Jonathan turned in. Now he would see if a few hours of practise could result in the men landing with dry feet, or relatively dry feet.

"Stroke, stroke, larboard back, starboard stroke," Jonathan called in a low voice. He used just enough volume for his crew to hear him over the pounding of the surf.

"All back together," urged Jonathan and the surge propelled the boat rapidly at the rocky shoreline. He turned the tiller at the last second, missed a large rock, and scraped between that large rock and another. The boat lodged fast, held by the rocks.

"Up forward, see if we can disembark here," commanded Jonathan.

The man in the bows jumped overboard. The surf varied between knee and chest high. "We can make it," he called in a low voice.

"Disembark," ordered Jonathan. The men grabbed their weapons and began the process of moving up to the bow, and over the side. Once they were on their feet, the next man passed down weapons and ammunition. Slowly the crew made it out of the surf to solid ground.

Another boat broached beside them. A third crashed into their stern. Jonathan secured three boats to his, and assisted the men in going from their respective boats through his to the beach.

A musket went off. Then silence for a few minutes. Then all hell broke loose. By this time, Jonathan had grabbed his musket and was on shore. He stopped and loaded the musket. He could see men in front of him working their way toward the walls of the fort.

From the top of the walls, the French were peppering the men with musket fire. All the firing was individual shots. There were no volleys.

Jonathan stood in a crouch and rushed forward. Musket balls went whistling past him. He dropped to the ground again. He found himself in an exposed position. He decided it was better to move than lie still in that exposed position. He would be more difficult to hit.

He made it to the base of the fortress walls. They were not high, but high enough that a man needed to be aided to climb them. He estimated they were about nine feet in height. Two men held a musket horizontal to the ground, while a third man stood on the musket and between their lifting and his jumping, men were gaining the wall.

French fire from the wall slackened off. More men were able to get on top of the walls. Then came something that Jonathan dreaded to hear - cannon fire. From the whizzing in the air above him, they were firing grape or canister against the men on the top of the wall. Then Jonathan heard the crash of a volley.

In the intensity of the moment, Jonathan realized what was happening. Just like boarders going over the bulwark of an enemy vessel, the defenders were below, firing up as soon as a target appeared. In this case instead of a bulwark, it was the stone wall. As soon as a man showed himself above the wall he was silhouetted against the night. Those remaining defenders that had manned the wall had withdrawn below and were firing up at the silhouetted shapes. That way they were safe from colonial fire, and extracted a heavy toll on the attackers. Additionally a single cannon, probably from the north face of the fort, had been turned and was firing at the same time at those above Jonathan.

Whoever was commanding the assault sent men further to the left and right to see if there was any possibility of attacking a more weakened enemy flank. The walls extended in both directions, with the area below the walls petering out to the sea. There was no possibility of a flanking move.

After a valiant effort on the part of many men, the decision to withdraw was made. Men started streaming to the boats. A line of shooters was placed on the slight rise in front of the boats. Their job was to snipe at the French to discourage them from manning the walls again.

Jonathan rushed back to his boat. He assisted men traversing his boat to get to boats further out. One by one men from his boat appeared. He motioned them to take a seat and wait. It allowed them time to regain their strength. He knew it would be a difficult pull out through the surf, and he still had to get the boat out of where it was wedged between the rocks.

The number of men rushing through petered out. He only had ten of his original forty men on board. All but one of the boats behind him pushed off. One broached. He and those on board ended up fishing a number of men from the water.

The men from the sniping line started to appear. Jonathan passed them through to the remaining boat. It departed. That left only his boat.

He quickly moved to the bow as he saw more men coming.

"Stay in the water. Pass your weapons up here. We're stuck fast, so if you want out of here you're goin' to have to push us off," shouted Jonathan.

Weapons were rapidly passed over, and men took up positions. Jonathan shouted, "Man your oars. Give way together and put your backs into it or we'll be guests of the French. You men in the water push with everything you got."

There was a significant motivation to get off the island. The boat resisted, but finally came loose.

"Hold steady," shouted Jonathan. "First two men - give a hand getting those men in. The rest of you - get ready to pull for your lives."

The men in the water were pulled unceremoniously over the side. Jonathan just grabbed each man and shoved him into a place.

"Grab an oar."

The men that had been fished out of the water from the broached boat were shoved in place as well.

"You're gonna row, it's the best thing to get you warm."

Finally, everyone was on board.

"Anyone left?"

"I'm the last man," croaked a shivering man who Jonathan shoved into position.

Jonathan agilely moved to the tiller.

"All ahead starboard, all back larboard." It was a shambles. Oars were crashing into one another. The surf hit, and they nearly capsized.

"Alright, look at me." When he had their attention, he raised his right arm, "This side is starboard." Then he raised his left hand, "This side is larboard. Everyone got it?"

"All ahead starboard, all back larboard." This time, it was much better. "Stroke, stroke."

They came around in time to meet the next big wave.

"All ahead together, and pull for all you're worth, the French are coming."

That was the motivation they needed. Despite being exhausted, these men pulled like champions, because the alternative was a prison cell and they knew it.

Jonathan did a head count. He had thirty five men aboard, but only about twenty of the ones he originally came with. He figured that probably the other twenty were still on Battery Island and would probably remain there forever.

It was a long hard pull. They pulled around Rocky Island, then headed south in the passage between Rocky Island and Green Island and then back toward the anchorage. The men were exhausted, wet, and had the fight torn out of them.

Jonathan didn't push them too hard. He could sense the mood. They were dejected. They had been defeated by the French and were ashamed.

"Ease oars. Take a break. We still have a ways to go," said Jonathan. He got up and moved forward. He pulled out his bottle of rum. He handed it to the first man. "Take a sip only, it's all I have and I want every man to have a sip."

The men were grateful, and surprisingly no one, not even the heavy drinkers among them, took advantage. Everyone had a sip. There was still some left when Jonathan sat down at the tiller again.

"I never asked," said Jonathan. "Is anyone wounded?"

"Nothing but a scratch," muttered one man.

"Take a look at him," said Jonathan quietly.

It was more than a scratch, but not mortal. Jonathan never took a sip from the bottle. He just passed it down to the wounded man. "There's not much left, so finish it, but send the empty bottle back down to me."

When the empty bottle was returned, he quietly said, "Give way altogether."

They continued rowing for another two hours to the anchorage.

Upon landing, he asked a couple of men to help the wounded man to the surgeon. He then looked for someone to report to that he had arrived with thirty five men. It took him some time to find anyone wishing to take his report. Everyone knew the assault had failed and wished to disassociate themselves from it. Finally, he found a duty officer who took his information.

Jonathan went searching for his tent. He found his ditty bag, pulled out a blanket, and collapsed asleep.

Chapter 26
Lighthouse Point

It was bright sunlight when Jonathan awoke. Wilson was not there. Jonathan saw that Wilson's kit was all properly stowed away in his ditty bag, so perhaps he had gone to get something to eat. Jonathan got up, went out and did his ablutions, and then went to the cook's tent to see if he could scrounge some food.

Surprisingly, there was no problem getting food from the cook, even though he found out that it was three in the afternoon.

The discussion in the cook's tent was about the attack last evening. Apparently sixty men had died. Another one hundred sixteen were missing and suspected of being taken prisoner. Jonathan took in the conversation idly. He did not know to whom to report, or what he was expected to do. In typical sailor fashion, he followed the sailor's unofficial motto - keep out of sight, out of mind, and never volunteer. In other words he kept a low profile and did not seek out any work.

When the evening meal came around, Wilson still had not shown up. Jonathan assumed then that Wilson had been one of the casualties. That did not mean that he was dead, only missing. He still could show up at some later time. As Wilson was a shipmate, Jonathan secured Wilson's ditty bag with his own. If he was dead, it was only fair that his goods be divided up by his mess mates or sold by auction, as was the normal custom. Jonathan however, made sure that the bowl he had loaned Wilson ended back in his own ditty bag.

Jonathan took in a long sleep. The next day, Jonathan was up early. He ventured out to see Louisbourg from the land side. He examined the breastworks that had been constructed to protect the colonial artillery. This artillery was firing periodically. Jonathan looked down in Louisbourg. There were a number of streets that followed the same trajectory as the shells being fired. A shell could rake the entire street, which meant that you wouldn't want to be in the streets when a shot was fired.

He moseyed on back to the encampment. He struck up a conversation with a colonial named Jeremy. After the normal topics of weather, food, drink, and women, the discussion got more serious.

"I don't understand why we are attacking Louisbourg. I would have thought there would be more to gain from taking Martinique or other French islands in the Indies," said Jonathan.

"Depends upon who is paying for the war," replied Jeremy.

"What do you mean? I thought that the crown was paying for the war," replied Jonathan.

"Well they are paying for some of it I suppose. Take a look around. How many British regulars do you see? And for that matter, how many ships are Royal Navy?" responded Jeremy.

"But if the crown is not paying for everything, then who is?" asked Jonathan.

"Massachusetts and a couple of other colonies, New Hampshire, and Connecticut," replied Jeremy.

"But why?"

"It's a question of money. Every time England and France have a spat, we get hurt. Now take the current troubles. All of New England relies heavily on the fisheries. Everyone knows that the best fisheries in the world are on the Grand Banks off Newfoundland. New England fishermen go there every season. But if you look at any map, you will see half way between the Grand Banks and New England is Louisbourg. The French can come out to attack our fishing vessels, take them, and retreat into Louisbourg where we can't get at 'em."

"In order to increase the time our fishing vessels stay on the Grand Banks, the New England merchants who are funding the fishing fleet set up a staging area closer to the Grand Banks. The first place it was set up was in Louisbourg itself. Back sometime around 1710 some treaty gave the entire island, what the French now call Ile Royale, to the French. We had to move our operations to Canso. Now last August, the French attacked Canso, took it, burned down the blockhouse that was there, and stole everything they could lay their hands on. They took it all back to Louisbourg. The damned privateers that operate out of Louisbourg have taken a number of our ships. All of this has cost the New England merchants, most of them from Boston, a lot of money. You can imagine what happened when a bunch of angry merchants went screamin' to the governor. The state built an army and navy. We intend on taking Louisbourg, and get rid of the French once and for all."

"What do you think is gonna happen?" asked Jonathan.

"We'll take Louisbourg and everything else that's French on this island," stated Jeremy.

"What happens then?" asked Jonathan.

"Not sure. I imagine that Louisbourg may take over from Canso for the fishing trade. It's got a better harbour, and is easier to defend. It all depends on London, and what they negotiate at the end of the war. Technically, the island still belongs to France. If London turns the island back over to the French, then we'll have to come back and do this all over again," responded Jeremy.

"Well, we still have to take it now," replied Jonathan. "I'm sure glad I'm not the one that has to storm those walls."

"Yeah," mumbled Jeremy, as he contemplated that fact.

On that note the conversation ended, each of them heading in their own direction. Jonathan headed back to his tent to grab his mess gear for the evening meal.

As Jonathan stood in line for supper, he was approached by a man. "Are you one of the sailors brought ashore to crew the rowboats?"

"Aye, sir," responded Jonathan. Because uniforms were scarce in the colonial formations, it was never clear whether the man to whom he was speaking was an officer or just a runner sent to fetch him. Jonathan always responded as if it was an officer. He got in less trouble this way.

"Come with me," said the man.

Jonathan stepped out of line, and followed the man down a few rows of tents to a larger tent. It looked like the same tent where he had found the duty officer when reporting back from the attack on Battery Island. He could see inside the tent. The place seemed loaded with officers. Jonathan immediately backed away from the tent and assumed a position close to attention.

The man was reporting to another older man who wore an officer's uniform.

Jonathan looked around and saw a couple of other sailors to the one side of the tent that he hadn't noticed when he arrived. He recognized at least one of them as another participant in the attack on Battery Island. He moved over to where they were standing.

"Any idea what's going on?" asked Jonathan.

"Your guess is as good as mine," responded one of them.

The officer in uniform came out of the tent and approached them. "We have need of some of your skills again. Report back here at six tomorrow morning with all of your kit. We will be moving to a different location." With that said, he turned and walked back into the tent.

Jonathan looked at the others. He rolled his eyes and said, "I guess I'll see you tomorrow morning." He then left to go back to the cook's tent and get something to eat. While there, he spoke to the cook about getting something to eat in the morning.

After eating he went back to his kit and prepared it for his departure in the morning. He sat down in the fading sunlight by himself, away from everybody. He pulled out, and unwrapped, the folded oilskin to view the pocket watch. It was the first time he had taken a detailed examination of it. It was a beautiful looking piece. What he couldn't understand was the key on the chain. He examined the case of the watch and saw no place where a key could be inserted. The key was a mystery. Was the key for something else that the French officer had? Jonathan didn't know and remained puzzled by it.

Jonathan set about cleaning the watch. He paid close attention to what he was doing, because he wanted to make sure no salt water had further damaged the watch. As he was moving his hands over the rear of the watch, the back plate of the watch popped. He turned the watch over to examine it, and found it was hinged. Underneath the plate were two places to insert the key. He inserted the key and gently turned. Nothing happened. He flipped the watch over and again gently turned the key. The minute hand moved. He then tried the second hole and gently turned the key. He felt increased tension. He continued to gently turn the key. The watch started to make some noise. He turned it over and regarded it.

The watch was working. He had a working watch! Over the next half hour he played with the watch slowly and carefully figuring out how it worked. He was amazed. He had never seen this level of workmanship. He felt truly honoured to have such a beautiful piece.

He carefully wrapped the watch back in oilskins and secreted it back in his money belt. He was a contented man when he went back to the tent to sleep.

In the morning, after eating, he quickly packed his kit and headed down to the big tent. Sometime after he and the others had arrived, the same officer who had addressed them last evening came forward.

"Men, we have located some French cannon that were dumped or otherwise abandoned. These cannon are under a few feet of water near the shoreline. Our orders are to raise them, and move them to Lighthouse Point. An emplacement is then to be built. The cannons will be mounted in this emplacement and then we will bombard Battery Island until it surrenders. Your skills as seamen will be required to raise these guns, and then hoist them into the Lighthouse Point emplacements when they are ready to receive them."

"We are going to take a number of longboats and set up an encampment near Lighthouse Point. We will be taking men with us who will establish the base camp, and build the emplacements while we recover the cannons."

"Could I have a show of hands of those who commanded a longboat during the Battery Island attack?" asked the officer. "Right, those of you who have raised hands will command another boat to get us to Lighthouse Point. Follow me."

Jonathan picked up his gear, slung it over his shoulder and followed the officer down to the boats at the shoreline. He went over to a boat. He dropped his ditty bag, took off his shoes and put them in the bag, then tossed the bag into the boat. About sixty men came forward. He directed them to launch the boat. Then they climbed aboard. It was very crowded, and the freeboard was lower than he would have liked it, but the sea was relatively calm. The only challenge would be getting through the surf on the way out, and landing at Lighthouse Point.

With so many hands, there was no problem pulling through the surf. After a bit, the quality of the rowing steadied to an even pace. Like the other boats were in the water, they threaded their way through the anchorage and turned for the run to Lighthouse Point. The major difference between this trip and the previous one was that it was light, and Jonathan could see the destination. Unfortunately, the French could also see them, so Jonathan swung out further to seaward to be at the extreme range of the French guns.

As soon as he swung to seaward, there came moans and growls of disapproval. Other boats were taking a more direct route. Jonathan grinned at the men, "You'll thank me if those French guns open up. Those other boats are well within range, and I'm thinkin' the French won't miss the opportunity."

Sure enough in a few minutes the shriek of cannon balls could be heard. Many heads turned to look at those boats that were closer inshore. The French shot wasn't particularly accurate because of the range, but they were close enough to scare the occupants of the boats. Those boats turned and put considerable effort into rowing to get out of range. A couple of additional French salvos hastened them.

After watching the frantic attempts of the inshore boats to get out of the range of the French guns, the men turned to Jonathan with new respect in their eyes.

The remainder of the journey was routine. Not knowing where the officer wanted the encampment, Jonathan waited offshore until the boat carrying the officer arrived. It had been one of the boats that had been inshore.

A location on the seaward side of the point was used to land. This ensured the landing point was outside the arc of fire from the French guns on Battery Island. It also meant that if necessary ships could move close inshore for support.

The sunken guns were in the harbour at what had previously been a careening beach. The officer wanted to take the boats to the sunken guns and get right to work. It was pointed out to him however, that they would have to pass in front of the French guns covering the entrance passageway. Jonathan suggested that this was not advisable in daylight. After having just endured the French fire, the officer concurred with this assessment. The boats would have to be moved that night.

The men moved inland. They picked a spot for the encampment and began to clear the area for tents, erected them, established latrines, and posted a picket. The men were then split into two groups. One group went to start the gun emplacements. The second group that included Jonathan and all of the sailors headed off to locate the sunken guns.

All the sailors had plenty of experience in hoisting heavy loads, but there had been yardarms from which to suspend the block and tackles. Here there was nothing. To add complexity, the cannon would be difficult to secure, and much heavier because of the water pressing them down. It would be like raising two anchors at the same time.

After some time, the cannon were located. They were in ten to twelve feet of water, about forty feet off shore. The water was freezing, and very dark. Much of the work would have to be done by feeling around with hands.

There was considerable discussion on the best method of raising these cannon. Jonathan proposed lashing two longboats together, then building a deck across them, and building a derrick on that deck. Because of the weight, a multiple pulley system was needed.

The process would be for a diver to take chain down and wrap the chain at the mouth and base of the cannon, and attach the two. The pulley hook would then be attached to the fulcrum of the chain. Men on the raft would then hoist the cannon. Once clear of the water, a long boat would glide in underneath the cannon. The cannon would then be lowered into the longboat. Then at night the cannon would be rowed around to the new emplacements and off-loaded.

A new carriage would have to be constructed. They wouldn't know what size until the cannon had been raised. During the off-loading process, the cannon would be dropped into the new carriage. The carriage would then be skidded up to the new emplacements. Once in place at the emplacement, the carriage would be levered up and trucks installed.

The cannon would then have to be prepared for firing. This included worming it out, checking the touchhole and firing a reduced charge to test the gun. Once this was complete, the gun would be considered ready for action.

Concurrent with these operations, gun equipment would have to be acquired and brought ashore. Rammer, sponges, shot, wads, and powder would have to be off-loaded from a ship and man-handled to the new emplacements.

The first order of the afternoon was to start dropping trees. Wood was needed at the careening site for the deck and derrick of the recovery platform. At the new emplacement location, wood was required for the emplacements, and the new carriages.

Before dark, the crew at the recovery location departed, leaving a small party for security. As they worked their way back to the encampment, a direct path was cut through the bush.

The boats, ropes and pulleys were organized for the night's journey. Jonathan had a quick bite to eat and fell asleep. It was a short rest for at midnight, he was roused and they set forth. They had muffled the oars and pins on the longboats. Thankfully, the wind was up and masked their movement as they threaded their way through the harbour passage. There were no shots fired.

Leaving the security party had been a good idea. Without them, they would have missed the location completely. The boats were put into the shore and secured. The security party was relieved and everyone not in the security party moved back to the encampment.

Jonathan cursed a thousand times during that night march to the encampment. He had left his shoes in his ditty bag. Walking through the brush in his bare feet, hardened though they were, was painful. He now understood the value of the footwear many of the colonial frontiersmen had. These were called moccasins. They were light, but protected the feet from jabs and sharp edges. They were quiet and smooth so nothing caught on protruding shrubs. He had seen two types. One type, the more common were low, like a slipper. The other type ran halfway up the calf.

Jonathan vowed to see if he could find someone willing to trade for a pair. He asked the cooks to spread the word that he was looking for a pair of moccasins.

The next morning, after another trek through the bush back to the recovery site, the work began in earnest. By noon, the longboats were lashed together, deck lashed in place, and the derrick base prepared. When they quit for the day, everything was in place for hoisting.

The second day, volunteers to dive were sought. There were few takers. Few knew how to swim. The water was freezing, and the work was ten to twelve feet under the surface. After a single dive a man would surface shivering like a leaf. Jonathan was smart enough not to volunteer for this job.

By the end of the day, they managed to recover a single cannon. It was a 12-pounder. They left it in the boat.

Jonathan walked over to the new emplacements. He was under orders from the officer at the careening site to ensure everything was ready to receive the recovered cannon that night. It took over forty minutes to reach it. When he got there, he realized they had no means of off-loading the cannon.

He spoke to a colonial gunner who appeared to be in charge of making the gun carriages. After a few minutes, Jonathan proposed constructing another derrick for off-loading. The gunner and Jonathan worked with a crew of men and had the derrick constructed before dark. This was not sufficient for off-loading. They still had to rig a block and tackle. This took a lot more time in the dark than Jonathan anticipated. He still had to go back to the recovery site and bring the cannon around. He was just preparing to go when a challenge from the shore indicated the boat had been brought around by someone else.

Jonathan supervised the unloading of the gun using the new derrick. As the gun was gently lowered onto the new gun carriage, Jonathan breathed a sigh of relief. He had a couple of men cut some pine branches from trees further back in the bush, and draped them over the derrick to hide it from curious French eyes.

While he was finishing his work, the gun was skidded up to the new emplacements by over a hundred men hauling on the lines.

Jonathan headed back to the encampment. He hadn't eaten since breakfast the previous morning, so he was hungry and exhausted. He had barely reached the base camp when he ran into the officer in charge of the careening site.

"Smith, where the hell have you been? You were supposed to bring the boat with the recovered cannon around to the point. You weren't there so I had to send Markleson," badgered the officer.

Jonathan replied exhaustedly, "Sir, when I got to the point to coordinate the movement, I found there was no way of off-loading the cannon. I got a crew of men together and we built a derrick. By the time I got the block and tackles rigged, it was midnight or later. I was just preparing to head back to the recovery point when the sentry spotted the longboat."

"We got the longboat off-loaded and sent it back to the recovery point. The gun was placed on a new carriage and skidded up to the emplacements. It's in-place and ready to be tested tomorrow."

The officer hesitated and then spoke, "Well, next time, make sure you inform me so that I know what's happening."

Jonathan just looked at him, "Aye sir." He knuckled his forehead and walked away. There was no chance of getting any food, so he just found his blanket, rolled in it and fell into an exhausted sleep.

The next day's routine was similar, only this time, Jonathan grabbed some extra food that he could munch on in case he missed another meal. He still had not adapted to the army way. Meals were at breakfast and in the evening, he supposed because they were marching in between. He was used to a major meal at dinner, and light meals at breakfast and supper. As a consequence his stomach growled a lot.

He asked around before everyone set off for the day's activities to see if anyone had a second set of moccasins that they would be willing to trade. Nobody he spoke to had anything to offer. He headed off to the recovery site. They managed to recover two 12-pounders and a number of balls over the course of the day.

When he arrived back in the encampment early that evening, he grabbed some food. He was heading off to get some sleep before rowing the boat taking the recovered cannons around to Lighthouse Point. He was intercepted by an old man in buckskins. The man looked sixty, but with the white-grey beard it was impossible to tell.

"I hear tell one of you sailor boys is interested in trading for a pair of moccasins," sputtered the old man.

"That's right, I am interested. I find it hard on my feet going through the bush," replied Jonathan.

The old man nodded, "Whatcha ya got to trade?"

"How about a bottle of rum?" said Jonathan. At the sound of rum, the old man's eye's blazed, and he involuntarily smacked his lips.

"Ya got this rum with ya?"

"It's close by. What about the moccasins, will they fit me?" asked Jonathan.

The old man pulled out a set of moccasins. Jonathan tried them on. They were worn, but still in reasonable condition. A slight adjustment with the cord and they fit perfectly.

Jonathan smiled, "Stay here, I'll be right back."

The old man obviously had been tricked before. He just shook his head, "Just leave the moccasins here while you go, so's you don't wander too far."

Jonathan smiled. He wasn't offended in the least. He took off the moccasins and handed them back to the old man. He headed off to his tent, found his ditty bag, and recovered the rum. He went back to the old man, and finalized the deal. They both departed, happy to have something that each could appreciate.

Jonathan put the moccasins on, rolled in his blankets and dropped off to sleep. At the appointed hour, he and the crews of both boats left the encampment. They got to the recovery point, boarded the boats and shoved off. The trip to Lighthouse Point and back was uneventful. The crews trudged back to the encampment and rapidly drifted off to sleep.

The next couple of days continued the same as the previous days. They only recovered eight cannon in total. But after testing, each of these cannon was found to be serviceable.

At the end of the day, as the men were getting their supper from the cook's tent, a rumour started going around. The general, Pepperrell, had ordered that heated shot be fired into Louisbourg. This was the main topic of discussion as the men sat in groups consuming their meal. There were some against it, but the majority were for it. Anything that weakened the enemy and caused him to surrender before these men had to storm the walls was considered alright. Jonathan looked at it from both sides. He favoured the men's perspective. He would not want to storm those walls. He vividly recalled the attack on Battery Island. He could only think that storming the real fortress would be resisted more fiercely. If that could be avoided by burning a few homes, then so be it.

An extra day was spent ferrying powder and shot from cargo vessels offshore to the new emplacements.

On June 17th, the guns in the new emplacement on Lighthouse Point commenced firing against the French fortress on Battery Island.

After watching the firing for an hour or two, Jonathan tired of it. He could not see if the shots were causing much damage. It had to be hard on the French morale. He could see that the colonials were in good form. Some faces that he recognized from the night of the attack expressed a 'take that you bastards' attitude. There was no mercy in their hearts for the French on the island. They had lost friends and acquaintances in the Battery Island attack. This was retribution.

The firing continued intermittently all through the daylight hours. Jonathan was called to carry powder and shot to refresh the guns. He took his turn as part of the gun crew on a gun for part of the afternoon.

There was not much else to do except support the guns. For ten days the guns continued to fire against the island. On the other side of the harbour, the guns continued to fire directly into Louisbourg. On June 25th, news reached Lighthouse Point that a substantial breach had been made in the west gate of Louisbourg.

Jonathan figured the assault was only a matter of hours away. Again he was thankful that he was at Lighthouse Point, so he would not have to take part in storming the walls or forcing the breach.

As the dawn broke on June 26th, Jonathan and the men around him went through their normal routines. After breakfast he moved up to the emplacements. The gun crews were preparing to commence the morning firing.

The guns on the other side of the harbour still had not commenced firing. That was odd, for they usually commenced firing before the guns on Lighthouse Point. As time ticked by, they remained quiet. Still, no order was given to commence fire. Jonathan wondered what was going on.

About halfway through the morning, news was received that Louisbourg had offered terms of surrender.

Chapter 27
Aftermath

As news of the surrender of Louisbourg spread, a great cheering by everyone at Lighthouse Point erupted. Everyone stood down. There would be no requirement to move powder or shot today. Jonathan headed back to the encampment to his tent and prepared his kit.

Not much happened for most of the day. Around supper time, a more senior colonial officer arrived from the other side of the harbour. He called all the officers together and briefed them. All within earshot heard heated protests. This got everyone on edge. Finally, the senior officer came out and stood on a barrel to address all the men. They crowded around to hear him.

"Men, the French commander of Louisbourg has offered Articles of Capitulation to General Pepperrell and Commodore Warren. They have accepted. Louisbourg is ours."

The men again cheered and tossed hats into the air. Backs were slapped and there were a lot of hoots and whistles. The senior officer raised his hands to ask for silence. Slowly, the noise subsided.

"As part of the terms, the French will turn over the fortress. The French residents of Louisbourg will be offered 'unmolested' safe passage back to France with their property on board British ships."

The excitement and enthusiasm of a minute ago now turned to anger and fury. Jonathan was surprised at the depth of anger being expressed by the colonials. He turned to the man beside him, "Why is everyone so mad? We won."

The man next to him was bitter, "What did we win? We fought for nothing!"

"I don't understand," said Jonathan.

"You obviously ain't one of us," spat the other man. "We took all the risks, put up with all the hardships just so we could get a portion of the spoils of Louisbourg. Now they even took that away from us."

Jonathan realized something instantly. He was not considered one of 'them', because he had to fight as ordered. They didn't. They came voluntarily to fight, expecting to gain part of their compensation from loot taken out of Louisbourg. Now this had been denied to them.

It also occurred to Jonathan that he might be singled out as a target for their anger. He decided it was time to make himself scarce. He edged out of the gathering and headed to his tent. He hoped, that if he stayed bottled up in his tent out of sight, that he would be forgotten and thereby avoid the wrath of the colonials. Just to be safe however, he kept his knives within easy reach.

Jonathan remained tense for the entire night as the fury slowly abated. He thought it was a good thing there were no spirits available. If these men drank in their current state of mind, it would get a lot more dangerous than it was currently.

Since he did not dare sleep, the night provided him ample opportunity to think things over. The mental activity also helped him stay awake.

Jonathan's main concern, besides staying healthy until the anger of the colonials passed was what he should do with regard to his future. He was in probably the best position to run that he had been since being pressed. He therefore needed to decide whether to stay with His Majesty's navy or to run.

He started by summing up where he was currently at, in terms of his finances and skills, as these were all that he had to use to live on. He was relatively flush with funds, having close to seventeen pounds in his possession. Since the average person had an annual income of less than that, he effectively had a year's wages in his possession. He was also owed nearly a year's wages from His Majesty, plus prize money. When he would be able to collect on those wages was a large question in his mind. He also had other items such as the pocket watch that could be traded for necessities.

Jonathan had great skills as an able seaman, but these could only be used on a merchantman. Working on a merchantman would significantly increase the probability of being caught if he ran. He had limited skills as a farmer or a woodsman. He was good as a trader, but in order to prosper in that area, more capital was needed. He certainly didn't have access to additional capital at the present.

At the present time he could move freely, as there were no guards to stop him. With the British taking over Louisbourg however, he couldn't stay here. He would surely be caught as a deserter. He was also dressed as a sailor, and was readily identified as such. Jonathan reasoned that he could easily obtain suitable clothes from some of the colonials.

There was the possibility he could travel back to Boston or somewhere in the colonies with some of these men. He was reasonably sure that they would hide him until they sailed, and then again when they landed.

There was a possibility that there would be special guards in Boston looking for men when the fleet returned. He had heard that the Royal Navy had pressed men in Boston. He had heard that there had been a number of desertions in Boston from Royal Navy ships. It was likely therefore, that they were alert for deserters in Boston. He would be at risk getting to Boston, disembarking at Boston, and staying in Boston. He would have to move swiftly into the countryside.

His concern was about his lack of the skills needed to survive in the Massachusetts countryside. He just didn't know what he needed to know.

It was a hard decision - to stay or to run. And Jonathan simply couldn't make that decision with the information he had at the present.

By breakfast, a degree of normalcy or at least of resignation had overcome the encampment. Men that he had worked with the past fortnight, and had feared last night, once again became hospitable.

As Jonathan sat down with these men, he wondered what would happen to him today. The fighting was over. There was no need for him on land. He would be expected to return to his ship, wherever his ship was. He hadn't seen it in a number of days. But would that be today, or did he have additional time to come to a decision?

He had barely started to consider his options when they were rudely taken away from him. A colonial officer approached him.

"Smith, you are to report to the longboat. It's taking all seamen back to their respective ships. Get a move on. Grab your kit and get down to the boat."

Off Jonathan went, back to the Mermaid and the sea.

Historical Notes

Life in 1740's England was more challenging than it is today. Class was very important. Class implied power, and many of the upper class were intent on maintaining that power. Those associated with that power often took liberties that may not have been known about by their employers.

Tenant farmers in many cases had to fork over a high portion of their annual harvest to pay for rent. In those years, as it is today, when the harvest was bountiful, prices were depressed by over-supply. Since transportation was difficult and costly, the sale of the harvest was generally conducted locally. Few tenant farmers had the capability to sell outside their local market. Buyers were limited in most local markets (e.g., it was usually a buyer's market in which the buyer controlled the prices paid). It was rare that tenant farmers were able to progress further ahead financially.

Tenant farmers often supplemented their diet by snaring. Any food acquired from such means resulted in more food on the table or it replaced produce that could subsequently be sold to supplement the farmer's income. Even marsh land was rented so fowl and other animals could be legally hunted, as indicated by advertisements in Rye newspapers of that period. Where the land was devoid of game, because of years of continuous hunting, the possibility of poaching on someone else's land increased.

Local squires had larger land holdings. Invariably some of these holdings were pasture for animals. Game tends to be more plentiful in pastures, as opposed to ploughed fields. Since pastures were limited on tenant occupied holdings, the larger land holdings of the local squires were more lucrative targets for poachers.

Impressments for the Royal Navy were legal. In reality, those pressed were generally men who could not afford to challenge the system, or were unlikely to pose such problems. Recruitment figures presented to Parliament during the 1740's, indicated that twenty five percent of all Royal Navy sailors were pressed. Another thirty percent were listed as volunteers (after pressed men and separate from another category of volunteers listed before pressed men). The rationale for listing these two separate volunteer categories is unknown. It is possible this second category of volunteers were pressed, but when offered the opportunity to volunteer, changed their enrolment status. Based on these numbers, it may well be that between fifty and fifty five percent of Royal Navy sailors during this period were recruited via impressments. It would also help explain the high level of desertion.

HMS Winchester was a fifty gun line-of-battle ship, launched in May 1744. She operated in home waters for some time, and then was sent to the North American station. She was in Boston in April and May of 1745 after the colonial fleet had sailed to Canso. In May 1745, newspaper reports indicated seventeen men deserted from her ranks in Boston.

The reader may question why messing arrangements and the watch system were discussed repeatedly throughout the book. With respect to the watch system, everything on a Royal Navy vessel and most merchant vessels revolved around the watch system. Any new recruit must adapt to this system, no matter how foreign it might be to them.

Rations and messing arrangements at the time were also significantly different from those with which any 'landsman' was accustomed. There was only one hot meal per day at dinner (noon hour), and only if the fires were not banned because of the presence of gun powder or bad weather. The rations were limited. There were only four days of varying menus (e.g., four different meals). Each hot meal averaged around fifteen hundred calories. Additional calories came from the spirit ration and ship's biscuit or bread, sometimes called hardtack. Additional challenges with food occurred due to spoilage and shrinkage. A twenty pound sack of ship's biscuit could shrink to eleven pounds after a few months of storage. Also, for every pound issued, the purser got his one-eighth share. Under this system, if a man was entitled to two pounds of beef, then at most he could expect to be issued only twenty eight ounces instead of thirty two ounces. All food was dried for long term storage, and salted in the case of fish or meat. All meat was boiled, for two reasons. The first was to soften it, and the second was to remove as much salt as possible. Fat that boiled off the meat as it was cooking in the big copper cauldrons was skimmed-off and sold as slush by the cook.

Given the physical activity of the men, the rations were barely substantial enough to cover daily essentials. Growing boys were under nourished. And anyone brought onboard with excessive fat usually lost it soon enough. Over time however, man will adapt to his rations, as did all seamen. There was a general concept at the time that Royal Navy sailors were better off than many in that they had 'three square meals' each day. While the rations were limited and unvarying, seamen were in fact, better off than many others on land.

The spirit ration was a selling point in the Royal Navy. Any captain who interfered with the spirit ration was toying with the morale of his men. Loss of the grog ration was also a punishment that was effectively used by many captains. Hoarding and trading in the rum ration was common practice, but officially outlawed because of the dangers of drunkenness. Jonathan was initially a non drinker. The loss of his spirit ration by trading was not an imposition upon him. This was especially true when it could be used to obtain something on which Jonathan placed a greater value. During this period, all ship's crew except those signed on as boys were entitled to the rum ration. In later years, the entitlement was changed so that those under the legal age of the period were not entitled to the rum ration, but were compensated an equivalent value.

Development of seaman skills was critical because of the high number of new men 'recruited' with few seaman skills. Typical training for a seaman was to pair him with a more experienced seaman and have the experienced man impart his knowledge to the other. Today this is known as on-the-job training or OJT. Many consider OJT as the best type of training. It certainly was well employed by the Royal Navy for decades. There are two major drawbacks to this type of training however. The first is that it takes a longer time to train an individual using this method. The second issue is that standards fluctuate. The source of your training is an indicator of your potential skill level. If you have a poor teacher the resulting skills will be poor. More formal training was accomplished in some areas such as gun drill, but in general, formal training and standards were lacking. This was one of the reasons that it took a long time to train ordinary and able seaman. At the present time, all countries with a naval presence complete training using formal courses and standards, and use OJT to improve the skill level taught during formal sessions.

In Jonathan's case, he was trained by the best available and forced to repeat the work or skill until it became automatic in a more formalized setting (i.e., during his supposed 'punishment'). He also completed OJT concurrently, thus employing the best elements of both training styles. He had to give up his free time to achieve this, but he was ordered to do so. It's the primary reason he is able to advance much faster than the norm.

The captain of a ship was responsible to ensure he 'recruited' sufficient men to man his ship. Only in special circumstances was he levied to provide men. If levied, any commander will assess his men and protect those he considers essential to his operation. Various contagious disease outbreaks did occur on ships at the West Indies stations. Since it was critical, especially during wartime, to maintain naval patrols / functions, any area commander could exert his authority to ships under his command to order transfer of crews. While HMS Winchester was not under the direct command of the commander in Antigua, it behoved the captain to comply in some degree. The Royal Navy was a small organization at the top, and one never knew where a station or area commander would next appear. Politics are ever present in the Royal Navy!

The operations against Louisbourg were made primarily for economic reasons. Once France and England again initiated armed conflict in 1744, called King George's war by the English, New England began to lose money. Louisbourg was the major French ice-free port in North America. France had spent considerable funds and effort to fortify it. Strategically, it protected the entrance into the Gulf of St. Lawrence, and hence New

France. It was well-positioned to interdict any fishing fleet activity between the Grand Banks and New England.

New England merchants, with a strong Boston influence, were losing money from ships captured by Louisbourg-based privateers. In August 1744, French forces attacked and captured Canso. Since Canso was the major transhipment point for the New England fishing fleet, and had been largely financed by Boston money, it was a major blow to New England.

A further consideration for attacking Louisbourg was that after Canso had fallen, prisoners of the Canso raid were taken to Louisbourg. They had an opportunity to assess the defences and conditions of the defenders. Some of these prisoners were exchanged. With this exchange valuable information came into the possession of the New Englanders. Some of this information included the fact that the soldiers at Louisbourg had mutinied, and were not trusted by the leadership.

In order to further inflame New Englanders, the religious card was played. There had always been distrust between Protestant New England and Roman Catholic France and New France. Those individuals wishing for war promoted these differences and incited opposition to possible French papist acts. As a result New England was in a fervour to attack the French. Finding men willing to fight was easy. Men were recruited for little or no pay. Instead they were offered the spoils of Louisbourg as compensation.

The Massachusetts legislature, as well as the legislatures of Connecticut and New Hampshire funded most of the Louisbourg campaign. Boston merchants assisted with ships and stores. A request was sent to Antigua to gain the assistance of the British fleet. At first a refusal was given, but then orders from England made support of the New England attack possible.

Winter is not a good time to be on the North Atlantic. At that time of year there are issues with ice in the Annapolis Basin, the Gulf of St. Lawrence, and on the St. Lawrence River. A winter campaign, while possible, was not enthusiastically embraced. It was thought that the spring of 1745 offered a better chance.

France traditionally pulled the majority of its larger vessels from North America in the fall, and sent them back in the spring. It was thought that any attack on Louisbourg should be made before the French vessels returned in the spring, bringing with them more soldiers, and more supplies.

Ice from the Gulf of St Lawrence was heavy in the spring of 1745. It drifted out into the Atlantic and was driven ashore all along the eastern coast of Ile Royale (Cape Breton Island). Entrances to most harbours were blocked.

When the New England fleet finally sailed for Louisbourg, it had two reasons to stop at Canso. The first was to liberate Canso, and the second was to wait until the ice was sufficiently clear to allow landings at Louisbourg.

Canso was made the base of operations. From Canso, New England ships of war were sent to each French port/harbour along the coast of Ile Royale (Cape Breton Island). They captured and/or burned everything at each outpost. Despite the close proximity of Canso to Louisbourg, the commander at Louisbourg, acting Governor Louis du Pont Duchambon, was not aware of the impeding invasion. Even the blockading ships he saw off the coast he believed were French ships waiting to enter harbour, but blocked by the ice.

HMS Mermaid (40) was one of three heavy ships that sailed from Antigua on 13 March 1745 to support the action against Louisbourg. HMS Superb (60) (the flagship of Commodore Warren) and HMS Launceston (40) were the other two. They reached Canso on 23 April 1745, where they were joined by HMS Eltham (40) which had sailed from Boston. Warren took command of the entire navy element. He finished the job started by New England ships by sending other ships to French ports and destroying them.

Commodore Warren just touched at Canso. He never even dropped anchor. He stayed long enough to obtain information about the current status of the fleet, and what actions had already been taken. He then proceeded north up the coast of Ile Royale (Cape Breton Island) to Louisbourg just a few hours away. His intent was to blockade the harbour.

The dates of the Louisbourg operations vary depending upon the source. Various reports written, either at the time or in later years, use conflicting dates, primarily because it was not always clear what calendar was used by the recorder. The Gregorian calendar (New Style) replaced the Julian calendar (Old Style) beginning in 1582, but was not fully adapted in all countries for at least 200 years. Thus we see the landings occurring anywhere from 01 May to 10 May 1745 depending upon which calendar is used. The surrender occurred between 16 and 26 June. To standardize, the dates based on the new style have been used (e.g., landings on 10 May, surrender on 26 June). One thing that is common is that the length of the siege was six weeks and five days.

After capturing Canso in the fall, French forces were next heading to Annapolis Royal in the Bay of Fundy. This was the only other English settlement of size in Nova Scotia at that time. The main French attack against Annapolis Royal however, was not launched until early April 1745, concurrent with the attack by English forces on Louisbourg. It thus deprived Louisbourg of additional troop support.

The British landings took place on 10-11 May in Gabarus Bay about five miles southwest of Louisbourg. The masts of the British ships could be seen from Louisbourg, so a small force under Pierre Morpain, the naval commander at Louisbourg sallied forth to investigate. They were kept at bay by the New Englanders and forced to withdraw back to Louisbourg.

For the first few days of the siege, the majority of action was capturing and burning outlying farms. After a while, the New Englanders began to construct batteries and breastworks opposite the West Gate of Louisbourg.

Louisbourg had a battery, called the Royal Battery, sited deep within the harbour, far from the actual fortress. The Governor believed this fortress was not defensible, so he ordered its evacuation. The fort was not destroyed however. When New England troops captured it, they found stores and spiked 42-pounder cannons. They drilled out the spikes of the cannons, moved them to the low hills west of the main fortress (i.e., opposite the West Gate), and turned them on their previous owners.

The French did mount one effort to retake the Royal Battery, but it was a sad affair and had no impact on the campaign.

Like any sea blockade, the blockade of Louisbourg could occasionally be penetrated by daring captains with fast ships. On a number of occasions ships did get in or out of Louisbourg. Others were captured. The most notable of these was the French ship-of-the-line Vigilante of 64 guns. Le Vigilante was carrying 500 regulars, 40 cannons and 1000 barrels of powder as cargo for Louisbourg and was unaware of the siege. She spotted HMS Mermaid off the coast and engaged her. Mermaid, being a smaller ship ran, but she ran with a purpose. While being chased by the Vigilante, HMS Mermaid ran directly back to the fleet to get support to take Vigilante.

When Vigilante saw the fleet, she immediately turned to head back out to sea. Mermaid attacked. She was joined by Massachusetts, Shirley, Superb, Launceston, and Eltham. Among the logs of the different ships the times differ. It appears that the Mermaid was initially engaged near 1300 (one pm) and finally took possession of a beaten and battered Vigilant just before 2100 (nine pm). Jonathan therefore earned some prize money. The Vigilant was bought into the Royal Navy. Captain Douglas of the Mermaid was given command of the Vigilant as a reward for his actions in taking her.

During the siege of Louisbourg the majority of all engagements were artillery duels. The French became more restrained in returning cannon fire over time as they conserved their remaining powder. One of the larger engagements occurred on the night of the 6th / 7th of June. On this evening New England troops assaulted Battery Island. They were repulsed with heavy casualties - sixty dead and one hundred sixteen taken prisoner.

The New Englanders were not inclined to assault Battery Island again. Instead they opted to bombard the position into submission. Batteries were setup in emplacements on Lighthouse Point, and bombardment commenced on June 17th, 1745. It is not clear how many guns were sited on Lighthouse Point, or the origin of these guns.

There are references to sunken cannon that were found at a careening point in the harbour at Louisbourg. These cannons were known to the French authorities. Efforts to raise them by the New Englanders during the siege did occur, and it is believed that these cannon were used at the Lighthouse Point battery.

The use of heated shot against the main town of Louisbourg was a sore point between British regulars and colonial troops. The regulars believed it to be morally wrong, and against the known covenants of war. The colonials, many having experienced just how brutal warfare could be against the natives, had no such qualms. Since this was largely a colonial army commanded by colonial General Pepperrell, heated shot was used.

By the June 24th, having withstood five weeks of artillery bombardment, seeing supplies run down, and having no hope of reinforcement, the influential citizens of Louisbourg petitioned the Governor to surrender.

The Governor distrusted the majority of his troops. By this point he had lost the confidence of the civilian population, as indicated by the petition. Within forty eight hours a substantial breach was made at the West Gate. He therefore had few options. The Governor approached the British with an offer in the form of the Articles of Capitulation on 26 June 1745.

A critical point of the Articles of Capitulation was that French residents of Louisbourg were to be granted safe passage to France 'unmolested' (i.e., with their property/possessions undisturbed) in British ships.

General Pepperrell knew he would lose men storming the fortress. He also probably had concerns about what would happen if battle-crazed men with a strong religious revulsion of Papists were forced to fight their way into the fortress. Trying to check or control them at that point would be impossible. He also had to consider his army's perception of compensation of loot from Louisbourg. Furthermore he had British regulars, both Army and Royal Navy, to consider. If he proposed to continue the siege and storm Louisbourg just because the New Englanders wanted loot, he would likely lose British regular support, which might include the Royal Navy. General Pepperrell therefore decided to accept the conditions.

When the New Englanders heard that they would not get any loot from Louisbourg as promised when they signed up, they felt betrayed. Anger, fury and open hostility were quite evident. Jonathan was smart to disappear, as the New Englanders looked to vent their anger.

About the Author

Alec Merrill served thirteen years in the Canadian Forces as an officer. Using this experience in the private sector, he established the training program for the North Warning System which provides NORAD with surveillance and early warning capabilities across the Canadian arctic. Alec completed three years as the Chief of Emergency Services for Fisheries and Oceans Canada which includes the Canadian Coast Guard during events such as Hurricane Juan, and Katrina. He has been a management consultant for over twenty years.

Made in the USA
Lexington, KY
08 February 2015